D1012182

©ENNIS

DEEP LONGINGS

She circled around him and rested on her knees before him, her hands at his cheeks. "I have never allowed myself to love a man," she murmured, her dark eyes imploring him. "I am a princess with duties to my people. But I care for you. You have aroused in me feelings and needs that, until you, were unfamiliar to me. I thought that making love might fulfill these needs. All of these feelings, this sort of hunger, are so new to me. I have never been with a man in this way before. I have never found a man I would offer myself to. But you are different, my sweet Charles. Everything you have stirred within me is so deliciously sweet."

She leaned into his embrace. She wrapped her arms around him. "Charles, make love to me," she whispered. "Please make love to me."

SAVAGE LONGINGS

CASSIE EDWARDS

LEISURE BOOKS   **NEW YORK CITY**

A LEISURE BOOK®

February 1997

Published by

Dorchester Publishing Co., Inc.
276 Fifth Avenue
New York, NY 10001

Printed in the United States of America.

These lonely days are slipping slowly by...
The memories, so soft, always make me cry.
Memories of sunshine, laughter, and rain...
The loving, the heartache, the letting go, and the pain.

Thousands of pictures pass through my mind...
Lying with you in the robed bed I left behind.
Your world and mine were so close, yet so far...
Now here I stand wishing on the North Star.

My heart cries out for your gentle embrace...
I wish I could look upon your face.
I pray you are happy, healthy, and well...
Coming soon to deliver me from this lonely hell.

I pray that time draws near, my love...
I pray for strength from the Man Above,
"Hurry, my love, my heart cries nearly aloud...."

—HARRIET LUCAS GARNETT
Poet and Friend

Dear Reader,

At the end of my previously published book, SAVAGE SECRETS, I introduced the character Snow Deer, who is, in truth, my great-grandmother. SAVAGE LONGINGS is Snow Deer's story...how she fell in love with a white man and left the Cheyenne world to live out the rest of her life in the white world. Much of SAVAGE LONGINGS is true, yet some is fiction. I have woven both truth and fiction together and feel that if she were alive today, Snow Deer would be proud of being remembered in such a fond way by her great-granddaughter.

In SAVAGE LONGINGS I have also written about a special house that was located in Bloomfield, Illinois. This was the real house that Snow Deer shared with her white husband, Charles Franklin Cline. I visited this house often as a child (long after my great-grandmother's death). Just a few years ago, I went back to the house one last time because I had been told by my father (Snow Deer's grandson) that the house was soon to be demolished to make room for a new highway. While wandering by myself through the house, I didn't feel alone. It was as though the ghost of my past were there, leading me from room to room. When I entered the parlor, a loose brick at the front of the fireplace drew me to it. I carefully slid the brick out. Behind it I found a treasure! Yellowed love letters my great-grandmother had written to my great-grandfather while she was away from him for a short while, visiting her Cheyenne relatives in Kansas.

I knew then that fate had purposely led me there that day to those letters. In them my great-grandmother's love for my great-grandfather lives on, forever!

I hope you will enjoy their love story, which appears on the following pages.

Always,
CASSIE EDWARDS

SAVAGE LONGINGS

Chapter One

Bloomfield, Illinois—1881

"C.C., I think that's the last of 'em," Bill Eckert said as he tossed a bag of letters down to Charles Cline from the open door of the railroad car. "Seems your pa's post office is gettin' more letters than usual these past several months. Where's the population growin', C.C.? Bloomfield still don't look no larger than a pea."

Charles set the leather letter bag on the ground with the other two that Bill had already thrown down to him. He smiled at Bill as the railroad man jumped from the mail car. The door closed behind him, and the others stayed in the car, preparing for the next mail stop down the line.

"No, Bloomfield isn't where the settlers are coming," Charles said, squinting as Bill stepped up to him. "Vienna, just up the road, is where most are going. It's a fine town. It's quite pretty with its new homes and fancy lattice work."

"Vienna's tryin' to imitate the big cities, huh?" Bill said, chuckling. Then he placed his fists on his hips and frowned at Charles. "C.C., if you'd wear your damn glasses, you wouldn't have to squint to see me." He gazed at the gold frames of the eyeglasses which were just visible in Charles's shirt pocket. "Put 'em on, C.C., before you ruin your eyes. I ain't no pretty thing you need to impress."

"I hate those spectacles," Charles grumbled, raking his long fingers through his thick brown hair, which lay just above his blue denim shirt collar. "I swear, Bill, I truly believe that if I don't wear them, I'll teach my eyes how to see as good as they did when I was a kid."

"Too damn bad about that blow to the head when you were playing softball last year, C.C.," Bill said. "I'd hoped by now your vision would've returned one-hundred percent. Perhaps it still will." He slid a gold watch from his vest pocket and studied the time, then turned and stared at the engineer as he let out a loud whistle from the train's engine.

"I think George Wesley is trying to tell you something," Charles said, waving at the engineer.

"Yep, it's time to make the rest of our run with the mail," Bill said, smoothing his thick hands down the front of his black fustian coat. He winked at Charles. "C.C., there's the prettiest thing waitin' on me at the end of the line. I think I just might be takin' wife number two sometime soon."

Bill started to walk away, then turned and gazed at Charles again. "When will weddin' bells be ringin' for you, C.C.?" he said, his green eyes twinkling. The breeze picked up Bill's fire-red hair and fluttered it around his freckled face. He nodded toward a small white church half a mile down the road. "Any pretty things in that there Baptist church on Sunday morning?"

"Yeah, there are plenty of pretty girls," Charles said. He picked up one of the leather mailbags and slung it over his left shoulder. "But that's all they are, Bill. Girls. There aren't that many who are of marrying age."

"How about the larger Baptist Church in Vienna?" Bill said over his shoulder as he ran toward the caboose. The train had started up, and the cars were rattling, the wheels groaning, as they began slowly rolling along the tracks.

"I stay loyal to my own church, Bill," Charles said, lifting a second mailbag and swinging it over his other shoulder. "I see no reason to give my tithing money to a church that I don't support."

"If that's where you can find a fit wife, you'd best forget about which church gets your ten percent each Sunday," Bill said. He hopped up on the caboose steps and waved at Charles as he rode past him. "C.C., you ain't gettin' any younger, you know. You ain't no spring chicken. I'm workin' on havin' a second wife. You ain't yet taken a first!"

"I know!" Charles shouted. "I know!" He waved at Bill as the train rattled on down the tracks away from him.

He then lifted the third mailbag and sauntered away from the railroad tracks, toward the white picket fence that enclosed the backyard of his parents' large home.

Charles thought about what Bill had said. Tall, broad-shouldered, and heavily muscled, and twenty-eight years old, Charles had always drawn the attention of women. Many openly flirted with him.

He appreciated such notice. But he had been too busy to concentrate on women. He had his garden and blacksmith shop to tend to. He also helped his father at his post office when there was more mail than his father could handle.

"And now there's Uncle Hiram," Charles whispered to himself, swinging the gate open.

Deep in thought, he entered the spacious, fenced-in yard. He was leaving that very day, traveling to Kentucky to get his Uncle Hiram. He was Charles's mother's brother, soon to turn eighty-one.

Charles was going to bring his Uncle Hiram back to Bloomfield so that Charles's mother could care for him. She had received a letter a few days before from Hiram's daughter, Elissa, informing her of Hiram's failing health. It had been made quite clear in the letter that Elissa no longer wanted to be bothered with him.

Charles grew bitter as he thought about Elissa, whose personality had seemed to change of late. He could hardly believe that the girl he had once known would want to be rid of her father. Charles would never believe that she would mistreat her father, mentally or physically, yet the letter had made it clear that she no longer wanted to care for him. So Charles had volunteered to go and get Uncle Hiram. Charles's blacksmith chores and his garden came second to family.

Just down the road, halfway between the church and his parents' house, was his own small plot of land, where he had built himself a comfortable cabin. His blacksmith shop was at the rear of the cabin, and past that was his garden.

"Yes, all seems to be going well for me," Charles told himself. "The only thing lacking is a wife."

Yes, he thought, he just might have to reconsider going into Vienna to take a look around for a woman.

He knew that the church was the best place to look. The ladies there would be upright, decent, Christian women, unlike those who frequented the saloons and showed their thighs to the gents at the bawdy houses.

"I want a wife as decent as my mother, that's for sure." Charles smiled at his mother's utter sweetness. She never thought of herself. She was always looking out for the interests of others.

The smell of chicken frying on the cook stove in his mother's kitchen wafted through the air from the open window, and Charles inhaled deeply. Nothing smelled as good to him as fried chicken. He could eat it at every meal and never grow tired of it.

He knew that his mother had spent the past two days preparing food for his journey to Kentucky. He knew that the buckboard wagon was already loaded with canned goods, fruit, cheese, loaves of freshly made bread, and today, as the chicken fried, there were several cherry pies cooling on the window sills of her kitchen.

As he walked around to the back of the house, he looked about him, at the tranquility of his surroundings. There were many fruit trees in the yard. The cherries were red and ripe. Also there were many flowering shrubs and trees, as well as varied blooms in the flower gardens.

He stepped around a chicken that scurried past. He looked toward the hen house, where dozens of eggs were laid each day. A rooster that he called Lucky strutted in front of the building, his head held high.

His gaze shifted to a smaller shed—the family outhouse, where the walls were papered with pages from the Sears, Roebuck catalogue, and where bees and horse flies were always a threat to one's behind.

He looked then at the huge red barn, where hay and feed were stored for his father's livestock. He smiled as he gazed at the hog pen that ran around one whole side of the barn. He was glad that the wind was blowing away from the fat, grunting animals. On days when the breeze blew unfavorably for the Cline family, nothing, not even the wonderful aroma of his mother's cooking, could diffuse the unpleasant smell of the pigs.

But, he thought with a grin, the sausage and bacon from the animals made the smells worthwhile.

"Charles! Charles Franklin!"

Charles's mother's voice brought his eyes around. He looked up at the porch, where his mother was waving her apron at him.

"What is it, Mother?" he asked, hurrying his pace.

A warm feeling filled his heart as he gazed at his mother. She was someone who always had a kind word for everyone. She was fifty now. Her brown hair, which she wore in a tight bun atop her head, was just now becoming sprinkled with gray. Her brown eyes were soft and warm.

She had lost her tiny figure some years ago from enjoying her own cooking too much. Yet her face still revealed how beautiful she had been when she met and married Charles's father so many years before.

"Son, I want you to get started on your way to Kentucky before it turns dark," Patricia said, smoothing a fallen lock of hair back into her bun. "The fried chicken is finished. I have it in a basket in the wagon. The pies are also in the wagon. Have you packed your clothes?"

"Yes, I've packed," Charles said, moving up the steps to the porch. "I'm ready. I just wanted to get the mail for father first."

Jacob opened the screen door and stepped out from the kitchen onto the porch. "Son, let me help you with those bags," he said, slipping one of them off Charles's shoulder. He frowned at Charles. "C.C., you aren't wearing your eyeglasses. You know what the doctor said. You have to retrain your eyes. The only way to do that is to wear your spectacles."

"I hate . . ." Charles began, but his father interrupted him.

"Don't say it, C.C.," Jacob scolded. He gave Charles another frown. "Just please listen to reason, Charles Franklin Cline."

Patricia sidled up next to Charles, stood on tiptoe, and kissed his cheek as Jacob went back inside the house. "Your father has spoken," she then whispered. "Wear them, son. Please? On your journey to Kentucky, wear your glasses."

"I will," Charles promised, then walked inside behind his mother, stepping into a kitchen full of the delicious aromas of all sorts of cooked food. He looked around.

Since his mother loved to spend time in the kitchen cooking, Charles's father had made sure that she had all the modern conveniences. She had one of the latest cook stoves, with an attached oven. She had many built-in cabinets, long counters on which to prepare her foods, and a long oak table large enough to seat fifteen people. She always preferred having her guests eat in the kitchen rather than in her fancy dining room.

"Charles, you've got to promise to be extra careful while on your journey to Kentucky," Patricia fussed as she walked beside him out of the kitchen, into the well room.

When Charles's father had drawn up the plans for this house, he had made sure their deep well would be housed inside the house, for the convenience of his wife during the long, cold months of winter. Whenever she wanted water for cooking or bathing, it was there, easily drawn up in buckets while standing in the warmth of the house.

Also, she kept her perishables in buckets lowered into the cool depths of the well, so that whatever was being stored there rested just above the water line.

"I know you are worried about Indians," Charles said. "Mother, the Shawnee have lived in those parts for years and have caused no problems. I'm sure the Cheyenne, who are new to Kentucky, are just as peaceful in their behavior."

"Still, don't take any chances, son, if you see Indians approaching you," Patricia said, her voice drawn.

"I'll be careful," Charles said, sliding the other mailbag from his shoulder as they walked into the mail room, where mail was sorted into tiny cubbyholes built along the wall.

Charles's father was the postmaster for the area—not only for Bloomfield, but also for all the surrounding farms. Some people even came from the outskirts of Vienna to receive their mail at this post office. When Jacob built his home, he had placed the living quarters at one end, the post office at the other.

"The only way you will be able to identify Indians approaching you is by wearing your glasses, son," Patricia said, giving him a pleading look.

Not wanting to show his frustration at being reminded so often of his poor eyesight, Charles ignored his mother's continued reference to it. He slid the mailbag from his arm onto a counter, then lifted the other one up beside it.

But knowing that his mother was still watching, and wanting to please her, Charles sighed to himself, took his gold-framed eyeglasses from his pocket, and placed them on the bridge of his nose.

He turned and smiled down at her. "There, does that make you feel better?" he said, his dark eyes twinkling when he saw her relief.

Patricia lifted her hand up to her son's cheek and gently patted him. "Never think that eyeglasses take away from your handsomeness," she murmured. "Just look at yourself. You are always so fresh and neat in your denim breeches and shirts. And those boots, son. You keep them so shiny, a person can almost see his reflection in their toes. With your skin so bronzed by the sun, and with such perfect features, what woman would not look past the eyeglasses and see the true man?"

"Patricia, haven't you spoiled C.C. enough?" Jacob said, chuckling as he started pitching letters into their appropriate cubbyholes. "No wonder he's being so choosy while looking for a wife."

"Please quit calling my Charles C.C.," Patricia said. "I hate nicknames, Jacob. Absolutely hate them."

"Mother, I don't mind the nickname," Charles said. He drew her into his embrace and hugged her. "And don't worry so much about me."

But he understood her concerns. He was her only child. If she lost him, she would have a hard time accepting the loneliness that would follow. A mother needed a child to nurture, even a grown son. Hugs seemed to be very important to his mother. He would always stay close to her. Always.

He gave his mother one last hug, then went to his father. "Father, I've got to go," he said.

"I placed your travel bag in the wagon," Jacob said, giving Charles a bear hug. "Son, please be careful."

"Now who worries about who?" Charles said, chuckling. "You're almost as bad as Mother."

"Yes, I know," Jacob said, easing from Charles's arms. He smiled broadly, so that his thick gray mustache quivered above his lips.

They all went outside. Jacob and Patricia stood on the wide front porch as Charles settled down on the seat of his wagon.

Charles peered over his shoulder and chuckled at the amount of supplies his mother had placed in the wagon. The fried chicken and the fresh cherry pies already made his mouth water for them.

He then gave his mother and father a last, lingering stare. "I'll be home as soon as I can," he said. He smiled when his mother blew him a kiss.

He snapped his horses' reins. The team took the buckboard wagon in a wide circle, then headed away from the house.

"God speed, son!" his father shouted at him.

"Son, I'll pray for your safe return!" his mother cried.

Finally on his way to Kentucky, Charles rode down the dirt road that led him past his cabin, then past the beautiful white Baptist Church with its tall steeple reaching into the sky. Remembering what Bill had said about Charles being in need of a wife, he gave the church a look over his shoulder.

Nodding, he gazed ahead at the road that stretched out before him between thick rows of elm and maple trees. "Yes, it's time," he whispered. "When I return, I'll begin my search for that perfect lady."

Yes, he thought, it was time to take a wife. But he had a journey of family responsibility to make first.

His smile faded when he recalled his mother's concerns about Indians. Well, he had his own concerns, and they were not entirely over Indians. There were ruthless outlaws and murdering trappers all through the state of Illinois and into Kentucky.

He slid a hand over to his holstered pistol, which rested at his left hip.

On the seat of his wagon, at his right side, lay his rifle.

At the far back of the wagon, buried beneath blankets, was a shotgun.

"I'm ready for whoever might decide to accost me," he whispered. His lips lifted into a smug smile. "Just let 'em come!"

Chapter Two

Kentucky

The Cheyenne village was pitched in a broad bottom. Trees, like a solid wall of green, surrounded the village on three sides. On the fourth side lay the Ohio River, which ran like a crawling snake through the forest.

It was the moon "When Cherries Are Ripe," when most Cheyenne women renewed their lodges. The tepees stood white and clean beneath the late-afternoon sun. Beside each lodge, the outdoor cook fires had been rekindled. Yellow flames licked the logs and churned gray columns of smoke skyward.

In all quarters of the camp women came and went from the river, carrying water to their lodges for the preparation of the evening meal.

Inside the large tepee at the far end of the village, strong words were being spoken in council.

Snow Deer sat with her proud chin lifted beside her father, Chief Blazing Eagle. Across the council fire from Snow Deer and her chieftain father sat Chief Rain Feather from a neighboring Shawnee tribe.

As Chief Rain Feather spoke his mind, the knuckles of his hands turned white in rising anger at how he was being received by the Cheyenne. Snow Deer did not for one moment allow him to see her uneasiness over his heated words as he repeated why he was there.

Unlike the other, more youthful, Shawnee braves, Rain Feather was a small, squat man, whose eyes were beady and whose aging skin was drawn tight over his bones.

In truth, Rain Feather disgusted Snow Deer. He had already had three wives who now walked the roads of the hereafter. None of those wives had given Rain Feather children. He saw Snow Deer as someone young, strong, and vital, perhaps his last chance to bring him an heir.

Snow Deer, who had no desire to marry anyone just yet, was glad that her father was standing up for her today so that she would not have to speak to this small, aging Shawnee chief.

And still she would not allow him to see how his stares were unnerving her, how his presence nauseated her. She looked past him, as though he were not there.

As his voice droned on, with promises of making Snow Deer a happy wife who would never want for anything, she noticed how the sun was bathing the outside of her father's council lodge with its amber light, spreading a soft glow across the inside of the hide covering.

She gazed slowly around the council lodge, where pictures of various forest animals had been

23

painted. Beautiful blankets were rolled up along the walls. Plush pelts hung from the rafters. It was a meeting place of the Cheyenne people, where weddings were performed, and where angry disputes were settled.

Her father's heated words brought Snow Deer's attention back to the matter at hand. She turned a slow gaze toward him. She blushed when she heard him determinedly defend her against a man no Cheyenne woman would want to marry, much less a Cheyenne princess!

"My daughter is a young woman of strong heart and soft, smiling eyes, who brings joy to the lives of my Cheyenne people," Chief Blazing Eagle said, his voice tight.

He leaned forward on his soft buffalo-robe couch with its sloping willow rests at each end. "She wishes to stay here among her people, *not* go to a Shawnee camp where she knows no one," he said firmly. "Her gentle words soothe the elderly of our village. She gives her heart to the elderly. She makes them feel as though life is still worth living although some can no longer walk, or see."

"*Huh*, your daughter *is* all of those things, and *is* capable of stirring one's heart into feeling young and vital again," Chief Rain Feather said. He gave Snow Deer another stare, which sent cold chills down her spine.

Rain Feather slid his eyes back to Blazing Eagle. "That is why I have singled your daughter out from your other women to be my wife," he said smoothly. "I, too, would enjoy her soft, smiling eyes. My people, too, would enjoy having her in their midst."

"This is my daughter's life we are discussing," Blazing Eagle said tightly. "She lives it as *she* chooses to live it."

Refusing to allow the Shawnee chief to sway him, Blazing Eagle looked over at Snow Deer. She had grown into a beautiful woman since that day he first saw her at the age of eight winters when her dying mother had brought her to live with him.

His first wife, whose name he would not even think or speak, had deserted Blazing Eagle and her son, Whistling Elk, many moons ago. When she left, she had taken with her a child growing inside her womb who belonged to her husband, Blazing Eagle.

A cruel, spiteful woman, she had not told Blazing Eagle when his daughter was born. It was only after Blazing Eagle's first wife knew her days were numbered that she had brought Snow Deer to him. Only then!

It had hurt him to know that he had lost his daughter's first seven winters!

Blazing Eagle had cherished his daughter from the moment he first saw her. And now that she was twenty winters, he cherished her no less. Besides her generous, warm heart, she had classic, beautiful features. She was tall and proud. Her eyes were so dark brown that they were almost black.

Today she wore her sleek, raven-black hair in long, thick braids which were ornamented with little fringed rolls of deerskin tied to the outside of the braids, close to the head. Sprigs of sage were tied on the outer sides of the rolls of deerskin.

Her tanned deerskin dress reached to halfway between her knees and her ankles. Midway between the waist belt and the border of the dress there was a wide decorative band. Two rows of blue beads ran across the front above the belt, with ornaments of porcupine quills hanging from them. Her leggings, which were painted yellow, were fringed at the bottom and up the sides. Her moccasins were worn on delicate, slender feet.

Blazing Eagle slid another slow gaze over at Rain Feather. "My Cheyenne people have ofttimes been coerced into doing that which did not please them," he said sternly.

Blazing Eagle's eyes were sharp as he glared at Rain Feather. "This chief now, forevermore, protects his people's pride and dignity, so that they, and especially my daughter, will not be humiliated again," he said flatly. "I protect them not only from the whites, but also from men with red skin who bring gifts that they feel might fool the Cheyenne into doing again what they do not see as best for them."

"You are wrong to compare Chief Rain Feather with any other red-skinned men, or whites," Rain Feather retorted. His eyes narrowed as his anger rose. "My gifts for your daughter today are gifts from my heart . . . from my very *soul*."

Rain Feather looked from Snow Deer to her father, then fixed his gaze on Snow Deer again. "Snow Deer, you saw the gifts," he said, his voice drawn. "You saw the canoe that I made especially for you. Did you not see the designs of deer along the birch-bark sides of the vessel? Carving them took this Shawnee chief many days and nights of hard labor. I carved them myself to make the gift more special for you."

He straightened his back and folded his arms across his bare chest. "Did you not also see the pelts inside the canoe?" he said stiffly. "These, too, I prepared especially for you. The white rabbit pelts can be worn on special occasions, or slept on during your . . . wedding night. I offer even more than that. You saw the gifts that I placed along the banks of the river, did you not? What woman could refuse such gifts?"

Rain Feather slid Blazing Eagle a slow gaze. "What father could refuse them for his daughter?" he said, his jaw tight.

"This father and this daughter appreciate the time you took to prepare such gifts, but this father and this daughter still wish for you to return them to your village and look elsewhere for a wife," Blazing Eagle said.

He slid a hand over to Snow Deer and twined his fingers through hers to lend her the added reassurance that he would never give her up easily to *any* man!

"You are wrong to treat this powerful Shawnee chief with such disrespect," Rain Feather hissed. "You are new to this land. I was born here! How can you feel that you can cast this Shawnee chief aside as though his words are only whispers in the wind? It is best that you think more carefully about this than you do today, or . . ."

"Are you voicing threats to this Cheyenne chief?" Blazing Eagle said, his eyes two points of fire. "If so, you had best reconsider. I no longer allow anyone to threaten me. To live in peace I have wrongly moved my people from place to place. First I dislodged them from our Wyoming homeland and took them to Canada, where the winds blew too cold and deadly for them. I then led them to Kansas near a place called Dodge City, where outlaws outnumbered the stars in the sky! I have brought them to this gentle land called Kentucky, and this is where we will stay. This land holds not only promise of bountiful land for growing crops, but also many forest animals to hunt. No one will ever force us to leave *this* land."

Blazing Eagle rose slowly to his feet. He was dressed in only a breechcloth and moccasins, his chest still as broad as when he was a young warrior falling in love with a beautiful white wife. He stood tall over the small Shawnee chief. "Our council is over," he said. He folded his arms across his chest. "Talk is over. Go and fill your canoe with gifts wrongly brought to my daughter. Take them and your canoe away from the shores of my people."

Hearing Rain Feather's sharp, shocked intake of breath, and suddenly afraid of what he might do to retaliate for being humiliated today, Snow Deer watched him warily as she slowly rose to her feet beside her father.

She hid her trembling hands behind her back as Rain Feather rose quickly to his feet, his eyes revealing his hatred not only for Blazing Eagle, but now also for Snow Deer.

"You were wrong to come to this land of the Shawnee," Rain Feather hissed. He reached down and grabbed a blanket that he had brought to sit upon while in council. He quickly slid the blanket around his narrow shoulders. He gave Blazing Eagle, then Snow Deer, one last, lingering stare, then stamped from the council house.

After his dramatic departure, the only sound in the lodge was the popping and crackling of the logs in the fire.

Outside, Rain Feather's voice rose above the commotion of the village as he shouted at them to step aside. Then he walked on toward the beached canoe that he had hoped would belong to the Cheyenne princess.

Snow Deer looked up at her father. "He is a man scorned, who might seek vengeance," she said, shivering at the thought.

Blazing Eagle turned to her and gently placed his hands on her shoulders. "If you allow yourself to fear this man, he will have caused even more damage to our lives than if he had married you," he said sternly. "Do you not know that he meant to intimidate you, so that you would carry the fear of him around inside your heart, so that, in time, you would marry him because you feared what he might do, not only to you, but also to your people?"

Snow Deer flung herself into her father's arms. "Oh, *Ne-hyo*, I cannot help but be afraid," she cried. "We have only recently established our home here. It would be horrible for our people to have to move our lodges again. I had hoped that this would be our home forever. I do love it so."

"As do I," Blazing Eagle said, gently caressing her back through her buckskin dress.

Then he held her away from him. Their eyes locked. "Again I implore you not to allow that Shawnee chief to put such fears and doubts inside your heart," he said. "Forget him. Forget everything that happened today. Remember *this*, my eldest daughter—we will not allow anyone to send us away from this land that we have found to be good for our people. If we have to bring our war clothes and war paints out of their parfleche bags to keep our feet planted on this soil, we shall do so."

"War, *Ne-hyo?*" Snow Deer said, paling. "Never have you spoken of warring before." She yanked herself away from her father and doubled her fists at her sides. "I hate that Shawnee chief! I hate him!"

Snow Deer spun quickly around when a soft voice spoke up behind her. She gazed at the woman who had raised her as her daughter since the death of Snow Deer's true mother. Snow Deer had grown to love this white woman, her father's beloved wife. Called Becky, she was everything to Snow Deer, her mother in every way.

"Daughter, hate is a word that I have never heard breathed across your lips before," Becky said as she stepped further into the council house, out of the shadows. Becky went and stood between Snow Deer and Blazing Eagle, looking from one to the other.

"I purposely did not sit in council with you, husband, because I knew what you were planning to say to Rain Feather," Becky then said. "Darling, it is apparent that he did not react favorably to what you said to him. I watched him storm through the village as he rushed toward his canoe. He was rude to everyone. He even shoved children who got in his way."

She turned to Snow Deer and placed a gentle hand on her cheek. "And, daughter, I am sorry you were given cause to have such harsh feelings for the Shawnee chief," she said softly. She drew Snow Deer into her arms. "Hatred is a destructive emotion. It eats away at one's soul. Please cast it out of your heart. Forget the Shawnee chief as though he does not exist. Go about your daily activities as you always have. The Shawnee chief will soon forget his anger. He will look elsewhere for a wife."

"I fear he won't," Snow Deer said, slipping away from Becky's embrace. "If not, he . . ."

"As I said, we will do what we must if he decides to pursue this further," Blazing Eagle said, interrupting her.

Becky turned to Blazing Eagle. "While at the trading post getting supplies, I questioned Clifton Wise, the owner of the post, about the Shawnee," she murmured. "He assured me that Chief Rain Feather's band of Shawnee are peaceful. There has never been warring in these parts. I wonder, though, if Rain Feather has ever been given cause to hate, as he has today?"

Blazing Eagle took Becky's hands. "Wife, we will not worry about such things unless given cause," he said softly.

Snow Deer gave them both soft hugs, then left the lodge and went to her own personal lodge, where she lived alone, in the tradition of a Cheyenne princess. The sun had lowered in the sky. The evening air was cool for August.

Shivering, she started a fire in her fire pit, then sat down on thick pelts and stared into the slowly burning flames. No matter what her father said, she could not get Rain Feather's angry words and flashing eyes off her mind. She and her father had humiliated the Shawnee chief! Surely he would retaliate in some ugly way!

"Can I sit with you by your fire?"

The small, sweet voice drew Snow Deer's eyes quickly to the raised entrance flap. When she saw Burning Snow, her twelve-year-old sister standing there, she smiled and held out a hand for her.

"Yes, come and sit with me," Snow Deer said. "You are exactly what I need. You always make me smile."

Holding her doeskin doll with its braids of corn-silk in her arms, Burning Snow came into the te-pee. Hugging the doll to her chest, she sat down beside Snow Deer and looked up at her sister. "That mean Shawnee chief shoved me to the ground as he hurried toward his canoe," she said, curving her lips into a pout. "Was he mean to you, too, Snow Deer?"

"He shoved *you*, the chief's daughter, to the

31

ground?" Snow Deer gasped, anger filling her heart.

"Yes. I guess I got in his way," Burning Snow said, lowering her eyes. "Sometimes I think I get in everyone's way."

Snow Deer felt a sudden ache in her heart as she drew Burning Snow into her embrace along with the doll. Sometimes Snow Deer did not know quite what to say to her sister. She never wanted to say anything to her that might hurt her feelings. Burning Snow had been born with a slow mind. Some who were cruel teased her about being "simple."

But no one in the Cheyenne village shamed the chief's daughter in such a way. It was mainly white people at trading posts. They knew no better than to poke fun at someone who did not catch on quickly to some things that were said.

"Never think that you are not loved," Snow Deer murmured. "You are in no one's way, ever. I'm so proud to have you for a sister. Mother and father are so proud to say you are their daughter."

Burning Snow slipped from Snow Deer's embrace. "You and mother and father are truly proud of me?" she asked. Her eyes implored Snow Deer for an answer that would make her feel needed.

"Very," Snow Deer said. She reached a hand out to smooth a fallen lock of hair back from her sister's eyes. "You are loved so very, very much."

Satisfied, Burning Snow sighed, then looked seriously up at Snow Deer. "The Shawnee chief was mad because you said you would not marry him?" she softly questioned.

"Yes, very," Snow Deer said, nodding. She leaned closer to the fire and shoved another log into the flames. "And I guess I would be just as mad if someone treated me as coldly as I treated him."

She turned to her sister. "I cannot imagine how many hours he spent carving those lovely figures on that canoe that he brought today as one of the bride-price gifts," she murmured. "That alone would give him much cause to be angry with me and father."

"The canoe was pretty," Burning Snow said, nodding. "I went down to the river and looked at it. I ran my fingers over the deer pictures. *I* would have loved having it."

"Yes, I would have loved having it, also," Snow Deer said, sighing. "But I would never want it for the reason it was made for me. I would never marry Rain Feather for *any* reason."

"A man you can love will come for you one day," Burning Snow said, nodding slowly. She giggled. "I wonder what he will look like? Surely he will be muscled and handsome, like father."

"Yes, perhaps one day I will find such a man as that," Snow Deer said, smiling at her sister. "But until I do, I shall enjoy being a Cheyenne princess."

"If a man came tomorrow who stole your heart, would you marry him?" Burning Snow asked softly.

"Tomorrow?" Snow Deer said, gently kneading her brow as she thought over the question.

She laughed softly. "No man will come tomorrow or the day after that who would suit my fancy as a husband," she said. "So let us stop talking about it."

Burning Snow clutched her doll to her chest and climbed up onto Snow Deer's lap. She cuddled close to her. "Sing me a song or tell me a story?" she whispered. "I so love these special times when it is just me and you."

"I also enjoy these special times," Snow Deer said, holding Burning Snow more closely. "And I shall tell you a story of the stars in the heavens and what they represent."

Content, Burning Snow smiled. She closed her eyes and listened.

For the moment, even Snow Deer was able to forget the fear of the Shawnee chief that had been etched into her heart today. There was only now, and her adorable sister, whose needs outweighed all of Snow Deer's fears.

But Burning Snow had brought something to Snow Deer's mind that kept nagging at her as she told the story in soft words. She wondered if she ever *would* find a man she could love. A man she would want to marry.

Of late, Snow Deer had been feeling restless, sometimes fantasizing about how it might be to be held, to be kissed, to be adored, as her mother was adored by her father!

She had, of late, become aware of a strange, hungry gnawing at the pit of her stomach whenever she wondered about this thing called "love."

Yes, she did feel as though she was ready to fall in love, if only the right man would come along!

She smiled at the direction her thoughts had taken while innocent ears had been listening to an innocent tale!

Chapter Three

Having arrived at his cousin Elissa's house just in time for dinner, Charles sat stiffly at her luxurious dining table. A bounteous feast was spread over the long oak table, filling the air with the aroma of a smoked turkey that was studded with pecans and bronzed and gleaming with a buttery, cider-honey glaze.

Charles looked at the mouth-watering food, which would usually tempt him into digging right in. Besides the turkey with its cornbread-and-sausage stuffing, there was his favorite corn relish, pickled cabbage, cranberry walnut relish, and glazed garlic. There was also a casserole of grits, smoked oysters, and glazed vegetables with fried parsnips.

He expected also to be tempted with one of Elissa's thoroughly indulgent desserts, like fresh raspberries swimming in wine sauce.

The table was spread with a crisp, white linen

cloth with matching napkins overflowing with lace, and set with china on which were painted designs of beautiful violets on a white background. Silver candlesticks sat at each end of the table, and tapered candles gave a mellow golden light. In the center of the table were two cut-glass decanters. One contained port and the other dark sherry.

Charles's appetite scarcely ever needed whetting, and he should have been ravenous after his long ride from Illinois. But he had no appetite whatsoever. When he had arrived at his cousin Elissa's house and seen the true condition his Uncle Hiram was in, he had become quickly disheartened. In fact, he was afraid that his uncle would not make the journey back to Bloomfield alive.

"Charles, you have scarcely touched your food," Elissa chided. "That's not like you."

She paused, and when Charles did not answer her, she tried another approach to bring him out of his ugly mood. "Charles, try a little of the brandied cranberry sauce on your turkey," she said, gesturing with a sweep of a hand toward it. "The sauce is in the sauceboat to the left of the platter of turkey."

"How could you allow your father's condition to deteriorate so much?" Charles suddenly said, glaring over the table at Elissa. "Lord, Elissa, he's your *father*. How could you allow him to lie in a bed so long that . . . that . . . he has bed sores on his . . ."

"Charles, please," Elissa murmured, interrupting him. With an expensive silver fork clutched between her fingers, she toyed with the food on her plate as she avoided Charles's accusing stare. "Please don't condemn me so quickly."

"I shouldn't have cause to condemn you at all,"

Charles said tightly. He slid a slow, heated gaze toward his cousin Gerald. "Gerald, I expected more from *you*. When you brought Uncle Hiram into your home, I was confident that he would never have to worry about anything again."

Charles sighed deeply. "I now know that I was wrong in that belief," he said thickly.

As Elissa began another attempt at explaining away her father's condition, Charles could hardly bear to listen. He stared at her, wondering if this was the Elissa he had known as a child. She had never been pretentious. She had loved the simpler ways of life.

But now she lived in a grand style, in a huge mansion, illuminated by broad windows that opened on a view of distant hills where many horses grazed on Kentucky bluegrass among white fences.

All through the house Gerald and Elissa's riches were flaunted, from the gilt-framed pictures that lined the walls to the expensive woolen rugs that covered the oak floors. Even the fireplaces in each room were not ordinary; they were each surrounded by silvery-blue slate.

Unlike Charles's mother's home, which was comfortable, hospitable, and unpretentious, Elissa and Gerald's home made one feel as though one should not even sneeze for fear of soiling something fancy.

Upon entering this house, one was swept away not only by the sight of the plush furnishings and wall hangings, but also by a stiff-collared butler with a strange foreign accent.

"Charles, are you listening to me?" Elissa said.

Elissa's troubled voice brought Charles out of his reverie. "You were saying . . . ?" he said tightly.

"Well, my word, Charles, I feel as though I have

been wasting my breath trying to explain my father's condition to you," Elissa snapped.

He did not respond immediately. He was enjoying her annoyance too much to make things easy on her.

His gaze slowly swept over her as though he were looking at her for the first time. She was the same age as he, a woman whom he had adored at one time, whom he had privately loved. She was of medium build; her hair, which was swirled atop her head in a fancy chignon, was a strawberry-blond color. Her round face, with its short nose which turned slightly up at the end, was tanned from spending more of her waking hours out of doors than inside her house.

This evening she wore a low-cut satin gown that revealed a mite too much of her milky-white cleavage, and a diamond necklace and earrings that sparkled beneath the light of the candles.

His gaze shifted to Gerald. He irritated Charles even more than Elissa did. He was a pompous bore who this evening was dressed in an expensive suit with a diamond sparkling in the folds of his ascot. His collar-length dark hair was sleeked back from his narrow face. His chin seemed permanently lifted, which was his way of saying that whoever he was speaking with was beneath him.

Charles sighed. His fingers clutched the long stem of the etched wine glass with its gold rim. He could hardly wait to return to Bloomfield, where life was ordinary and sweet. He only hoped and prayed that he could get his Uncle Hiram there before he died. Perhaps if his uncle could feel his sister's loving arms holding him again, he just might emerge from that black void that he had escaped to.

"Charles, you are being rude to my wife," Gerald

said, his eyes narrowing as he glared at Charles. "Your attitude is uncalled for. Must I remind you that you are a guest in our house?"

"I shall be taking Uncle Hiram away from this place tonight, as soon as I see that he has been fed a decent meal," Charles said, shoving his chair back and quickly rising.

"You will leave tonight?" Elissa said, getting up slowly from her chair.

"As I see it, the sooner the better," Charles said, walking solemnly from the room.

He went outside and stood on the spacious front porch. He clasped his hands on the railing and stared into the darkening shadows. It was his intent not to travel far with his uncle tonight. He would find a suitable inn on the outskirts of Paducah. He and his uncle would stay there until early morning, when he would begin his true journey home.

The rustling of the skirt of Elissa's dress made Charles stiffen as she came and stood beside him. He recoiled when she placed a gentle hand on his arm. His jaw tightened when she began talking softly to him.

This time he listened, for she seemed to be the Elissa he remembered when they came together as children for weekend visits, laughing and playing, or going horseback riding. He tried not to think of when they had grown older and had become awkward in each other's presence, when their unspoken feelings for each other had made them self-conscious.

"Charles, I'm sorry for so many things," Elissa murmured. She slid her hand up to his face. She placed her palm against his cheek. "Please, Charles, turn and look at me. Please listen."

Wanting desperately to love Elissa as he had in

innocent childhood, Charles turned slow eyes her way. Bits of memory, like snatches of a song, floated between them as their eyes met and held.

"Elissa, how could you have changed so much?" Charles blurted out. "How could having wealth have changed you into someone I no longer know? How could it have made you neglect your father? Lord, Elissa, Uncle Hiram is pitiful!"

"Yes, he is certainly that, Charles," Elissa said, lowering her hand and her eyes. "But he's been that way for far longer than Gerald and I have had our wealth. Even when I spent almost every waking daylight hour trying to make Father comfortable, and trying to make his mind function again, he had become someone foreign to me. His mind left him long ago, Charles. His ability to think, to speak, to walk . . . all of those things were gone before Gerald and I found ways to make ourselves rich."

"I can't believe that," Charles said. He placed a hand under her chin and brought it up, so that her eyes met the questioning look in his. "It hasn't been that long since I last saw Uncle Hiram. He was all right then, Elissa."

"Charles, you've been so busy, you have lost track of time," Elissa said softly. "C.C., it's been eight years since you last saw me *or* my father. And as I recall, Father fought hard then not to show you how his mind was slipping into a strange sort of dark void. I watched him. He forced himself to be attentive, to act alert to all that you said to him. It was shortly after that when it all came tumbling down around him."

"But, Elissa, those bed sores on his body must mean that you rarely get him out of bed," Charles said, his voice drawn. "How can you explain that away?"

"C.C., I hire nurses to come each day to bathe him, to get him out of bed, to take him for walks through the woods in his wheelchair," Elissa said, tears welling in her eyes. "Every day he is taken to see the horses. Although even they no longer bring light into his eyes, I make sure that he sees the horses that he once loved with all of his heart."

"The bed sores, Elissa," Charles persisted. "They seem to make everything you are saying a pack of lies."

"C.C., it hurts me so that you don't believe me," Elissa said, a sob catching in her throat. "Do you know that it takes only a few hours in bed each day to cause bed sores? Neither I nor the doctors or nurses have found a way to prevent them. It hurts me deeply to see them. My heart has wept to see my father slowly deteriorate right before my eyes."

She wiped tears from her cheeks. "C.C., I know that my father hasn't much time left to live," she said. "I don't think I can bear it. This is why I am asking you to take him away. My pain will not disappear in his absence, but it might be lightened somewhat."

She again placed a gentle hand on Charles's cheek. "Charles, your mother might bring something back inside my father's mind," she said softly. "Please understand that we must make this last attempt at bringing him some happiness at the end of his journey on this earth."

Hearing the genuine pleading in her voice, Charles swept his arms around her and held her close. "Elissa, Elissa," he said. "I knew that you couldn't have changed as much as it seemed you had."

"C.C., my life might look easy to you, but it *isn't* at all as it seems," she murmured. "Yes, I have a mansion for a home. I have vast land. I own many beautiful horses. And I can say that my husband and I are wealthy. But nothing comes without a price. I have worked so hard to help make our stud farm what it is today, I find it hard now to find joy in it."

Charles slid her away from him. He held her hands. "What are you saying?" he said thickly.

"I am not well, Charles," she said, sighing. "Before we could afford to hire men to help with our horse-breeding chores, I worked by day caring for father, then by night catching up with things that should have been done during the daylight hours. I didn't get enough rest. I, not Gerald, worked long hours in the cold night air. My lungs have paid the price."

She swallowed hard and looked away from him. "I am in the first stages of consumption, Charles," she said, her voice breaking. "I am not sure how long even *I* have on this earth."

Charles paled.

He clasped her shoulders with his fingers.

She gazed slowly up at him.

"Yes, Charles, I am dying," Elissa said, an uncontrollable shiver of fear racing across her flesh. "It is a blessing of sorts that father isn't aware of what is happening. He would be devastated to know my condition."

Charles yanked her into his arms and held her protectively to him. "Isn't there anything that can be done?" he said, his voice breaking.

"When my condition worsens, and it is obvious to all who see me that I have consumption, I could go and live in an asylum," she said softly. "But I refuse to. I love my horses too much. I want to spend as much of my remaining time with them as possible. They are my heart and soul, Charles."

"Lord," Charles said, finding this almost too hard to accept. He slowly held her away from him. "What about Gerald? What does he say about all of this? What does he want you to do?"

"Gerald has turned into someone I hardly know anymore," Elissa said. Her eyes filled with tears once again. "He's taken to gambling. He spends long hours away from home at night." She swallowed hard. "I even suspect now that there is another woman involved in his life."

Anger filled Charles. "I can't leave you here with him," he said. He glanced past her. He gazed through the parlor window and saw Gerald sitting, leisurely smoking a cigar and sipping a glass of port.

"This is where I want to be," Elissa said, her eyes following the path of Charles's gaze. She stared at her husband. "It doesn't matter to me anymore what Gerald does. As I said, my horses are my life. It makes me so proud when I see a foal being born into this world, knowing that one day it might be a famous racehorse. I have always been careful with the blood lines when I breed my horses so that I will be raising a winner."

"The stud farm has become quite profitable for you," Charles said. He turned and gazed into the shadows of the vast reaches of pasture land. He could see the horses being led, one by one, by grooms to the stables. He could see the lamplight in the stables and could hear the contented wickering of horses that were already housed there for the night.

"These animals have given me such contentment," Elissa said, nodding. "It has given me such a sense of accomplishment to see my foals grow into beautiful racehorses! I have so enjoyed riding them, myself, for pleasure. We have a bond, my horses and me. They, more than my husband, will feel my absence when the good Lord calls me home."

Charles again drew her into his arms. "Knowing how you feel about your horses will make it easier for me to leave you here," he said. "But before I leave, I think I have some talking to do with Cousin Gerald."

Elissa drew quickly away from Charles and looked up at him with warm, soft eyes. "No, I'd rather you didn't," she said. "There's no need. Just leave it be. I don't need him."

Charles said nothing more, but inside his heart he was thinking about Gerald, who surely was waiting to bring another woman into this house that had been built with Elissa's sweat, blood, and tears.

Yet Charles knew that he had no control over anything that Gerald did now, or in the future. Just knowing that Elissa accepted things that were, and would be, was all that mattered to him.

"Please change your mind about leaving so soon," Elissa said, standing on tiptoe to brush a kiss across his cheek. "Please stay one more night, C.C.? It will be our last together."

Hearing her say the words that he knew now to be true tore at his very soul. He grabbed her again and held her close. "I'll stay for as many nights as you wish," he said, his voice breaking.

"Just this one night will satisfy me," Elissa murmured. "Then I think it best that you get father to Bloomfield. I so badly want him to have some time with your mother before he dies."

Charles closed his eyes, trying to shut out the sadness, for he was almost certain that his uncle would not live through the long, arduous miles of the journey to Bloomfield.

But if he did make it there, Charles feared his mother's reaction when she saw her brother in this condition. She often spoke of her brother and his laughter and ability to tell jokes.

Those days were long past for Uncle Hiram.

"I'll stay this one more night. Your father and I will be leaving tomorrow shortly after breakfast," Charles said thickly.

"Thank you, Charles," Elissa murmured. "Thank you."

She slipped away from him and smiled up at him. "C.C., had you not been my cousin, you know that I would have latched on to you long ago," she said, her eyes locked with his. "I would have chosen you over Gerald for a husband."

"I would have been honored to have you for a wife," Charles replied warmly.

"When *are* you going to take time enough to find yourself a wife?" Elissa asked.

"I've been thinkin' on it, Elissa," Charles said, laughing softly.

"C.C., some lucky woman is waiting out there somewhere for you," Elissa said, smiling up at him. "I just know she'll be beautiful."

"I look for more than beauty in a wife," Charles said. Then he laughed softly as he looked at Elissa. "But don't think that will be something I'll overlook, either."

"That sounds more like my Charles," Elissa said, laughing. "As children, I watched your eyes going to the most beautiful girls in the park when we were there picnicking. I saw the appreciation in your eyes."

"You know me so well," he said, chuckling, glad to find something lighthearted to talk about. But seeing how young Elissa was, and knowing that

45

she was dying, made him realize that life was not indefinite. He most certainly could not waste any more of his years without a wife.

He would begin looking for her right away.

Chapter Four

The air was sweet with fragrance from the wild rose vines that twined across the forest floor and up the trunks of the trees. The wild turnips were growing on the hillsides, and the chokeberries were ripe along the river.

Their moccasins as silent as field mice, the young Cheyenne maidens walked through the knee-high grass. The view of the Ohio River was clear through the trees at their left side.

Snow Deer walked beside her sister, Burning Snow, her eyes wavering as she glanced over at her. Today was no different from all the other times when Snow Deer had taken Burning Snow with her on a root-digging expedition. Slow, not only in her way of thinking, but also in everything she did with her hands, Burning Snow had dug only a few bear roots and wild turnips today.

Protective of her younger sister, and not wanting her to feel any less proud of her roots than the others, whose baskets held so many, Snow Deer smiled. What she was going to suggest to the other maidens had been done before without their holding a grudge against Burning Snow for being slower than they.

Yes, Snow Deer thought, she would once again propose that everyone there should divide into two groups and gamble for the bunches of roots.

Everyone would understand why she suggested the game, and everyone, loving Burning Snow, would agree.

It would be only Burning Snow who would not understand the purpose behind the gambling. To her it would just be something else to laugh and have fun with.

In the end, she would carry home with her as many roots as her friends!

But before suggesting their gambling game, Snow Deer continued onward with her friends and sister, enjoying the loveliness of the day. She gazed heavenward and sighed at the beauty of the sky, with not one cloud marring its blue serenity.

The sunshine was mellow.

The wind, smelling of the river and the trees, was soft. It gently fluttered the fluffy tips of Snow Deer's hair ornaments, which she had made from rabbit fur dyed yellow and red. The wind blew against her face, as though it were a mother's caress.

It was such a beautiful day that it was easy to forget the Shawnee chief who had disturbed the tranquility of her father's council house. She forced herself not to think of what he might do to retaliate for being so humiliated while in Cheyenne council.

"I dropped my basket of roots," Burning Snow

suddenly cried, drawing Snow Deer out of her reverie.

She looked quickly down at Burning Snow, who was on her knees gathering her few roots into her tiny hands and slowly placing them back inside her basket.

Everyone was quiet as they circled around Burning Snow and Snow Deer, their eyes showing their understanding of Burning Snow's disabilities. Except for a few foolish young braves at the Cheyenne village, none had ever shown pity toward Burning Snow. Only love.

Pink Willow edged close to Snow Deer. "Burning Snow has so few roots," she whispered, so that Burning Snow could not hear. She smiled over at Snow Deer. "As we have done before, do you wish to play the gambling game again so that she will enter the village with many bunches of roots in her basket?"

Snow Deer reached a hand to Pink Willow. She twined her fingers through hers as she smiled at her. "You are a dear friend," she murmured. "Yes. I was thinking the same. Let us, you and I, suggest the gambling game."

Loving Burning Snow, everyone soon agreed to the game.

As Burning Snow watched, her eyes wide with excitement, the maidens divided into two groups. Pink Willow plucked her root-digger from her basket of roots and held it out before her, to be the first one to pitch it.

The root-digger was a slender, sharp-pointed implement which was used to thrust into the ground to pry out the roots. Each digger was made of ash, the point sharpened and hardened in the fire. There was a knob at one end to protect the hand.

Everyone grew quiet when Pink Willow pitched her root-digger as far as she could throw it.

Then everyone began laughing and talking as each one took a turn trying to hit Pink Willow's digger with her own. If only one of the maidens' root-diggers hit the one that had been thrown first, her side would win. If a root-digger from each side hit Pink Willow's digger, the game would be a draw. If none of the root-diggers that were thrown hit Pink Willow's, the game would also be a draw.

Either way, no matter who the winner was, their roots would be divided, for Burning Snow did not know enough about the game to understand who was the winner or the loser.

After everyone had taken a turn pitching her root-digger at Pink Willow's, and not one of them hit hers, or even came close to it, the game ended with much laughter as they each filed by Burning Snow's basket and placed one of their bunches of roots into hers, along with an occasional turnip.

Afterward, Burning Snow picked up her basket and smiled when she saw how many roots were there. She looked proudly up at Snow Deer. "I won the gambling game again," she said, her eyes shining. "See? I now have as many roots as you! I even have turnips for our mother's table!"

"Yes, and both she and father will be so proud of you," Snow Deer said, placing a gentle hand on her sister's sleek copper cheek. "I'm proud of you."

"I'm going to run on ahead and show mother and father my basket!" Burning Snow said excitedly.

Snow Deer frowned, for she always wanted to keep her sister near when they were away from the safe confines of the village.

Gazing ahead, she could see the outer fringes of

the village through a break in the trees. She sighed to herself, thinking they were close enough for it to be safe.

"*Huh*, go on and show mother and father," Snow Deer said, her sister's innocent, sweet smile filling her with gentle warmth. "I will be there shortly."

Burning Snow laughed gaily as she broke away from the maidens and ran onward, toward the village.

Still enjoying the loveliness of the forest, where butterflies flitted about with their delicate wings of varied beautiful colors, and where birds sang overhead in the birches and cottonwoods, Snow Deer slowly dropped back from the others, to enjoy the wonders of nature.

A hummingbird darted past, only inches from Snow Deer's nose; she stopped to watch its flight into a mimosa tree that was thick with luscious pink flowers. She gasped with delight when several other hummingbirds swarmed around the flowers, ignoring the bees that were there also for a sweet meal of nectar.

Lost in her enjoyment of this sight, Snow Deer was not aware of being left behind. She was fascinated by the way the wings of the hummingbirds continued to flutter as they thrust their long bills into the depths of the flowers, instead of landing like a butterfly, to relax while enjoying the meal.

Snow Deer looked quickly over her shoulder. When she saw her friends moving away from her, drawing close now to the village, she started to run to catch up with them, but something flashing at her right side within a thick stand of forsythia bushes drew her eyes there.

She could not imagine what might be flashing

mysteriously in the bushes unless someone had dropped a mirror there, or perhaps a piece of jewelry.

Filled with curiosity, she was lured away from the path, toward the mysterious light. It seemed that the sun was causing the fluttering light as its rays reflected from whatever lay there.

The flashing suddenly stopped.

Snow Deer's pace slowed as she stiffened and looked more intensely into the bushes where she had seen the light. A warning went off inside her brain when she saw the bushes rustle strangely, as though someone might be there.

But then again the flashing light was there, making her forget the dangers of being alone in the forest. She stared at the mysterious light as it flashed into her eyes, as though it was a beacon luring her onward.

A wave of fear swept through her, and the skin at the back of her neck prickled in warning. Her heart skipped several beats and she stopped suddenly when she noticed more movement in the bushes.

She gasped with alarm when two rough-looking white men stepped out of the shadows. Their buckskin clothes were soiled, wrinkled, and blood-stained, and one of the men was laughing throatily as he held a mirror so that it still captured the shine of the sun in it.

It was obvious to Snow Deer that the men had used the mirror to lure one of the Cheyenne maidens away from the others. She felt foolish that it had been *she* who had been duped in such a manner. In the past she had always been so careful.

Before she could make a fast retreat, or scream for help, one of the whiskered men grabbed her and held her tight, while the other man dropped the mirror and tied a filthy handkerchief around her mouth.

A cold fear filling her veins, Snow Deer dropped her basket of roots and struggled to get free as the other man tied her hands together behind her.

When the man released her, she ran only a few feet before the other man ran after her and, laughing boisterously, caught her.

Her eyes flashing over the gag, Snow Deer gave the men a look of defiance.

"Seems we have a feisty one on our hands, Luke," one of them said. He chuckled as he raked his thick hands through his greasy, shoulder-length brown hair. "We'll have us a good time with 'er tonight. She's probably never been with a man before. We'll introduce her to things she never imagined could happen to a redskin squaw."

Hearing what they had planned for her, knowing that she was going to be raped not only once, but many times by these filthy, evil, women-hungry men, Snow Deer managed to wrench herself free from the man's grip. She tried to run again, but Luke was too quick for her. He grabbed her, turned her to face him, then raised a foot and kicked her in the belly, sending her rolling backward down the embankment, toward the river.

"We've wasted enough time foolin' with 'er here," the first man snarled. "Come on, Luke. Grab 'er. Let's get 'er to the canoe and get out of here a'fore she's missed at the village. We need to get downriver before stoppin' to have our fun with 'er."

"I'm hot as hell for 'er, Zeke," Luke said, bending over Snow Deer, leering into her face.

Snow Deer turned her face away, choking on the strong stench of the whiskey on his breath.

She groaned when he yanked her to her feet by

her long braids and began half dragging her farther into the shadows of the forest, Zeke following close behind them.

Soon she realized that Luke had made a wide turn and was now making his way through the trees toward the shine of the river. When she saw a large canoe beached on the rocky shore, and saw the bloody pelts piled high in the canoe, she understood too well who these men were.

Trappers.

Cackling, Luke lifted her and dropped her down next to the bloody pelts.

She cringed and looked away from the pelts, not only because of their stench, and not only because the blood was oozing from them into the hem of her lovely skirt, but because these trappers had killed needlessly today. They had taken many pelts.

Cheyenne hunters went forth solemnly and with reluctance when they left for the hunt, for it was the Cheyenne's belief that killing any creature disturbed the harmony of the world. Cheyenne warriors always made proper prayers to the animals they killed, so that they didn't cause offense.

But these white men surely knew not the art of praying, nor knew any remorse when they killed.

And today they did worse than reduce the animal population. They had abducted a Cheyenne princess!

They planned to defile her body and then perhaps to kill her!

Snow Deer lowered her eyes and closed them as the canoe was shoved away from the shore. She tried not to listen to the men laughing and poking fun at her. She tried not to listen as they planned what they were going to do with her, and how.

Tears came to Snow Deer's eyes, for she saw no

way to save herself. There was no trail being left for her father to follow. The men were carrying her away by water. Each dip of the paddles, each splashing wave of the Ohio, took her farther and farther away from life as she had always known it.

She felt an utter hopelessness such as she had never known before.

Chapter Five

"Mother, Mother!" Burning Snow cried excitedly as she entered her parents' large tepee. "See what I have brought for you? Many roots. I even have turnips for you!"

Becky sat on a soft mat made of willow twigs at the inside of the tepee where she had rolled up the bottom of the buckskin covering so that she could have some clean, fresh air in her lodge on this warm August day. She looked quickly up at her younger daughter and smiled at her exuberance. She knew that once again Snow Deer had managed to see that her younger sister would have as many roots as the others who had gone on the root-digging expedition.

It pleased Becky that her two daughters were so close, that they loved each other so much, even though they were only half-sisters. Having different mothers had not mattered to them. They shared a father and a great love for each other.

As Burning Snow plopped down beside Becky, Becky saw that her daughter's thoughts had already strayed from her basket of roots. She was mesmerized now by the lovely beads that Becky had begun to slide on a long coil of string before using them to decorate a dress that she had made for Burning Snow.

"Mother, the beads are beautiful," Burning Snow said, setting aside her basket. Her long, slender fingers went to the beads as Becky held them up for her to see them better. She ran her fingers over them, sighing.

"Sweetie, the beads are for the doeskin dress that I made for you," Becky said.

"A dress?" Burning Snow said, her eyes widening with joy. "Thank you, Mother. I love new dresses."

"Daughter, do you not remember watching me make the dress?" Becky asked, her voice drawn. "Do you not remember sewing a few stitches of sinew on the dress yourself?"

"No, I remember nothing of a dress, nor of helping you," Burning Snow said. She clasped her hands on her lap and smiled at Becky. "But I would love to help you when you begin sewing the beads on the dress. May I?"

"Yes, you may," Becky said, swallowing hard. Her heart always ached for this daughter, whose mind was too slow to comprehend many things. Rarely did Burning Snow maintain interest in anything for long. It seemed her mind would not rest as it jumped from thought to thought. Her attention lasted for only moments at a time.

It was hard for Becky to believe that Burning Snow could not remember having helped sew the dress! At the time, she had marveled over the softness of the doeskin and its whiteness.

Yet Becky knew that nothing should surprise her about her daughter's lack of memory. She had noticed it as soon as Burning Snow was old enough to talk.

And Becky was now afraid that it would never be any different for her daughter. It was up to Becky and Blazing Eagle to keep her safe, for it was doubtful that she would ever be able to marry or have a normal relationship with a man.

"And so you had a good time today while digging roots?" Becky said, again stringing beads as Burning Snow watched with wide, curious eyes.

"Yes, I always have a good time while I am with my sister Snow Deer," Burning Snow said, again reaching over to touch the colorful beads. "She will love the beads, too, Mother, don't you think?"

"Yes, she will love the beads as much as you," Becky said, looking toward the entrance flap, then back at Burning Snow. "Where *is* your sister? She always stops in for a short while after seeing you safely home."

Burning Snow frowned as she tried to recollect when she had last seen her older sister.

She then shrugged. "I do not know where Snow Deer is," she said nonchalantly. She looked at her mother with innocently wide eyes. "Should I know?"

Becky sighed. She reached a hand over to Burning Snow's face and gently stroked it. "She'll be here soon," she murmured. "I'm sure she stopped to talk with her friends before coming inside to visit with her mother."

Blazing Eagle came into the lodge with a bow that he had been fashioning while sitting outside with the other men, chatting.

Becky looked up at him and smiled, then gazed with admiration at the bow. "You carve bows so beautifully," she murmured. "Our son Whistling Elk gets his skill at carving from you." She gazed up at Blazing Eagle. "Where is Whistling Elk? I haven't seen him all day."

"He is visiting a friend just outside Paducah," Blazing Eagle said, laying his bow aside. "There is a white woman. She lives on a farm. Whistling Elk saw her one day while horseback riding. He stopped. They became acquainted. I believe he is interested in her, my wife."

"He never told me about a woman," Becky said, raising an eyebrow.

"Sons do not discuss matters of the heart with mothers," Blazing Eagle said, chuckling.

He knelt down beside Burning Snow. "Young daughter, where is your older sister?" he asked softly. "I did not see her arrive at the village with the other root diggers. Where is she, Burning Snow? She was to see you safely home."

Burning Snow turned blank eyes up to her father. "I do not know," she said softly. She looked past Blazing Eagle and stared at the entranceway, then gazed into her father's eyes again. "She is not here? Why is she not here, Father?"

Frustrated, yet not wanting his younger daughter to see his frustration over her inability to remember when it was so important, Blazing Eagle patted Burning Snow's shoulder.

He then turned troubled eyes to Becky. "I fear something has happened to Snow Deer," he said. He saw the fear mount in his wife's eyes. He held a hand out for her. "Come. We will go and question the others. Surely Pink Willow will have answers for us about Snow Deer. They are best friends. Best friends watch out for each other."

"Blazing Eagle, you don't truly think anything has happened to Snow Deer, do you?" Becky asked, laying her sewing aside. She took Blazing Eagle's hand as she rose to her feet.

"If she is not here, what else am I to think?" Blazing Eagle said, his voice drawn.

Burning Snow scrambled to her feet. "Where is Snow Deer?" she asked, her eyes suddenly wild. "Where is my sister?"

Realizing that Burning Snow had sensed his alarm, Blazing Eagle turned quickly to her. He clasped his hands on her shoulders. "Burning Snow, there is no need for panic," he said. "There is an explanation for everything. I am certain your sister has not come to any harm."

Burning Snow swallowed hard. She smiled weakly and nodded. "She is all right," she said, her voice softer.

"Yes, she is all right," Blazing Eagle said. He looked past Burning Snow, into Becky's eyes. "Wife, I think it is best if you stay here with Burning Snow. Keep her here until I return. I might be gone for a while."

Becky's fear was like ice around her heart, for she knew now that Blazing Eagle thought something terribly wrong might have happened to Snow Deer. He had watched the girls return from the root-digging expedition without Snow Deer. It was evident now that something must have happened to her!

"Yes, I shall stay here with Burning Snow," Becky said, finding it hard to control her feelings. Yet she knew that she must—for her younger daughter's sake. Burning Snow was easily disturbed by violent emotion. Blazing Eagle and Becky had learned long ago to keep their moods light around her.

Blazing Eagle went to his supply of weapons and grabbed his rifle. Then he paused before

Becky, gave her a soft kiss, and left the lodge with long, determined strides.

Becky drew Burning Snow into her arms. She could feel the desperation in Burning Snow's embrace, which proved that her daughter *did* know more than she was saying aloud. This time it seemed that Burning Snow knew that an outburst on her part would be useless.

Blazing Eagle went to Pink Willow's parents' lodge. He called Pink Willow's name, bringing her quickly out to stand before him, her eyes questioning.

"Snow Deer did not arrive home from root-digging with you and the others," Blazing Eagle said. "Why is that?"

Pink Willow's dark eyes widened. "I did not know that she was not with us," she said softly. "We were all laughing and talking. I paid no attention to anything else."

"I saw your return," Blazing Eagle said, clutching his rifle tightly. "And she was not with you." He cleared his throat nervously. "When do you last recall seeing her?"

"Right after we played the gambling game," Pink Willow said. "Snow Deer and I schemed together to make sure that Burning Snow had as many roots as the others. After the roots were placed in Burning Snow's basket, we all proceeded toward the village. I remember Burning Snow running on ahead of us. But I do not remember anything else about Snow Deer. We were all having fun. I . . . thought . . . she was there with us, enjoying the fun herself."

Blazing Eagle's eyes narrowed angrily. "Friends watch out for friends," he said, his teeth clenched. "Is Snow Deer not your best friend?"

Pink Willow took a shaky step away from him.

She nodded. "Yes, my very best," she said, her voice breaking. "I . . . would . . . never want harm to come to her."

Seeing how his anger was affecting Pink Willow, and wishing now that he had guarded his anger and words more carefully in the presence of the young maiden, Blazing Eagle placed a gentle hand on Pink Willow's shoulder. "It is true that neither of you is the other's guardian," he said solemnly. "Return to your lodge. Help your mother with the chores. But send your father outside to me."

Pink Willow nodded anxiously. She turned and entered her large tepee. Her father, Red Bow, came out quickly.

"What is this about Snow Deer?" Red Bow asked.

"I fear harm has come to her," Blazing Eagle said somberly. "Get your rifle. We must take many warriors and search for Snow Deer."

Red Bow nodded.

Soon Blazing Eagle led the search party away from the village, retracing the steps of those who had returned a short while ago from their root-digging.

When they reached a place where the crushed grass led away from the path made by the others, they followed more slowly, watching carefully until they came to a thick stand of forsythia bushes.

There they found a mirror.

There they found signs of a recent scuffle.

There they found Snow Deer's spilled basket of roots!

Blazing Eagle's heart bled with despair. Now he was certain that something had happened to his beloved daughter.

His heart thudding like a thousand drumbeats,

Blazing Eagle led his men past the forsythia bushes and followed the trampled grass into the forest, then on to the river.

Blazing Eagle turned to Red Bow, his eyes filled with sorrow. "She has been taken away by river," he said solemnly.

Then his sorrow was replaced with anger. "There is only one man who would steal my daughter away from her people!" he cried. He lifted his rifle above him. "Rain Feather! He is a man scorned! He is a man filled with humiliation over Snow Deer's rejection of him! His humiliation has led him into foolish actions today! He has taken my daughter away! He has abducted her!"

"Surely he is not so foolish," Red Bow said, staring down the long avenue of the river. "Surely it was someone else. Rain Feather knows he could not take your daughter to his village without you coming for her."

"He is blinded with his humiliation and would not think past what his heart has told him to do," Blazing Eagle said, his jaw tight.

He looked from warrior to warrior. "We must paddle our canoes downriver to Rain Feather's village," he said tightly. "Pity Rain Feather if he has taken Snow Deer, my daughter, your *princess*."

They hurried back to the village.

Without taking the time to explain to their wives where they were going, they boarded their birch-bark canoes and headed downriver.

Blazing Eagle's muscled arms could not move the paddle quickly enough, for he knew that each moment that his daughter was away from him, she was at the mercy of a madman, for any man who thought that he could get away with abducting her could be no less than mad!

He lifted his eyes heavenward and said a silent prayer to the Supreme Being, asking *Maheo* to get him to his daughter before her beautiful body was defiled by a man with a black, evil heart!

Chapter Six

The buckboard's wheels rattled and creaked as Charles rode slowly beside the Ohio River, watching for the ferry landing where he would find the paddle-wheeler ferry that would take him across from Kentucky into Illinois.

When he heard a low moan, he looked quickly over his shoulder at his Uncle Hiram. Charles had made him a thick padding of blankets in the wagon and had laid him there for the journey to Bloomfield. His uncle was not strong enough to sit beside Charles.

With tender care, Charles had carried his uncle to the wagon. He had made him as comfortable as possible on the blankets, and then had drawn one over him, up to his chin.

Charles had managed to make a tent-like canvas covering over his uncle so that he would not be exposed to the sun, but he made sure there was enough space for air to circulate.

Charles could see now beneath the canvas covering, which was tied from the back of the wagon to his seat. He saw that his uncle was asleep. He frowned when he saw a slow stream of drool rolling from the corners of his uncle's mouth.

When his uncle moaned again, and Charles heard strange rattling sounds coming from his lungs, panic seized him. His uncle was dying! The death rattles were signs of his imminent death! And there was nothing he could do to help him.

"Uncle Hiram, please hang on," Charles begged. "Please don't die on me."

The sound of paddles splashing in the river at his right side drew Charles's eyes quickly to the Ohio. He drew a tight rein and brought his wagon to a quick halt.

He frowned as he gazed at the three occupants of the canoe. Two of them were men. The pelts piled high in the canoe proved the men were trappers.

Charles gazed at the other occupant, taken aback when he saw that it was an Indian woman. His eyes widened when he noticed that her mouth was gagged.

"Lord," Charles gasped. "They've abducted the woman!"

Just then he caught sight of a huge limb rolling through the water, approaching the canoe from behind.

He jumped when the limb crashed into the back of the canoe, the jolt sending the Indian woman into the river along with many of the pelts.

As the trappers yelped and hollered and tried to stay aboard the canoe themselves, it was obvious they had forgotten about the woman.

Charles hadn't. He was already in the river swimming toward her. He kept an eye on her as she bobbed up and down in the water. He could tell that she was half dazed. When she had fallen overboard, her head had hit a huge boulder thrusting up from the river bottom.

Charles reached the woman just in time. She had gone beneath the surface just within his reach.

His heart racing, he reached down and grabbed her.

After he had her positioned in the crook of one arm, he yanked the gag from around her mouth.

She began to cough and choke.

Her eyes flew open, and she stared frantically at Charles.

"You're going to be all right," he reassured her, now fumbling with the rope at her wrist, glad when it fell off and floated away in the water. "Just relax. I'll take you to shore."

He was relieved that the woman didn't fight back. She closed her eyes and relaxed as he took her toward the riverbank.

When he reached the rocky bottom where he could stand up, he gently positioned the Indian woman in his arms and carried her out of the water.

As he laid her on the ground, he waited for her eyes to open again. When they didn't, he worried that she might have lost consciousness. Not knowing what to do next, almost desperate with concern over the woman, Charles knelt over her and gazed at her.

Never had he seen anyone so beautiful.

Never had he been this close to an Indian woman before!

Her raven-black hair, with its heavy braids that must hang almost to the ground when she walked, framed a face of beauty—a face of perfect features. He could not help being taken, body and soul, by her loveliness.

He reached an arm beneath her and raised her somewhat from the ground. "Can you hear me?" he asked softly, his gaze never leaving the loveliness of her face. "Miss, can you hear my voice?"

He was relieved when her eyes fluttered open.

When she closed them again, Charles did not worry as much as before. It was obvious that she was exhausted from her ordeal in the water.

As she laid her head against his chest, he could see where she had hit the rock. There was a small amount of blood oozing from the wound.

Charles took a handkerchief from his rear pocket and noticed that it was already soaking wet. Gently, he washed the blood from her head and hair.

Still she slept soundly.

Charles glanced at the wagon, where his uncle lay somewhere near death.

He gazed again at the Indian maiden. He had no idea where she came from, or from which tribe she had been abducted.

And he had no time to waste searching for her people. His uncle was quickly slipping away. He had to think of his welfare before anyone else's. He *must* make an attempt to get him home before he died!

Charles gazed at the woman again, his eyes traveling over her attire. She was dressed in a beautifully tanned deerskin dress and leggings. Her moccasins were intricately designed and beautiful.

He did not want to let his eyes linger on how her wet buckskin dress clung to her shapely figure so tightly, revealing her beautifully rounded breasts, her tiny waist, and her tapered thighs.

He felt that to look at her tempting curves would be taking advantage of the woman whose privacy had already been violated by two white men. He did not want to be placed in the same category as those who took what was not theirs!

But, oh, she was so captivatingly beautiful.

And, apart from the forbidden love of his past, this woman was the first to stir him. He knew that if he were given the chance, he could love her.

He stared at the river, where he had last seen the canoe. He recalled the two trappers. He wondered how long this woman had been with them.

How many miles had she been forced to travel with them as their captive?

Had they harmed her in any way?

That last thought made his heart beat angrily. If the trappers had defiled this Indian maiden, surely she would be afraid of him, too, when she fully awakened.

While Snow Deer lay in a dark void of semiconsciousness, she heard an eagle up in the sky. He seemed to be whistling and coming nearer and nearer, descending in a circle. Just as the eagle came very close, she awakened.

She became quickly aware of a throbbing in her head. Groaning, she reached her hand up and flinched when she found the lump.

Aware of not being alone, she slid her gaze slowly upward and found the white man staring down at her. For a moment, it was as though the handsome white man's eyes held her as if by a spell.

When he looked as though he was ready to speak to her, her senses seemed to return. She recoiled and yanked herself free of him.

Her gaze roamed slowly over the stranger, and she saw that his clothes were as wet as hers.

Cassie Edwards

"Where am I?" she murmured, surprising Charles by speaking perfect English. "Who are you? Why are we both wet?"

Charles's eyes wavered and his heart went out to her when he realized that she remembered nothing, not even the fall in the river! She didn't recall his saving her. So certainly she wouldn't recall having been abducted.

"My name is Charles Cline," he said, yet he did not approach her again for fear of frightening her. For the moment, she seemed too puzzled by her inability to recall things to be really afraid of him.

"Can you remember your name?" he asked softly.

"No, I cannot tell you my name," Snow Deer said, confused over her inability to think clearly. Was she incoherent with fear?

Or was it something more, for she truly felt no threat in this white man's presence? She seemed to have lost her ability to remember things.

She groaned and closed her eyes when the pain in her head worsened. She lowered her head and slowly shook it back and forth. She again reached her hand to the lump.

"How was I injured?" she said, her voice drawn.

"You don't remember falling from the canoe, do you?" Charles said, daring to place a gentle hand beneath her chin, lifting it so their eyes could meet. Oh, Lord, he thought to himself. She was so very pretty, with soft, large eyes like an antelope's.

"I do not remember anything," Snow Deer said, a sob catching in her throat. "Tell me how I got here. Why are you with me?"

He softly explained how he had seen her in the canoe with two trappers. He told her that she had been gagged and that her wrists had been tied together. He explained how the limb had hit the ca-

70

noe, the jolt of it throwing her from the birch-bark vessel.

He told her that he had saved her.

"I wish I could take you home, to your true people, but if you can't remember who they are, how can I?" Charles said, raking his fingers through his wet hair in frustration.

He glanced nervously over at the wagon, then into Snow Deer's eyes. "I have to get my uncle home," he said, his voice drawn. "Yet I can't leave you here."

Still confused, and afraid to be left alone, Snow Deer grabbed his hand. "I want to go with you," she murmured. "I . . . I am afraid to be alone. I am so confused as to why I cannot remember things."

"The blow to your head has caused your temporary lapse of memory, but I am certain that soon you will regain it," Charles said. He gazed down at her. He was amazed at her total trust in him. Perhaps that was how the trappers had managed to abduct her. She seemed so innocently sweet and trusting!

"After I get my uncle to my parents' house, I will try to help you remember things," he said warmly. "When you do, trust me when I say that I will return you to your people."

Snow Deer gazed up at him. She studied the face of this white man whose words were so kind, whose heart seemed so pure and giving. She smiled and kept looking at him, entranced by his handsomeness. She felt a strange sort of fluttering in the pit of her stomach.

"Charles is your name?" she said softly.

"Yes, Charles Cline," he said, gazing over at her. "But some call me C.C."

"C.C.?" Snow Deer said, cocking an eyebrow quizzically. "That is a strange sort of name."

Charles laughed throatily. "Yes, so my mother says."

He stepped up to the side of the wagon, then reached down and slid the tent covering back enough so that he could take a good look at his uncle.

His heart sank, for his uncle's condition seemed to have worsened.

The death rattles were more pronounced. His uncle's skin was a pale gray. Drool rolled in a steady stream from both corners of his mouth.

"He is ill," Snow Deer said, gazing down at Uncle Hiram. "Is he dying?"

"Yes, I'm afraid so," Charles said thickly. He looked over at her. "This is my uncle . . . my Uncle Hiram."

"Uncle Hiram," Snow Deer murmured, her eyes sad as she watched Hiram's unsteady breathing. "I wish I knew ways to help him."

"Yes, me too," Charles said, pulling the canvas covering back in place.

He went to the back of the wagon and pulled out one of his travel bags. He opened it and took a change of clothes from it.

Then he looked at Snow Deer. "I have enough clothes for both you and I to have something dry to wear," he said. "Would you like to change out of that wet dress? All I have to offer you is a pair of my breeches and a shirt."

"I do not remember much, but I do know for certain that a woman does not wear man's clothes," Snow Deer said stiffly, then climbed onto the seat. "A blanket will feel good, though."

Charles reached inside the wagon and grabbed a blanket. He took it to Snow Deer. He watched her wrap herself in it, then he went and stood behind some bushes and changed his clothes. He stared at his boots and groaned. His best leather boots had been given a soaking!

But having no change of shoes with him, he struggled into them again.

He tossed his wet clothes in the back of the wagon, checked his uncle one last time, then climbed aboard. He reached down on the floor where he had left his eyeglasses before going to save the woman. He hesitated to put them on, thinking they might make the maiden think less of him.

But needing them to be able to keep a close eye on things around him, he slid them onto the bridge of his nose.

Before lifting the reins, he looked over at the lovely woman, smiling when he was able to make her features out more clearly now that he wore his eyeglasses. Lord, with the aid of his glasses, he saw just how uniquely beautiful she was. She was so pretty, it almost made his heart stop!

She had curled up on the seat next to him and had already fallen asleep. He could not help continuing to stare at her.

Then a thought came to him that made him grow cold inside. Surely those who loved her were looking for her. What if they came upon Charles riding along the trail and they saw her with him? Since she had no recall of her past, how would she react to them? Wouldn't Charles be blamed for everything?

Frightened, he snapped the reins and sent the team of horses into a fast pace along the riverbank. He saw the importance of getting across the river as soon as possible.

Yet he was not all that sure which side was the safest for his travels. He was not sure where this Indian maiden's people made their camp. In Illinois? Or Kentucky? He wasn't even sure which tribe she was from—Cheyenne or Shawnee?

He had no idea where he should travel to truly be safe now that he had involved himself in an Indian maiden's life.

He looked over at her again. He knew that, deep down, where his desires were formed, he would chance anything for her!

Chapter Seven

Once their canoes were beached just downriver from Rain Feather's Shawnee village, Blazing Eagle and his warriors moved stealthily through the forest. The village could now be seen through a break in the trees a short distance away.

Blazing Eagle had been in council with Chief Rain Feather more than once and knew which lodge was his. Knowing that it was at the center-most point of the horseshoe-shaped configuration of tepees, he made a sharp turn right and nodded at his warriors to follow him.

When they arrived where the trees stopped and the Shawnee village began, they halted their steps. The warriors gathered around Blazing Eagle for further instructions.

"I will go first to Rain Feather's lodge," Blazing Eagle whispered, looking from man to man. "I will take a look inside. If I nod once to you, encircle the village and ready yourselves for a battle, for I will have seen my daughter in his lodge."

He smiled as he looked at the chief's tepee. Like those in his own village, the bottom of Rain Feather's lodge had been rolled up about a foot, so that fresh, cool air could circulate inside the lodge.

He again looked at his men. "If I do not find my daughter in the chief's lodge, I will nod twice to you," he said. "That is my command for you to come to me. We will enter the village together. We will go to the chief and demand council. While in council I will get the truth from him."

His warriors nodded, then watched as Blazing Eagle ran quietly toward the back of Rain Feather's lodge.

When he came closer to the tepee, he dropped onto his belly and crawled in a snake-like fashion until he was close enough to be able to see inside, without having to place himself in danger by going all the way in.

The sun was sending its light through the canvas of the lodge, as well as down its smoke hole overhead. That light was enough for Blazing Eagle to see who was in the lodge.

He had mixed feelings when he saw that his daughter was not there. Sitting just inside the open entrance flap was an elderly woman. She was stringing beads. He knew her to be Wind Woman, Rain Feather's grandmother.

Beyond her, sitting in view just outside the entrance flap, were Rain Feather's mother and sister. They were preparing a hide for tanning.

Everything seemed normal.

Yet could he trust how things appeared to be? It could all be pretense. If Rain Feather had abducted Snow Deer, he would know that Blazing Eagle would come to see if his daughter was in the Shawnee village.

Realizing that being there alone was getting more risky by the minute, he turned and nodded twice to his warriors.

They rushed forth. He rose to his full height.

"We must make a normal entrance," Blazing Eagle said tightly. "Although people will question why we beached our canoes out of sight of the village, those who ask will soon know the answer, for I will ask about my daughter directly."

"The weapons we carry will alert them that we have arrived without friendship in our hearts," Red Bow said.

"That is true," Blazing Eagle said, nodding. "But that is good. If my daughter is being held captive, the Shawnee will know we have come to take her home with us again. Should they choose to fight, we will fight. Should they decide to have peaceful council, they shall have peaceful council."

He walked square-shouldered away from his men, around the back of the many lodges, and came to the entrance where they found Rain Feather and his warriors standing protectively along the whole front of the lodges, which faced the river.

"Your canoes were spied downriver," Chief Rain Feather said, stepping forth from the throng of men. He held a rifle. His free hand was doubled tightly into a fist at his left side. "We have waited for you. Why have you come in secret? Why are you carrying weapons?"

"Why does anyone carry weapons?" Blazing Eagle asked. "Why do you think Chief Blazing Eagle feels a need today to carry his?"

"There is no reason I can think of unless you have chosen to become the enemy of the Shawnee," Rain Feather said, stepping closer to Blazing Eagle. "It would not be hard to look on you with enmity, you whose daughter turned her eyes away from this proud chief!"

"And so you still are bitter over my daughter's decision to refuse you as a husband?" Blazing Eagle said, his heart beginning to thump wildly within his chest.

He looked past Rain Feather, into the village, and slowly let his eyes roam over the many lodges. If his daughter was a captive, she would be hidden in one of those lodges.

When his gaze stopped at one tepee in particular, whose covering was not opened for air around the bottom, his heartbeat quickened even more. Surely that was where he would find his Snow Deer! She was being kept well hidden, so that no one could sneak up behind the lodge and have easy access to peer inside!

"There are other women besides your daughter, women who would willingly be the wife of the mighty Chief Rain Feather," Rain Feather said, drawing Blazing Eagle's eyes back to him.

Blazing Eagle's eyes narrowed as he watched Rain Feather nonchalantly shrug his shoulders.

"And, Blazing Eagle," Rain Feather said, laughing mockingly, "I would imagine there are many women more beautiful than your daughter. So do not think this chief's heart is affected one way or another by what your daughter has chosen to do."

Blazing Eagle was taken aback by Rain Feather's attitude, and then it came to him like a thunderclap that Rain Feather must be putting on a show of indifference because deep inside his heart he still truly cared about Snow Deer!

Blazing Eagle would not let Rain Feather play this game any longer.

"I demand to have council with you today," he said flatly. He took a step toward Rain Feather and looked steadily down into the short Shawnee's eyes, watching his reaction.

"No one demands anything of Rain Feather," Rain Feather hissed. He motioned toward the river. "Your canoes await you. Go to them!"

"Then you refuse council with Blazing Eagle?" Blazing Eagle said, glaring at Rain Feather. "Do you not know that this decision to turn your back on Blazing Eagle today will make all councils between us from this day forth impossible?"

"That is the way of enemies," Rain Feather said, thrusting his face up into Blazing Eagle's.

Blazing Eagle's blood raced like hot fire through his veins. He placed a hand on Rain Feather's shoulder, drawing gasps from both factions of warriors when he gave Rain Feather a shove away from him.

"Enemies we are then," Blazing Eagle growled. He dropped his hand to his side. "And since we are declared enemies, do not think that my warriors and I will back away today like frightened children."

As quick as lightning, Blazing Eagle had the barrel of his rifle thrust against Rain Feather's abdomen. Out of the corner of his eye he saw that his warriors were quicker than the Shawnee. His warriors' weapons were aimed at the Shawnee, and their fingers were on their triggers, ready to shoot them.

"Now tell me where my daughter is," Blazing Eagle said, his voice filled with a seething anger. "She is here, is she not? Take me to her!"

Blazing Eagle saw Rain Feather's surprise. This gave Blazing Eagle cause to believe he had been wrong to think that Rain Feather had stolen his daughter. The surprise had leapt too quickly into

Rain Feather's eyes. Blazing Eagle could tell that it was genuine.

Yet he did not lower his rifle.

He first would hear what Rain Feather had to say.

"Why would you think that Snow Deer is in my village?" Rain Feather asked, raising an eyebrow.

"She has been abducted," Blazing Eagle said, his rifle still steady on Rain Feather. He had to find some way to bring a measure of peace between them again before commanding his warriors to lower their firearms . . . before he lowered his own.

"And so you thought that I had abducted her?" Rain Feather said. He lifted his chin proudly. "You think that this powerful Shawnee chief is that desperate to have your daughter as a wife? *No* woman is worth warring over. Not even your daughter."

Rain Feather laughed throatily. "And how do you think I would have hidden your daughter from you when you came looking for her?" he said, his eyes filled with amusement. "You do not put much faith in this chief's intelligence, do you?"

"I would have guessed you would soon be changing the location of your camp and that you would take your captive with you, far enough away for her father never to find her again," Blazing Eagle said. "You could even have taken her somewhere and hidden her until your move was made."

That possibility suddenly seemed all too likely. Again he thrust the barrel of his rifle into the Shawnee's abdomen. "I was wrong to listen to you when you so cleverly gave me cause to doubt my own intelligence," he growled. "You *do* have my daughter. You *have* hidden her! Your whole village will pay for the sins of one man, their *chief*."

Blazing Eagle shouted over his shoulder at his warriors. "Take those Shawnee warriors and tie them in the middle of the village! I will then bring their chief and we will stake him on the ground until we have the answers we seek! There will be no more pretense! No more lies! No council!"

Rain Feather gasped as he watched his warriors being forced at gunpoint toward the center of the village. There were no others in the village to stop them. He had been foolish enough to have all of his warriors come and stand with him at the entrance of his village!

His eyes wide, he gazed up at Blazing Eagle. "You are wrong," he said, his voice drawn. "Your daughter is not here! Do not carry your foolishness any further! I can thus far overlook a father's desperate actions. But if you humiliate my warriors in the presence of their wives and children, somewhere down the road, Cheyenne, you and your people will pay!"

Seeing the logic in what Rain Feather said, Blazing Eagle shouted to his warriors to stop.

"If you stop this now and return to your village without any more wrongful threats and accusations, I will see to it that my earlier words about being your people's enemy are forgotten," Rain Feather declared. "I will even volunteer to join you on your search to find Snow Deer. I am more familiar with this land and the river than you. My people have been here for many generations. If your daughter is still in this area, she will be found."

Feeling foolish for having taken his anger against the Shawnee chief this far, Blazing Eagle sighed heavily and lowered his rifle to his side:

"She is not here," Rain Feather reiterated. He

placed a gentle hand on Blazing Eagle's shoulder. "If she was, I would hand her over to you, for I see your grief . . . I can even feel it. I would not wish to be the cause of such grief." He swallowed hard. "I am not a father, but I would die for my sister."

"I was wrong to come like this to your village without proof," Blazing Eagle said, his eyes holding Rain Feather's. "And by doing so, I have wasted time. Those who took my daughter have been given a chance to get farther away with her down the long avenue of the river."

"I shall send many of my men up and down the river to help in the search," Rain Feather said. "Perhaps together we shall find her."

"Any help will be appreciated," Blazing Eagle said. "Thank you, Rain Feather."

Many canoes slid into the water, belonging to both Shawnee and Cheyenne. Up and down they went, mile after mile, sometimes even retracing parts of the river where they had already been. They even went up small tributaries that led away from the river.

Still Snow Deer was not found. The search was finally disbanded. The Shawnee went one way down the river, to their village. The Cheyenne, the other.

His shoulders slumped, his eyes downcast, Blazing Eagle entered his lodge. He stopped and gazed from Becky to Burning Snow, then broke the news to them that it seemed that Snow Deer might be lost to them forever.

Becky broke into soft sobs as she leaned into Blazing Eagle's embrace. But she didn't stay there for long. Burning Snow burst into a loud wailing behind her.

Becky turned with a start. Blazing Eagle rushed past Becky and gathered Burning Snow up into his arms. He rocked her back and forth as she clung to him, crying.

"It is my fault!" Burning Snow wailed. "I should have stayed with my sister!"

Blazing Eagle stopped and placed a hand beneath his younger daughter's chin. "Do not blame yourself," he said softly. "You are not responsible. Those who abducted your sister are the ones to blame! Never you!"

"I remember! I remember! Had I not been so anxious to show my roots to Mother, I would have stayed at Snow Deer's side," Burning Snow cried, not to be dissuaded about the guilt she felt over her sister's absence. "She always looked out for me. Why could I not have looked out for her?"

Becky and Blazing Eagle's eyes locked. They shared each other's silent despair about one daughter's disappearance, yet felt some hope for their other daughter. This was a first for Burning Snow! The shock of the moment seemed to have unlocked her ability to remember!

Chapter Eight

As the wagon rolled on toward the ferry landing, Charles gazed over at the Indian woman. More and more he worried about taking her away from her people, her way of life. What if she never remembered her past?

What was he to do with her?

Certainly he could not turn her loose, unaware of who she was, or with whom she belonged! She was now his responsibility. That had to mean that he must take her home with him.

"But what then?" he whispered to himself.

A thought sprang to his consciousness that made a warmth spread through his veins. He had only recently begun to think about his need for a wife. Could fate have sent this woman, this beautiful Indian woman, to him for that purpose?

Even now, as she slowly emerged from her long nap, he was again taken by her loveliness. He could not help staring at her as the blanket fell from around her when she stretched and yawned. Her dress was now dry and hung more loosely around her breasts, but he could still see their perfect roundness, even more so when she raised her arms above her head to stretch.

Aware of how she was affecting him, knowing that he would most certainly welcome her into his home as his wife, Charles looked quickly away from her.

His blood raced hot and fast through his veins. He wanted this woman.

Yes, he thought, smiling, he would take her home with him. He would be gentle and kind to her. He would woo her into loving him.

And then they would share marriage vows.

The thought of sharing more than that with her made him feel dizzy with a passion that he had never felt before.

Now fully awake, Snow Deer gazed at the white man. Her memory had fully returned, but there was no fear inside her heart when she looked at him, for she would never forget his gentleness toward her when he saved her from the river. While going in and out of consciousness after her fall in the river, she had been aware of someone's arms around her, protective and caring.

When she had awakened long enough to see whose arms she was in, she had found the kind face of this man who now sat at her side. She had not even been afraid of him then, a total stranger. Anyone who would risk his own life to save a woman could not be evil.

He was nothing like those filthy trappers who had held her captive. When she asked this white man to return her to her home, surely he would do so without question.

She was glad that the white man, whose name

she now recalled was Charles, still looked away from her so that she could study him more carefully. While he had held her in his arms earlier, she had seen enough of him to know that he was handsome. Although his skin was that of a white man, it was bronzed tan, which had to mean that he spent much time outside. That made her smile, for a man should be at one with nature.

She looked more closely at him. His sculpted features stirred strangely delicious feelings within her. The set of his jaw, his straight nose, and his perfectly shaped lips were beautiful for a man.

She noticed his eyeglasses. She did not see that they made him any less handsome. Her father's white friend, Judge Newman, also wore spectacles. No spectacles could take away Judge Newman's handsomeness. As she gazed at Charles, he turned toward her. She saw warmth, compassion, and kindness in his dark brown, deeply set eyes.

And she could not help recalling how she had, more than once, seen Charles looking at her as though he adored her . . . and she was nothing but a stranger to him!

That had to mean that feelings had been awakened within him for her, as hers had been for him.

Charles felt the woman's eyes on him, studying him. He swallowed hard, for never had he been under such scrutiny before by a woman! He wondered why she suddenly found him so interesting. What was she thinking as she gazed so intensely at him? Did she find him unattractive?

Or was all of this deep study only because she had never been with a white man before who treated her kindly?

Surely the trappers had treated her as if she were a heathen savage!

Or was it something else?

His hand went quickly to his eyeglasses. Lord, *now* he knew what she was staring at. The damnable eyeglasses!

He tore them off, then looked quickly over at her when he felt her hand touching the hand in which he held his glasses.

"Do not remove them because of me," Snow Deer said softly. "I do not find them bad to look at. Please wear them so that you can see well enough to get you where you are going."

"How did you know what I was thinking?" Charles asked, stunned. "How do you know about eyeglasses and why they are worn?"

"My father has a friend whose eyes do not see as well as others see," Snow Deer said. "I have seen this man become uneasy about his glasses. Your uneasiness seems the same."

Charles laughed softly and placed his glasses back on. "I hate these damn things," he said. "And, yes, I am self-conscious about them."

"Self-conscious . . . ?" Snow Deer said softly. "What does that mean?"

Charles saw her sweet innocence and felt himself slipping deeply under her spell. "It means uneasiness," he said softly. "I did not like you seeing me wear them."

"Why should you care how I feel?" she asked, her eyes dancing.

He laughed softly, then looked away from her, his pulse racing.

"My name is Snow Deer," she suddenly blurted out, drawing Charles's eyes quickly back to her.

His insides melted when she smiled at him.

"Yours is Charles," she murmured. "Or would you rather I call you C.C.?"

"Whichever you prefer," Charles said, again swallowing hard.

Then his eyes widened. "You remembered your name!" he exclaimed. "Your remembered mine, even my nickname. You remembered things about your father's friend and his eyeglasses. That has to mean that your memory has returned."

"Yes, I now have full recall of everything," Snow Deer said, her smile waning. She looked away from Charles, and over at the river. "I was with my friends. We were headed home from root digging. I saw a strange, flickering light. I left my friends to see what it was. It was the trappers. They lured me to them with a mirror."

Her eyes flashed as she gazed over at Charles again. "I was foolish to allow it," she said in a low voice. "They took me captive."

"How long were you with them?" Charles asked, finding it strange to be talking to her so comfortably, as though they had known each other forever.

"I was with the evil trappers for only a short while," Snow Deer said. She reached up and touched her hair, grimacing when she discovered that several locks had fallen free of her braids.

Charles looked guardedly at her. "Then you were not harmed by them?" he asked.

Knowing what Charles might be referring to, understanding that she *would* have been raped had she spent much more time with the trappers, Snow Deer lowered her eyes, her face pink with the heat of a blush.

"Only my pride was harmed," she murmured. She reached a hand to the bump on her head. She lifted her eyes and smiled at Charles. "And my head, but the river rocks caused that."

"Yes, the river rocks," Charles said, laughing softly. Then he frowned. "Does it still hurt?"

"Somewhat," Snow Deer said, nodding. She

eased her hand from the lump and smoothed the blanket away from herself. She frowned as she gazed at her dress. "It seems my dress was more harmed by the spill into the river than Snow Deer."

"Dresses can be discarded; Snow Deer can't," Charles said, not realizing the seriousness with which he said this until he saw her look quickly up at him, her eyes softly questioning him.

He looked away from her, suddenly clumsy in her presence. It was certain that she affected him in ways no woman had ever affected him before. He had never felt this intensely even about Elissa those long years ago when he had been enamored of her.

But he knew that he could do nothing about his feelings for Snow Deer. Now that her memory had returned, he had no choice but to return her to her home.

Yet, how could he do that? It would delay getting his Uncle Hiram to Bloomfield!

He was uncertain what to do. He felt a duty to this woman whose honor had already been compromised. Yet he had a duty to his uncle, and to his mother. His mother was anxiously awaiting her brother's arrival.

Snow Deer was aware of Charles's sudden silence. "What has made words become silent upon your lips?" she asked softly.

"I'm worried about Uncle Hiram," he said, glancing over at her. "I need to get him to Bloomfield as quickly as I can. I was headed for the ferry that would take me across the Ohio into Illinois when I saw you thrown overboard into the river. I must get him to his sister so that they can be together one last time before . . ."

A quick panic seized Snow Deer. She scarcely heard what else he was saying. If she crossed the river on the ferry with him, he would be carrying her farther and farther away from her people! The land called Illinois was on the other side of the Ohio. She wanted to stay on the Kentucky side—the side of her people's village!

Yet she understood Charles's deep concern for his Uncle Hiram. The old man was dying. Charles wanted to get him to his mother's house so that the elderly man could be with his sister before he began his long journey on the hereafter road!

If she asked Charles to return her home first, then the old man might die before he reached his sister.

And Snow Deer understood the strong feelings between brothers and sisters. No one could be more special to her than her older brother, Whistling Elk. She knew the importance of Uncle Hiram being with his sister one last time.

Yet if she traveled farther and farther away from her people, she would be causing her family needless concern for her.

Snow Deer turned on the seat and lifted the corner of the canvas cover which hung protectively over the elderly man.

She gasped and dropped the canvas back in place and looked quickly over at Charles. How could she tell him that the old man had already died? That his uncle's eyes were locked in a death stare?

Snow Deer did not know how to tell Charles. She did not want to see the despair that news would bring to his beautiful eyes. She did not want to inflict hurt on his heart!

Yet she had no choice. The elderly man was dead. There had to be a burial. It was too hot to take a body very far without . . .

Charles was aware of a change in Snow Deer's

mood. She was scarcely even breathing as she looked at him. He had done nothing to frighten her. So why was she behaving so strangely?

"What's wrong?" he asked as he gave her a quick glance. "Why are you looking at me like that?"

"How can I tell you . . . ?" Snow Deer said, her eyes wavering.

"Tell me what?" Charles said, his eyes imploring her. When he saw her take a quick glance over her shoulder at the canvas cover, his heart skipped a beat. His uncle! He had seen her lift a corner of the canvas and look down at Uncle Hiram, then turn quickly around again.

His pulse racing, Charles snapped the horses' reins and guided them in a wide right turn away from the river.

When he had the wagon beneath a thick stand of cottonwood trees, he jumped from the seat and rushed around to the side of the wagon.

His jaw tightened as he lifted his hands toward the canvas covering. Trembling, he hesitated before raising it.

Snow Deer came to his side. "Shall I do it for you?" she murmured. She understood that he needed someone now, as she had needed someone when she had been near death in the river.

Charles was taken aback by her sweet kindness. It was as though she could feel his fear and pain. It was as though he and Snow Deer shared each other's thoughts, as though they had known and cared for each other forever!

Could love truly come that quickly between two people? he wondered. Could it come between two people of different skin colors and beliefs?

He was brought out of his reverie when Snow Deer eased the covering aside. He was catapulted into despair when he saw his uncle's death stare, the dreaded death rattles inside his lungs having died with him.

Unable to look any longer at his Uncle Hiram, Charles turned away and held his face in his hands. He was so distraught that he could hardly bear the sad pangs of loss that stung his heart.

Seeing Charles's sadness, Snow Deer went to him and moved into his embrace. She placed her cheek on his chest and hugged him.

"Do not despair so," she murmured. "Do you not know that your uncle is now in a better place than either you or I? He is where the birds' songs never end. He is where the skies are always blue. He walks among those who have gone before him. His reunion with his ancestors is a happy one, as yours will be one day when your own spirit leaves your body."

Hearing her earnest words of comfort, and feeling her arms around him and her cheek pressed gently and trustingly against his chest, Charles lost his heart and soul to her. His arms slid around her and held her against him. He lifted her chin so that their eyes could meet. In her eyes he saw such compassion, such understanding. . . .

And even more. True, she could be showing such affection for him because he had saved her. But he knew that there was far more than gratitude in her eyes and smile. He sensed that she cared for him in a deep, passionate way, the same way he cared for her.

"Thank you," he said, his voice breaking. "Thank you for caring. God has blessed me with your presence. It makes my uncle's passing not quite so heart-wrenching."

"I have lost loved ones, also," Snow Deer said, thinking back to when her mother had left her with her father. "It is not easy, yet it is something one must accept. Life goes on. And so must yours."

Charles eased from her arms. He gazed at the wagon. "My mother," he said, his voice drawn. "She so counted on me bringing her brother to her. I've let her down."

"Perhaps because of time taken for me?" Snow Deer said softly.

Charles turned quick eyes to her again. "No, not because of you," he said. "You see, the time it took to save you was only a fraction of the three days' ride I have yet to make before reaching my home in Bloomfield."

He reached his hands to her cheeks and touched them. "Lord, had I not been where I was when you fell into the river . . ." He paused before continuing. "I am so glad that I was there to help you."

"It was destiny that led you there," Snow Deer said softly. "Yours *and* mine."

Afraid of where their feelings were taking them, Snow Deer felt a desperate need to change the subject. She had never considered the possibility of falling in love with a white man.

She reached up and took Charles's hands from her face, held them for a moment, then slid her hands free and gazed at the wagon. "What are you going to do now?" she asked quietly.

"It's too far to Bloomfield for me to wait and bury my uncle there," Charles said, nervously raking his fingers through his hair. "Yet I hate to bury him this far from home."

He then lifted an eyebrow. "And how *can* I bury him?" he blurted out, looking over at Snow Deer. "I have no shovel."

"No shovel is needed," Snow Deer said. She was familiar with many ways of burying the dead, having seen different customs on her people's journeys from one land to another in their quest for a peaceful homeland.

"First wrap your uncle in blankets," Snow Deer said. "Then we shall bury him beneath rocks so that his body will be safe from predators."

They chose a place of burial close to where a great field of golden sunflowers grew. Charles recalled how his uncle had loved sunflowers, their leaves so bright green, their yellow petals more lovely and delicate than gold.

Now, as Charles went sorrowfully through the burial, many finches, their feathers almost as yellow as the petals, hovered over the field of sunflowers, while bright red cardinals swept down and picked at the brown seeds.

Charles and Snow Deer worked together until Uncle Hiram lay beneath a protective covering of rocks.

"Now to pray over him," Charles said, kneeling down beside the grave. Before he began his prayer, Snow Deer's soft voice broke through. He looked quickly over at her. She was kneeling beside him, praying to her Great Spirit for Uncle Hiram. She then sang a song in her Indian tongue.

Her lilting voice, the utter sweetness of it, and the fact that she showed such caring for someone else, for a perfect stranger, brought tears to Charles's eyes.

Touched deeply, he wanted to reach over and draw her into his arms, to again thank her.

But he had his own prayers to say, his own good-byes, his own grief to get through. Now it was not as hard. Snow Deer had lightened his load, had helped ease the pain that circled his heart.

Silent, Snow Deer stood up and walked away

from Charles and let him have his time with his uncle.

She stopped, turned, and watched him speak his words to his God. She listened to his prayer, having heard her white mother praying in the same way when she had felt sad, or had lost someone dear to her heart.

Because she had been raised by a white woman, Snow Deer had learned many ways of the white people. That had made it easier for her to trust this compassionate, wonderful white man, and she whispered a soft prayer of thanks to *Maheo* that she could allow herself to care for this man. He was so different from the men who had abducted her and wished the worst for her because she was a woman with copper skin.

She would never forget how the trappers had mocked her as they had taken her down the long avenue of the river!

Wiping tears from his eyes, Charles rose from the grave site.

He took one last look, then turned to walk away, but stopped again when Snow Deer knelt down beside the grave and laid a bouquet of sunflowers upon the rocks.

"Please smile down upon Charles from the spirit world and let him know that you are all right," she said, addressing Uncle Hiram's spirit.

Suddenly, as the sun shifted lower in the sky, a ray of sunshine broke through the leaves of the trees overhead and flooded Charles's face with its brilliant warm light.

Snow Deer rose to her feet and smiled at Charles. "The sun's caress is your uncle's," she murmured.

Stunned by how it did seem that her request

had been answered, Charles raised a hand to his cheek and touched it.

"It is real enough," Snow Deer said, moving to him, taking his free hand. "Loving your uncle as you did, do you not know that he will always be with you? He is also now with your mother."

Before Charles had the chance to say anything, Snow Deer straightened her shoulders and smiled up at him. "You know my name, but did I not tell you that I am a Cheyenne princess?" she blurted out, her pride showing in how she lifted her chin.

"No, you didn't tell me," Charles said, his voice filled with the awe that he felt for her.

She was so special . . . someone he could never let go of!

She was exactly the type of woman he had been looking for all of his life. She was not pretentious like most of the women he had met. She was pure, through and through, and so sweet it made his heart melt every time she opened her mouth and spoke to him!

He only hoped that she cared as deeply for him.

If so, he had her family to convince that he would cherish her, if they would allow her to be his wife.

He wondered if the Cheyenne would welcome him into their village and into their princess's life—or would they see him as a threat and turn him away?

Chapter Nine

"A Cheyenne princess?" Charles repeated.

"Yes, my father is a Cheyenne chief," Snow Deer said, an intense pride leaping into her eyes. "Chief Blazing Eagle. Do you know of him?"

The discovery that her father was a powerful Cheyenne chief sent a warning through Charles's heart. He hoped that she would have a chance to explain to her people that he was a friend. Otherwise, when they saw her with him, they might decide he was responsible for her abduction. He wondered if he should just take her near to her village and let her return the rest of the way alone.

But no, he would never do that. He had never acted the coward. And he did not want to give her cause to think little of him. He wanted to marry her. To do that he must first make peace with her people!

"No, I don't know your father," Charles said softly. "But only because I don't live in Kentucky.

I am sure if I had asked Cousin Elissa whether she knew of your father, she would say that she did."

"Cousin Elissa?" Snow Deer asked. "Who is Cousin Elissa?"

Charles looked over at the grave. His eyes lowered, and then he looked up at Snow Deer again. "She is Uncle Hiram's daughter. She lives on a large horse-breeding farm in Kentucky." He laughed throatily. "I think Elissa knows everything about everybody. She has always been inquisitive . . . a little bit too nosy."

"Inquisitive?" Snow Deer said, looking wonderingly into Charles's eyes. "I am not familiar with that word." She shrugged before he had a chance to explain. "But I do not know many of the white man's fancy words even though my mother is white and has taken much time to teach me the things of her world and read to me from her books."

Charles's eyes widened. "Your mother is white?" he said softly, a sudden hope filling his heart. If her mother was white, that had to mean that Snow Deer's father held no deep grudge against whites in general. Perhaps he would not be repelled at the thought of his daughter loving a white man.

He smiled. "I should have known that someone close to you was white," he said. "Your English is perfectly spoken."

"She is not my true mother, yet in my heart, she is," Snow Deer said, confusing Charles.

Before he could ask her to explain, she looked up at the sky, then gazed with a soft frown up at Charles. "It will soon be dark," she said. "I wish to return to my people today. But I am lost. I am not certain how far I was actually brought down the river. I might not reach my village before nightfall.

98

If you do not mind, I would much rather arrive home by daylight."

"Whatever you wish," Charles said, enjoying the trust she showed him. He gazed up at the sky. The sun had lowered behind the trees. It would soon drop behind the distant hills.

He reached a gentle hand to Snow Deer's arm. "We will travel until it gets dark," he said. "Then we can stop and make camp."

He lifted a hand to her cheek and gently cupped it. "You won't be afraid to spend the night with me?" he asked softly. "I *am* a stranger, you know."

"You are not a stranger to Snow Deer," she said, reaching a hand to his, covering it. "You are what my mother would call a 'white knight.' White knights save women. You saved me, did you not?"

"Yes," he said, chuckling at the idea of being compared to a knight. "And I would do it over and over again if given cause to."

"Then, *sire*, lead me onward into the night," Snow Deer said, giggling.

"I can tell that your mother told you the story in depth, perhaps many times?" Charles said.

"My mother brought her book knowledge to not only her family, but also our people," Snow Deer said, now walking toward the wagon. "I am eager for you to meet her."

She smiled at Charles as he placed his hands at her waist and lifted her into the wagon. "And she always welcomes council with white people," she murmured.

After getting settled on the seat, she watched Charles walk around the back of the wagon, then climb aboard beside her.

"Father will also enjoy making your acquaintance," she said, clasping her hands together on her lap. "He will wish to give you many gifts for having saved his daughter's life."

Charles lifted the horses' reins. He glanced over at Snow Deer as he snapped the reins and sent the horses on their way, this time away from the ferry landing. "I expect no gifts for saving you," he said softly. "That you are alive and well is all that matters to me." He glanced at her head. "How is your head feeling?"

She reached a hand to the lump. "Still sore, but I am so happy to be alive, I scarcely feel it."

She looked over her shoulder at the grave that was being left behind and Charles's eyes followed.

"Rest in peace, Uncle Hiram," Charles said, his voice breaking. "I will always remember you and love you."

Snow Deer gazed over at Charles. "The most sacred region of the Cheyenne universe is *Otatavoom*, the blue sky lodge, the blue sky space," she murmured. "There resides your Uncle Hiram."

She paused and smiled when he looked over at her. "You see, Charles, the color blue visually represents *Maheo*, the Supreme Being," she explained. "Your Uncle Hiram is with *Maheo*, riding the clouds with him as though they are one being, despite the difference in the color of their skin."

"You see your Supreme Being, your God, as having copper skin?" Charles asked.

"*Huh*, as I am sure you see your God with white skin," she murmured.

"Yes, that is how I have always envisioned God when I am praying to him," Charles said, nodding.

"He was a special man?" Snow Deer asked softly.

"God?" Charles asked, raising his eyebrows.

She laughed softly. "No," she murmured. "Your Uncle Hiram."

He laughed, then nodded. "Yes, Uncle Hiram

was a fine man," he said. "He always took time for
me when I was a young lad whom others saw as
only a pest."

He nodded again. "Yes, Snow Deer," he said,
swallowing hard. "My Uncle Hiram was *very* special."

They chatted constantly until the sky began to
darken.

Charles rode onward for just a while longer,
then stopped when he came to an overhang of
rock that could serve as a protective cover. Wolves
roamed this land. Wild boars were known to frequent these woods.

Charles had learned, while on his outings, to
stay alert even while he slept by a roaring campfire. He had almost learned how to sleep with one
eye open.

"I think this'll do," he said, looking over at Snow
Deer. He expected to see some apprehension in
her eyes at the idea of spending the night with a
man she scarcely knew. But he saw nothing akin
to uneasiness. She had spoken from her heart
when she told him that she trusted him.

It made him feel proud to have such trust from
such a woman as she. He would never prove her
wrong!

Charles helped Snow Deer from the wagon, his
heart skipping several nervous beats when her
breasts brushed against his chest as she slid past
him to place her feet on the ground.

Then she laughed and talked with him as they
gathered firewood.

Once the yellow flames of the campfire licked
the twigs and churned black smoke skyward, and
the horses had been unleashed from the wagon
and tethered close to the river so that they could
graze on the knee-high Kentucky grass and drink

from the river at will, Charles and Snow Deer went on a hunt together.

"I am not a brave, yet my father took me often on the hunt with him," Snow Deer said as she walked beside Charles through the forest. "I enjoy everything out of doors, especially the hunt."

Charles looked over at her, impressed by her anew. He doubted there was anything she couldn't do.

"Look!" Snow Deer said, grabbing Charles by an arm. "Do you see the deer over there? How it is so keenly watching something that it has not sensed our approach?"

"Yes, I see it," Charles said. He frowned down at her. "Snow Deer, I'm not hunting for anything as large as a deer. I want something smaller."

"That is my reason for pointing the deer's actions out to you," Snow Deer said, yanking on Charles's arm to stop him. "Just wait and watch. Soon you will see a rabbit."

Charles peered through his eyeglasses, then cocked an eyebrow when a rabbit hopped up beside the deer, nonchalantly feeding on the same thick mound of grass that the deer was again munching on.

"A rabbit," Charles said, eyes wide. He looked down at Snow Deer. "How did you know?" he asked softly, so that his words would not startle the rabbit.

"A good Cheyenne hunter watches all animals, for one animal often betrays the presence of another," she said. She shrugged. "I could tell by where the deer's eyes were directed, so low, and by the fact that he showed no fear, that the animal near him was probably a rabbit."

Charles chuckled, lifted his rifle, and fired.

The rabbit fell into the soft cushion of the grass.

The deer bounded away and was quickly hidden in the brush.

Soon the roasting rabbit was dripping its tantalizing juices into the fire as Charles and Snow Deer watched it cook on a makeshift spit over the flames. A pot of coffee sat in the hot coals, its fragrance filling the night air.

Snow Deer drew a blanket up around her shoulders. "Tell me about your family," she said, looking over at Charles who sat at her right side. "Then, if you wish, I will tell you more about mine."

"Yes, I would love to know everything about you and your family," Charles said, hardly able to take his eyes off her beautiful face.

The glow of the fire on her copper cheeks, and in her dark eyes, made her a vision of loveliness.

She had unbraided her hair and washed it quickly in the river. It now lay in a thick black sheen over her shoulders, reaching down her back to the ground.

Charles had enjoyed their time in the forest while hunting for their evening meal. He would never forget her soft, lyrical laughter. He would never forget her smile when she suddenly looked over at him and grew quiet.

Yes, something had awakened between them that neither one could deny. He just hoped that her feelings for him were strong enough that she would leave her people and promise to be his wife as soon as they returned to Bloomfield.

He smiled when he thought of the little white Baptist church up the road from his cabin. Never would he have thought that when he did take a wife, she would be Indian!

He prayed that she would say yes, when he asked her!

Needing to shift his thoughts away from his longing to hold her, to kiss her, Charles swallowed hard and gazed into the dancing flames of the fire. "My father is a postmaster," he said.

"What is a postmaster?" she asked. "That is another word that I am not familiar with."

"Does your white mother ever receive mail from her relatives?" Charles asked, thinking this might be the best way to explain.

"Yes, and she enjoys sending written words on pages back to them," she murmured. "Especially my Uncle Edward, who is my mother's brother. He lives in a place called Saint Louis. His wife's name is Marilyn. My Uncle Edward and my mother send written words on pages quite often to one another. Even I know how to send words on pages. It is an enjoyable thing to do."

She placed a finger to her chin in thought. "Also, Charles," she said, before he had a chance to speak again, "my family receives such words from Judge Newman and his wife, Waterfall, from where they live in Boston."

Snow Deer smiled at Charles. "Yes, many such written pages are exchanged between my mother and her friends and relatives."

She laughed. "My father was surprised one day when he received written words from Fish Hawk, my father's best friend from childhood days."

"It sounds like your parents have many friends and relatives who correspond with them," Charles said. "That's nice, Snow Deer. There is nothing quite like receiving mail from those you love."

"Correspond?" Snow Deer questioned.

"Yes, correspondence and mail are one and the same," he said. He lifted a log and slid it into the hungry flames of the fire. "And my father makes sure the mail reaches those who correspond with one another. He is called the postmaster."

He smiled over at her and leaned back on an elbow. "When my father built his house in Bloomfield, he built his post office on one end, the living quarters on the other. It serves him and my mother very well."

"Do you look like your father?" Snow Deer asked, turning to lie on her stomach on a blanket, propping her chin in her hands as she gazed adoringly at Charles.

Charles chuckled. "Some say I look like my father, and some say I look like my mother," he said softly. "Either way is quite a compliment, for I love my parents from the bottom of my heart."

"You are filled with love, are you not?" Snow Deer asked, a sensual shiver coursing through her when his eyes met hers and held. "I have met many men in my lifetime, but none as dear and sweet as you." She laughed softly. "Except for my father and brother, that is. In many ways, in your behavior, you remind me of them."

Charles's heart swelled with pride at such a compliment coming from someone he wished so much to impress. He was so touched by what she had said, he felt too clumsy to reply.

Snow Deer was aware of how her compliment had affected Charles. To make things relaxed between them again, she hurriedly interceded. "Do you have a sister or brother?" she asked, moving to a sitting position. She drew the blanket more snugly around her shoulders; the night air beside the river was damp.

"No, I was not blessed with a brother or sister," Charles said. "But I never felt any emptiness in my life because of this. My parents filled that gap. We have been very close. And now that they are older, I have become the protective one, whereas, while

I was growing up, they were *my* protectors."

"I can tell there is a special bond between you and your parents by the way you speak of them with such warmth," Snow Deer said. "There is such a bond between myself and my parents, as well as with my brother and sister."

"Oh?" Charles said. "So you do have a brother and sister? What are their names? Are they older? Or younger?"

"Whistling Elk is my older brother and Burning Snow is my younger sister," Snow Deer said with much pride.

Her smile faded when she thought of Burning Snow and her affliction . . . of her slowness. It had always concerned Snow Deer when she thought of her future and of living elsewhere when she married. Burning Snow had grown to depend on her. Even now she imagined that Burning Snow was devastated over her older sister's absence, perhaps even blaming herself for it.

She looked over at Charles. She now knew that this was the man she wished to marry. He was the one for whom she would give up the title of princess.

Yet to do so would also mean that she would have to live far from her family. It would be especially hard to leave her sister.

But perhaps this might be best for Burning Snow. If she did not have Snow Deer there, she might become more independent.

Feeling somewhat awkward over where her thoughts had taken her, Snow Deer grew quiet and looked away from him. Perhaps she had been a mite presumptuous to think that this white man would want an Indian for a wife.

"The meat is done," she said, glad to have something to draw them away from where their conversation had led them.

Feeling her awkwardness, aware of his own, Charles went to his wagon and took some tinware from a travel bag. He smiled when he lifted one of his mother's pies into his other hand, wondering if Snow Deer had ever eaten cherry pie.

He set the pie and the utensils on a blanket before the fire. He watched Snow Deer's eyes widen when she gazed down at the pie.

"Cherry pie," she said, smiling at Charles. "It is my mother's and father's favorite pie. Mother makes them while the Cherries-Are-Ripe moon is high in the sky."

"Cherries Ripe Moon?" Charles softly questioned.

"Yes, now, the month the whites call August on their calendar," Snow Deer said, nodding.

"Oh, yes, I see," Charles said, laughing softly. Then he nodded. "Cherry pie is also my parents' favorite," he said. "And mine."

The ice had been broken again between them, and they fed on the roasted rabbit and the pie, and sipped coffee.

"I think I forgot to tell you *my* occupation," Charles said, moving his empty plate aside.

"Occupation?" Snow Deer said. "What is 'occupation'?"

"Occupation means how I am employed," Charles said, laughing softly when even that word seemed unfamiliar to her. "It means how I spend my day making a living. My work."

"Oh, I see," Snow Deer said, nodding. Then she shoved her plate aside and wiped the grease from her lips with the back of her hand. "How do you make a living? Do you hunt and sell your pelts?"

"No, I'm no trapper," Charles said. He took another sip of his coffee as he thought back to the men who had abducted her. He wondered where the trappers were now, whether or not they were still a threat to anyone. "I am a blacksmith and a farmer."

He smiled when he saw that she understood the meaning to both of those words. They chatted a while longer; then he noticed that her eyelids were becoming heavy with the need of sleep.

"I think it's time to call it a day," he said.

He went to the wagon and brought out several blankets, then took them and made two separate pallets.

Snow Deer yawned and stretched her arms over her head. "I am so very tired," she murmured.

Charles gestured with a hand toward one of the pallets. "Come and snuggle," he said, smiling at her. He reached for his rifle. "I shall make sure you are safe through the night."

Snow Deer went to the blankets and made herself comfortable. "But you need rest also," she murmured.

"Don't worry about me," Charles said, going to his own blankets across the fire from hers. "I'll do just fine."

Snow Deer smiled again, then sighed as her eyes slowly closed.

But she found that she could not sleep for long. She could not help waking up and looking at Charles through the dancing flames of the fire.

When she found him gazing at her, too, she blushed.

Her heartbeat quickened with a desire that until now was unfamiliar to her. Then, afraid of her feelings, she rolled over and placed her back to Charles.

She wondered about these new feelings and

how they made her heart beat like distant thunder inside her chest.

She smiled and closed her eyes, enjoying the deliciousness of these feelings . . . enjoying knowing that she had finally found a man who could stir such feelings inside her!

Chapter Ten

Snow Deer did not know how long she had slept when a rustling noise in the nearby bushes brought her instantly awake. She stiffened when she heard something that sounded like snorts.

"Wild boars," she whispered to herself, fear of the wild hogs causing the hair to rise at the nape of her neck.

She leaned up and looked toward the bushes, then sighed when there were no more noises. Whatever had been there seemed to have moved onward.

She gazed through the low-burning embers of the campfire and saw that Charles was asleep. His rifle lay on the ground next to his face, his hand still clutched around it.

She turned on her side and watched him. She smiled, for he looked so innocent, like a child, in his sleep. His lips were slightly parted, revealing his white teeth. He had removed his glasses, and his lashes lay on his cheeks in his sleep.

While he slept, she was tempted to go to him and run her fingers over his sculpted features. She wished to press her lips against his, so they could be warmed by his in a kiss.

Distant lightning flashed in the sky in lurid zigzags. Thunder rolled and rumbled across the heavens and in the ground beneath Snow Deer's pallet of blankets.

She looked quickly away from Charles and peered into the darkness when a coyote howled close by.

When she looked upward, on the high, rocky crevice beneath which she and Charles had taken refuge for the night, she saw the flash of the coyote's eyes. Instant fear leapt into Snow Deer's heart.

She scrambled out of her blankets and went to Charles. When she saw that he was still asleep, she picked up his rifle and raised the barrel into the air and fired it, purposely not aiming at the animal. She just wanted to frighten it away.

Charles awoke with alarm. He rose quickly to his feet, then saw Snow Deer standing there with his rifle, smoke spiraling from the barrel.

"What happened?" he asked, quickly grabbing his eyeglasses from his pocket and putting them on. He looked at the rifle, then at Snow Deer. "What were you shooting at?"

"A coyote," Snow Deer said, easing the rifle into his hand. "It was close. I frightened it away."

A slow smile quivered onto Charles's lips. "And I was supposed to keep *you* safe through the night," he said, laughing softly. "Thanks, Snow Deer. I guess I've learned my lesson. I can no longer brag about being able to sleep with one eye open."

"One eye open?" Snow Deer said. "I have never seen anyone sleep with one eye open. How could one sleep that way?"

Charles was charmed by her innocence, by her not knowing when he was serious. He loved this innocence about her. He loved *her*.

Again lightning flashed in the heavens. Thunder rolled. Snow Deer looked quickly at the sky, then gave Charles a worried look. "Storm warriors are throwing their lightning sticks to earth, shaking the ground with their thunder. I am afraid of storms," she murmured. "I do not think I can go back to sleep while the lightning flashes in the heavens." She looked down at his blankets, then looked questioningly into his eyes. "Can I sleep with you in your blankets?"

Charles was stunned by her question, by this absolute trust in him. Surely she didn't know how a woman's body next to a man's affected him, especially a man who was so enthralled by the woman.

Yet seeing her shivering, seeing her real fear of the storm, Charles reached a hand out for her. He would not allow himself to be tempted by her nearness. If she trusted him this much, he would prove to her that her trust was well-founded!

"Yes, you can share my blankets with me," he said, his whole body growing warm with desire when she slid her hand trustingly into his. "But I promise you, Snow Deer, I won't go to sleep again tonight. I'll keep better watch than before."

"If you wish, I can stay awake instead of you," Snow Deer said, slipping beneath his blankets, reveling in the warmth that remained there from his body.

"No, I think you have been my bodyguard long enough for one night," Charles said, chuckling.

The damp coolness was seeping into his clothes, giving him a chill, so he knew that he had no choice but to get beneath the covers with Snow Deer.

He removed his glasses and placed them in his eyeglasses case this time, then put the case in his travel bag.

He could not deny the thumping of his heart at the thought of having her so close as he slid in beside her.

And when he turned on his side, and she moved up behind him and pressed her body against his so that her breasts pressed against his back, he closed his eyes and gritted his teeth. It was pure hell having to restrain himself from turning to her and grabbing her and kissing her.

"Charles, your body is so warm," Snow Deer murmured, snuggling closer. "Thank you for sharing your heat with me."

"Think nothing of it," was all that he could say. His loins ached from this need that he could not deny, but must continue to fight with his every heartbeat.

"Charles?"

"Yes?"

"Do you think I am pretty?"

Again he closed his eyes and gritted his teeth as a shiver of passion swept through him.

"Very," was all that he could say, for fear of revealing the huskiness of his voice.

Snow Deer slid both her arms around him. She hugged him to her. She closed her eyes in the ecstasy of having his hard body next to hers. She slowly ran her fingers over his chest, feeling his muscles through his denim shirt.

Recalling how she had wanted to touch his lips and his face earlier as she watched him sleep, she got the courage to slide her hands upward. Her heart pounded as her fingers touched his lips.

Charles's eyes flew wide open as he felt her fingers on his lips, and then the curve of his chin, and then his cheeks. "Lord, Snow Deer, what are you doing?" he could not help saying, for the fires she was awakening in him were almost burning out of control.

He was not sure how much longer he could fight this desire!

Never had he wanted a woman as he did now!

He wanted to taste her lips! He wanted to touch her breasts! He wanted to taste her nipples!

"I am sorry," Snow Deer said, yanking her hand away. She turned away from him, placing her back to him. "I did not mean to upset you."

Charles sighed heavily. He wiped beads of nervous perspiration from his brow, then turned over and placed a gentle hand on her arm.

Slowly he turned her to face him.

"Snow Deer, you didn't upset me in the way you thought you did," he said, his eyes sweeping over her face, seeing her as mystically beautiful in the soft glow of the dying campfire. "I'm not angry over you . . . you touching my face, or anything else that you did. It's just . . . just that I am a man. You are a woman." He swallowed hard, then placed a gentle hand on her cheek. "Lord, Snow Deer, everything you do makes me want you."

Snow Deer's heart flooded with desire for him, and it was the first time she had ever felt such a need for any man. Oh, but there was such an aching need gnawing at the pit of her stomach. She was at a loss for words; now she truly knew that he desired her, too!

Charles guessed that he had been too open, for she seemed suddenly shy, for whereas always before she had been so open with him . . . *too* open.

He continued gazing at her. He had never found anyone he wished to marry before because he just had not met that perfect woman . . . and perfection was what he was after.

Well, to him, Snow Deer was perfection tonight beneath the stars and firelight!

Snow Deer melted beneath Charles's steady stare. She could see such adoration in his eyes! She was more and more aware of his needs, which matched her own. She had always wondered how it would be to want a man the way her mother wanted her father! She had seen their looks of love. She had seen them enter their lodge and drop their entrance flap to give them the privacy needed for lovemaking.

She had always wondered how it felt to make love! She had always known that she would never be with a man in such a way, unless she loved him with every ounce of her being!

She loved Charles this much.

He loved her.

She reached a hand to his cheek. She pressed herself close to him and brushed a kiss across his brow. Her breasts ached strangely and she pressed them against his chest, causing rapture to leap into her heart.

"Snow Deer, what are you doing to me?" Charles whispered, reaching up and twining his fingers through her hair as he brought her lips to his.

His whole body turned into one thunderous heartbeat when she returned the kiss with abandon, her body gyrating against his as soft moans came from her lips.

A warning went off inside Charles's mind when he felt the fire moving in hot waves through his body, dangerously stirring his loins. He was fully aroused now.

Breathing hard, his hands trembling, he moved away from Snow Deer and hurriedly left the pallet.

Almost blinded with need of her, he walked quickly away from the campsite down to the river, then knelt beside it and attempted to steady his nerves.

Stunned by how quickly things had changed between them, Snow Deer lay there for a moment, then left the blankets and went to him.

She circled around him and rested on her knees before him, her hands at his cheeks. "I have never allowed myself to love a man," she murmured, her dark eyes imploring him. "I am a princess with duties to my people. But I care for you. You have aroused in me feelings and needs that, until you, were unfamiliar to me. I thought that making love might fulfill these needs. All of these feelings, this sort of hunger, are so new to me. I have never been with a man in this way before. I have never found a man I would offer myself to. But you are different, my sweet Charles. Everything you have stirred within me is so deliciously sweet."

She leaned into his embrace. She wrapped her arms around him. "Charles, make love to me," she whispered. "Please make love to me."

Charles was stunned speechless by her openness, yet he knew that this was not something she made a habit of. She had said that all of this was new for her. He saw such an innocence in her invitation to make love with her, an innocence that made her need of him so endearing!

And loving her, adoring her so much, he would not take advantage of the moment. Still, as before, when she had told him how she felt about him, he wondered if her feelings for him might be only gratitude.

And he didn't want her to mistake gratitude for love. He never wanted her to feel as though she owed him something for having saved her from drowning in the river.

He placed gentle hands on her shoulders and eased her away from him. He gazed into her eyes, fighting his hunger for her.

But before he could speak, she said something to him that made denying her anything almost impossible.

"Charles, do you not want me?" Snow Deer asked, her eyes filled with a savage longing. "Do you not hunger for me as I do you?"

"I do want you," Charles said softly. "I do hunger for you. But Snow Deer, it is not right to rush into . . . into making love only because your body tells you it wishes to. I would rather wait until you are certain of your feelings for me."

"I could never be more certain than now," Snow Deer said, yet she was touched deeply that he would not take advantage of the moment, when most men would have thought only of themselves. To her he was so courageous. He was such a gentleman!

"Charles, I love you enough now to know what I want," Snow Deer murmured. "I love you even more than before because you do not see me as only a body that you can use."

She crept into his arms and hugged him, placing her cheek against his chest. "Please, Charles, hold me?" she whispered.

He wrapped his arms around her and held her that way for a while; then, when he was aware that she had fallen asleep, he slid his arms beneath her and carried her to the blankets.

After he had her snuggled beneath the blankets, he sat down beside her and watched her.

Then he lay down beside her beneath the blankets, and this time he allowed himself to enjoy it, when in her sleep, she curled up next to him.

His heart soared and sang as he held her.

Chapter Eleven

A loud clap of thunder awakened Snow Deer with a start. She raised herself on one elbow and looked around her. The realization of where she was, where she had slept the entire night, and with whom, caused her eyes to widen. She had slept so soundly, once she had finally gone to sleep, that she had forgotten she was not in her bed in her lodge back at the village.

When she recalled that she had slept with Charles, she looked quickly at the pallet, where only his impression was left in the blankets.

A quick panic seized her when she discovered that he was gone.

What if he had decided to go on to his home in Illinois? she worried. Would he have left her to find her own way home alone?

Her fear that the two filthy trappers might be out there somewhere made her skin crawl!

A lurid flash of lightning in the heavens above

her and the ensuing clap of thunder took her eyes to the sky. On the far horizon, she could see the blueness of early morning, yet overhead the sky was black from the impending storm.

She shivered and hugged herself when another bolt of lightning came straight down from the sky and crashed into the earth not far from the campsite. The thunder was so loud, the impact so strong, that the ground seemed to be swaying beneath her.

"Snow Deer, you've awakened," Charles said, coming up from behind her.

Startled, she turned quick eyes to him. She was so relieved to see him, she jumped to her feet.

But she stopped herself just short of what instinct demanded. She wished to be held by Charles this morning. For a moment she had thought he had abandoned her. Instead he was there, with two platters of food held out before him.

She looked past him. He had started a new campfire farther up the bank from the river. Probably he had not wanted to waken her.

The wind had changed its direction and now brought to her the wonderful fragrance of coffee cooking over the leaping flames of the campfire.

"Are you hungry?" Charles asked, offering her one of the platters of food. He glanced skyward, then frowned at Snow Deer. "We'd best eat quickly and be on our way. It won't be long before the sky opens up and gives us a dousing."

Snow Deer took the platter of food. She walked beside Charles up the embankment, welcoming the warmth of the fire as she sat down beside it with Charles. It felt more like late September this morning than August. The air was chill. The wind was just now beginning to howl through the trees overhead.

Eating quickly, yet enjoying the cheese, bread, and fruit because she was so hungry, Snow Deer watched Charles as he poured himself a second cup of coffee. This morning he wore a fresh, clean shirt and breeches. His hair was perfectly groomed to his collar. His handsome face was sleek and shining with a fresh shave, his glasses perched on his straight nose.

She gazed at his boots. He had them so freshly waxed, she could almost see her reflection in them.

She watched him take faster gulps of his coffee, aware that he was looking heavenward every time a fresh bolt of lightning seared the sky. Like her father, Charles was a man of controlled moods, yet she could see his concern about the storm. They had no true shelter from the rain. And she still had no idea how far she was from her village!

When the first rain drop hit Snow Deer on the cheek, she winced.

Charles looked at Snow Deer, and then jumped to his feet, offering her a hand. "I have the horses ready for travel. I have everything in the wagon except for our blankets and our breakfast plates and the coffee pot. You get the blankets. I'll cover up everything in the wagon as best I can. Then we'd best be on our way."

As more rain drops hit Snow Deer's face, she ran and grabbed the blankets, then met Charles at the wagon. He handed her a large leather rain cape that had been packed for his uncle.

As she slipped into it, he swung one around his own shoulders and fastened it at his throat.

He helped Snow Deer onto the seat, then ran around and climbed aboard himself.

"Let's ride!" he shouted above the continuing rolls and claps of thunder. He snapped the reins. The team of horses lurched, then took off at a brisk pace.

Aware of leaving the river behind, Snow Deer gave Charles a questioning stare. "Where are you going?" she asked, gripping the cape at her throat and holding her head down against the hard wind. "If we leave the river, I will not be able to lead you back to my village."

"We must leave the river long enough to seek shelter," Charles said, glancing over at her. "This storm is going to be a hellish one. I should have awakened you earlier, when I first saw the clouds building."

"Why did you *not* awaken me?" Snow Deer asked, her eyes locked with his.

"You were sleeping so soundly," Charles said. "Just like a princess in a story book." He smiled. "I know now that I should have kissed you to awaken you."

A sensual thrill swam through Snow Deer at the thought of how it would have been to be awakened by his kiss. It would have been a heavenly way to start the day.

Yet she had to guard against these feelings that were overwhelming her. This was some sort of fantasy world she was living in at this moment. Soon it would be just a memory, for although she loved this man with all of her heart, she knew that it was an impossible dream to think they could have a life together. Their lives were so different!

A sudden rush of hard rain, as if the gods had overturned huge buckets of water in the heavens, caused Snow Deer to stop thinking about impossible dreams. The rain was so hard, she was blinded by it.

And she could tell that the horses were also frightened by the rain and the incessant lightning and thunder. They were suddenly moving erratically through the mud that had swollen up through the sparse grass. Their hooves were slipping and sliding.

"Hang on!" Charles suddenly cried, yanking and jerking on the reins.

Before Snow Deer had the chance to ask why, and before she could grab onto the seat, one of the wagon wheels crashed into a large pothole.

The wagon moved onward.

The one wheel that had broken from the wagon stayed behind.

The crazed horses refused to pay heed to Charles's tightening of the reins or his shouts.

Snow Deer tumbled over the side of the wagon and landed in a morass of mud and grass.

Quickly she sat up and watched the horses dragging the three-wheeled wagon onward, food and supplies flying in every direction over the sides and out the back.

And then she sighed with relief when the wagon came to a shuddering halt.

She rose slowly to her feet and watched Charles sit for a moment with his head hung. Then, slowly, he left the wagon, staring at what was left of it and his precious supplies.

Snow Deer went and stood beside him. They exchanged silent stares.

Charles saw how cold Snow Deer was. He quickly drew her into his embrace. "Damn the storm," he muttered beneath his breath. "Damn the wagon. Damn the *horses.*"

"But, Charles, at least the storm has stopped," Snow Deer said, trying to console him when she realized that the rain had suddenly ceased.

"Yes, thank God for small blessings," Charles said.

He held her for a moment longer, then stepped away and looked around at all of his belongings, which were strewn along the ground.

His eyes fixed on a cherry pie that lay upside down in the mud, the filling of the pie like red tears across the ground.

Then he laughed throatily. "That wasn't what my mother had planned for that pie," he said, gazing at Snow Deer. "But there's no use in crying over spilled . . . pie."

He chuckled, but then grew somber again. "Can you ride a horse?" he asked. He slipped the rain cape from around his shoulders and laid it across his arm.

While wiping his eyeglasses dry with the tail end of his shirt, he noticed how Snow Deer's long black hair had grown wavy in the rain, and how she looked even more beautiful with the rain droplets still clinging to her lovely cheeks and thick, long eyelashes.

"Not all Cheyenne women ride horses," Snow Deer said, seeing disappointment leap into his eyes.

"But remember, Charles, I am a chief's daughter," she went on. "I am a princess. Time was taken to teach me many things other Cheyenne women do not know how to do."

"Yes, I should have known that before asking," Charles said, sighing with relief.

"While you unhitch the horses, I shall gather up what has not been ruined by the rain and the fall from the wagon and place the usable supplies in your travel bags," Snow Deer said, removing the cumbersome rain cape.

She slung it over one arm, then proceeded to

pick up supplies that she knew they should have for the rest of the journey.

She was relieved when she found some fruit that had not been damaged. She even found a slab of cheese still wrapped and tied in a linen cloth.

After everything was placed on the horses, and blankets had been tied on instead of saddles, Charles went to Snow Deer and drew her into his arms. "I'm sorry the rest of the trip won't be as comfortable as it was earlier," he said.

"I am Cheyenne," Snow Deer said softly. "I have learned how to survive many hardships, not only nature's, but also those caused by man."

"Yes, I'm certain it has not been an easy road you have traveled, being Indian," Charles said. He was aware of how those words had silenced her, and wished he knew better things to say at such awkward times.

He looked at the horses as they nervously pawed the muddy ground. He then gazed at the sky, wincing when he saw that the clouds had gathered again to pelt them with more rain, wind, and lightning.

He looked at Snow Deer. "We'd best see if we can find that shelter I was talking about it," he said thickly.

Snow Deer looked at the swirling clouds. A shiver raced across her flesh.

Then she walked quickly to the horse.

Keeping a close eye on the sky, and peering in all directions for a cave or a barn, they rode onward.

Just as the rain began in earnest again, they spied a farmhouse a short distance away through a break in the trees. It sat high on a hill away from the Ohio River, which was inclined to spill over its banks.

"You should have kept the cape on!" Charles cried through the noise of the thrashing wind and the rain that was now falling in torrents. He laughed into the air. "Damn it, I should have kept *mine* on."

They rode up the steep hill toward the farmhouse. When they reached it, Charles quickly dismounted and ran up the steps onto the porch, then knocked on the door.

The door creaked slowly open. Charles peered down at a tiny woman whose eyes were wide with fear.

"Can we seek shelter in your barn, ma'am?" he asked, motioning with his hand toward Snow Deer who shivered atop her horse, her shoulders hunched against the wind.

"I'd ask you and the lady in out of the rain to get warmed and dried by the stove, but I'm alone. My husband has gone into town for supplies," the woman said, her eyes moving slowly to Snow Deer. She stared at her. "I've been warned about strangers."

She squinted her eyes up at Charles. "My husband especially warned me against Indians," she said in her wispy voice.

She moved her gaze over Snow Deer again. "She is Indian, ain't she?" she spat out.

Hating prejudice of any sort, Charles sighed. "Yes, she's Indian," he said. He made a mock salute toward the woman. "Thanks, ma'am, for your hospitality. Me and my wife will accept your offer of shelter in the barn."

He purposely stood there for a moment longer to see the woman's reaction to his reference to Snow Deer being his wife. He laughed when he saw the utter shock that he had expected in her eyes, then hurried from the porch and grabbed his reins.

"She's offered the use of her barn," he said, grabbing Snow Deer's horse's reins. He led the animal toward the barn, his own trailing behind him.

And when they were inside, their horses tied in the stalls, Charles searched around until he found a lantern that was fueled with kerosene. He took a match from a box and lit the lantern, then held it out and looked slowly around him, his eyes stopping on a ladder that led up to the loft.

"There should be plenty of fresh, dry straw up there," he said. He looked over at Snow Deer and saw that she still trembled from the cold and her wet clothes. "Go on. I'll follow you."

He held the lantern up to guide her way.

After she was safely in the loft, he climbed up and sat down beside her.

"I'm so cold," Snow Deer said, her teeth chattering as she hugged herself fiercely.

"I'll go and get my travel bags," Charles said, already crawling back toward the ladder. "Surely the blankets are still dry."

He returned with the bags. He took out two blankets, one for Snow Deer and one for himself.

He looked away from Snow Deer, to give her privacy while she removed her wet clothes.

"I am covered now," Snow Deer said, drawing his eyes back to her.

She watched his eyes flit from her clothes, which she had hung up on a rail, to her, knowing that he realized she was naked beneath the blanket.

It gave her a strange sort of thrill to know that only a blanket lay between herself and his hands!

She shook off such shameful thoughts. "Now it

is your turn to remove your wet clothes," she said softly. Their eyes locked. "I shall give you the same privacy you gave me."

She turned her eyes away. Her spine was stiff and she scarcely breathed as she heard the rustling of his clothes as he removed them. Her pulse raced to know that he, too, wore nothing but the blanket. He spoke her name, letting her know that she could turn and look at him.

Her face hot with a blush, Snow Deer turned her eyes slowly to him. He had removed his clothes as well as his eyeglasses and now wore a blanket. She did not draw away when he slowly reached a hand toward her. She sucked in a wild breath of anticipation when he circled his fingers around the hand that clutched the blanket to her.

When he slowly lowered her hand and the blanket slid down her body, revealing her full nudity to him, she knew that she should be shocked, and that she should stop this thing that had begun between them.

But all of her inhibitions were swept away when his hand brushed against one of her breasts, drawing a gasp of pleasure from deep inside her throat.

This time he was initiating the lovemaking, not she. She was . . . allowing it.

Without reservation, shame, guilt, or thoughts of the future, she reached over to him and slid his blanket down from his body.

When she saw his manhood, curiosity made her reach out and touch him.

Charles groaned with pleasure and slid his hand over hers, guiding her into slow up-and-down movements on him. She closed her eyes with ecstasy when his mouth covered her lips in a sweet, yet demanding kiss.

She moved her hand from his manhood and

stretched out on the soft bed of sweet-smelling straw. She swept her arms around his neck when he blanketed her body with his.

"I love you," Charles whispered, his tongue then flicking across her luscious lips.

When he entered her slowly with his throbbing member, Snow Deer was keenly aware of this entrance causing her some pain.

But his kiss, his hands on her breasts, made her forget the pain. It soon changed into something sweet and wonderful as he began his slow strokes within her.

"Tell me you love me," Charles whispered, as he placed his lips over one of her ears. He flicked his tongue inside, smiling when she shivered with sensual pleasure.

"I love you, and it will be forever," Snow Deer whispered back.

"I am the first man with you," Charles whispered, his breath hot on her ear. "I . . . will . . . be the last."

"Yes, you are the first and there will never be anyone *but* you," Snow Deer whispered back, clinging around his neck. She drew in a breath of wild pleasure when he leaned down and sucked one of her nipples between his teeth. She combed her fingers through his wet hair.

"My body is warming up," she said, laughing softly. "Thank you, Charles, for thinking of ways to do this."

He looked into her eyes and chuckled. "It was not all that hard," he said. "I have wanted you since that very first time I saw you."

"But, Charles, I offered myself to you and you refused," Snow Deer said, pouting softly.

"As I should even now be thinking twice before continuing," Charles said, leaning away from her.

She slid her hands around him and splayed her fingers across his buttocks. "Please stay with me," she murmured. "Kiss me. Make love to me. You have unlocked feelings within me I never knew existed."

"No woman before you ever stirred my heart as you have," Charles whispered, then swept his arms around her and held her close against him as he thrust himself deeply into her. As he began his rhythmic strokes, her body answering his in her own rhythmic movements, he kissed her.

When thunder rumbled outside, and the wind howled, and the lightning flashed, Charles and Snow Deer were not aware of it.

They were soaring on beautiful white clouds of rapture.

Chapter Twelve

Still basking in the afterglow of lovemaking, Charles and Snow Deer cuddled beneath a blanket, the straw soft beneath them.

"The rain has stopped," Snow Deer said, slowly running a hand over Charles's muscled back.

"Has it?" Charles said, gazing down at her. He chuckled. "I hadn't noticed."

"Your thoughts are on Snow Deer?" she murmured, now sliding her hand around to run her fingers through his thick curls of black chest hair.

When she had first seen his bare chest, and the hair that spread across it from breast to breast, she had been intrigued, for no Cheyenne warrior ever allowed hair to grow on his chest.

But she hadn't questioned Charles about this. She just accepted this as another difference between white and red men.

She was glad, though, that Charles's face was smooth and clean of bristly stubble, the same as a Cheyenne warrior's. She wondered, though, if he plucked the whiskers, or had some other means with which to remove the hair from his face. She hoped one day to know not only this about him, but everything else.

Charles took her hand from his chest and kissed its palm. "Yes, my thoughts are of you," he said huskily. "I doubt that I shall ever be able to think of anything else again."

He wanted to ask her to marry him. But he understood that this was all happening abnormally fast . . . especially his thoughts of marrying her.

But nothing about this relationship was normal. Her skin was red. His was white.

And if he didn't solidify their relationship before she was among her people again, he might never have her. Her people, especially her father, might talk her out of loving him.

Yet even though he was aware of this possibility, he felt that the timing still wasn't quite right.

He had read enough books about Indians to know that a bride price was always paid for an Indian's daughter. He would approach the question of his marriage to her in the custom of the Indians. He would meet with her father first, and speak his feelings for her to him, then later return with a bride price that would be more than enough for her father to release her into the care of another man.

Snow Deer was filled with her own concerns as she thought of how much she loved this white man, how quickly this love had come into her life. She had heard other women talk of experiencing love at first sight. She had scoffed at their talk, thinking the women foolish to love so quickly.

But here she was, one of those "foolish" women,

loving so much that her insides ached from the intensity of it!

How could she approach her father and tell him that she wished to be this man's wife? If she married Charles she would be caught between two worlds—the red and the white—and she would have to find a middle road that wouldn't compromise her traditional beliefs.

Her father would tell her that she had not known Charles long enough to truly know how he would treat her once he had her away from her world.

How could she tell her father that she was willing to risk much to be with this man?

And what about Burning Snow? she despaired. Her little sister depended on her so much!

Not wanting to be faced with these questions now, when she knew her people were surely frantic over her absence, Snow Deer wrapped a blanket around her shoulders and rose quickly to her feet. "We must be on our way," she said, seeing a look of surprise enter Charles's eyes at her sudden change of mood.

She turned away from him and avoided his questioning stare. She went to her dress and touched it, groaning. "It is still too wet to wear," she said. "I itch even now from having worn my dress wet yesterday."

She turned and gazed down at Charles. "But I must hurry home," she murmured. "I guess I have no other choice but to wear the wet dress as I did after my spill into the river from the canoe."

Charles was still in a state of disbelief over her sudden mood swing. He stared up at her.

Then, seeing that she was determined to be on her way, and understanding that she must be concerned about her parents, he rose to his feet.

He reached over and ran his fingers over his breeches, discovering they were still as wet as when he had removed them. "Seems we both must change into something else," he said, going to his travel bags.

He unsnapped one of them and searched through his belongings, soon bringing out two clean and dry shirts and breeches.

He turned to Snow Deer and held out a shirt and pair of breeches for her. "I know you abhor the thought of wearing men's clothes, but you must wear something besides the wet dress or I might be delivering you to your parents with the sniffles," he said softly.

"The sniffles?" Snow Deer said, hesitating to accept his offering of clothes. Although she owned many pairs of leggings, when she wore them, she also wore a skirt or dress. She was not certain that she wished to dress totally as a man!

"You might catch a cold," Charles explained softly. "Or pneumonia."

"Oh, I see," Snow Deer said, gazing at length at the clothes he still held out for her. She paused for a moment longer, then shrugged her shoulders and took them. "Thank you."

She giggled as she laid the shirt aside long enough to slip into the breeches. "When my father sees two men with breeches approaching his village, he might not recognize that one is his daughter," she said. "It will be amusing to see his expression when he realizes that it is Snow Deer who dresses like a man."

Enjoying these final moments with Snow Deer before venturing outside again, Charles didn't bother yet to get dressed himself. But he did place his eyeglasses on. He just watched Snow Deer and laughed to himself when she yanked on the breeches. She was almost swallowed whole by them.

Holding the waist of the breeches away from herself, Snow Deer looked up at Charles. "They are so big," she said softly. "They will fall off as I try to walk."

"I'll make them fit," Charles said.

He looked around at the things in the barn that he might use for a belt for her breeches.

When he saw a small strip of rope hanging on a nail a few feet away, he went and got it. He then looped the rope around her waist and tied it securely in the front.

"They look so funny," Snow Deer said. The pants were puckered strangely around her waist where the rope held them in place.

Then she gazed past her waist, at the floor where her bare feet were hidden beneath the pants. She giggled when she tried to take a step, her feet tangling in the denim fabric of the breeches.

"I'll make that all right, too," Charles said, bending before her. He rolled up the pants legs, making a wide cuff in them.

He stood up before her and smiled into her eyes. "Now I think you can navigate well enough," he said. His gaze lowered. His pulse raced at the way she innocently stood there with her breasts exposed, her shyness having been vanquished by her total trust and love for Charles.

Swallowing hard, fighting off the urge to cup her breasts in his palms, Charles reached for his shirt and shoved it into her hands. "I think you'd best get the shirt on, also," he said. "I'll hurry into my own clothes."

He looked over at the walls of the barn, where wide cracks revealed to him that the sun was now out, sprinkling its beams onto the floor along the wall. "I do believe the weather might cooperate with us now, so I can get you back home," he said.

Those words . . . "back home" . . . sent his eyes back to Snow Deer. Their eyes met and held. He could see her indecision in her gaze. He understood that she was uncertain what to do when she finally was home and her parents saw that she was all right. The word marriage had not been spoken between them, yet surely she wanted this as much as he! Her feelings for him had poured from her heart as they held each other and made love.

Even now, just being together, working out problems as they were faced with them, it was clear they were meant to be together forever.

"Charles, you are looking at me so strangely," Snow Deer said, slowly slipping the shirt on. Her heart pounded, as she sensed his passion, his needs. His eyes seemed to tell her what he was not saying aloud.

"There is so much I wish to say to you," Charles said, reaching a hand out for her, then dropping it back to his side. He turned his eyes away and hurried into his clothes.

"Charles, say what your heart is feeling," Snow Deer said, going to him, slowly buttoning his shirt for him as their eyes again met and held. "Never hold in your feelings for me. You know how much I love you. I want to know all of your thoughts. I want to share everything with you. Is that not what love is? Total sharing?"

"Are you saying that you . . . ?" Charles began, but the voice of the farm woman shook them out of their reverie.

"I think it's time you two be on your way," the lady said, her tone unfriendly. "My husband ain't returned yet. I'd feel safer if you weren't here for me to fret over while I'm alone in the house 'cept for my cat."

Recalling the woman's prejudice against Indians, Charles's jaw tightened. He took Snow Deer's hands, squeezed them reassuringly, then winked at her. "I think we've worn out our welcome here," he said. He nodded toward the blankets, then her dress. "We'd best gather everything up quickly and go before the woman decides she has another companion in her house—a *rifle*."

Snow Deer nodded. She slid her hands free and slipped on her moccasins. She rolled her dress up and tucked it inside one of the travel bags. She then rolled up the blankets and placed them also in the bags.

She followed Charles down the ladder.

When she reached the bottom, she turned and gazed at the woman. "Thank you for the use of your barn," she murmured, flinching when the woman gave her a nasty glare.

"Just be on your way," the woman said, lifting her chin haughtily. "I don't want nothin' to do with the likes of you two."

Charles untied the horses, secured the travel bags on them, and helped Snow Deer onto the gentle mare.

Quickly mounting his own horse, he stared down at the woman as she stepped aside.

He then rode out of the barn, with Snow Deer following closely behind him.

He looked over his shoulder at the woman as she left the barn, her eyes steely gray as she glared at him. He smiled devilishly when a thought came to his mind.

He wheeled his horse around and drew a tight rein as he gazed back at the woman. "Oh, yes, I forgot to tell you, ma'am, that a band of Cheyenne are following close behind us," he said, the lie tasting like sweet syrup as it passed across his lips. "They'll be asking for the same hospitality you gave me and my wife."

When he saw the instant fear that leapt into the woman's eyes, he threw his head back in a fit of laughter.

Then he rode onward and sidled his horse close beside Snow Deer's.

"That was a shameful thing to do," Snow Deer said, giggling. "She will be afraid for the rest of the day, just waiting for the Cheyenne warriors to arrive and ask for lodging in her barn."

"She deserves to be afraid," Charles said spitefully. "The prejudiced biddy."

"At least she gave us lodging out of the rain, Charles," Snow Deer said softly.

"Only because she was afraid not to," Charles said.

"I enjoyed my time with you in the barn," Snow Deer said, feeling a blush rising from her neck to her cheeks. She lowered her eyes bashfully. "If my mother knew what I've done, she would be ashamed of me." She looked quickly up at Charles. "I have never been loose with men. Please believe me."

"A man knows," Charles said, reaching over to gently touch her cheek. "So stop fretting over it. And don't worry about anyone knowing what we shared. It's our secret."

Again he was tempted to ask her to marry him, to prove to her that he was not a man who thought lightly of making love, or who was afraid of committing himself fully to a woman. And he must convince her that she was the first woman he had wished to make a commitment to!

Yet now was not the time for such talk. They

needed to be alone, so that while he told her of his feelings for her, he could hold her and brush soft kisses across her lips and throat.

His heart pounded at the thought of how soft her body had been against his . . . how wonderfully her breasts had filled his hands!

And, ah, the taste of her was surely better than the sweetest stick of candy!

"You are suddenly quiet," Snow Deer said.

He quickly thought of an excuse for his silence. When he told her that he could not live without her, it would be at a time when they were free of horse leather and glaring sun. When he proposed to her, it had to be where there was sweetness and starlight!

"I am wondering where the damn river is," he said, as he jerked his reins and guided his horse in another direction.

Snow Deer kept up beside him. "Follow me," she said, inhaling to get the whiff of the river that she was so familiar with. Because her village was situated along its banks, she was as one with it. She knew its smells. She knew its moods. She knew its path.

And that path would eventually take her home. She only hoped that it would not be too much longer before she reached her village. It made her heart ache to think of how her parents might even now believe that she was dead!

Soon the river came into view down a steep embankment. Beaming with pride at having found it, Snow Deer smiled at Charles. "The Ohio," she said, gesturing toward it with a sweep of a hand.

"How did you know?" Charles asked in amazement.

"I smelled it," Snow Deer said, laughing softly.

"Smelled?" Charles arched an eyebrow, then he

smiled and rode on with her beside the river, knowing that he would have to understand that the ways of this woman would often differ from his.

Yes, he had much to learn about this woman who was a Cheyenne princess! As she had much to learn about his life as a white man. When he took her home to be his wife, she would be faced with many changes. He hoped that she adapted well to changes!

They rode onward at a brisk clip now, Snow Deer's need to get home as quickly as possible the prime thing on her mind. Sometimes she broke away from Charles and rode on ahead of him.

He would quickly catch up with her.

Again she would break away, unaware of even doing it. She kept her eyes straight ahead, watching for familiar curves in the river, for familiar terrain. She knew that she could not be far from home now. The evil trappers had not had her in their canoe for that long before she spilled over the side.

As she and Charles rode past some steep cliffs and thick clusters of forsythia and lilac bushes, six heavily armed Indians suddenly appeared, on foot, from behind the brush, their rifles aimed at Charles.

Charles looked quickly over at Snow Deer. He questioned her with his eyes as she slid out of her saddle and went to the Indian who seemed in charge of the others. He was a small man, older than the rest, with skin drawn tightly over his face like shoe leather. His dark hair was drawn back from his brow with a beaded band. His thin, sunken chest was bare, and he wore only a breech clout.

Charles could not believe that this leader could

be Snow Deer's father. When Charles had thought of her father, he had envisioned a handsome, muscled warrior. Nothing like this man whose eyes cut deep and cold when they looked at him.

Snow Deer rushed to Rain Feather. "Rain Feather, what are you doing?" she shouted, struggling with the Indian's rifle as she tried to get it away from him. "Rain Feather—"

One of the Shawnee warriors grabbed Snow Deer from behind and held her against him. With one arm, he held her firmly around her waist; he clasped his free hand around her mouth.

She wriggled to get free. She kicked. She shoved at the man's arms and hands.

She looked wildly over the Shawnee's clasped hand at Rain Feather as one of his warriors yanked Charles from his horse.

Her eyes widened and she stiffened when Rain Feather raised his rifle and hit Charles across the back of the head with its butt. A scream froze in Snow Deer's throat as she watched Charles crumple to the ground, unconscious.

Rain Feather turned to his warriors. "Hurry to the canoes!" he shouted, then gazed with smiling eyes at Snow Deer. "When I take you to your father he will reward me by giving you to me for a wife!"

Snow Deer managed to bite the warrior's hand. She laughed as he yelped and dropped it away from her mouth, and at the same time released his hold on her waist.

She stepped up to Rain Feather and spoke into his face, their eyes level with one another. "You stupid Shawnee," she spat out. She slapped Rain Feather on the face. "This man saved me! He was taking me home!"

She fell to her knees beside Charles and cradled

141

his head on her lap. "Charles, Charles," she crooned, gazing down at him, her hand caressing his brow.

She screamed when Rain Feather grabbed her by the hair and yanked her away from Charles. "*I* will take you to your father," he said, his voice filled with venom. "Not the white man!"

"Rain Feather, please!" Snow Deer screamed as he dragged her away from Charles, then nodded to one of his more powerful warriors to carry her.

Snow Deer fought against the warrior's hold as he began carrying her away from Charles. She pounded his chest with her fists. She bit his shoulder.

Nothing she did persuaded him to go against his chief's commands.

Snow Deer strained her neck and looked over the warrior's shoulder as she was carried farther and farther away from Charles. "Charles!" she cried, tears flowing down her cheeks. "Oh, Charles, please be all right!"

Just as they reached the beached canoes, there was a rustling in the brush beside the beach.

Snow Deer heard a pistol cock.

She screamed when sudden gunfire broke out.

Her spine stiff, her eyes wide, Snow Deer watched as one by one the Shawnee warriors fell to the ground.

She screamed again as she fell to the ground when the warrior who held her was also shot.

She looked over at Rain Feather. He lay on his belly unconscious, blood seeping from a shoulder wound and from the back of his head. She could tell that the head wound was not fatal. The bullet had only grazed the flesh. She knew also that the shoulder wound was not fatal. He would live.

She tried to scramble to her feet to seek shelter

from the crazed assailants. But she was not quick enough.

"You!" she gasped when the two grizzly trappers who had abducted her earlier stepped out into the open, smoke spiraling from the barrels of their pistols. Their eyes squinted wickedly down at her as they smiled.

"Thought you could get away from us, eh?" Jake said, chuckling as he poked her in the breast with his pistol. "Well, missie, we thought you *had*, until we saw you bein' carried by the injuns toward the canoes we were gettin' ready to steal."

Zeke came and stood over Snow Deer. "My, oh my, but don't you look different in men's clothes," he said, chuckling. "But no less a woman as I sees it."

He looked at Jake. "Ready one of them canoes," he said, nodding at the canoes. "Our lives ain't worth spit if we're caught here with these dead savages."

"You worthless, heartless heathens," Snow Deer hissed, as Zeke grabbed her by one arm and yanked her to her feet. "When my father catches up with you, there will be no pity spared you when you are sentenced to death."

She smiled. "I shall be the one who slips the hangman's noose over your heads," she said.

"Shut up," Zeke said, slapping her across the face.

Jake yanked her away from Zeke. "Stop that, you idiot," he shouted at Zeke. "No need in infuriatin' her more than she already is."

"Since when do you call the shots?" Zeke demanded.

"Since you got us in all of this trouble by suggestin' we travel down the river in canoes," Jake spat out. "When we finally reach our home, I never

143

want nothin' else to do with the likes of you."

Snow Deer only half listened to their arguing as she was thrown into one of the canoes. She looked at the fallen Shawnee, then looked past them. She could not see Charles where he had been left to die.

She lowered her eyes as tears flowed down her cheeks.

She cradled her face in her hands, sobbed, and murmured Charles's name over and over again as she felt the canoe start its journey down the river.

Gradually, her sobs lessened and she began to absorb the conversation between the trappers. She learned that after she had fallen into the river, they had been pushed onward for a while longer by the large limb, then had been dumped, themselves, into the Ohio.

Weaponless, and with nothing left of their belongings, they had traveled upriver by foot until they had come upon three trappers earlier that morning. As the trappers had been busy preparing their many valuable pelts for transporting in their canoe to the nearest trading post, they had not noticed Jake and Zeke sneak up and steal two of their pistols. The trappers had been taken off guard. Two of them had been shot by Jake and Zeke. The third had fled in the canoe, leaving Jake and Zeke with many valuable pelts, but no way to transport them.

It was fate that had led them to where Snow Deer had confronted Rain Feather and his men. They had taken delight in shooting the Shawnee warriors, laughing over and over again at their luck to have found Snow Deer again.

Now they were planning to paddle the Shawnee

canoe back to where they had left the pelts. Snow Deer smiled grimly. Perhaps while they were busy loading the furs, she would have an opportunity to escape.

Chapter Thirteen

Out again searching for Snow Deer, Blazing Eagle and his warriors inspected every inch of the land for any signs of his daughter. Never would he give up searching for Snow Deer. He would never believe that she was dead.

He knew his daughter was strong enough to face any challenge. She would fight with every ounce of her being to survive whatever or whoever stood in the way of her returning home.

Blazing Eagle and his men had taken canoes out this morning to continue the search. He had just beached his canoe when he heard distant gunfire. There was not only one gunshot, but several. Moments later, Blazing Eagle was running through the forest in the direction of the gunfire, his rifle clutched in his right hand, his warriors on both sides of him, their own firearms poised for firing.

Red Bow looked over at Blazing Eagle. "Everything has grown quiet," he said. "Surely we will

146

not find anything more than hunters who are now busy skinning animals."

"Something deep inside my heart tells me that it is something more than a man on a hunt," Blazing Eagle said, frowning as he and Red Bow wove their way around first one tree, and then another, their moccasined feet quiet on the thick cushion of dead leaves beneath the trees.

"We will soon be there," Red Bow said, looking ahead as they pushed their way through the thick brush.

Blazing Eagle stiffened when he saw a break in the trees a short distance away, where on the left the blue shine of the Ohio River could be seen, and on the right an incline that led to a stretch of ground thick with knee-high Kentucky bluegrass.

Red Bow squinted his eyes to try to see movement in the clearing, where he hoped to see one or more men bent over their kill, casually skinning it.

But he saw nothing. Just space and light, and trees and grass, and huge sunflower plants.

Blazing Eagle, who was somewhat taller than Red Bow, strained his neck to see if he could glimpse what lay ahead. He muttered to himself when he found that the height and size of the flowers blocked his full view of the land on the far side of them. Wanting to get around the sunflower plants instead of going through them, where swarms of bees buzzed, Blazing Eagle made a sharp turn right and ran up a slight incline, then turned again and ran toward the clearing.

When he stepped out of the thickness of the trees and brush, his footsteps faltered and his eyes widened.

"A white man," Blazing Eagle whispered, staring at the man who lay on the ground, on his stomach.

He knelt beside Charles and studied him, his eyes raking over him. "This man has not been shot," he said, gazing quickly at Red Bow as he knelt on Blazing Eagle's right side. His warriors made a wide circle around them, their gazes locked on the white man.

"There is blood in his hair," Red Bow said, reaching a slow hand toward Charles, his fingers touching the wet blood on Charles's hair.

"Who then, fired the rifle?" Blazing Eagle asked. He frowned down at Charles, then looked around for a weapon, finding none. "He could not have done the shooting. There is no weapon."

"Then who . . . ?" Red Bow questioned.

Charles was slowly emerging from unconsciousness, the drone of voices from somewhere close by sounding as though those who spoke were inside a deep, narrow well.

He groaned when he felt the throbbing of his head.

He moved his right arm beneath him and slowly pushed himself over onto his back.

"He awakens!" Red Bow gasped, his eyes wide as he watched the white man turn over.

Blazing Eagle's jaw tightened. He rested on his haunches as he watched the white man's eyes slowly open.

Charles jolted when he opened his eyes and discovered many Indians standing around him, two others resting on their haunches close beside him, their midnight-dark eyes staring at him.

In flashes, like lightning erupting inside his memory, lighting up the black, blank spaces that the blow to his head had caused, Charles recalled what had happened.

The Indians!

Snow Deer!

The one called Rain Feather!

He recalled how Snow Deer had defied the small, elderly Indian. And how the Indian had ignored her when she started to explain that Charles was a friend!

He glared at these Indians, thinking they were a part of the group who had obviously taken Snow Deer away, for she was nowhere in sight.

"Where did Rain Feather take Snow Deer?" Charles blurted out, moving quickly into a sitting position as he glared at the two Indians who were the closest to him. Something told him that one of those two Indians was in charge.

The question, the mention of Rain Feather and Snow Deer in the same breath, caused Blazing Eagle's breath to catch in his throat. He inhaled a quick breath, then leaned closer to the white man.

"You speak my daughter Snow Deer's name," he said. "Why? How do you know her? And why would you ask about Rain Feather, about him taking Snow Deer? Why? How would you know anything about Rain Feather or my daughter?"

Charles was taken aback. "You are Blazing Eagle?" he asked guardedly. "You are Snow Deer's father?"

Growing impatient, Blazing Eagle clasped a tight hand on Charles's shoulder.

"Answer me," he said, as his men closed in closer around Charles. "How do you know my daughter? Why do you speak her name in the same breath as that of the Shawnee chief, Rain Feather?"

Charles swallowed hard when he heard the click of the rifles as the warriors prepared them for firing. He looked slowly from warrior to warrior, yet

149

saw nothing but the gun barrels that were leveled at him.

He looked quickly up at Blazing Eagle. He couldn't talk fast enough to please himself. "I saved your daughter from the river," he said. Then he explained everything that had happened between himself and Snow Deer, except for their passionate moments together.

He explained about Rain Feather suddenly appearing, about how Rain Feather would not allow Snow Deer to explain that Charles was her friend before he knocked Charles unconscious.

Charles looked in the direction of the river, unable to see it from his position. "The Shawnee must have taken her away by river," he said, his voice breaking to think that he had been unable to protect her. But the Shawnee warriors had appeared so quickly. There had been no chance to react any more swiftly than he had.

Suddenly Charles was aware of something else. He reached a slow hand to his eyes. His eyeglasses weren't there. They had been knocked off when he was hit on the head.

Yet . . . yet . . . he was seeing everything perfectly well, as though he was peering through the corrective lenses of the eyeglasses!

Miracle of miracles, he had regained his sight! And the blow to his head seemed to be the cause!

He reached his hand to the lump at the back of his head, wincing when touching it caused pain to shoot across his scalp.

He lowered his hand and looked up at Blazing Eagle. "I . . . can . . . see," he murmured, amazed. "Lord, my eyesight has returned!"

Blazing Eagle silently watched him, unable to share his obvious joy.

If Snow Deer was being taken down the river,

he did not even want to think of how far Rain Feather could have gotten by now. Blazing Eagle knew not how long this white man had been lying there, unconscious.

Then a thought sprang to his mind that sent spirals of dread through him. "The gunfire," he gasped, looking toward the river. "I forgot about having heard the gunfire!"

He felt suddenly queasy. Had his daughter struggled too much when she was carried toward the river by the Shawnee? Could Rain Feather have grown tired of fighting with her? Had he finally decided she was not worth the trouble she was causing him after all?

"There were many shots fired," he whispered to himself, wondering if he would find his daughter with many bullets in her lovely flesh.

"Gunfire?" Charles said, glad when Blazing Eagle dropped his hand away from his shoulder.

He watched Blazing Eagle rise quickly to his feet. His eyes wonderfully focused, Charles watched the Indians leave him and run toward the river.

Charles paled, and a sick feeling assailed him when he again repeated, "Gunfire?" A quick agony grabbed at his heart.

He bolted to his feet and ran toward the river.

What if the Shawnee had killed her? The phrase kept running through his mind. He envisioned her lying there on the bank of the river, dead.

Charles had seen enough to know that Snow Deer hated Rain Feather. Charles had seen her utter defiance of him. Had she been too defiant? Had he murdered her because of it?

When he arrived where he could look down at the river embankment, his footsteps faltered and he stopped at the sight of what did lie there: pools of blood soaking the earth beneath the Shawnee warriors.

Relief washed through him when he realized that Snow Deer was not among those who lay sprawled on the ground. But where was she? Who had taken her? Rain Feather and his warriors were dead.

"The trappers," he said, his teeth clenched. He doubled his hands into tight fists at his sides. "Those damn trappers!"

He broke into a mad run, forgetting the throbbing of his head in his despair at what might now happen to Snow Deer. "Lord," he whispered, looking heavenward. "She is everything good on this earth. Protect her as though she were one of your angels sent from heaven to spread goodness among mankind! To me, she *is* an angel! She is my beloved!"

When he reached the death scene, he stopped and stared slowly around him. He hoped that at least one of the Indians might be alive to tell what had actually happened!

Then he flinched and stiffened when he heard a slow, agonized moan. His gaze swept over the fallen men again, searching for the one who was still alive!

He watched as Blazing Eagle knelt quickly beside Rain Feather and turned him slowly over, onto his back.

"Blazing Eagle," Rain Feather said, his voice a mere whisper. "Snow Deer! She . . ."

When Rain Feather's words fell away and his eyes closed again, Charles rushed over and knelt down opposite Blazing Eagle.

Ignoring Blazing Eagle's gasp of surprise, Charles grabbed hold of Rain Feather's long black hair. He yanked it, bringing Rain Feather's eyes open again in a fearful stare. "You son-of-a-bitch, God has spared you only so that you can tell us what happened to Snow Deer," he said, his eyes narrowed angrily as he glared at the aged Shawnee. "Tell us! Who took Snow Deer? Did they take her away by river? Or were they on horses?"

Rain Feather inhaled a quavering breath, then spoke. "Two whiskered men came and ambushed the Shawnee. It was for the Cheyenne princess they did this. They took Snow Deer away," Rain Feather stammered. "They reeked of dead animals and white man's firewater. Their clothes were unclean. There was blood dried on their clothes."

"How did they take her?" Blazing Eagle said, his voice tight. "By river? Or on horseback?"

"If you see fewer than five beached canoes, then they took one of our canoes down the river," Rain Feather said.

Charles dropped his hand from the Shawnee's hair and looked quickly at the canoes. When he counted only four there, his heart sank. In his mind's eye he recalled Snow Deer falling into the river again. He saw her bobbing up and down in the water, her mouth gagged, her arms tied behind her.

Then he glared at the tiny Shawnee chief. "If you hadn't interfered, nothing would have happened to Snow Deer," he shouted, drawing Blazing Eagle's eyes quickly around to stare at him. "I was taking her home. I would not have passed the place where the trappers found you with Snow Deer!"

Seeing the intensity with which this white man spoke about Snow Deer, and knowing that he had saved her once before, Blazing Eagle felt a camaraderie with him.

Then his thoughts were altered when he heard

Rain Feather's explanation as to why he had taken Snow Deer from the white man.

"Blazing Eagle, I was going to deliver Snow Deer to you," Rain Feather said. "Look around you, Blazing Eagle. I have lost my friends today while trying to save your daughter. I did not know that this white man was a friend of Snow Deer's. I thought . . . I was doing the right thing. I wanted to prove to you that I am a friend, not a foe! I sacrificed today for *you*, for your friendship."

"But instead you caused my daughter to be taken away by those who will possibly rape, then kill her," Blazing Eagle said, his teeth clenched.

"Father! Charles! I am all right!"

The sound of Snow Deer's voice caused Charles and Blazing Eagle to jump to their feet.

Both men sighed, laughed awkwardly, then held out their arms for her, each vying for her sweet embrace.

Chapter Fourteen

Knowing that the trappers were close behind her, Snow Deer looked frantically from her father to Charles. Her heart sang to see that Charles was all right.

She had managed to escape from the trappers when they'd gone ashore to load their stolen pelts, leaving her alone in the canoe. But she'd only paddled a short distance when she heard them shouting her name. Afraid they would shoot her, she'd beached the canoe and set off running back to where she'd left Charles.

She could hardly believe it when she saw both her father and Charles in the clearing. But the trappers were now just behind her.

"You bitch!" Jake shouted in the distance. "You'll be sorry. When we catch up with you, you'll wish you were dead!"

Jake's shout alerted the Cheyenne and Charles of the approach of the trappers. The Cheyenne, all but Blazing Eagle, rushed away to meet the trappers' approach.

After a moment's hesitation as she looked from Blazing Eagle to Charles, Snow Deer ran to her lover and flung herself into his arms.

"Charles," she sobbed, clinging to him. "Dear Charles, I thought we would never be together again. Oh, Charles, I prayed to *Maheo* that you would be all right."

Blazing Eagle scarcely breathed as he stood beside Charles and watched his daughter show such deep emotions toward the white man. Her love for him was in her voice and in the way she clung to him.

Blazing Eagle was stunned. His head swam as he tried to accept this side of his daughter that he had never seen before.

He found it hard to believe that his daughter could love so quickly when all along she had not allowed herself to love at all. Now, like her father, she had fallen in love with someone with white skin!

No, he could not believe what his eyes were telling him. Always before, she had scoffed at the men who tried to bring her into a serious relationship. She had always claimed a devotion to her title of princess, which made her turn a cold shoulder to anyone who even hinted at marriage.

Never would he have guessed that a white man could be the one to change those things about her—a white man who looked down at her and held her with adoration in his eyes.

"Had anything happened to you . . ." Charles said, his voice breaking. He held her more strongly, ignoring the stare of her father. She was all that mattered at this moment. They had both had a scrape with death today. They had both survived it.

"I would not allow anything to happen to me, for that would take me away from *you*," Snow Deer said, leaning just far enough away so she could see his handsome face. She lifted a hand to his cheek. "I love you so."

Those words cut like a knife into Blazing Eagle's heart. He stared at his daughter a moment longer, then turned and walked slowly away, feeling a deep loss of a kind he had never felt before.

Charles saw Blazing Eagle's despair. His eyes wavered; then he unwound his arms from around Snow Deer and framed her face between his hands. "I think you'd best go to your father," he said gently. "He's hurt, Snow Deer. He fears he has lost you."

A quiver ran across Snow Deer's flesh when she turned and saw her father walking away from her, his head hanging in dejection.

Shame swam through her at the realization that she had wounded her father in such a way. She stifled a sob of regret behind her hand, for never did a daughter love a father as much as she.

Feeling almost desperate in her flight, Snow Deer broke away from Charles and ran to Blazing Eagle. She reached out and grabbed his hand.

"Father!" she cried. "Oh, Father, please, I am so sorry!"

Charles watched Blazing Eagle turn to Snow Deer. He watched her lunge into his arms and hug him tightly as she continued to apologize to her father for having ignored him.

Charles observed how father and daughter clung to each other, demonstrating a bond so tight that it frightened him.

He inhaled a deep, trembling breath. He had not

expected Snow Deer to be so apologetic at having chosen him over her father for that brief moment.

Something deep inside told him that he might not have won her after all. Perhaps her father's anguish would make her think twice about leaving her family to marry him!

He now regretted not having already asked her.

His thoughts and worries about Snow Deer were swept aside when the Cheyenne warriors came back, bringing the two whiskered men with them. One of them was scarcely conscious as blood dripped from a head wound that had been inflicted by the butt end of a rifle. The other man held on to his chest; blood seeped from between his fingers from a knife wound.

Snow Deer heard the approach of her father's warriors and the groans of the injured trappers. She swung away from her father and glared at the evil white men.

Then she told her father everything, from the moment she had first been abducted by the trappers until now.

"Not only did they kill the Shawnee," Snow Deer said, peering over at Rain Feather, "the trappers killed white men, too. Their bodies are downriver a short distance."

Several warriors went to check on the murdered white men.

Rain Feather limped to one of his canoes, gave Blazing Eagle a lingering stare, then climbed aboard and paddled himself away, to return later for his fallen comrades.

Charles went to Snow Deer and bravely slid an arm around her waist and faced Blazing Eagle.

Snow Deer gazed up at her father, awaiting his acceptance of Charles's attention to her.

"Your name is Charles?" Blazing Eagle asked quietly.

"Yes, Charles Cline."

"But some call him C.C.," Snow Deer quickly interjected, her pulse racing as she noticed the way her father's eyes shifted often to Charles's possessive hold of her. Uneasy at Blazing Eagle's frown, she slowly slid free and stepped away from Charles.

She was very aware now of Charles's eyes on her. She did not look his way, for she did not want to see the questioning in his gaze.

She was torn between two men!

Between two worlds!

Smiling, Blazing Eagle relaxed when he saw Snow Deer step away from the white man. "C.C. is a strange name," he said, tightly gripping his rifle.

"So I've been told," Charles said, clearing his throat nervously.

Snow Deer looked quickly up at Charles again. "Your eyeglasses," she blurted out. "Did they get broken? You are not wearing them."

Charles turned toward her. "No, they aren't broken," he said softly. "I just don't need them any longer. I see perfectly well without them." He reached a hand out for her, then brought it back to hang limply at his side. "I see everything, Snow Deer, even inside your heart."

"What do we do with the trappers?" Red Bow asked, interrupting the strained moment between Charles, Blazing Eagle, and Snow Deer.

"Tie them and take them back to our village," Blazing Eagle said. He watched as his other warriors returned, their arms heavily laden with the dead white men's rich pelts.

"Father," Snow Deer said, drawing her father's

attention back to her. "I would like Charles to be invited to our village. Will you please do the asking?"

Blazing Eagle's head turned toward her. He saw the silent pleading in her dark eyes.

Then he looked at Charles. "You are to be rewarded for having saved my daughter," he said tightly. "Return with us to my village. There will be a celebration in your honor."

Pleased by her father's generous offer, excited that Charles would be able to meet her mother and sister, Snow Deer almost clapped her hands with glee. She held back, yet sent Charles a wide smile.

That smile was what Charles needed, even more than Blazing Eagle's invitation to the Cheyenne village, to have some hope again for himself and Snow Deer.

"Thank you," he said, holding a hand out to Blazing Eagle. "It would be my pleasure to go with you and Snow Deer to your village."

Charles felt the stiffness of Blazing Eagle's handshake, knowing then that he had a long way to go before convincing this man to accept him.

He gazed at Snow Deer, then looked at Blazing Eagle again as he slowly slid his hand away. "But I expect no celebration, no reward of any sort for rescuing your daughter," he said, reveling in the touch of Snow Deer's hand as she slipped it into his. "Knowing your daughter, being lov—"

He stopped short of saying the word "loved," for fear of stirring up Blazing Eagle's wrath even more!

Instead he said, "Getting to know your daughter is payment enough."

He felt Snow Deer's fingers tighten in his and

knew that she understood why he had not gone further.

"This father repays any kindness paid to his family," Blazing Eagle said. "There will be a feast. There will be a celebration. There will be gifts."

Blazing Eagle ignored the fact that his daughter now held hands with this white man. He would have a talk with Snow Deer. He must make her realize the hardships she would face loving a white man! Adapting to the white man's way of life could be too hard for a princess who had known only Cheyenne ways.

Snow Deer looked through the brush and saw that their horses were still tethered safely there, then smiled up at her father. "Father, Charles and I will follow on horses as you glide down the river in your canoes," she said softly.

Her suggestion caused a cold look in her father's eyes. Yet she stood firm in her decision. She felt that Charles needed her support at this time.

"We have come far in our canoes," Blazing Eagle said stiffly. "You would be more comfortable in a canoe. Let the white man ride alone on his horse."

"Father . . ." Snow Deer pleaded, her voice soft and lilting.

"Go with the white man," Blazing Eagle then said, sighing heavily. "But stay close by the river-bank where you can see our canoes as we travel down the Ohio toward home. I do not want you out of my sight—*ever* again."

Those words cut into Charles's heart, making him truly anxious about his future with Snow Deer.

When she looked at him, and he saw the same worry in her eyes, his blood ran cold. When she returned home and was surrounded by her people who adored her, *would* she truly be able to leave them, to live the life of an ordinary white woman?

He was beginning to doubt it. . . .

Chapter Fifteen

Shortly after Charles arrived at the Cheyenne village, and everyone saw that their princess was alive and well and knew that Charles was responsible for her safe arrival home, feast shouts had risen into the air.

After the feast was announced, he had watched the children of the village running around, laughing and chatting among themselves, excitement building as the working men and women put away their tasks and prepared for the long night of celebration.

At sundown, everyone gathered around a big fire built against the darkening sky.

Soon whole sides of meat were tied to thick poles and hung over the fire. Women took turns slowly swinging them back and forth through the flames, while other women hurried about pulling armfuls of weeds and strewing them along the ground for people to sit on.

Charles shifted his weight on a white deerskin where he sat beside Snow Deer as braves, decorated with their fine feathers, rose to dance around the fire. The night sky was clear and beautiful, the breeze soft and gentle. The smoke from the tepees floated gently away, and the feathers of the braves fluttered gracefully as they danced around the fire.

Charles peered across the fire and became unnerved when he found Chief Blazing Eagle staring back at him through the flames from the pallet of blankets and rich pelts that he shared with his wife.

Although Charles had already smoked a pipe of peace with Blazing Eagle, he did not feel comfortable about it. He did not see a trace of acceptance in the powerful Cheyenne chief's eyes.

Charles saw resentment—keen resentment.

Charles's gaze moved to Becky, the chief's wife. When she looked his way and smiled, he sighed. He was relieved that at least he might have *her* in his corner when he spoke of his intentions toward Snow Deer.

He returned Becky's smile, then leaned out a bit and looked past Snow Deer at her little sister, Burning Snow, who sat at Snow Deer's right side. He stiffened when he saw how Burning Snow clung to her sister's arm. There seemed to be desperation in the way she held on to her, as though she was not about to let go of her again.

Snow Deer had only moments ago explained to him how Burning Snow held herself accountable for Snow Deer's disappearance, and why. It seemed that Burning Snow wanted to make this up to her sister by proving that she was would never desert her again.

If he had found disapproval in Blazing Eagle's

gaze, he had seen it twofold in Burning Snow's eyes as she glared at him. Charles had to wonder how this young maiden would react when she heard that Charles's intentions were to take Snow Deer away from this village—and her—forever!

As the weaving dancers circled around the fire, their bare feet stamping the ground in time with the music being played on several drums, Charles looked out beyond the fire and the dancers, and observed the cone-shaped lodges that stood about him, so quiet and remote in the moonlight.

He looked into the shadows at the far right side of the village, where the two trappers were stretched out on the ground, their wrists and ankles tied to stakes.

Their severe wounds had not even been seen to, and the trappers had been placed there until votes were taken as to how they would eventually die.

He looked quickly again at Chief Blazing Eagle. He realized that Blazing Eagle had seen him looking at the imprisoned men. Did Charles see a gleam in the chief's eyes? he wondered. Could the chief have the same sort of plans for Charles?

Again Charles shifted his weight on the deerskin. He folded his legs before him and clasped his hands on his knees, the knuckles white from his tight grip. He held his chin high, thinking that surely the Cheyenne chief would not allow his people to shower him with gifts for saving their princess if he was planning to harm him. The gifts lay, even now, in Snow Deer's private lodge. She had told him that she would help place them in his travel bags just prior to his leaving.

He had laughed softly at that suggestion, knowing that no bags were large enough to carry away all that he had been given by these generoushearted people—pelts, blankets, stores of food, fancy clothes, jewelry, and even moccasins!

He wore one of the fringed buckskin outfits tonight, as well as the beaded moccasins.

He gazed at Snow Deer and saw how her beautiful buckskin dress clung to her shapely body, and how her lovely hair was drawn back and braided, with white rabbit fur woven into the braids.

All evening she had smiled, her eyes twinkling in her happiness.

Snow Deer turned to him. "Are you happy, Charles?" she whispered. She winced and turned to look quickly at Burning Snow when Burning Snow's fingers bit into her arm in an attempt to draw Snow Deer's attention away from Charles.

Charles stiffened as he watched the quiet words being exchanged between sisters. He couldn't hear what they were saying. The loud drumming drowned out their soft voices. But he could see a silent battle in Burning Snow's eyes as she argued with Snow Deer.

"Why did you do that?" Snow Deer whispered as she eased her sister's fingers from her arm. "Burning Snow, you hurt me. Never have you done that before. Why do you now?"

"You look at that white man with too much favor," Burning Snow said, her lips curving into a pout.

"Why should I not?" Snow Deer said, stunned by her sister's obvious rejection of Charles.

"White men stole you away," Burning Snow said. "White men cannot be trusted!"

"Burning Snow, *this* white man saved my life," Snow Deer softly argued. "How can you compare him with the filthy, murdering trappers?"

"All white people are bad," Burning Snow said, her eyes filled with a sudden fire. "This man who sits at your side cannot be trusted. He will hurt you."

Snow Deer's lips parted in a gasp. "I cannot believe you are saying these things," she said. "Burning Snow, our *mother* is white. We have many white friends."

"Mother's skin, as well as that of our special white friends, is white, yet in their hearts, they are all Cheyenne!" Burning Snow declared.

"Burning Snow, you must forget these harsh feelings about Charles," Snow Deer said. She reached for her sister's hand and held it over her heart. "Do you feel my heart beating inside my chest?"

Burning Snow nodded. "Yes, I feel it," she murmured.

"Well, sweet sister, each of those heartbeats is for the white man who sits at my side," she said. She refused to allow the alarm that entered her sister's eyes to sway her determination to make Burning Snow understand her feelings for Charles. "I love him, Burning Snow, as our mother and father love each other."

Burning Snow gasped. Her face paled. She yanked her hand away from Snow Deer's and leapt to her feet. Sobbing, Burning Snow ran past the fire and threw herself down beside Becky.

Charles scarcely breathed as he watched while the young girl who seemed to hate him was pampered and consoled not only by her mother, but also by her father.

Charles looked quickly over at Snow Deer. "Why does your sister hate me so much?" he asked, imploring Snow Deer with his eyes. "I know that my skin is white. But your mother's is white. Doesn't that give your sister cause enough to trust me?"

Snow Deer took Charles's hand. Although she

knew that it was not appropriate to leave a celebration that was being held in honor of them both, she had the need to be alone with him. She had to try to patch up the hurt that had been inflicted on his heart this evening by a small sister who had not even the ability to reason things out.

"Come," Snow Deer said, giving Charles's hand a soft tug. "Let us go where we can be alone . . . where we can talk. I believe I can explain things to you about my sister that might help you understand."

"I'm not sure that's possible," Charles said. He rose beside her and ignored the stares they drew as they walked away from the circle of Cheyenne people. "If so, there is also your father, Snow Deer. It is in his eyes how much *he* dislikes me."

Snow Deer smiled but did not answer his questions just yet. Instead, she led him past the lodges, and to a slight rise of land, to a rock she always visited when she needed solace and solitude. It was her place to pray to *Maheo* when she needed advice about life.

"Please sit," Snow Deer said. She swept the fringed hem of her skirt up as she eased down onto a patch of ground that was covered with soft green moss.

Charles sat down beside her. She took one of his hands and laid it on her lap, her fingers intertwined with his.

"There is so much I need to explain to you," she said, then looked away from him, up at the sky. "There are many mysteries in life that are hard to explain." She gestured with her free hand toward the sky. "Look heavenward, Charles. See the stars tonight? The stars are a beautiful mystery." She looked over at him. "And so is the place where eagles go when they soar out of sight."

She paused and nervously cleared her throat, then spoke again. "There are many mysteries of life that slowly unfold around you," she murmured. "As for my father—Charles, you must remember that I am his first-born daughter. I am a princess. He would choose someone quite unlike you for me if he thought that I would allow it."

"I am that undesirable in his eyes?" Charles said, raising an eyebrow.

"Not you," Snow Deer softly explained. "The color of your skin, and the location of your home. Is it not far from this village? Just how many days would you say it would take for my parents to travel so that they could sit and laugh with me if I went with you to live in your lodge?"

Charles's heart skipped an anxious beat. She was talking to him as though she was seriously thinking of returning with him to Bloomfield! Certainly she had thought about it!

"Yes, my home is some distance from your father's," he said, looking deeply into her dark eyes. "It is three days' travel on horseback."

"See then why my father has cause to resent you?" Snow Deer said, softly touching his cheek. "He would miss seeing my face every day. He would miss talking with me as fathers and daughters talk."

She looked slowly around her, at the wide expanse of land on all sides. "Also, although Father is a man of peace, he resents many things the white men are responsible for," she said, her voice drawn.

She looked into his eyes. "With the arrival of white people on the land of the Cheyenne many moons ago, the words 'hate', 'mistrust', and 'injustice' became familiar to our people," she murmured. "Yet, as I have said, my father has walked the path of peace. He even married a woman with white skin. But it is his daughter he must now think about. He does not want to lose me to a life that will be filled with customs very different from the Cheyenne's. He wants me to carry on the tradition of the Cheyenne when I have children. He knows that would be impossible if I chose to live in the white man's world."

Snow Deer lowered her eyes. "Also, my father would miss watching me with . . . with my little sister."

Charles noticed that the mention of her sister had put a soft melancholy in her voice, a hesitation. She even now looked downward, instead of into his eyes.

Slipping his hand free of hers, he placed a finger beneath Snow Deer's chin and brought her eyes up. "There is something about your sister that you have not yet told me, isn't there?" he asked softly.

Eyes wide and shining with tears, Snow Deer slowly nodded.

"What is it?" Charles persisted, his eyes searching hers for answers.

"She was not born as lucky as you or I," Snow Deer said, her voice filled with a sudden sadness.

"What do you mean . . . not as lucky?" Charles asked.

A short distance away, the celebration continued in the village, the drums beating, the people singing, the feet stamping. From somewhere off in the distance a wolf bayed at the full moon. An owl hooted.

"My sister was born slow in every way," Snow Deer said softly. "She cannot remember well. She cannot . . ."

Her voice broke; then she continued. "There are so many things about my sister that are hard to explain," she murmured. "Except that she has always depended on me, Charles. I have always been nearby, to speak for her, to do things for her. Now do you understand why she sees you as a threat? It is not only because your skin is white. It is because you are a *man*, who perhaps seeks a wife."

Charles sat quietly for a moment and allowed all of this to sink into his consciousness. His fears were now twofold that Snow Deer might not, in the end, accept his proposal of marriage, especially if she felt desperately needed by her sister.

Yet he could not allow anything to stop him from trying!

He had to find a way to persuade her that she should not live someone else's life!

He had to convince her that she had a life of her own!

"Your sister is right," Charles said, his voice drawn. He framed Snow Deer's face between his hands. "Beautiful Cheyenne princess, I *do* want to take you away. I want you to be my wife."

Snow Deer's heart raced and her knees grew weak with passion as his hands slid down and he cupped her breasts within them. She closed her eyes and sighed as he caressed her breasts. Her face grew hot with a blush.

"Can you tell me that you do not want me?" Charles said, his hands now at her waist, drawing her soft, pliant body against the hardness of his. "Haven't I awakened fires within you that you cannot deny?"

"Yes, yes," Snow Deer whispered, forgetting everything when his lips came to hers in a frenzy of passionate kisses.

Chapter Sixteen

The sound of horses approaching drew Charles and Snow Deer quickly apart. They turned just in time to see two horses passing below the hill on which they sat, the moonlight revealing the faces of the riders.

"Whistling Elk," Snow Deer said, her eyes wide.

She scarcely breathed as her gaze swept from her brother, Whistling Elk, over to the other rider, a golden-haired woman.

"You know them?" Charles asked, peering through the darkness to get a better look. He saw that one rider was a warrior. The other was a beautiful white woman.

"I know the Cheyenne warrior," Snow Deer said, rising to stand beside Charles as he stood. She gave Charles a worried glance. "He is my brother. But the woman?" She looked down at the woman again as she rode on toward the village. "No. I do not know her."

She began to hurry down the hillside. "I must get back to the village," she said, her heart pounding as she wondered who this woman might be, and how she might be received into the Cheyenne village. This was surely the woman Whistling Elk had gone to see just outside of Paducah. Surely there was more than an infatuation with her, or he would not be bringing her back to be among his people.

"Where are you going?" Charles said, catching up with Snow Deer. He grabbed her hand and stopped her. He placed a hand at her waist and turned her to face him. "Darling Snow Deer, we were just about to—"

"Yes, and it was wrong," Snow Deer said, swallowing hard. "I should have not left the celebration. It was wrong to even think of making love at such a time as this." She placed a gentle hand to his cheek. "My handsome Charles, so often you make me forget who I am, and what is expected of me. Our worlds, Charles, differ so. I must stay with mine. You must return to yours."

"No," Charles gasped. "You can't mean that."

Snow Deer gave him a lingering stare, then yanked her hand free and ran away from him.

Stunned, almost numb, feeling forlorn and defeated, Charles stood and watched her as she ran into the village; her brother and the woman were already there.

The music had ceased.

The singing and dancing had stilled also, with the arrival of the chief's son and his golden-haired woman.

"Perfect timing," Charles grumbled to himself. "Now the chief is going to have double cause to be upset. Not only does his daughter choose someone out of their race, but now his son does also."

173

He ran his fingers through his hair, sinking more and more into despair as Snow Deer's words played over again inside his head . . . that their worlds differed and that she had actually asked him to return to his, and that she would stay with hers!

"No, I can't give up that easily," he told himself, doubling his hands into tight fists at his sides.

He strode on to the village, then took a shaky step backward when he saw the anger in Chief Blazing Eagle's eyes and heard it in his voice as he spoke to his son.

"You have already taken this woman as your wife?" Blazing Eagle said, his teeth clenched as he looked from Whistling Elk to the golden-haired woman.

Blazing Eagle's eyes flashed with a deepening anger. "She is . . . with *child?*"

Low gasps reverberated throughout the crowd of Cheyenne as they watched and listened.

Snow Deer felt an icy-cold dread enter her veins. And not so much because of her brother bringing a pregnant woman home to his people, but because she was *white*. That could make her father hate Charles more than ever.

She lowered her eyes, now realizing that what she had said to Charles moments ago had been the only way it could be. She could not add to her father's distress by marrying a white man herself. Even though she wanted to, with every ounce of her being, she had to fight this need, this love that was so dear to her heart! She had to be strong and prove that she was Cheyenne through and through, and that the Cheyenne's best interest, as a whole, came before *her* needs.

Seeing how this news was affecting Snow Deer, Charles went and stood at her side.

But when he tried to take her hand, to give her some reassurance, some comfort, she jerked it quickly away, and his spirits fell, and with them all hopes of ever having her as a wife.

Yet he stood his ground. He stayed beside her and listened to a father's wrath against a son who had disappointed him.

"*Naha*, my son, you who would one day be chief, would marry without giving your parents the courtesy of knowing the woman first?" Blazing Eagle said. He ignored Becky's hand as she tugged on his arm to remind him that he was shaming his son in front of the entire village. "And what bride price did you pay for her, *Naha?*"

"None was required," Whistling Elk finally said, taking his wife's hand and gently gripping it. "My wife, Sharon, was courted in the tradition of white people, not Indian. She was married in the white man's tradition."

Charles watched Blazing Eagle take a shocked, shaky step away from his son.

Becky felt her husband's despair, and she understood it, for he had planned so much for Whistling Elk. He had even begun readying him for chieftainship.

But having gone so far as to marry the white woman somewhere besides in his village, among his people—that was what cut deeply into her husband's heart. And for Blazing Eagle to know that his son had loved this woman this deeply for so long without having shared her with his family, so long now that she was with child, was perhaps something that Blazing Eagle could not forgive.

Whistling Elk stepped away from his wife. He went to his father and started to place a hand on his shoulder, but paled when Blazing Eagle stepped far enough away to keep him from it.

Whistling Elk dropped his hands to his sides. "*Ne-hyo*, my wife's parents would not allow me into their life by any path other than that which I have taken," he said. "Had I not married her among her people, she could not have been my wife." He held his chin high. "And, *Ne-hyo*, had I not expected such a reaction from you as I received here today, I would have confided in you long ago about my woman."

Whistling Elk turned a slow gaze his mother's way. "*Nah-koa*, I would have told you about the child, for I know how you feel about children," he said with much love and devotion in his voice and eyes. "You love and adore them. I know that you will adore mine and Sharon's child, yet Father . . ."

Unable to keep the tears back any longer, Becky flung herself into Whistling Elk's arms and hugged him. "I know," she sobbed. "And I'm sorry that you were put in such a position as this. I just wish you could trust that the hurt your father is feeling will be short-lived. We could have shared all of this with you. All of it."

"Then you understand?" Whistling Elk said, looking past his mother's shoulders into his father's sulking eyes.

"Yes, and as soon as your father's hurt is lived through, he will also understand and accept your wife into his heart," Becky said. She eased from her son's arms. She took him by his hand and led him a step closer to Blazing Eagle. "Blazing Eagle, our son needs your approval."

Blazing Eagle folded his arms across his chest, his jaw tight, his lips tightly pursed.

"Blazing Eagle, when did our son ever disappoint you?" Becky asked softly, her eyes imploring her husband. "Did he not learn the ways of the hunt quickly? Did he not learn all things Cheyenne in a way that made his chieftain father proud?"

"Apparently he was not taught Cheyenne traditions well enough," Blazing Eagle said. "Perhaps the blood of his *true* mother, who is also Snow Deer's mother, runs too thickly in his veins, for she was also a traitor to her people!"

Becky paled and watched Blazing Eagle turn and stamp away. Hardly ever did Blazing Eagle refer to Whistling Elk's true mother! Becky had been his mother for so many years now, it seemed he truly *was* her son.

She was hurt that Blazing Eagle would refer to his first wife now.

Everyone in the village was stone quiet. Scarcely could a breath be heard. A wolf's howl in the distance seemed to be an omen, sending shivers across everyone's flesh.

Becky stood and stared at her husband as he entered his magnificently large tepee; then she turned slow eyes up at Whistling Elk. "I'm sorry," she said, a sob catching in her throat.

She walked past him and took Sharon's hands. She peered into blue, frightened eyes. "My husband, your husband's father, will soften in his mood toward you," she murmured. "Go with Whistling Elk to his lodge. You are his wife. You are carrying his child. Do not allow despair and fear to spoil what you have found together."

"He can't resent me because I am white," Sharon said, her voice soft and lilting. "For *you* are white."

"Yes, I am white, but from the beginning I gave up everything of my past life to be with Blazing Eagle," Becky said softly. "I did this willingly because I loved him so much. It looks to Blazing Eagle as though it was Whistling Elk who gave up too much to be your husband. That might make

Whistling Elk look less strong in the eyes of his people."

Sharon lowered her eyes. "I should not be blamed for that," she said. "It was my father who forced this upon us."

"Yes, I know," Becky said. "But even that makes Whistling Elk look weaker in the eyes of the Cheyenne."

Sharon began crying. She turned and rushed away, then stopped when she collided with someone. Trembling, she gazed up into Charles's dark eyes.

Charles stared down at her, seeing her loveliness, and understanding how any man might forget tradition to have her. Then he let her go and turned and walked stiffly toward the small makeshift lodge, a lean-to, that had been offered him for his night's lodging. Snow Deer had pleaded with him to stay with her in her lodge. She had even had all his gifts taken there, to encourage it. She had said that she was a princess. A princess had the right to have anyone she wished sleep in her lodge.

He had laughed softly at her determination, saying that he doubted that her people would think kindly of him if he stayed with her in her private tepee.

Now he was glad that he had not gone there even for one moment. He would have stirred up the wrath of the Cheyenne chief even before his son arrived home with a pregnant white wife!

When Charles reached the lean-to that sat beside the river away from the village, he numbly began gathering up his supplies. He felt soulweary to know that he had lost at love a second time in his life. First Elissa. Then Snow Deer!

After having witnessed Blazing Eagle's wrath,

Charles did not wish to put Snow Deer in the same position as her brother.

Yet a part of Charles wanted to fight for her, to tell Blazing Eagle that he should not expect his children to live wholly Cheyenne now when the world was not wholly Cheyenne! The white world lay all around Blazing Eagle and his people! How could he expect his children not to react to it?

It confused Charles how Blazing Eagle could so easily forget that he had reached out into the white community himself to take a wife.

Then he reminded himself of what he had heard Becky tell Sharon—that Becky gave the white world up for Blazing Eagle.

Charles could never do that. He was as loyal to his family as Snow Deer was to hers.

No, he thought sadly, there could be no compromises. He could never turn his back on his family. He doubted she ever would.

On his knees in the lean-to, he angrily rolled up a blanket and shoved it into his travel bag. "I'll go to that Baptist church in Vienna as soon as I get home," he told himself "I'll pick me out a wife. I'll forget Snow Deer."

"Charles . . . ?" Snow Deer said, breaking through his train of thought as she crawled into his lean-to.

Charles's knees almost buckled beneath him at the sound of her voice, at the realization of her nearness. He stiffened and refused to look at her. "Snow Deer, I saw enough tonight to last me a lifetime," he said. "I now know that it wouldn't work between us. I'm going home."

"I wish I could beg you not to," Snow Deer said, stifling a sob behind a hand. "But I cannot do that. My father's hurt is deep. I cannot add to it."

She placed a soft hand on his shoulder.

179

"Charles, please turn around and look at me," Snow Deer said softly. "Charles, please?"

Charles sighed heavily.

Then he turned and locked eyes with her.

"Charles, our worlds are too far apart," Snow Deer said, flicking a tear from her cheek as it rolled from the corner of her eye. "But I do love you. And . . . and I promise I shall never, ever love again."

Charles searched her eyes.

He then gazed slowly at her face, at the features that made his heart spin with rapture. He framed her face between his hands and kissed first one cheek, and then the other. He so badly wanted to tell her that if she would leave with him, he would give her the best of everything. He would make her happy.

But he knew that those words and emotions would be wasted.

She had made her mind up.

She had made her choices.

And they did not include him.

He gave her another lingering stare, then grabbed his travel bag and crawled past her.

Once outside, he stood up and went to his horse, secured his bag, and swung himself onto the steed's back.

"Charles!" Snow Deer cried as she watched him ride away at a gallop.

She held her hands out for him.

"My Charles," she whispered, then went limp and fell to the ground, crying. She felt empty, totally empty.

Tears fell from Charles's eyes as he rode into the darkness of the forest. He felt like a coward, for he had not even fought for Snow Deer!

Yet he knew that the fight had been lost as soon

as Blazing Eagle guessed Charles's intentions toward Snow Deer. Charles would never forget the contempt in Blazing Eagle's eyes as he had glared at him through the flames of the fire during the celebration earlier that evening.

"No, Snow Deer, it just wasn't meant to be," he whispered. "It just wasn't . . . meant . . . to be."

He sank his heels into the flanks of the horse and rode onward, focusing his thoughts elsewhere. He had more heartache ahead of him, when he revealed to his mother that her beloved brother was dead and buried somewhere along the trail.

"It seems that life is a never ending series of heartaches," Charles whispered, the loneliness he was feeling almost too much for him to bear.

He gazed down at what he wore. The sight of the Indian attire cut deep into his heart, for it was a rude reminder of what he had lost.

He drew a tight rein, stopped his horse, and leapt to the ground.

His anger and hurt overwhelming him, he ripped off the buckskin shirt in one hard yank and tossed it aside. Then he removed the fringed breeches and moccasins and threw them over his shoulder.

Totally nude, he lifted his tear-filled eyes heavenward. "Why, Lord?" he cried. "Why did you allow me to love so deeply, then take her away from me?"

Chapter Seventeen

Her lodge fire having burned down to soft, glowing embers, with only an occasional spark igniting a lone piece of wood that had not been burned entirely to ashes, Snow Deer sat beside the pile of gifts that her people had generously given to Charles.

Tears streamed down her cheeks and her hands trembled as she reached over and touched a buckskin shirt that was embellished with beautiful beads in the designs of forest animals. When one of the women of the village had given this to Charles, Snow Deer had envisioned him in it as they rode toward his home in Illinois.

She had made so many plans inside her heart as she watched Charles's face light up in a happy glow as Snow Deer's people paid homage to him during the celebration.

"Where are you now?" she whispered. Filled with a savage longing, she took the shirt and hugged it to her bosom. "Charles, Charles . . ."

When she saw a shadow just outside her entrance flap as the moon outlined a man's figure there, Snow Deer's throat constricted with the sudden hope that Charles had changed his mind and had returned to spend another night with her.

Yet she had not heard any horse arriving at the village. Her heart skipped a beat and she wondered who it might be.

Had one of the trappers escaped from his bondage?

When she had looked their way, before entering her lodge for the night, they were still prone on the ground, awaiting their judgment day.

"Sister, it is I, Whistling Elk," a voice said softly, quickly erasing Snow Deer's fears and apprehensions. "I would like to talk with you if you are still awake."

"Yes, brother, I am awake," Snow Deer said. She placed the shirt back on the pile of gifts. "Please enter. I, too, need to talk."

Whistling Elk, with his hair unbraided and hanging halfway down his back, and wearing a long buckskin robe, brushed the flap aside and stepped into the soft shadows of Snow Deer's tepee.

Snow Deer rose to her knees and reached her arms out for Whistling Elk.

He moved quickly to his haunches and drew her within his embrace. He held her while she cried, then when she only sobbed, he held her away from himself and gazed deeply into her eyes.

"Your tears are not for your brother and his wife," he said. "They are for the white man who rode from our village shortly after my return."

"*Huh*, they are for Charles," Snow Deer said, wiping tears from her face with both her hands.

She gave Whistling Elk a questioning stare. "How did you know . . . ?"

"While father was berating me over my choice of wives, I saw him look often at the white man whose eyes held only you in their depths," Whistling Elk said softly.

Whistling Elk took Snow Deer by her elbow and led her down beside the fire pit, where he sat beside her. He lifted a log and placed it into the embers of the fire. He took a stick of wood and stirred the coals around, creating small fires along the larger log; then he slipped this piece of wood into the fire pit also.

"This white man saved my life," Snow Deer blurted out, drawing Whistling Elk's eyes quickly back to her.

She took him by the hand.

She twined her fingers through his and told him the whole story.

"I was wrong to let him go," Snow Deer said, sighing heavily, her shoulders slumping. "I have lost the only man I have ever loved . . . or ever will love." She shook her head slowly back and forth. "What am I to do? I know now that I cannot live without him, yet . . . yet I have surely lost his love. He is a man rejected!"

Whistling Elk gripped Snow Deer's hands and drew her eyes back to him. "You and I will go to Father," he said, his voice eager. "We *must*. We should not let another night pass into day without making him understand our feelings about those we love. Then, Snow Deer, no matter whether he listens or not to reason, or shows any understanding over wanting to accept what makes us, his children, happy, you must go after the man you love. There is only one true love in a lifetime. If you lose that, you shall never know the meaning of happiness again, or of devotion."

Snow Deer had never thought much about Whistling Elk being so knowledgeable of life before. He had always seemed too intent about the hunt, about all things that warriors do, to think about things like love and devotion.

She was seeing a new side of her brother tonight—one that she admired and would never forget.

Then her heart sank as she thought of their father, and how he had spoken so vehemently to Whistling Elk over his choice of women, and how he had stared so angrily at Charles, who was there to take his daughter away from him.

"Father will not listen to reason," Snow Deer said, hiding her face in her hands. "No, Whistling Elk, it is no use going to Father. He might even see us both as traitors."

"Then that is more reason than ever to go to him and talk to him and convince him how wrong he is to have this attitude about the people our hearts have led us to love," Whistling Elk said.

He slid one of her hands from her face and gently tugged at it. "Come, sister," he urged. "We must go now and talk to Father. I fear tomorrow might be too late. By then he will be even more set in his ways. By then your man will have traveled so far from our village that you might never find him."

Snow Deer's lips parted in a gasp. "You truly think that I should go after Charles?" she murmured, rising slowly to her feet as Whistling Elk kept a firm grip on her hand.

"If you wish for your tomorrows to be blessed with children born of a true love, yes, you must go after the white man," Whistling Elk said. He stood before her and smoothed her sleek black hair back from her face. "I am a skilled tracker. I will ride with you. I will help you find him."

"You have always been so understanding, so . . . so caring," Snow Deer said. She moved into his embrace, reveling in the strength of his arms, which matched the strength of his convictions.

Oh, how she adored her brother! He had never let her down.

Nor would he ever!

"I love you, sister," Whistling Elk said, his voice breaking. He placed gentle hands on her shoulders and held her away from him. "And so does Father. He would never want to be guilty of leading you down the sad road of life. We will go to him and not leave his lodge again until he realizes that what we wish of life is no less than what he wished of it when he met the white woman he took as his wife. He understands true love . . . true need. After he hears us both spill out our feelings to him, how can he deny us anything, especially the ones we wish to share our futures with?"

Snow Deer nodded, grabbed a fringed shawl, and left her lodge beside her brother.

When they reached their parents' lodge, and they saw through the buckskin fabric of the tepee that a fire still burned high in the fire pit, sending steady spirals of gray smoke high into the heavens, Whistling Elk and Snow Deer exchanged slow smiles. They understood by the fire that sleep was not coming easily to their father.

"Father is rethinking every word he spoke to me tonight," Whistling Elk whispered to Snow Deer. "He is rethinking every sour glance and stare that he gave your white man. I am certain he is not proud of his behavior. It is not like him to be a cold and uncaring man. Mother has surely reminded him of this more than once since they entered the privacy of their lodge tonight."

"And poor Burning Snow," Snow Deer said softly. "She might be the most confused of us all. Rarely has she seen her father lift his voice in anger or disappointment toward his children. Not understanding so many things, she must be wondering about what might have caused her father to change into someone she doesn't know."

Whistling Elk gave Snow Deer one last comforting hug; then he called softly.

"Father, it is Whistling Elk and Snow Deer outside your lodge," Whistling Elk said softly. "We wish to have family council with you. Will you allow it?"

Becky was the one who drew back the entrance flap. "Come inside," she murmured. She smiled at Whistling Elk and then Snow Deer. "Your father and I have been talking. He has much to say to you both."

She reached up and kissed Whistling Elk on the cheek. "*Naha,* your father is changing his mind about many things," she murmured. "Go on and sit beside him. He will tell you how he truly feels."

Whistling Elk gave his mother a gentle hug, then walked past her and sat down beside his father. His back straight, his legs folded before him, he waited for Snow Deer to sit on his father's other side before speaking.

Snow Deer hugged her mother.

"Snow Deer," Becky returned a generous hug, then smiled at Snow Deer as she stepped away from her. She nodded toward Blazing Eagle.

"Snow Deer, go and sit beside your *ne-hyo,*"

she whispered. "I will go and see if Burning Snow is still asleep. I will sit there with her while you and Whistling Elk talk things over with your father."

Snow Deer watched Becky walk to the farther shadows of the lodge, where Burning Snow slept soundly in her blankets; then Snow Deer went and sat down at her father's left side.

"All a father ever wants for his children is their happiness," Blazing Eagle said, slowly sliding one hand toward Snow Deer, the other toward Whistling Elk. "Even if a father must make sacrifices, his child's happiness must come before anything else."

He looked from Snow Deer to Whistling Elk. "Were you not happy as children?" he asked, his voice breaking.

They both nodded their heads eagerly.

"Then I want the same happiness for you as adults," Blazing Eagle said, slowly nodding. He inhaled a deep, quavering breath. "I was wrong to voice so openly my discontent over your marriage with the white woman, Whistling Elk. If she is what makes you happy in your adult life, it was wrong of me to speak against it."

Blazing Eagle looked over at Snow Deer. "And the man who saved you, who now loves you, is a kind, generous, and caring man," he said, his voice drawn. "I was wrong to make him feel less than appreciated. He is a man deserving of a woman like you."

Snow Deer's eyes widened and her heart beat like distant thunder to see her father so humble in his apologies.

And to know now that he was even ready to accept not only Whistling Elk's wife but also

Charles into the lives of the Cheyenne, seemed too hard to believe.

Blazing Eagle squeezed both his children's hands. "I give you both my blessing," he said.

He turned and looked over his shoulder at his wife. He smiled when he saw the tears of joy spilling from her lovely eyes.

Panic seized Snow Deer. She slid her hand free and bolted to her feet. "Charles!" she cried, eyes wild. "If he crosses the river, I may never find him."

Blazing Eagle rose to his feet. He placed gentle hands to her shoulders. "You love him enough to want to leave tonight to find him?" he said, his voice drawn.

"Yes. If not, I may never see him again!" she cried. She looked past him at Burning Snow. The commotion had awakened her.

Seeing Burning Snow looking at her in such a questioning way gave Snow Deer a feeling of guilt inside her heart, for Snow Deer knew that she was hurting Burning Snow by leaving, more than she could ever hurt her father.

But Snow Deer had thought it over and knew that her life should be shared with Charles!

Burning Snow had to find a way to understand!

Snow Deer gave Becky a lingering stare, then smiled when she saw Becky draw Burning Snow into her arms and comfort her.

Yes, Snow Deer concluded. Becky would make even this wrong right!

"If you know this is what you absolutely want to do, then I will help you find Charles," Blazing Eagle said, drawing Snow Deer's eyes quickly back to him. "It is because of me that he is gone."

"It was I who sent him away," Snow Deer said, swallowing hard.

189

"But it was I who made you feel as though you must," Blazing Eagle said. He drew her into his arms and hugged her. He looked past her shoulder at Whistling Elk. "Son, go and explain to your wife that you will be gone for a while. I want you to ride with me and your sister to help search for her white man. You are the best tracker among all the Cheyenne. You will find the white man."

Whistling Elk smiled broadly from Snow Deer to his father, then left in a rush.

Becky led Burning Snow over to Snow Deer. "I think Burning Snow has something to say to you," she said, gently shoving Burning Snow closer to Snow Deer.

Burning Snow smiled softly up at Snow Deer. "I love you, Snow Deer, and want you to be happy," she murmured. "Please be happy, Snow Deer? For me?"

So grateful that Becky had found a way to make Burning Snow accept that Snow Deer would be leaving, and why, Snow Deer fell to her knees and hugged her sister against her. She ran her fingers through her sister's lustrous long hair. "Yes, I will be happy," she softly cried. "For you, I shall be *very* happy with the man of my heart."

Snow Deer moved quickly to her feet when she heard horses just outside her parents' lodge. She looked at Becky, hugged her, then turned toward her father. "I love you so much for this," she said, then left the lodge with him and Whistling Elk.

As she mounted her gentle mare, Snow Deer looked from Becky to Burning Snow. "I will miss you," she said, her voice breaking.

"God be with you," Becky said. She dropped to her knees and wrapped Burning Snow in the warmth and comfort of her arms.

Snow Deer smiled and nodded.

Then she swung her horse around and rode off at a hard gallop with her brother and father. She looked heavenward, wondering if Charles might be staring at the stars even now, recalling how she had spoken of their mysteries to him.

"Please, *Maheo,* let me find him," she whispered in a low, fervent prayer.

Chapter Eighteen

Too restless to sleep, Charles shoved his blankets aside and sat up. Brushing some blanket lint from his denim breeches and shirt, he gazed at his campfire. So distracted was he, he had almost allowed the fire to go out.

After sliding bits and pieces of twigs into the smoldering embers, and then larger pieces of broken limbs, Charles drew a blanket around his shoulders.

Still despairing over having left Snow Deer behind, he put his face in his hands and sighed. "Did I give her up too easily?" he whispered.

Yet he couldn't think of anything he might have done to change her mind.

If only Whistling Elk hadn't arrived with his white bride, surely things would have been different, he thought.

Yet, even before their arrival at the village, Charles knew that Blazing Eagle had surely been plotting ways to keep his daughter from loving a white man.

The neighing of his horse caused Charles's head to jerk up from his hands. Scarcely breathing, he peered into the dark shadows of the night, trying to see what had caused his horse to behave as though someone or something were near.

Then Charles's heart skipped a beat when he heard the sound of horses approaching a short distance away.

He glanced quickly at his campfire, cursing himself for having rekindled the flames. They were now shooting high in the sky, casting a golden glow into the heavens, a beacon for all intruders in the night to follow.

The fire was too high to extinguish, and the horses were drawing closer and closer. Charles tossed his blanket aside and grabbed his rifle.

Hunched over, hoping not to be seen as the riders approached from his left side, Charles ran stealthily into a thick stand of brush.

His heart pounding, he waited for the riders to appear in full view. If they were renegade Indians or outlaws, who rode under the cover of darkness to do their dirty deeds, he knew that he did not have a chance in hell of surviving.

Not unless he got off the first round of gunfire.

And, by damn, he *would*, he assured himself. He was a sharpshooter. His father had taught him how to shoot when he was first old enough to hold a heavy firearm in his hand.

"Come on, bastards," Charles whispered through gritted teeth, his rifle poised for firing. "Just . . . come . . . on. Show your beady eyes to Charles Cline."

His horse whinnied again, causing one of the approaching animals to answer in kind. Charles heard the distinct sound of someone cocking a firearm.

"Whistling Elk, do not be hasty with your firearm," Snow Deer whispered as she leaned over to speak to her brother. "It might be Charles's camp."

"Did you not say he was headed for the Illinois side of the river?" Whistling Elk whispered back.

"*Huh*," Snow Deer said, nodding. "But perhaps something detained him before crossing the river. Please put your pistol back in its holster."

She sighed with relief when her brother did as she asked, even if he had done it with reluctance.

"Daughter, it is wise never to take chances when you come up on a camp in the night," Blazing Eagle said, sidling his horse closer to Snow Deer's. He placed a hand on the rifle in the gunboot at his right side, yet hesitated before removing it. "If it is Charles, we will immediately lower our firearms. If it is not, stay back away from any confrontation we might get into."

"But, father—" Snow Deer began, then flinched in alarm and drew a tight rein when someone jumped out of the shadows before her father had a chance to arm himself.

Snow Deer's heart sank, when the stranger's rifle caught the reflection of the fire, showing that it was aimed at them.

Snow Deer peered hard through the darkness in an attempt to see the stranger's face. But because of the way he was standing, shadowed by low-hanging branches of trees, she could not make out any of his features.

Charles peered up at the riders but could not see their faces. They were shadowed by the low-hanging branches of the trees overhead.

"Don't come any closer," he warned gruffly. "And don't go for your firearms or I'll blow you clean out of your saddles." He motioned with his rifle. "Dismount. Step into the light of the moon. Let me see your faces."

Snow Deer could not believe her luck!

For a moment she was speechless over having found Charles so easily!

Then she spoke, her voice quavering in her excitement.

"Charles, it is I, Snow Deer," she cried, sliding quickly out of her saddle.

She ran to him, and as he dropped his rifle to the ground, she flung herself into his arms. "Oh, Charles, I've found you," she sobbed. "I've found you."

Blazing Eagle and Whistling Elk watched, their mouths parted, as Charles and Snow Deer clung to each other, their kisses frenzied and passionate.

"Snow Deer," Blazing Eagle then said, his voice drawn with weariness. "Snow Deer!"

Hearing her father's voice, Snow Deer came quickly to her senses. Bashfully, she slid away from Charles's arms and turned slowly to look up at her father.

Charles stood stiffly and looked from Blazing Eagle to Whistling Elk, yet his heart was singing, for Snow Deer had come to him!

That had to mean that both Blazing Eagle and Snow Deer had had a change of heart. Snow Deer had surely decided to forfeit her life as a Cheyenne princess to take on another important title—to be a *wife*.

"Father, we have found Charles," Snow Deer said, her fingers trembling with happiness as she twined them together behind her. "I am so happy to have found him!"

Stoic and calm, Blazing Eagle dismounted and tied his horse's reins to a low limb. "Yes, we've found Charles," he said, then walked toward Snow Deer, his eyes lingering on Charles.

Charles stepped closer to Snow Deer. He slid an arm around her waist, for he found it so hard not to touch her.

She was his!

She was going to be his wife!

How could anyone be as happy as he was at this moment?

"Charles, we would like to have council with you," Blazing Eagle said, placing a gentle hand on Charles's shoulder. "Although the hour is late, would you grant us this council?"

"Most certainly," Charles said, squaring his shoulders in his pride over this moment, when a great Cheyenne chief was soon to relinquish his prized possession, his eldest daughter, to the care of a white man—to *him*.

"Come and sit by the fire," Charles then said, motioning toward the campfire that was still blazing high, feeling blessed now that he had thought to rekindle it. That had surely helped lead Snow Deer to him through the darkness of night.

Snow Deer ran on ahead of them. She grabbed two of Charles's blankets and laid them on two sides of the fire.

At first her father just crouched before the fire, watching the flames. Then he sat down beside Whistling Elk on a blanket.

Snow Deer sat on a separate blanket with Charles, opposite the fire from them. She was where she belonged and she felt as though she were sailing on clouds of rapture high in the sky, to know that she would soon be this wonderful man's wife. She did not see how she could ever have thought that she could live without him!

Oh, how grateful she was to her father for allowing it!

As Snow Deer waited for her father to begin speaking, she leaned close to Charles. "I thought you would already be across the river into Illinois," she whispered. "Had you been, I might have never found you."

"I missed the ferry," Charles whispered back. He smiled over at her. "It was fate that led that ferry across the river before my arrival. It kept me on the Kentucky side so that you *could* find me."

"I am so happy," Snow Deer said, beaming as she smiled up at him.

She looked over at her father when he began to speak in his "council voice," solemn yet sincere.

"My daughter has given up much to come to you," Blazing Eagle said gravely. He folded his arms across his chest. "Do you give an oath to this Cheyenne father that you are deserving of such a woman as Snow Deer?"

Embarrassed, not used to singing his own praises to anyone, Charles's face flooded with color. "I will make her a good husband," was all that he could think to say. "I will protect her with my life. She will not want for a thing."

"I do not ask you to spoil her," Blazing Eagle said, his eyes now having softened into a quiet warmth. "But I do expect that her comforts will be seen to. I do expect that your caring for her runs as deep as her parents'—even more deeply, since you will be her husband."

Blazing Eagle clasped his hands on his knees and leaned forward. "You do plan to marry her soon?" he asked.

"Yes, soon," Charles said, sliding a hand over to take one of Snow Deer's. He gazed into Snow Deer's eyes. "There is a pretty white Baptist church down the road from my house. There we will speak our vows."

"I would have rather she was married in the Cheyenne tradition, but as all things change as life changes, this change, too, I must accept," Blazing Eagle said, sliding his son a knowing, apologetic gaze.

He then looked at Snow Deer and Charles again. "Tell me about your lodge. Is it large or small? Are your parfleche bags filled with good eats for my daughter? Do you have warm enough pelts to keep her comfortable during the snow months of winter?"

There were so many questions so suddenly that Charles's head felt as though it was spinning. But he knew the importance of answering each question to satisfy Blazing Eagle, so he thought hard to give him one answer at a time.

"My lodge is a cabin made of logs," Charles slowly explained. "There are four rooms—the living room, the kitchen, a bedroom, and a storage room where I keep supplies that always last the long, cold winter months."

He cleared his throat nervously, then continued. "I do not use pelts for warmth in the winter. I use warm blankets. Also I do not use parfleche bags for storage," he said softly. "I have a cellar beneath the floor of my kitchen. There you will find bags of potatoes, carrots, turnips, onions, corn, and all the things that I grow in my garden."

"Also, there are many canned foods in my cellar," he softly explained. "Cherries, apples, and peaches from our trees, and green beans, peas, and other vegetables from the garden."

"Canned food?" Blazing Eagle said, lifting an eyebrow. "What does that mean?"

"My mother places vegetables and fruits in glass

jars and seals them tightly with lids to keep them from spoiling," Charles slowly explained. "Food stored in these jars can be kept many long months without spoiling."

"Hmm, interesting," Blazing Eagle said, kneading his chin.

"I shall learn the art of canning from your mother?" Snow Deer asked anxiously, her eyes wide as she gazed up at Charles.

"Mother will teach you many things of our white world that I, as a husband, cannot teach," Charles said, nodding. "She will enjoy teaching you how to sew on her sewing machine."

"Sewing . . . machine . . . ?" Snow Deer said, eyes wide.

"It is a machine that women use to sew their clothes instead of doing it by hand," Charles said softly. "Indians use sinew to sew their clothes together. White women use thread."

"Yes, mother uses both sinew and thread, but she has no sewing machine," Snow Deer said. She moved to her knees and faced Charles. "I am so excited to see such a thing as a sewing machine. Can I see it soon?"

"Yes, soon," Charles said, as always before finding her innocence so endearing and sweet.

"Tell us more about the new things you will bring to my daughter's life," Blazing Eagle said, truly interested.

Charles began explaining his daily routines to the Cheyenne chief, then explained what his mother did to pass her days, which would be the same for Snow Deer.

"Snow Deer will be happy," he said, completing his description of his life. "My family will welcome her with open arms. They will love her as I love her."

"Father, I will love them as I love Charles," Snow Deer said softly. She turned smiling eyes to Charles. "I will devote my life to Charles Cline."

"As I will devote mine to Snow Deer," Charles said, bringing one of her hands to his lips and kissing it.

"Council is over," Blazing Eagle said abruptly. He rose slowly to his feet. "Snow Deer, come to me."

Snow Deer scrambled to her feet and went to her father. She welcomed the strength of his arms as he wrapped her within them.

"You will return home whenever possible to be with your family? Your people?" he said, his voice drawn. "You will return to us and share your new life with us?"

"Yes, whenever the weather allows it, I will return home and tell you everything of my new life," Snow Deer said, clinging to him.

"Are you afraid of this new life that lies before you?" Blazing Eagle asked, still holding her.

He knew that once he let her go, it could be many, many sleeps before he saw and held her again. The distance would be too great for her to travel home as often as he wished.

This, also, he would have to endure and go about his daily business comforted only with thoughts of her happiness in her new life with the man she loved.

Her happiness was all that mattered to Blazing Eagle.

Snow Deer eased from his arms and turned to gaze at Charles. Her eyes lingered on him.

Then she turned beaming eyes up at her father. "No, I am not afraid of anything, not as long as I will be with Charles," she said softly. "Charles makes all my fears blow away in the wind."

They embraced again.

Then she went to Whistling Elk. "My big brother, I will miss you so," she murmured. She slipped into his arms. She reveled in his closeness. She would miss him with every beat of her heart.

"As I will miss you," Whistling Elk said.

Snow Deer gave her brother one last, fierce hug, then went and stood beside Charles as her father and brother mounted their steeds.

She tried to be brave and not cry as they rode away and gave her one last look over their shoulders before they were out of sight, deep in the shadows.

Snow Deer stood and strained her neck to see them until the sound of their horses' hooves could no longer be heard.

Then she turned to Charles.

Laughing, she flung herself into his arms. "I am yours!" she cried. "You are mine!"

Chapter Nineteen

"I can't believe you are here," Charles said, gently holding Snow Deer away from him. His gaze moved slowly over her.

Then his eyes locked with hers. "I thought I had lost you," he said, his voice breaking with emotion. "How . . . what . . . changed your mind? You seemed so determined not to leave your people."

"A part of me is still there, *always* there," Snow Deer said softly. "But I just could not live without you, Charles. My life would never have been complete had I not come to you."

Charles yanked her against his hard body. He held her close. "You know now, don't you, that since you *have* come to me, I shall never again let you go?" he said huskily, his nose against her cheek, inhaling the sweet fragrance of her skin.

"I will never leave you again," Snow Deer whispered, then placed her hands at his cheeks and brought his mouth to hers.

"Kiss me. Hold me. Make love to me," she whispered against his lips.

"The hour is late," Charles said, yet he could not deny the passion that was quickly overwhelming him.

"The hour makes no difference to me," Snow Deer said. "I want you now. Oh, Charles, I need you so much."

"I will marry you soon," he whispered against her lips.

"Yes, soon," Snow Deer whispered back, her voice quivering in her excitement.

She swirled in a storm of passion that shook her innermost senses when he kissed her. His arms held her so close, she felt as though she were an extension of his body.

Twining her arms around his neck, she clung to him when he gripped her waist and slowly led her down onto the blankets beside the campfire, his lips never leaving hers.

She shivered sensually when one of his hands slid up inside her dress and left a trail of fire along her flesh as he moved his fingers slowly upward along her inner thigh.

And when he reached the hot, wet place between her legs, and splayed his hand over it, slowly, gently grinding his hand against her, Snow Deer's breath caught.

Needing more, hungering for it, she reached down and circled her fingers around his hand and led his fingers where she throbbed with need of him. "Please caress me there," she whispered against his lips, her cheeks hot with ecstasy.

Charles leaned slightly away from her and watched her eyes as his fingers swirled on her woman's center. He smiled when he saw how passion-heavy her eyelids became the more he caressed her.

Realizing that he was watching her, Snow Deer smiled and closed her eyes, moaning when he slid a finger up inside her.

As his finger moved in a slow inward and outward motion, her hips gyrated to the rhythm of his movements. Her lips parted; her eyes still closed, she leaned her head back and allowed herself to enjoy being transported to another world. All the apprehensions she had felt earlier were banished from her life forever.

"Snow Deer . . ." Charles said, bringing her out of her pleasurable reverie.

She opened her eyes and gazed up at him, then watched as he stood over her and slowly began to discard his clothes.

Her heart pounding, her knees weak with passion, she rose and stood before him.

Trembling, she reached down and grabbed the hem of her dress.

Standing beside the warmth of the fire beneath the velvet rays of the moon, she drew the dress slowly up her body, then wriggled out of it and tossed it onto the ground. She then removed her moccasins and set them aside.

Her breath caught in her throat when her eyes moved upward and she saw Charles's full arousal as he tossed his last piece of clothing aside.

Her eyes twinkling, Snow Deer drew nearer to Charles. Smiling, she slowly ran her fingers over his hard body, beginning at the broadness of his shoulders, then downward through his thick patch of black chest hair, then lower across his belly.

She giggled when she noticed how her touch caused him to suck in his breath with pleasure.

Then she grew quiet and her smile faded when her hands slid further downward, through another patch of dark hair, then gently touched his manhood.

Charles stretched his legs out slightly on each side of himself, his spine stiffening; a deep groan swept up from the depths of his throat when she wrapped her fingers around his throbbing member.

She leaned into his embrace and kissed his chest, her tongue flicking one of his nipples, as she moved her hands on him.

She licked her way up to his lips, then kissed him with an unleashed passion that equalled nothing she had ever felt before.

Knowing they would soon be man and wife, and knowing that they would be spending their lives together, made her feel free to love him without reservation.

Charles was breathless with the ecstasy of the moment. His lips were on fire with her kiss. His body was one massive heartbeat as her hands burned into his throbbing member, moving on him, bringing him closer to that moment of sheer ecstasy.

Knowing that he was far too close to that point of no return, and wanting to experience it while inside her, Charles placed gentle hands on her shoulders and eased her hand away from him.

Then he swept her fully up into his arms and held her for a moment, so grateful that she was there with him. Then he laid her down on the blankets and eased his body down over her.

Again her hand reached out for him.

Smiling up at him, her pulse racing, she guided him inside her.

"Lord, lord . . ." Charles whispered, gritting his

teeth. "Nothing could ever feel as good as the way your warm walls suck and cling to my . . ."

For wont of the correct word to describe that part of his anatomy, Charles chuckled, then crushed her lips beneath his mouth in a fiery kiss.

As he filled his hands with her breasts and began his eager thrusts inside her, he kissed her long and deep. He moved slowly within her, then powerfully. Her hips gyrated, moving, rocking, her pelvis pressing against his.

Squeezing her breasts, he rolled the stiff, resilient nipples beneath his palms.

Then he slid his mouth downward, across the lovely column of her throat, then lower, to a breast.

His tongue swept over the nipple, drawing a lazy moan from somewhere deep inside Snow Deer. He tugged at the nipple with his teeth, then flicked his tongue again over it.

Snow Deer slid a hand gently behind his neck and led his mouth to her lips. Their bodies strained together hungrily as they kissed and fell back into a wild, dizzying rhythm of lovemaking. Together they awaited the one moment that would bring them together as one heartbeat, one soul, one being.

Then, suddenly, Charles placed his arms gently around Snow Deer and turned with her until she was lying above him, her breasts pressing into his chest.

"Straddle me," he whispered, holding himself inside her as she slowly rose above him.

He reached up and cradled her breasts within the palms of his hands. "Just sit there," he said huskily. "I shall do the rest."

When he began his powerful thrusts up inside her, his lean, sinewy buttocks lifting rhythmically from the ground, Snow Deer sighed, leaned back, and closed her eyes.

She gasped throatily when his fingers gently pinched her nipples, causing them to throb sensually.

Overcome with a feverish heat, she sighed with pleasure as he bucked even harder into her, her legs spread out on each side of him, giving him better access to her throbbing center.

Then again he shifted their positions. He guided her to her hands and knees, then moved up behind her on his own knees.

Snow Deer cried out with ecstasy when he entered her again in one deep, wild thrust from behind. Dizzy with the building passion, she hung her head, gasping. Her hair thrashed from side to side each time he thrust himself more deeply into her.

Then again he moved her. He positioned her on her side then stretched out behind her. Lifting one of her legs, resting it over his thigh, he entered her anew.

He closed his eyes, the wild ripples of passion overwhelming him as she met his thrusts with thrusts of her own. He reached down and caressed her swollen bud, drawing a series of moans from deep within her.

Then again he changed their positions. He rose over her and blanketed her with his body.

In one thrust he rode her again, her legs wrapped around his waist, moving with him. He feverishly kissed her breasts, then twined his fingers through her long hair and drew her lips to his.

With one final, deep thrust, her hips straining to draw him even more deeply into her this time, their spasms began.

Charles's body stiffened, then plunged.

Snow Deer cried out as she shoved herself against him, receiving his seed deeply inside her.

After their bodies became still, and Charles had rolled away from her to stretch out on his back to get his breath, Snow Deer crawled over and snuggled next to him.

"Our lovemaking was so wild tonight," she whispered. She giggled as she leaned up on an elbow to gaze at Charles. "We were like two wolves mating."

He laughed throatily as he placed a gentle hand on her cheek. "Perhaps we *were* wolves tonight," he said. "I feel strangely like howling."

Snow Deer giggled and snuggled closer to him. She rested her cheek against his powerful chest. "I still cannot believe that I am here," she murmured. "Pinch me to prove that I am."

"Lord, I think what we just experienced together should be proof enough," Charles said, laughing softly.

He stared into the flames of the fire. "I wish we could stay here and live out the rest of our lives alone, living only for each other," he said, his tone of voice now serious.

He turned toward her.

He nestled her close as he wove his fingers through her hair, slowly stroking. "But such thoughts are selfish," he said softly. "I have my family. You have yours."

He framed her face between his hands. "And soon we shall have children," he said, his eyes gleaming. "I hope we have a daughter first and that she is the exact image of you."

"Charles, I am not sure that is too wise a wish to make," Snow Deer said, her eyes imploring his. "I have not thought much about what prejudices

Thrill to the most sensual, adventure-filled Historical Romances on the market today...

FROM  LEISURE BOOKS

As a home subscriber to Leisure Romance Book Club, you'll enjoy the best in today's BRAND-NEW Historical Romance fiction. For over twenty-five years, Leisure Books has brought you the award-winning, high-quality authors you know and love to read. Each Leisure Historical Romance will sweep you away to a world of high adventure...and intimate romance. Discover for yourself all the passion and excitement millions of readers thrill to each and every month.

Save $5.⁰⁰ Each Time You Buy!

Each month, the Leisure Romance Book Club brings you four brand-new titles from Leisure Books, America's foremost publisher of Historical Romances. EACH PACKAGE WILL SAVE YOU $5.00 FROM THE BOOKSTORE PRICE! And you'll never miss a new title with our convenient home delivery service.

Here's how we do it. Each package will carry a FREE 10-DAY EXAMINATION privilege. At the end of that time, if you decide to keep your books, simply pay the low invoice price of $16.96, no shipping or handling charges added. HOME DELIVERY IS ALWAYS FREE. With today's top Historical Romance novels selling for $5.99 and higher, our price SAVES YOU $5.00 with each shipment.

AND YOUR FIRST FOUR-BOOK SHIPMENT IS TOTALLY FREE!

IT'S A BARGAIN YOU CAN'T BEAT! A Super $21.96 Value!

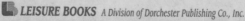 LEISURE BOOKS A Division of Dorchester Publishing Co., Inc.

GET YOUR 4 FREE BOOKS NOW — A $21.96 Value!

Mail the Free Book Certificate Today!

4 FREE BOOKS

A $21.96 VALUE

Free Books Certificate

YES! I want to subscribe to the Leisure Romance Book Club. Please send me my 4 FREE BOOKS. Then, each month I'll receive the four newest Leisure Historical Romance selections to Preview FREE for 10 days. If I decide to keep them, I will pay the Special Member's Only discounted price of just $4.24 each, a total of $16.96. This is a SAVINGS OF $5.00 off the bookstore price. There are no shipping, handling, or other charges. There is no minimum number of books I must buy and I may cancel the program at any time. In any case, the 4 FREE BOOKS are mine to keep — A BIG $21.96 Value!

Offer valid only in the U.S.A.

Name _____

Address _____

City _____

State _____ *Zip* _____

Telephone _____

Signature _____

A $21.96 VALUE

If under 18, Parent or Guardian must sign. Terms, prices and conditions subject to change. Subscription subject to acceptance. Leisure Books reserves the right to reject any order or cancel any subscription.

4 FREE BOOKS

Get Four Books Totally FREE — A $21.96 Value!

PLEASE RUSH
MY FOUR FREE
BOOKS TO ME
RIGHT AWAY!

Leisure Romance Book Club
P.O. Box 6613
Edison, NJ 08818-6613

AFFIX
STAMP
HERE

I might face among your people when they realize that you have brought me, an Indian, home to be your wife. But I am thinking about it now, now that it will soon be something real to face. I fear what they might think or do once we have children. If the child looks more Cheyenne than white, might not the child be resented by the white children of your community?"

"Children can be cruel, that is true," Charles said, nodding. "But we shall make the best of things, should that happen."

Snow Deer moved to her knees, accepting a blanket when Charles gently placed it around her shoulders. She gazed down at him, her eyes filled with wariness. "But Charles, what will everyone think of me, a Cheyenne, when they see me as a part of your life?" she asked, her voice drawn. "You spoke of marrying me in a church. Will your people allow it?"

Charles twined his arms around her waist and brought her down beside him again. "Yes, they will allow it," he said, then chuckled. "Or else I will fill their breeches with buckshot."

Snow Deer wrenched herself away from him. The blanket fell away from her shoulders as she sat up. "I am serious, Charles," she said, her lips forming a pout. "We must talk this over now, for soon I will enter your community beside you on horseback. Can I expect stares? Can I expect to feel unwanted?"

Charles saw her genuine concern.

He sat up and placed his hands gently on her arms, gently unfolding them. "My dear woman, who will soon be my wife, don't you know that we can look past all stares and prejudices as long as we have each other?" he said, his voice solemn. "Yes, it might take time for everyone to get used to seeing an Indian woman in their midst, for, you see, you will be the first." He placed a hand at her cheek. "But as soon as they get to know you as I know you, how could they not forget their prejudices and love you as well?"

"You do think it will happen that way?" Snow Deer asked, her eyes wide.

"I not only think it, I know it," Charles said, drawing her into his embrace again. "Now will you just relax and enjoy knowing that we have each other? And knowing that we will soon be married and have children?"

"One thing spoils the moment," Snow Deer said softly.

Charles held her slightly away from him so that their eyes could meet again. "What is that?" he asked throatily.

"Upon your arrival, you have sad news to give to your mother about her brother," Snow Deer murmured. "Your mother will be sent into a period of mourning. I am sad for her."

Charles nodded. "I do dread telling her," he said, sighing deeply. "I wish it could have been different. Uncle Hiram was such a fine, lovable man. We all will miss him."

"Even I, and I never truly knew him," Snow Deer said. "I knew him only long enough to pray over his grave."

"Your prayers not only aided his ascent into heaven, but also helped me accept my loss," Charles said, again holding her. "Sweet Snow Deer, sweet, adorable Snow Deer."

Suddenly he was aware of her total silence, and her limpness as she lay against him. He smiled when he heard her deep, even breathing, realizing that she had fallen asleep in his arms.

"My darling . . ." he whispered, easing her down between the blankets.

He gazed at her for a while, then entered the blankets behind her.

He slid an arm around her and held her. Before long he fell asleep himself, smiling.

Chapter Twenty

It was mid-morning three days later when Charles and Snow Deer drew a tight rein on the road in front of Charles's parents' house. The sun was bright. The sky was blue. There was a slight breeze that rustled Snow Deer's unbraided hair as she stared at the sprawling white house that sat back from the road beneath the shade of huge oak trees.

"A . . . house and it is so large," she stammered. "And look at the beautiful shrubs and flowers in the yard at the front of the house."

In awe of everything, she looked past the house, where the white picket fence ran down to the railroad tracks.

She gasped when she saw chickens pecking in the yard beneath the shade of the many fruit trees. "Charles, what are those small white creatures?" she blurted out, never having seen chickens before.

Charles had sat there purposely quiet so that he could enjoy watching Snow Deer's reaction to this new life that he was offering her. He had come to his parents' house first, before going to his own, to let them know that he had arrived safely from Kentucky, and to give his mother the terrible news about her brother.

He had been so concerned about telling his mother the news, he had not even thought about Snow Deer's reaction to his parents' house.

Now that he had seen it, he was not surprised, for she had been raised in the small confines of a tepee. Surely she saw this house as a mansion.

She turned to Charles. "The house is so huge, your parents must get lost in it," she said, her eyes filled with wonder. She sighed. "Charles, it is beautiful."

He reached over and took her hand. "My mother is quite proud of it," he said softly. He chuckled as he gave the house a quick glance, and then looked at Snow Deer again. "But don't be fooled by its size. Remember that I told you that my parents' residence is in only half of the house. The post office is in the other."

"Only half is still large," Snow Deer said, again staring at the house.

Then she looked at Charles again. "Is this what your lodge is like?" she asked, eyes wide.

Charles's eyes wavered, wondering if she would be disappointed by the size of his cabin. He had not thought much about the size of one house over another. "No, not quite," he said, looking over his shoulder at his small cabin, which was a short distance down the road from his parents' house. He nodded toward it. "Snow Deer, that is my home." He turned slow eyes her way. "There's *our* house."

He saw her look at it, and then turn slow eyes back to his parents' house. He scarcely breathed as he awaited her comments.

"I am so glad," she said, sighing. "I prefer your lodge over theirs, for I would not like to live in a dwelling where I have to stop and think which direction to go to find my way around inside it."

Relieved, and finding what she said so sweet and endearing, Charles smiled. "Let's go on inside," he said, kissing her hand before releasing it.

Snow Deer followed him on her horse along the small rocky drive to the house.

She dismounted when he did and slung her reins around a hitching rail where he did the same.

Again she gazed up at the house, at the rambling front porch where a swing hung, swaying gently in the breeze. She also saw a white wicker rocking chair as well as two other white wicker chairs which sat in a small cluster beneath a wide window, through which she saw the loveliest of lacy white curtains.

She looked farther down the porch and saw another window. It had no curtains. Instead, there were iron bars like the ones she had seen in the windows of white men's jails.

She rushed to Charles's side as he reached out for her hand. She twined her fingers around his, her eyes not leaving the bars at the window.

Finally curiosity got the better of her. Just as they stepped up on that first step, she yanked at Charles's hand, drawing his eyes quickly to her. "Do your parents also have a jail here in their lodge?" she whispered, standing on tiptoe so that only he could hear the question.

She glanced quickly over her shoulder again at the bars, then looked questioningly up at Charles.

Charles had seen the direction of her gaze and now understood why she would ask such a question. He chuckled. "No, Snow Deer, my parents do not have a jail here at their house," he said. "Those bars that you see at the window? That is the post office window. The bars are a deterrent to robbers who might think we have more than mail to deliver."

Snow Deer's lips parted in a slight gasp. "Are you saying that there are outlaws in Illinois who rob people?" she asked, her voice wary.

Charles chuckled again. "My sweet Snow Deer," he said, placing a gentle hand to her cheek. "There are outlaws everywhere."

"Have any robbed your parents' post office?" she asked, but got no answer, for Charles's attention was drawn quickly to the door when his father opened it suddenly and stepped out onto the porch.

"Son!" Jacob said, holding his arms out for Charles. "Son! You are home!"

Charles hurried past Snow Deer and went to his father and embraced him. "Yes, I'm home," he said, knowing that the moment he'd dreaded had now arrived.

"I'm so glad you're safe," Jacob said, patting Charles on the back.

Then he eased from Charles's arms and looked first at Snow Deer, and then past her, his eyebrows lifting when he saw no wagon—and no Uncle Hiram.

Jacob stepped away from Charles, silently questioning him with his eyes.

Charles was not so much disturbed by his father's silent questioning as he was by the fact that his mother had not come outside with his father to greet Charles.

215

"Where's mother?" he asked warily. "Why didn't she come outside with you?"

Jacob nervously raked his lean fingers through his thinning gray hair. "Your mother—well, your mother is ailing, Charles," he said, his voice drawn.

Charles paled. "She's ill? What's wrong with her?"

"Some strange sort of fever, C.C.," Jacob said, turning to stare at the open door. Then he turned to Charles again. "Doc Rose can't seem to put his finger on just what *is* ailing her. The fever came quickly and just won't go away."

Charles started to walk past him, to hurry to his mother's bedside, but Jacob grabbed him by one arm. "C.C., before you go to your mother, I think you've a couple of things to tell me, don't you?" he asked, searching Charles's dark eyes for answers.

Charles looked past his father at Snow Deer, who seemed terribly frightened by having thus far been ignored. Then he thought about Uncle Hiram, knowing that his father had realized his absence.

He looked from Snow Deer to his father, uncertain who to go to first.

Loving Snow Deer so much, and feeling guilty for letting her feel isolated and alone in this new world that he had brought her to, Charles went to her and held her hand. Then he led her up the steps.

When he was standing before his father again, Charles nodded toward Snow Deer. "Father, I want you to meet my future wife," he said.

He slid an arm around her waist, to give her comfort. His father's alarmed response showed in his heaving gasp, and in the way he shuddered, as though a cold breeze had hit him in the face.

Jacob took a slow step away from Charles, his eyes still on Snow Deer.

Then, as though he hadn't see her or heard what Charles had said, Jacob frowned at Charles. "Where is your Uncle Hiram?" he asked. He looked at the horses, then at Charles again. "Where is my wagon? Where is my other horse? One of those horses does not belong in my stable."

"One of those horses is mine," Snow Deer said, finally breaking her silence. She was trying hard not to be wounded by the way Charles's father was ignoring her. He was treating her as though she did not exist, probably because he did not wish for her to be there if it meant she was going to be a part of their family. She had faced prejudice before and recognized it.

She knew that if her relationship with Charles was to survive against such odds, she had to pretend not to notice his father's dislike of her.

"Charles, I'm asking *you* about the horse and wagon, and about your uncle," Jacob said, again obviously ignoring Snow Deer.

Charles was stunned almost speechless by his father's attitude toward Snow Deer. He was acting as though she was not even there. His father had always been kind-hearted. He could not recall his father ever being a man of prejudice.

Yet Charles remembered how *he* had been treated by Snow Deer's father. After Blazing Eagle had realized Charles's intentions toward his daughter, he had shown a deep dislike for Charles because of the color of his skin.

Two worlds were colliding here, and Charles knew that he and Snow Deer were strong enough to cope with it, for their love was strong enough to go against all odds and survive.

"Father, when I arrived at Elissa's ranch, I discovered that Uncle Hiram was far worse than we originally thought," he said thickly. "I was concerned about him making the long ride from Elissa's ranch to our home, but . . . but . . ."

He paused, swallowing hard when he thought of Elissa's failing health.

"But what?" Jacob said, raising an eyebrow. "Spit it out, son. Don't leave me hanging."

"Elissa has consumption," Charles blurted out. "She's dying. She would not have been well enough much longer to care for her father." He again swallowed hard. "And Elissa wanted her father to see his sister one last time before he died."

"Elissa is dying?" Jacob said, paling. He hung his head. "Good Lord almighty."

"Father, I didn't get far before . . . before Hiram died," Charles said. His father's head jerked up at those words. "I had no choice but to bury him before I returned home."

Jacob stared at Charles for a moment longer, then turned and opened the screen door that led into the parlor. "Come on, C.C.," he said. "I don't know how your mother is going to take this news."

"Perhaps I should wait until later to tell her?" Charles said, stepping aside so that Snow Deer could enter the house before him.

Then he hurried to her side again, his arm sliding around her waist to give her the assurance that he knew she needed in this new environment. If his mother had not been ailing, Charles would have left quickly for his own home to give his father time to think about how he had treated Snow Deer.

But as it was, he could not put off seeing his mother. His heart ached for her, for never had he known anyone as sweet and gentle as Patricia Cline.

He glanced over at Snow Deer, amending that last thought. Snow Deer's personality was the same as his mother's. He prayed to himself that his mother would get well and love Snow Deer as Charles loved her.

Charles and Snow Deer followed Jacob down a long corridor with closed doors on each side. When Jacob stopped before one of the closed doors, he turned and stared at Snow Deer, then gave Charles a tight-lipped look.

Then Jacob spoke. "She'd best stay out here, son," he said. "I think your mother deserves only one shock at a time. Or else her heart might give out on her."

"She goes with me," Charles said flatly. He held Snow Deer's hand. "From now on, Snow Deer goes with me everywhere I go, Father."

Jacob angrily folded his arms across his chest and watched his son go into the room with Snow Deer. Then he followed and stood back in the shadows. He watched as his wife's eyes slowly opened.

"Son," Patricia said in a shaky whisper. She lifted a hand from beneath her blankets and touched Charles's face as he leaned down closer to her. "You're back. I was beginning to worry."

She looked past him, at the door, then questioned Charles with her eyes again. "Son, where's Hiram?" she asked softly.

Charles hesitated, then explained to her what had happened.

He bent low and held her as she began sobbing. She was so distraught, she had not yet even noticed Snow Deer standing there.

Snow Deer watched the tearful reunion, noticing that Patricia's face was deep crimson with fever. She knew she could find herbs to help combat the fever, outside beneath the trees across the road from the house. She would go and gather the herbs and teach Charles how to use them to help lower his mother's temperature. It was a remedy her father had taught her when people in her village suffered with high fevers.

She glanced at Charles's father as she walked past him. She straightened her back as she felt the heat of his eyes on her while she walked down the corridor toward the front door. She could not help being puzzled by this man's attitude toward her. Charles had spoken so warmly of him. He had told her that his father was a religious man, a man who practiced his religion every day of the week!

Then, she wondered sadly, if he was such a man of prayer, why did he resent her so much? She meant no harm to his family. She was no threat!

Then she thought of her own father and his attitude toward Charles. Blazing Eagle had acted much the same way that Charles's father was behaving toward her!

She hoped that as time passed, Charles's father's feelings would change, or she might want to flee back to live among her own people where she was loved and respected.

Running down the steps, and then across the spacious yard toward the road, Snow Deer smiled to think how grateful Charles's father was going to be when he saw that she had brought medicine to his wife that would make her temperature go down!

Pleased at the thought of earning Jacob's gratitude once he saw her kindness toward Charles's mother, Snow Deer rushed into the thickness of the trees and gathered herbs.

With her pockets bulging, her hands stained green from having pulled so many varied herbs from the ground, Snow Deer hurried back to the house and crept into the bedroom where Charles was still comforting his mother with soft words. Obviously he had not even noticed Snow Deer's absence.

"Charles?" Snow Deer said, her voice soft, yet anxious as she stepped up to Charles's side. "I have brought herbs for your mother. Show me where I can find water. I shall heat it over the lodge fire, then place the herbs in it for your mother to drink."

Jacob paled. He stamped over and stood beside Snow Deer. He pointed toward the door. "Out!" he shouted. "Get out with your hocus-pocus doctoring ideas! You'll not use any of that stuff on my wife."

It was then that Patricia's attention was drawn to the lovely Indian maiden. She watched Charles go to Snow Deer and sweep her out of the room, a protective arm around her waist.

"Who was that woman?" Patricia asked, her voice so weak it was barely audible. "Jacob, she's *Indian*. What . . . is she doing here? Why is . . . our Charles acting so protective of her?"

Jacob slid a chair up beside the bed. He took his wife's hand and held it. "Darling Patricia, that woman has come home with Charles to . . . be his wife," he said, stunned to see that Patricia's reaction to the news was not the same as his.

"His wife?" Patricia said, looking past her husband, at the door that Charles had closed between himself and his parents. "Why, she is ever so beautiful, Jacob."

Jacob paled, then hung his head.

Chapter Twenty-One

Snow Deer sobbed as she yanked herself away from Charles and ran out of the house without him. She was blinded by tears as she ran down the steps and went to her horse. Her fingers fumbled with the reins as she attempted to loosen them from the rail.

"Snow Deer, please . . ." Charles pleaded, catching up with her. He grabbed the reins from her. "Please don't allow my father to upset you like this. I've never seen him like this before. Surely it is because mother is so ill."

"I offered help, but he treated me badly," Snow Deer said. "Oh, Charles, tell me I was not wrong to come here to be a part of your life. If it is always like this, I will be so miserable."

"Things will get better," Charles said, drawing her into his arms. He stroked her back through her buckskin dress. "I promise you they will be better. I will have a talk with father. And mother—

222

oh, Snow Deer, there is not a prejudiced bone in her entire body. Once she is well, she will take you in her arms as though you were her very own daughter."

"She is so ill," Snow Deer said, easing from his arms. She wiped tears from her eyes as she looked at the house. "I know that I could have helped."

"Yes, I'm certain you could have," Charles said, helping her into her saddle. "But for now I think it's best if I go for Doc Rose. I'm going to tell him to come and take another look at mother. Surely he has something else that he can give her to help bring down her fever."

"Can I go with you?" Snow Deer asked as Charles swung himself into his own saddle.

"Do you know what I'd like for you to do instead of that?" Charles said, looking past her at his cabin.

"Whatever you want, I will do," Snow Deer said, following his gaze and seeing that he was looking at his lodge.

"I'd like to take you to our home, Snow Deer—yours and mine," Charles said. "You can get some rest while I'm gone. It's been a strenuous journey for someone who isn't used to staying in a saddle for so long."

Snow Deer managed a soft laugh. She reached back and rubbed a sore buttock. "Yes, I ache in places I've never ached before," she said, nodding. "Yes, take me home, Charles. I shall wait for you while you see to your mother's welfare."

Charles leaned over and kissed her, then rode with her to his house.

He watched her reaction as they entered his cabin. He stood back as she went to the over-stuffed furniture and ran her hands over the softness. Then she walked to the kitchen and stood awestruck by the cook stove, the shelves of dishes and pots and pans, and the table and chairs on which they would eat their meals.

Then he ushered her into the bedroom. He stood back and watched her as she pressed her hands into the soft feather mattress, turning to give him a wide smile of appreciation.

"It is all so grand," she murmured, then went to Charles and hugged him. "We will be so happy here."

They kissed, and then he led her into the parlor. He watched her as she again walked around the room, then knelt before the spacious fireplace.

"Your lodge fire will be much larger than mine ever was," she said, smiling over her shoulder at Charles.

Then her smile faded. She went to him and hugged him. "All of this is wonderful, yet so new to me," she said, her voice breaking. "And your parents. I cannot get them off my mind, especially your father's resentment of me."

"After he gets to know you, he will love you," Charles encouraged her softly.

He gazed at the door, then held Snow Deer away from him. "I truly must go now and get Doc Rose," he said. He placed his hands gently on her waist. "Will you be all right while I am gone?"

Snow Deer's eyes were wide as she nodded. "Snow Deer will be all right," she said softly. "Go. I will rest on the soft bed while you are gone."

Charles's eyes suddenly twinkled. "Snow Deer, tonight we'll spend our first full night together on that feather bed," he said. "You'll find it much softer on your back and behind than the ground as I make love to you."

"I will feel as though I am floating on clouds," Snow Deer said, giggling.

She grew somber after he kissed her and left her alone. Looking around the cabin, she felt foreign to herself. She stifled a sob behind her hand and wondered if she could ever accept this way of life. True, the lodge was one of many comforts. But it was so different from the way she was used to living!

"And his father," she whispered, a keen sadness sweeping through her. "I doubt he will ever accept me as his daughter."

Filled with doubt, and suddenly afraid, she turned and fled the cabin. She ran blindly through Charles's spacious garden, then rushed into the forest that stretched out behind the garden.

She was not sure where she was going.

She just had to get away!

Chapter Twenty-Two

Having achieved more than merely taking Doc Rose to see his mother, Charles beamed as he ran down the narrow dirt road toward his cabin. According to Doc Rose, his mother was better than when he had last seen her. He had given her a new type of medicine that had quickly brought down her fever.

She was going to be all right.

That made Charles feel as though a weight had been lifted off his shoulders. Yet something else made him eager to get back to Snow Deer. While Doc Rose had been seeing to his mother, Charles had taken his father into the parlor and had a long, serious talk with him about Snow Deer.

Charles had spoken to his father from the depths of his heart, explaining to him how much he adored and loved Snow Deer, and how nothing would change his mind about marrying her.

Charles had explained to his father about the

cool treatment *he* had received from Snow Deer's chieftain father, and how that had made him feel so empty, so hopeless, to think that he could not have Snow Deer as a wife after all. He'd used that example to show his father how Snow Deer must have felt to be treated as though she were not even worthy of Jacob's respect.

It had not taken long for Charles to convince Jacob to be more open-minded about Snow Deer, to allow her into their lives. Charles had listened, struck numb, when his father had explained about a massacre that had occurred many years ago—when his father's great-grandparents had been slain by Indians.

He had explained to Charles that that was why he could not take an immediate liking to Snow Deer, for she was Indian.

Charles had been overjoyed when his father gave him a bear hug and apologized for his behavior toward Snow Deer.

After Doc Rose left, Charles and his father had gone to Patricia's bedside.

Charles had again started pleading Snow Deer's case to his mother. But she had stopped him almost as soon as he began, saying that she would never make the young woman feel as though she was an intruder. She would welcome Snow Deer into her life with an open mind and heart.

The mood had grown light and gay when his mother had suddenly noticed how well he was seeing things without his eyeglasses, and he had explained that he no longer needed them.

He went further to explain about the blow to his head. Believing that it was the blow that had caused his suddenly improved vision, Charles joked that he had Rain Feather to thank for his regained eyesight.

Charles could hardly wait to tell all of this to Snow Deer. As he ran from the road, down the narrow gravel path that led to his cabin, he laughed into the air.

"She will make the loveliest bride ever seen in the history of our little Baptist church!" he cried, looking into the heavens.

He marveled at how blue the sky was. Never had it seemed this brilliant! Even the sun seemed to be smiling down at him!

And the breeze! It touched his face in a soft caress, causing him to close his eyes and recall the last time Snow Deer's hand had been on his cheek, lovingly caressing it.

He opened his eyes and stopped in mid-step when he found a gorgeous monarch butterfly, with velvety wings of orange, black, and gold, fluttering around his face, almost landing on his nose.

He laughed to himself as the butterfly fluttered past him. "Snow Deer would say that was an omen of some kind," he whispered to himself. "Of course, a good one, for everything is going to be perfect between us! Perfect!"

Smiling broadly, Charles opened the door to his cabin and rushed inside. He stopped, his smile slowly fading, when he found utter silence greeting him.

He looked slowly around the living room. Snow Deer wasn't there. He looked past the living room, into the kitchen. The sun was pouring through the window above the work counter, revealing that that room was also empty.

Then a smile quivered on his lips as he looked at the partially closed door that led into his bedroom at the far side of the house.

"She's still resting," he whispered.

He took long strides toward the bedroom.

He did not doubt that she would welcome being awakened, knowing that the news he brought would make their lives together so much easier.

He would never forget the hurt in her eyes that his father's rudeness had inflicted upon her. If only Charles had known about the Indian massacre, then he would have prepared Snow Deer, warned her that his father might not take to her so quickly.

Stopping just outside the bedroom door, Charles placed a hand on it and slowly shoved it open.

When it was open far enough for him to get a full view of his bed, with the window open beside it and the wind fluttering the sheer white curtains, his heart seemed to stop. The bed was empty.

He could tell that no one had even been on it. The patchwork quilt that he used as a bedspread had not been disturbed. It was as he had left it on the day of his departure for Kentucky.

"Lord," he gasped, paling.

He turned sharply and again looked in quiet desperation around the living room.

No. There were no signs whatsoever that Snow Deer had been there.

His gaze stopped at his travel bags, which sat just to the right inside the front door. Even they had not been opened.

A feeling of desperation seized him. Could she have run away?

He eyed the open door, then ran outside. Panting hard, he stopped and looked anxiously in all directions.

Which way would she have gone? he wondered. Lord, why did she go? Didn't she trust him enough to know that he would make things right for her?

His eyes went to the ground, hoping to see her

footprints, or perhaps some trampled-down grass, which would point his way to her.

But nothing. She was no heavier than a bird.

Slowly his eyes looked around him, trying to think as she might have thought when she chose her route of escape.

He gazed at his blacksmith shop. No. She would have no cause to go there.

He gazed at the barn, where his horses were stabled.

"The horses!" he said, swallowing hard.

He ran to the barn and soon discovered that none of his horses were gone. Wherever Snow Deer had gone, she had chosen to flee on foot.

He hurried out of the barn and stopped to look around again.

He gazed at his garden, then past that, at the deep shadows of the forest.

His heart skipped a beat.

Snow Deer was as one with nature. If she felt a desperate need to get away from this new life, surely she would seek solace among the trees.

She might even find something more there— shadows in which to hide as she fled from this life that she had decided to have no part of.

His pulse racing, Charles broke into a hard run. He ran down the furrowed rows of his garden where cornstalks were already shoulder-high.

He ran past the part of his garden where green beans were twining up the poles that he had placed there in the shape of tepees. The green beans hung from them, ripe, fat and green, ready to be plucked.

He ran past large orange flowers that would develop into pumpkins in time for Thanksgiving pies.

He caught the scent of the tomatoes that were

red and overripe on the vines, some mildewing as they lay heavy and neglected on the ground.

Finally he reached the cool depths of the forest. He wove his way in and around the trees where trumpet vines climbed heavenward, their flowers huge and beautiful, resembling orange orchids waving in the soft breeze.

He pushed his way through thicker brush. He cursed beneath his breath when thorns grabbed at the legs of his breeches.

Then he stopped and scarcely breathed when he heard a soft voice coming from somewhere close by.

"Snow Deer!" he whispered, relief rushing through him. He had found Snow Deer.

Following her lilting, soft voice, understanding now what she was doing, and why, he smiled and said a soft thank you to his own God that she had not left him.

She had sought solace in the forest.

She was praying to her *Maheo*, the god of the Cheyenne.

Not wanting to disturb her prayer, knowing how badly she had needed this time alone with her *Maheo*, he climbed the side of the hill where she prayed.

When he reached the summit, he stopped. Snow Deer was on her knees, her eyes lifted heavenward. He was touched deeply by the sight of her and by what she was saying.

He stayed there and listened, not wanting to intrude on her private moment, yet not wanting to eavesdrop either.

"*Maheo*, please hear my pleas," Snow Deer cried. "Give me strength to live as my heart wants me to live, with the man I will always love. Give me strength to understand those who are prejudiced against me because of my race, and because of the color of my skin. Give them a better understanding of me, a Cheyenne woman. Let them see past their prejudices."

She lowered her eyes and closed them. She folded her hands over her heart. "Oh, *Maheo*," she said, her voice breaking. "Let Charles understand my weaknesses when I cannot accept things as easily as he would wish me to. His life differs so from mine. Please give him patience. It is his patience and my courage that will make our life possible."

Charles watched Snow Deer rise slowly to her feet.

And when she turned to leave the hilltop and saw him standing there, his heart skipped a beat at the way she stood and stared at him.

He could not help believing now that it was wrong for him to have been there, listening.

He started to apologize, but before the words passed across his lips, she was there, in his arms, hugging him to her.

"My Charles," she murmured. "Did I frighten you when you found me gone? If so, I am sorry."

Charles held her close. "I was foolish to think that you had left me," he said, feeling her tense in his arms at his confession.

Snow Deer looked quickly up at him. She eased from his arms. "I will never leave you," she said, placing her hands at his cheeks. "But I must sometimes seek private prayer time. Do you understand my need to be alone with my prayers? Do you need such time alone also, with yours?"

"My praying is done at all times, at all hours of the day and night," he said softly. "I don't need to be alone, for more oft than not I pray to myself, not aloud. If I find a moment when a prayer is needed, I pray. My Lord listens even to those prayers that are not said aloud."

"My *Maheo* listens also when I speak to myself, yet I feel the need at times to speak my prayers aloud," Snow Deer said. She smiled at him. "If you ever wish to try praying on my hill, please do so."

"Your hill?" Charles said, smiling. "This is now your hill?"

"My chosen prayer place," Snow Deer said, her eyes twinkling into his.

"Yes, your prayer place," Charles said, again drawing her into his arms.

He enjoyed the closeness of the moment a while longer, then held her away from him, his hands at her waist. "I have brought you some good news," he said softly.

"What sort?" Snow Deer asked, arching an eyebrow.

"My mother is going to be all right, and my parents both wish to have you return to their house so that they can tell you that you are welcome there anytime you wish to go there, and to tell you that you are welcome in their lives," Charles blurted out, so happy he could not hold back until he had told her everything in one rush of words.

"Truly?" Snow Deer said, her eyes widening. "I am so glad for you that your mother is going to recover. But Charles, what did you say to your parents to cause this change toward me?"

"Not much coaxing was needed to bring my mother around," Charles said. He took her by the hand and led her down the side of the hill. "She saw you as something special and precious from the first time she looked at you. My father was a harder nut to crack . . ."

"Nut . . . to . . . crack?" Snow Deer said, interrupting him. She peered questioningly up at Charles.

"That's just a way of describing someone who is stubborn," Charles said, laughing softly. "Darling, about my father. I now know why he behaved so irrationally toward you. You see, long ago, before our time, his great-grandparents were slain in an Indian massacre. My father was told about the massacre when he was a child. He has always held deep inside his heart a grudge against all Indians."

Snow Deer stopped. She stepped in front of Charles. "He will always hate me?" she murmured. "In his heart, he will hate me?"

"I talked with Father," Charles said softly. "I persuaded him to forget his ill feelings. I made him know that you are a wonderful person, that you are no kin to those who killed his great-grandparents."

"And he asks to see me?" Snow Deer asked, her eyes wide. "He will learn to accept me and my skin color?"

"Yes," Charles said. "My father will accept you and he has asked for you to come to the house. I believe he has something to say to you."

Snow Deer's heart pounded anxiously as Charles led her through the forest, past his garden, and then out onto the dirt road. She looked heavenward and whispered a silent thank you to *Maheo*, for he had listened and had quickly granted her wishes.

She smiled. For a while she had wondered if by leaving her Cheyenne people behind she might also have left *Maheo* behind. Now she knew that he was with her at all times. He was still all things to the Cheyenne, no matter where they lived, or with whom.

"Your smile is radiant," Charles said as he

glanced down at Snow Deer. "I hope I am the one who caused it."

"You and *Maheo*," Snow Deer said, laughing softly.

Charles inhaled a deep sigh of happiness, then swept Snow Deer away from the road and hurried her into his parents' house.

His father was just inside the door, having stood there watching for Charles to return with Snow Door.

Snow Deer's heart pounded within her chest as she stood at Charles's side looking up at Jacob Cline. She sighed with relief when he opened his arms and drew her into a warm embrace.

"I'm sorry for having been so unkind to you earlier," Jacob said, his voice drawn. He then held her back from him, his fingers on her shoulders. "Young lady, you are welcome in my home. I welcome you as the woman who will soon marry my son."

Tears spilled from Snow Deer's eyes. "Thank you," she murmured, then turned to Charles when he spoke softly to her.

"Mother is waiting to see you," he said, his voice drawn with emotion.

Snow Deer wiped happy tears from her cheeks with the palms of her hands as she went with Charles into his mother's bedroom.

Her nose twitched at the strange smell of medicine that now hung heavily in the air. She recalled having offered the use of her herbs and how her offer had been refused, as though she was a witch of some sort wanting to bring evil into the life of this woman.

She brushed the memory aside, vowing to forget that hurt, for it was being made up to her now.

She stood at the bedside and smiled down at

Charles's mother. Even without the use of Snow Deer's herbs, the flush was now gone from Patricia's face. Her eyes were no longer hazed over with pain. There was love and laughter in them as she looked at Charles, and then at Snow Deer.

"My dear," Patricia said, offering Snow Deer a thin, white hand. "Come to me. Let me hug you."

Relishing these moments of acceptance, knowing that it could have been so different, Snow Deer knelt beside the bed. She winced when she smelled some strange sort of medicine smell on Patricia's breath, yet pretended it did not affect her and joyfully accepted the woman's arms around her neck.

"Snow Deer, Charles has told me so much about you," Patricia said, patting Snow Deer on the back. "My son loves you so much. I will also love you."

"Oh, thank you, thank you so much," Snow Deer murmured. She slid her arms beneath the frail lady and returned the hug.

Patricia smiled at Snow Deer as she slipped away from her and stood at the bedside beside Charles.

Charles's attention was drawn to the window when he heard the arrival of a horse and buggy outside. He peered through the curtain as the breeze lifted it, giving him a full view of the outdoors. He smiled.

"Seems supper has arrived," he said. He watched two women from the church step from the buggy and reach in the back for covered dishes.

"Who is it, son?" Patricia asked, unable to see from where she lay and too weak to rise from her bed.

"Alice and Hannah," Charles said, watching the

women moving up the steps.

"Such good women," Patricia said, smiling. "Such good Christian women."

"Yes, and I'm glad they are here," Charles said, whisking an arm around Snow Deer's waist. "Snow Deer, I want you to meet these women. They are mother's best friends."

Jacob left the room to greet the women.

Snow Deer's smile faded at the thought of meeting other white people so soon after getting over the hurt previously inflicted by Charles's father. She could not help being wary of more white acquaintances. To so many, Indians were looked at as heathens, as "savages."

She would die if she was made unwelcome by these women for whom Charles seemed to have such a fondness.

"Must I meet them now?" Snow Deer whispered in Charles's ear.

"You don't want to?" Charles asked, his eyes searching hers.

Snow Deer didn't get the chance to respond. The two women, with colorful hats perched atop their heads and floor-length, lacy cotton dresses swirling about their feet, came into the room.

They were quietly reserved as they peered toward the bed. "Patricia?" they seemed to say in unison. "Jacob said you are better. Can we see you for a moment?"

But before Patricia answered, both women's eyes darted to Charles, then slowly assessed Snow Deer.

Charles saw their quick reaction to Snow Deer by the way they softly gasped.

He held Snow Deer possessively at his side. "Alice, Hannah," he said, pride in his voice. "I wish for you to meet Snow Deer, my fiancée. I hope you

237

will help make the church beautiful for our wedding. I wish to marry Snow Deer soon."

"Charles, she is . . ." Hannah said, then stopped in mid-sentence. She smiled her usual sweet smile and held out a hand toward Snow Deer. "So nice to make your acquaintance. Snow Deer? Is that what Charles said your name was?"

"*Huh,*" Snow Deer said, her jangled nerves causing her to reply first in her Cheyenne tongue.

Then she quickly answered in the language these women were used to hearing. "Yes, my name is Snow Deer," she murmured. "It is good to meet you."

Charles scarcely breathed as he watched Hannah and Alice talking with Snow Deer. He was relieved to see that once the ice was broken, they showed signs of truly accepting her.

Snow Deer walked with them over to the bed as Charles stood back and continued watching.

"I have made friends with your friends," Snow Deer said, beaming as she smiled down at Patricia.

"I'm so glad," Patricia said, reaching a hand out for Snow Deer.

Snow Deer took her hand. She sent a quick smile over her shoulder at Charles.

Charles almost melted, his happiness at this moment was so complete.

Chapter Twenty-Three

It was *To-no-ish-i,* "Cool Moon Time."

Summer was turning to autumn. For the third time, Snow Deer looked anxiously from the open door for Charles to return home for the evening.

When she still did not see him, she became lost in thoughts of how things had transpired these past several weeks. As soon as Charles's mother's full health had returned, Snow Deer and Charles had been married in a small wedding ceremony in the beautiful white Baptist church down the road a short distance from Charles's house.

Snow Deer had known that the whole congregation attended the wedding not only out of respect for Charles, one of their deacons, but also out of curiosity to see the woman he was marrying—a Cheyenne princess.

Out of true respect and love for Charles, she had worn a dress far different from any she had ever worn before. She had accepted the dress that

Charles's mother had worn during *her* wedding ceremony. Although yellowed with age, it had been no less beautiful with its lace and pearl buttons, and its lovely veil, which Snow Deer had also worn to be a traditional bride for her husband.

Seeing the need to make certain changes in her life, she had accepted many other clothes from Charles's mother. Snow Deer now dressed as a white woman.

She found the crude shoes the worst to get used to. They squeezed her toes together painfully. The soles were so coarse and hard, she felt as though she were walking on stones.

Yet she had worn it all, even the high-collared dresses, and on Sunday, when she wanted to look her best to attend church with her husband, she had even worn the horrible corset that squeezed her insides unmercifully.

But today she was excited because she had truly mastered the wood-burning cooking stove in the kitchen that until today she had called a monster. She had prepared her first full meal for her husband on the stove today without burning everything so badly that it looked like scorched leather.

She had taken her time.

She had paid attention to Charles's mother's many instructions.

When she placed the frying pan on the stove, with lard spattering hot in it, she had known just exactly when to cook the meat, and for how long.

Supper was ready now on the kitchen table: meat, vegetables, potatoes, steaming hot coffee, and an apple pie.

She giggled to think of Charles's reaction to the pie. But she would allow him to believe that she had made the pie for only a few short minutes. She did not like to lie to her husband, even in things as trivial as that. As soon as he made his first surprised comments about the pie, she would confess to him that his mother had made it.

Sliding her hands up and down the front of her cotton dress, her flour-covered apron having just been discarded, Snow Deer opened the screen door and peered toward the blacksmith shop. It was just growing dusk. She could see no lamplight in the shop's windows, which surely had to mean that Charles had left.

"Where did he go?" she whispered, closing the screened door. She went to the living room and placed another log on the fire in the fireplace, then lit two kerosene lanterns, giving the lovely room a warm, intimate glow.

She looked toward the door again. She went to it and stepped out onto the porch to look at the garden. Everything had been harvested. Green beans were stored in glass jars in the cellar, thanks to several church women who had come and taken the vegetables home to can them for Charles and Snow Deer.

Corn hung in tied bunches from the rafters in the cellar, and there were many other vegetables in the cellar that would be used during the long winter months.

All that was left of the garden were the tilled rows, where only a few bent cornstalks had refused to be plowed under.

But she saw no Charles.

Sighing heavily, Snow Deer went back inside the house. She stood over the table, watching the steam rising from the dish of green beans, the boiled potatoes, and—

Snow Deer's thoughts were interrupted and she turned with a start when Charles came into the house in a rush, panting.

Cassie Edwards

"Snow Deer, I'm sorry I'm late," he said, yanking off his leather jacket. "Someone came at the last minute to shoe his horse. I rode with him down the road a bit. His horse seemed somewhat lame. I wanted to make sure it was all right before coming on home."

"Was the horse all right?" Snow Deer said, following him to the wash basin that sat on a stand beneath the kitchen window.

She was used to not being greeted with a hug and a kiss. Charles was an immaculate person. He had explained to her that after working with horses all day, he first needed to wash the horse smell from his hands before touching her.

"Yes," Charles said, soaping his hands and rubbing them briskly together. He smiled over at her. "It's just old age creeping up on the roan. I'm not sure how much longer he'll be around."

He inhaled deeply, then looked past her at the table. His eyes widened when he saw the food heaped on the platters. It smelled so delicious, his stomach growled with anticipation.

And something else. Snow Deer had set the table with fancy dishes and silverware that he recognized from his mother's hutch. He smiled, so grateful that his mother and Snow Deer had become so close that his mother would part with things that were precious to her.

"Charles, I had no trouble at all today with the stove," Snow Deer said, seeing how he was silently admiring what lay waiting on the table. Once his hands were washed and dried, she went to him and leaned into his embrace. "Husband, are you proud of me? See what I have made you for supper?"

Charles's heart thumped wildly within his chest as he slid his arms around her waist, and not because of the food that she had prepared for their supper, but because of her nearness.

He gazed at her lovely bronze face, her midnight-dark eyes that always stirred his insides. He noticed how she had drawn her black hair away from her face, tying it with a pink satin bow that matched the lace-trimmed pink cotton dress that made her look like an angel.

"Do you know what I want more than any food prepared on our kitchen stove?" he said huskily. He slid his hands around and cupped her breasts through her dress.

Snow Deer's breath quickened. She could feel a flush of excitement rise to her cheeks. "What do you want more than supper, husband?" she teased, moaning as he bent and showered kisses across the upper curves of her breasts, where they were revealed by the bodice of her dress.

"You," he said.

His lips covered hers in a frenzied kiss.

Snow Deer clung to him. She was becoming lost in a swirling passion. But both were brought out of their reverie when their stomachs growled at the same time, reminding them of just how long it had been since they last ate—and that their lovemaking could be more vigorous if their other hunger was fed first.

Laughing, they pulled apart.

"Our stomachs have spoken," Charles said. He took Snow Deer by the hand and led her to the table.

After they were both seated and coffee was poured into each of their cups, Charles eyed the food once again. He then gave Snow Deer a look of pride. "I see that my Cheyenne princess has kept busy today," he said, chuckling.

"And all for you," Snow Deer said, spreading her

linen napkin on her lap. She saw his eyes light up when he looked past her and finally saw the apple pie sitting in the shadows on a small table. She giggled, then told him the truth about the pie.

"Your mother brought it over a short while ago," she murmured. "Does it not smell delicious? Your father picked the apples fresh from their tree this morning."

"A pie made from Jonathan apples is my favorite," Charles said, then laughed when his stomach growled again.

He picked up his fork and pierced a piece of meat from the meat platter. He scooped huge spoonfuls of beans from a bowl, and then ladled out a good portion of boiled potatoes that were dripping hot with butter fresh from his mother's churn.

"It looks good enough to feed a king," Charles said.

He cut off a small piece of meat and slipped it between his lips.

As he chewed, his eyebrows rose. This was something different, he thought to himself, wondering what it might be.

After swallowing, he smiled at Snow Deer. "That was really good," he said. He waited for her to swallow her food, then asked, "Darling, what sort of meat was that? I can't seem to recognize the taste."

She watched him take another eager bite, then smiled as she matter-of-factly told him what he was eating.

"Muskrat," she said, her eyes widening when he suddenly sounded as though he were choking. She gasped when he reached for his napkin and spat out what remained of the meat in his mouth.

"Why did you do that?" she asked, still watching

him wiping at his lips with the napkin. "I thought
you liked the meat. Why would you spit it out?"

"Muskrat?" Charles said, shuddering at the
thought of having actually swallowed several bites
of the rat-like rodent. "You actually cooked muskrat for our supper?"

"Yes, why would I not?" Snow Deer asked, stung
by his quick change of attitude.

"Snow Deer, I . . . I have never known anyone
who eats muskrat," he said, his voice drawn.

"You know *me*, and I have often eaten the delicacy of muskrat meat," Snow Deer said softly.
"Today, while I was out walking, breathing in the
autumn air and enjoying looking at the patchwork
color of the leaves, I came across many muskrats
in the nearby marsh. I am skilled at catching
them, especially now, in the autumn, when they
are fat and lazy. I caught three and skinned them.
I then cooked them."

"Lord, Snow Deer, how . . . how did you get past
. . . the stink?" Charles asked incredulously.
Muskrats were known for the musky secretion
that came from the musk sacs in their compact,
heavy bodies.

"Snow Deer pays no attention to the smell," she
said, shrugging. She shoved the platter of muskrat
meat toward him. "Try again. Take another piece.
Take several bites. Think of something else as you
eat the meat, then tell me exactly how it tastes.
Think of rabbits. My people sell muskrat pelts.
They are known to the traders as 'marsh rabbits'."

"I don't know," Charles said, staring at the meat.

"For me, Charles?" Snow Deer pleaded. "We
have both been learning the ways of each other's
culture. I have adapted well, do you not think, to
yours?"

"Yes, very much so," Charles said, nodding.

Cassie Edwards

"Today," Snow Deer said softly. "With this muskrat meat, I am trying to teach you more of mine. Please eat. Please allow yourself to see just how delicious the meat is."

Charles hesitated a moment longer, then placed another piece of meat on his plate.

Stiffly, he cut off a small portion. When he began to chew, he tried to think of something pleasant, like honey being spread on a biscuit.

The more he chewed, the more he thought that the muskrat meat tasted even better than the fried chicken his mother was so skilled at cooking.

"You see?" Snow Deer said, beaming. "You *like.*"

Charles laughed softly. "Yes, I like," he said. He took another bite and actually enjoyed it.

"Charles," Snow Deer said between bites. "I have something to show you later."

He gave her a look of amusement, wondering what other surprises she had in store for him today, then continued the meal.

He gobbled down the apple pie in only a few bites.

He emptied his cup of coffee.

Then he went and lifted Snow Deer up into his arms and carried her to their bedroom. "Now to feed our other hungers," he said huskily.

He kissed her as he laid her down on the soft feather bed. His hands trembled as he slowly undressed her, then stood beside the bed and removed his own clothes.

"I have waited all day for this," Charles said, stretching himself over her.

His hands caught her breasts in their palms. His thumbs tweaked the nipples into tight buds. His tongue flicked over the nipples, his hands sliding down her body, causing her flesh to ripple beneath them.

"Take me," Snow Deer whispered, her voice quivering with emotion. Her eyes dark and knowing, she twined her fingers through his hair and brought his mouth to her lips. "Kiss me."

She abandoned herself to the torrent of feelings that washed over her as his body plunged into hers and he filled her with one deep thrust. His strokes within her were powerful and insistent.

She wrapped her legs around his waist, drawing him even more deeply inside her.

His hands cupped the rounded flesh of her bottom and molded her against him. He loved the feel of her smooth copper skin against his fingertips, his mouth drinking in the taste of her lips.

Snow Deer's fingernails raked lightly down Charles's spine. She reveled in the touch of his hard body against hers.

Sliding her hands along his flesh, around to his chest, she wove her fingers through his chest hair, then ran her fingers lightly and teasingly over his tight nipples, smiling when this drew a sigh of pleasure from deep within him.

His tongue brushed her lips lightly. "My beautiful Cheyenne princess," he whispered. "My wife."

His mouth brushed her cheeks and ears lightly. He tenderly kissed her eyelids.

"My husband, my husband," she whispered back.

She clung and rocked with the thrusting of his pelvis as he now loved her in a leisurely fashion, the press of his lips against hers as he kissed her again so warm, so wonderful.

When she felt the passion peaking, she gripped his shoulders.

Charles felt the heat rising, rising, then exploding within him. He held Snow Deer tightly to him as their bodies quivered and quaked together. He groaned as his seed spilled deep inside her.

The room was now dark, except for the glow of the fire visible through the doorway from the fireplace. They lay together and looked through the window at the sparkle of the stars in the heavens. The wind suddenly gave off a moan from outside as it whisked around the corner of the cabin.

"It won't be long before we'll see our first snowfall of winter," Charles said, cuddling her close. "Somehow this year I don't dread it as much."

"Why is that, Charles?" Snow Deer asked, stroking a slow hand down his chest.

"I have you to keep me warm," he said.

Remembering the surprise that she had for Charles, talk of cold weather having brought it to mind, Snow Deer sat up quickly and smiled down at him.

"Do you remember me telling you that I had something to show you?" she asked, her eyes dancing.

"Yes, I believe it was just after I discovered I was eating muskrat," he said as he leaned on his elbow.

She hopped from the bed and went to the dresser. Slowly she opened a drawer.

Charles sat up and watched her take something from the drawer.

When she turned and he could see in the light of the fire that she held a pelt in the full shape of a muskrat, with its small ears, its hind feet that were webbed and fringed with stiff bristles, and even its long, scaly tail, he recoiled.

"Snow Deer, don't tell me that . . ."

"Yes, it is a pelt taken from one of the muskrats that we ate for supper," she said, her eyes gleaming with pride. "Charles, just look at the pelt. I have the other two, also. I am going to make us each a pair of soft moccasins from them."

Scarcely breathing, she awaited his reaction.

"I can hardly wait," he teased, smiling.

He smiled even more broadly when he realized that she had not recognized the true meaning of his statement—that he, in truth, was only jesting when he said that he could hardly wait to have the moccasins made out of muskrat!

Ah, how he more and more loved her sweet innocence!

He reached a hand out for her. "Come back to bed?" he asked softly.

She started toward him, the pelt still in her hands.

"Uh, without the pelt, darling," he said, chuckling. "Without the pelt."

She giggled, laid the pelt aside, then leapt on the bed beside him. "Charles, I not only brought meat to our table from the muskrat kill, and have pelts for moccasins, but also I saved you from problems with muskrats," she said.

"How is that?" he asked, arching an eyebrow.

"Have you not had trouble with muskrats damaging your corn crop?" she asked. "My family has gone on the warpath against muskrats in Kentucky."

"I guess my corn isn't appealing to them, for no, I haven't ever had trouble with muskrats," Charles said, reaching a hand out for Snow Deer.

"Perhaps you blamed damage on other animals when all along it was muskrats," Snow Deer said, leaning forward and sighing as he placed his hands at her waist and lifted her over him, so that she was straddling him.

With her woman's center pressed against his abdomen, it did not take long for Charles to become fully aroused again. He held her by the waist as he shoved himself inside her.

They made long and leisurely love again.

Afterward, as they lay in the blissful aftermath of lovemaking, Snow Deer gazed up at Charles. "I just might have enough fur to make tiny moccasins for our child," she murmured.

Charles's eyes widened. He sat quickly up on the bed and reached for her. He sat her on his lap facing him. "Are you saying what I think you are saying?" he asked, his pulse racing. "That you are with child?"

Snow Deer's eyes wavered.

She lowered them.

Charles placed a finger beneath her chin and lifted it so that their eyes could meet and hold.

"Snow Deer, are you with child?" he asked softly.

"No, not yet," she said, sighing. "But I will be soon. I so badly want a child with you, Charles." She gazed at him with a hint of pleading. "Perhaps we made a child tonight?"

He reached his hands out for her and brought her into his arms and stroked the satiny soft flesh of her back. "Yes, perhaps so," he said softly, unable to deny the disappointment he felt to know that she wasn't pregnant *now*. He was beginning to wonder if she might have difficulty becoming pregnant. By now most women would have been with child!

"Are you disappointed in me that I am not with child?" Snow Deer asked, clinging.

"How could I ever be disappointed in you over anything?" Charles said, feeling bad now that she had somehow sensed his disappointment. He would guard his feelings better from now on.

"I love you so, Charles," Snow Deer said, placing her hands on his cheeks and drawing his lips to hers.

Her lips trembled as he kissed her.

Chapter Twenty-Four

"Christmas is near," Patricia said as she slid her hands into the washpan and washed another dish with a cloth. She gazed over at Snow Deer. "Dear, do the Cheyenne celebrate Christmas?"

Her hair drawn up in a tight bun atop her head, her back straight in her plaid wool dress, the stiffly starched white collar scratching her neck, Snow Deer peered from the window at the thickly falling snow, then looked over at Patricia when she realized that she had repeated her question twice.

"Yes, my family celebrates not only Christmas, but also Thanksgiving," she said, taking the freshly washed dish from Patricia. She carefully dried it with a soft cloth. "But only because my father's wife is white. She brought the tradition into my father's home."

Patricia looked quickly at the window when she heard some sleet pellets mixed in with the snow bouncing off the glass. "Lordie, lordie, I haven't seen this much snow in a coon's age," she said.

When Patricia turned to Snow Deer and saw a puzzled look on her face, she understood it was because of her reference to coons.

"Dear, so often I know you don't understand some of the ways I speak about things," she said. "It's just that I remember so many of my father's sayings, I find it hard not to use them myself. In time, you will know when I am serious, and when I'm not."

Snow Deer smiled. "Never guard your words while talking with me," she murmured, setting the dried dish aside. She took another wet dish as Patricia handed it to her. "I learn from you. I want to know everything about you and your family, so that I can please Charles."

"I know something that would make him truly happy," Patricia said. She wrung out the dishrag and draped it over the edge of the wash basin. She reached back and untied her apron and hung it over the back of a chair.

"What would that be?" Snow Deer asked, setting the last dish aside. She spread the dish towel on the counter to dry.

Patricia clasped her hands together before her as she gazed warmly at Snow Deer. "My dear, a *child*," she said. "Don't you know how badly Charles wishes to have a child? Don't you know how badly Jacob and I want to have grandchildren?"

Snow Deer's heart sank. She lowered her eyes. Several months had passed since her marriage to Charles and thus far she had not missed one of her monthly weeps! She was beginning to wonder if she *could* have children.

She knew that Charles was concerned about it,

for each time her monthly flow began, he seemed unusually quiet.

When she had questioned him about his quiet moods, he had brushed her off with something logical like worrying about the weather, the crops, or his blacksmith business.

She knew that it was because she could not tell him that she was growing a child from his seed inside her womb!

"Snow Deer, did I say something that I shouldn't have?" Patricia asked, slowly dropping her hands to her sides.

When Snow Deer turned her back to Patricia, Patricia's eyes wavered. She went to her daughter-in-law and slid her arms around her and gave her a warm embrace. "Daughter, daughter," she murmured. "I'm sorry if I said something that caused you pain."

Patricia had only recently begun to occasionally call Snow Deer "daughter" at certain times. She had urged Charles to talk to Snow Deer, to see if he might encourage her to take a white name, to keep people from staring at Snow Deer in public whenever she was called by her Indian name.

So far, Charles had refused to take his mother's suggestion. He always said that Snow Deer had already been faced with so many changes in her life, he was not sure if she would be able to tolerate such a change as that, or agree to it.

"I want children so badly," Snow Deer blurted out, clinging to Patricia.

"Dear, dear," Patricia said, interrupting her. "I shouldn't have spoken of it. I should have known that you wanted to have a child as badly as Charles."

Snow Deer eased from Patricia's arms. She wiped tears from her face with her hands. "Yes, I want children," she said, a sob catching in her throat. "But . . ."

"Dear, mother nature sometimes can be unkind," Patricia said, again interrupting Snow Deer, trying to take away her uneasiness about the subject. "Those of us who wish to have a house full of children sometimes are denied the pleasure. I . . . I wanted more children than just one. No matter how hard Jacob and I tried, we had only one child. I thank God every day that I was blessed with Charles. Never could a mother be as proud of a son as I am of Charles Franklin."

"And now you have a daughter," Snow Deer said, taking Patricia's hands and smiling at her. "And I promise you, Mother, you shall one day have many grandchildren."

"Yes, many grandchildren," Patricia said, forcing a smile, for she truly doubted now that Snow Deer would have children. Patricia had fought such battles of the heart over children. It was a draining thing, this desire to have children, then being denied them.

The truth was that Charles was adopted, something that neither Patricia nor Jacob would ever disclose to their son.

"And what are my two favorite women in the world talking about?" Charles asked as he burst into the room, all smiles. His footsteps and his smile faltered when he saw his wife's blood-shot eyes, knowing that they had to have been caused by tears.

"The snow," Patricia said, forcing another smile as she turned abruptly toward Charles. "I think we're in the midst of a blizzard, son."

"Yes, seems so," Charles said, his eyes still on Snow Deer. But he thought it best not to ask now what had caused his wife's tears. He would ask her in private, when he would not embarrass both his wife and mother by such prodding of secrets between women.

"Dishes done yet?" Jacob asked, stepping into the kitchen beside Charles. Locking his thumbs on his suspenders, he looked from woman to woman, then turned questioning eyes up at Charles.

Charles shook his head, to tell his father not to ask any questions about whatever had transpired in the kitchen before the men's arrival.

"Yes, the dishes are done and now it's time to dirty some more," Patricia said, laughing awkwardly. "I've made some mighty fine bread pudding. Snow Deer, would you mind carrying the coffee pot and cups into the parlor? I'll bring the pudding."

Snow Deer gave Patricia a soft smile. She was glad to have something to do to take away the strain that was evident in the kitchen. She took the coffee pot from the stove and set it on a silver tray, then also placed cups, saucers, sugar and cream, and spoons on the tray.

With Charles close behind her, she took the tray into the parlor and set it down on a coffee table with chairs arranged around it; a fire burned high in the fireplace close beside them.

Everyone settled down before the fire.

They ate in silence, their eyes darting to one another.

"I find cream so fascinating," Snow Deer finally blurted out, pouring some into her coffee. She needed something to talk about to break through the silence. "Even milk and butter. I saw cows before coming to Illinois, but I did not know what they were for except that white men butchered them and ate them."

"Do you enjoy the taste of milk?" Jacob asked,

stirring sugar into his coffee. "Of cream and butter?"

"I think they are all delicious," Snow Deer said.
"But I especially like this bread pudding." She
looked at Patricia. "You have taught me so many
things, Mother. Will you also teach me how to
make bread pudding?"

"I would be delighted to," Patricia said, nodding. Then she smiled mischievously at Snow
Deer. "Have you shown Charles his surprise yet?"

Snow Deer's eyes darted over to Charles, then
back at Patricia. "Shh, please," she softly encouraged. "Later tonight. I shall show him later tonight."

"What is this?" Charles said, eyebrows forking.
"Do I sense a conspiracy here between women?"

"Perhaps," Patricia said, her eyes dancing.

Finally the strained mood was broken. They
laughed and chatted. Charles and Snow Deer kept
exchanging glances. His were filled with curiosity,
wondering what sort of surprise his mother was
talking about.

Snow Deer's eyes were filled with a soft gleam,
so eager was she to show Charles what she had
made for him on the sewing machine that he had
recently bought for her. It matched his mother's,
with its foot treadle and ease of sewing with
thread.

Snow Deer was so fascinated with the machine,
she wished that Becky could have one, to ease her
daily sewing chores.

She became filled with melancholy when
thoughts of Becky and her father came to mind.
And Burning Snow. How Snow Deer missed her
little sister.

In Snow Deer's last letter from Becky, she had
said that Burning Snow was adjusting well

enough without Snow Deer being there to watch out for her. Burning Snow had made a new close friend. This friend had become Burning Snow's constant companion.

And as for Whistling Elk, Snow Deer's beloved brother, he and his wife had proudly announced the birth of a son, a son in the exact image of his father! He was Cheyenne in all features and skin color!

Hearing about her family always made Snow Deer somewhat homesick. She hoped that Charles might agree to take her home for a visit sometime in the spring.

"Snow Deer?" Charles said, breaking through her reverie. "I think we'd best head for home before we get snowed in here."

Snow Deer blinked her eyes nervously, then nodded at Charles. She set her saucer and cup aside and rose from the chair. She smiled a thank-you to Jacob as he brought her woolen cape to her and slipped it around her shoulders. She tied it at her throat, then slid the hood up over her head.

After her gloves were on, and Charles was dressed warmly for the outdoors, they hugged his parents and said good-bye, then went outside where the horse and sleigh awaited them.

As the horses struggled through the almost knee-high snow, Snow Deer lifted her eyes toward the heavens. She giggled as the snow settled on her face. "It feels like soft cotton, Charles," she said.

"I have always loved this time of year," he said, blinking snow off his lashes. "I have always loved snow."

"When I was a little girl, Becky taught me how to make snow angels," Snow Deer said, brushing snow from her face as it continued to come from the heavens in steady white sheets. "Have you ever seen a snow angel, Charles?"

"Don't think I have," Charles said, chuckling.

"Charles, please stop the horses," Snow Deer said, grabbing the reins.

"Why?" he asked, forking an eyebrow. "I might love this stuff, but right now, I'd prefer a warm fire over it."

"Please?" Snow Deer said, pleading with her eyes when he gently took the reins back from her.

Charles could never ignore anything she asked when she looked at him with such a soft pleading in her midnight-dark eyes. He laughed throatily. "Well, all right," he said, drawing a tight rein.

The sleigh wavered, slid somewhat sideways, then finally came to a halt.

"Come with me, Charles," Snow Deer said, taking Charles's hand. "I want to make you an angel."

"I don't need for you to make me one," Charles said, placing a hand at the nape of her neck and drawing her near. "Darling, don't you know that I already have an angel? *You.*"

"You see me as an angel?" she said, her voice almost a purr.

"My one and only," Charles said huskily. "Snow Deer, I'd much rather go home and climb in bed with you than play in the snow."

Laughing softly, she yanked away from him and jumped from the sleigh into the snow.

Charles watched, wide-eyed, as she fell back into the snow on her back, laughing, moving her arms up and down in the snow, making a design that resembled an angel's wings.

Unable to resist the sight of her lying there, so child-like, so sweet, Charles bolted from the sleigh. He went to her and spread himself over her, blanketing her with his body.

Their lips met in a frenzy of kisses.

Charles reached beneath the cape and cupped her breasts through her dress.

His knee parted her legs.

He slid a hand up her dress and heard her moan of pleasure when he stroked her woman's center.

"I want you," he whispered huskily. "Now. In the snow."

"Yes, yes," Snow Deer whispered, arching herself up against his hand when he splayed it across her patch of hair, his one finger thrusting inside her. She fumbled with his breeches, struggling with her gloved hands to unfasten them.

When she finally had his manhood released from its tight confines, she sighed and lifted herself toward him, her world melting away when he entered her in one deep thrust.

"This is a first for me," Charles whispered against her lips, chuckling. "It's surely only twenty degrees, we're having a blizzard, and here we are making love in the snow."

"I feel nothing but your warmth inside me," Snow Deer whispered back. "Charles, Charles . . ."

Chapter Twenty-Five

The fire crackled and popped on the grate as Charles and Snow Deer stood before the fireplace, laughing as they hurried out of their wet clothes.

"I can't believe we did that," Charles said, stepping out of his breeches.

"It is good to sometimes do something that might be foolish to some, fun to others," Snow Deer said. She trembled like a leaf as she slid her wet dress down her body.

"I'll get our robes," Charles said, hurrying into their bedroom and grabbing them from pegs on the back of the door.

When he returned to the living room, Snow Deer was standing as close to the fire as she could get, her arms hugging herself.

Charles gently slid the robe around her shoulders. She snuggled into it, then turned and gazed up at Charles as he slipped into his robe.

She was overwhelmed with remembrances of

only moments ago, when she was in passion's throes with her husband. She had never known that someone could love as deeply as she loved Charles. He brought so much to her life, his genuine caring the most important. She wished—oh, how she prayed—that she could bring him more—a child!

"I'm going to fix something special for my wife," he said, smiling at her over his shoulder as he walked toward the kitchen. "Have you ever drunk hot chocolate?"

"No, but anything that is hot will please me," Snow Deer said, unable to leave the warm security of the fire.

As she waited for Charles to come back to the living room, she gazed into the flames. She grew somber as she went over in her mind her recent discussion with Patricia.

It unnerved her to know that Charles's mother, perhaps even his father, were always watching her belly for signs of her being with child.

It did seem important to them, for Patricia did not seem to realize tonight, when she brought up the subject of children again, how many times these past days she had done this.

No one wanted a child more than Snow Deer, she despaired to herself. It would be the true culmination of her marriage with Charles.

A child would make their bond complete!

And a child was a blessing, a gift from a woman to a man.

Having married in the white tradition, Charles had missed out on many things. Had they married in the Cheyenne way in the Cheyenne village, Charles would have been given many presents, not only by Snow Deer's family, but by the village as a whole, since Snow Deer was the daughter of a chief, and a Cheyenne princess.

She thought back to the moment Charles was given the other gifts from her people. They had showered him with so many things for having saved Snow Deer from drowning in the Ohio River.

Those, too, had been denied him in the end, for when he left, he had not taken any of them with him.

"Hot chocolate for my lady," Charles said, interrupting Snow Deer's deep thoughts.

She swung around and looked, wide-eyed, at the two cups on a tray, and the steam spiraling from the dark brown liquid. She stared at the hot chocolate for a moment longer, then smiled and took one of the cups.

"It does look stimulating," she said.

She laughed at the word she had chosen to describe the hot chocolate, knowing by the gleam in Charles's eyes that he had also seen the double meaning in her choice of words.

Neither of them needed any more "stimulation" after what they had just shared in the snow.

Ignoring the cold, the snow, and the wetness that had spread through their clothes, they had made passionate love for longer than would they have, had they been on a bed. Somehow, that forbidden way of making love had made the pleasure that much greater.

"I hoped you might think it looks delicious," Charles said, setting the tray down as Snow Deer curled her feet beneath her robe and sat down in the chair closest to the fire.

"It does look and smell delicious," Snow Deer said, yet knew that it was still too hot to taste it. "I can see now why it is called hot chocolate. It is hot and it looks as though it is made of chocolate."

"It is made from cocoa," Charles said. "You have not seen the can of cocoa. When I bought it before I met you, I absently placed it way up high on a shelf. It got moved around until it was out of sight behind several other food articles."

He braved a sip of the cocoa, smiling over his cup as she, also, took a slow sip. He watched her as she got her first true taste of cocoa. He lowered his cup, laughing softly as she took another quick sip.

"I see that you approve," Charles said, himself now taking another drink.

"I wonder why Becky did not introduce my family to such a delicacy as this," Snow Deer said, gazing at the cocoa as if mesmerized by it. "It is truly wonderful."

"Perhaps your mother concentrated on those things that were not so frivolous," Charles said softly. "She saw the importance, I am sure, of seeing that your family got what was most necessary in your diet. Cocoa is not something a mother would think of while gathering food in the garden for her children."

"Yes, times have sometimes been hard for my family," Snow Deer said. She took another sip of the cocoa, her eyes locked on Charles over the rim of her cup.

"I have been more fortunate," Charles said, setting his cup aside. "My family is considered wealthy by the standards in which most people in this area live. Being a postmaster, Father is paid by the government. The pay has been more than adequate to get my parents what they need to be comfortable."

He laughed. "But that did not spoil them," he said. "They still spend much time making their own food instead of depending solely on that which you can buy in the stores. I'm proud of them for that, for their continued independence."

Again lost in thought about the conversation she had shared with Patricia earlier, Snow Deer only half heard what Charles was saying.

Charles saw that Snow Deer's mind had strayed. She was preoccupied. He could see just how distant her eyes had become. He saw a sudden sadness in their depths.

"Snow Deer, when I entered my mother's kitchen tonight, I interrupted something between you and her," he said softly. "Darling, I saw that you had been crying. I know that something my mother said upset you." He cleared his throat nervously.

Then he leaned closer to Snow Deer. "I told mother not to talk to you about that," he said, thinking he knew what his mother had said to Snow Deer. "I told mother not to ask you to change your name. That's what she did, isn't it, Snow Deer? She told you that it would be best for you to change your name into something more appropriate for living in the white community."

Snow Deer's spine stiffened. She could feel the color draining from her face at the mere thought of someone suggesting she change her name from Snow Deer to—to something else. She had *already* changed so much about herself to make her more acceptable in the eyes of the whites!

She wore their scratchy, stiff-collared clothes. She wore their shoes. She wore their dreaded corsets!

And she now often wore her hair in a tight bun atop her head instead of in braids, or hanging straight down her back.

"How could she even think I would do that?" she

finally blurted out. "My name is *me*. I could never part with it!"

Charles's shoulders slumped. He shook his head slowly back and forth. "Lord, that *was* what made you cry," he said. He then rose from his chair and went to Snow Deer. He took her hands and drew her up before him. He held her tightly to him. "No one is going to take your name away from you."

"Thank you for not being the one to ask," Snow Deer said, clinging.

"I *was* going to ask," Charles said, unable to lie to her about anything. He could feel her stiffen in his arms. He placed his hands at her waist and held her away from him so that he could look more clearly into her eyes. "But not until we had children that were of school age. Then I would have asked you if you liked the name Mame. I love it."

"You, too, see the need of a name change?" Snow Deer said, searching his eyes. Her gaze was filled with hurt and disappointment in the man she loved. It was the first time she'd ever felt this emotion about him. "You have even chosen the name?"

"Snow Deer, as I said, I would have never mentioned changing your name had I not thought Mother had already done it," Charles said. He wanted to bite his tongue for having misconstrued what Snow Deer and his mother had been talking about. "And I wouldn't have asked that of you for *many* years. We don't even have children on the way yet. It is only after they enter school that I can see the need for their mother to have a white woman's name. It would save confusion on our children's part when they were asked to explain why their mother's name was Indian."

"Are you saying that they might be ashamed to

have an Indian mother?" Snow Deer said, yanking away from Charles. She doubled her hands into tight fists at her sides. "Perhaps *you* are embarrassed to have an Indian for a *wife.*"

Charles reached out for her, but she took a quick step away from him, not allowing him to touch her.

He was stunned by her sudden anger and by how she had misconstrued everything he had said. That she was accusing him of being ashamed of her being Indian made him momentarily speechless.

But she still had plenty to say.

He stood silently watching and listening, his lips parted in wonder at how deeply hurt she was by what he had said, and . . . by something more.

As she told him that his mother had not mentioned changing her name, but had instead talked about her not being pregnant yet, he became aware of how hurt she was not only by the conversation but by the mere fact that she was not with child yet.

"I am making everyone unhappy," Snow Deer said, suddenly sobbing. She lowered her face in her hands. "No one likes my name. No one likes it that I am not pregnant. No one wants me to be Indian!"

Aghast at that last statement, Charles rushed to Snow Deer. He drew her into his arms. "Darling, darling," he said, caressing her back. "You are wrong about so many things, especially thinking that no one wants you to be Indian. No one has ever said anything against you being Cheyenne! They see you as special, as so sweet. The color of your skin means nothing to them! And as for your name change, that will never be mentioned again."

He slid his hands up and framed her face between them. He gazed lovingly into her eyes. "And as for children, yes, I am anxious to be a father, but not to the point that I wish you to feel inadequate because you are not yet pregnant," he murmured. "And my mother loves you, Snow Deer. She never meant to make you uncomfortable by speaking of wanting to be a grandmother. She sees herself as aging so quickly. And remember that only recently she was gravely ill. She fears that she might not have enough years with our children if we wait too long to have them."

"It is not that we are waiting purposely," Snow Deer said, a sob lodging in her throat. "We are trying. My body just is not ready yet to give us children."

"And no one will ever bring the subject up again," Charles said. "I shall have a talk with Mother. I'll ask her to refrain from mentioning children again to you."

"No, please do not do that," Snow Deer said, sighing. "It might make a strain between me and your mother, whereas normally, when children are not being discussed, we are so relaxed with each other. She has been so good to teach me so many things. . . ."

Her words trailed off as her eyes lit up. "Oh, Charles, I almost forgot," she said, stepping away from him.

"Forgot what?" he said, forking an eyebrow.

He was glad to see her smiling again. He would never hurt her for the world!

And even though she had asked him not to speak to his mother, he now saw that he must. There were many things that his mother must learn to refrain from speaking about.

And if it made his mother uncomfortable, so be

it. It was his wife's well-being that he must protect. He knew that she had been forced to adapt to many things that were uncommon to her and she had faced them all with a smile and willingness that proved that she was unlike any other woman in the world!

"I will be back in a minute," Snow Deer said, rushing toward the bedroom. She stopped and turned to Charles. "Please shut your eyes? What I have is a surprise."

Charles suddenly recalled his mother having asked Snow Deer if she had shown him his "surprise" yet. Too many things happening between then and now had made him forget her reference to it.

"Yes, I'll close my eyes," he said, chuckling.

"Now, for it will take me only a moment to get it," Snow Deer said. She smiled broadly when he closed his eyes and covered them with his hands.

She then hurried into the bedroom and opened a drawer, where she had hidden the garment that she had made for Charles on her new sewing machine.

Beaming, and stretching the blue denim garment out between her hands, she went back to the living room and stood before Charles. "Now you can open your eyes," she said.

She eagerly watched his expression as he opened his eyes and saw what she held out before her.

"A shirt," he said, his eyes lighting up as he reached for it. He turned the shirt from the front to the back, then turned it to the front again and gazed at Snow Deer. "I love it! Snow Deer, you can do anything. Anything!"

"I enjoyed very much sewing this for you on my new sewing machine," Snow Deer said, proudly squaring her shoulders. "I am so glad that you like it."

"I shall always treasure it," Charles said, again looking at the shirt.

He smiled to himself, thinking that she had not put all of her past talents behind her in favor of the more modern way of sewing. She had sewn many colorful beads on the front of the blue denim shirt.

Smiling down at her, he slipped out of his gown and put the shirt on.

Stark naked except for the shirt, he strutted around the room in front of Snow Deer.

Snow Deer watched him for a while, giggling, then went to him and snuggled into his arms. "I never thought it possible to be this happy," she murmured, pushing out of her mind any troubled thoughts that came to her about children, names, and mothers-in-law who were sometimes hard to please. Charles was all that mattered, and it did seem that she was making him happy enough!

She was so happy at this moment, she was giddy!

Chapter Twenty-Six

Charles and Snow Deer had lived together through one summer and autumn, and now even "Robe Season," winter, had passed.

It was now *mat-si-o-mi-ish-i*, April, the moon of spring, when the earth received the embrace of the sun, and when everyone would soon see the results of that love. Every seed was awakened and so was animal life.

"I've been waiting for this day all winter," Charles said as he pulled on a leather jacket. He smiled over at Snow Deer. "Today I begin readying the soil for planting. I love it. It'll be good to be outside again."

He slid an arm around Snow Deer's waist and drew her into his embrace. "But I must admit, I've enjoyed this winter more than any others," he said. "You were here to share the long, lonely nights with me."

"I am also going to share your time outside with

you," Snow Deer said, her eyes bright as she gazed up at him. "Husband, I am going to the garden with you and help you prepare it for the crops."

"No, I don't think so," Charles said, laughing softly. "Wife, in the white man's world, it is the man's place to prepare the garden for planting . . . even to plant the crops. The woman's place is in the kitchen, *cooking* them."

"In my world, the Cheyenne men and women work together as partners," Snow Deer said, not to be put off that easily. "The men and women share equally the work of the family, which also includes the planting of crops."

She eased from his arms, went to lift a shawl from a peg on the wall, and placed it around her shoulders.

Her chin held stubbornly high, she marched over and opened the door as Charles watched, his eyes wide with disbelief at her stubbornness.

"Coming, Charles?" Snow Deer said, turning to smile mischievously at him. "Working together forges a deeper affection between husband and wife, an affection which lasts to the end of life. Come. Let us work together this morning. Like you, I have looked forward to being out of doors. What better way to spend time in the fresh air of spring, than with my husband?"

When Charles still did not respond to her determination to go with him, she stepped away from the door and went to him. She placed a gentle hand to his cheek. "Husband, a Cheyenne man's favorite companion is his wife," she murmured. "Is it not the same in the white man's culture? Do you not see me as your favorite companion?"

Charles sighed. He took her hands and kissed first one palm, and then the other, then released her hands and reached around to slowly stroke her glistening black hair.

"Wife, you are, and always will be, my favorite companion. You are my very best friend," he said thickly. "I feel that we already have an affection between us that will last to the end of time, so please let me be about my business, and you, about *yours*."

Snow Deer went silent, knowing now that he truly did not want her to accompany him to the garden. She looked slowly around the house. Yes, there were things that needed to be done there. She had just thought she might do them later.

She now knew that today was as good as any to renew her lodge, a tradition practiced at her village.

She slipped into Charles's arms and gazed up at him, smiling. "Go on, husband," she murmured. "I understand. I have important wifely things to do here. You go and do your husbandly duties wherever they take you."

Wondering about her quick change of heart, Charles placed his hands at her waist and held her away from him. "What are you going to do today?" he asked, searching her eyes for answers. "It seems you've changed your mind too quickly after being so determined to help me in the garden."

"Just go on your way," Snow Deer said, removing his hands from her waist. "You have your chores. I have mine."

Silently questioning her with his eyes, Charles idly scratched his brow with his forefinger. He knew from her expression that she was not going to be doing just ordinary chores today.

Yet he felt that it was best not to question her. He had already chanced causing a strain between them by being so adamant about her not going

273

with him to the garden. He would just have to take his chances and discover whatever sort of "surprise" she might have in store for him when he returned home for dinner.

He was becoming used to her "surprises," most of which sprang from their different beliefs and cultures.

"I guess I'll go now," Charles said, still gazing questioningly down at her.

"Yes, go," Snow Deer said.

She took him by his elbow and led him to the door.

Charles stared at her as he walked backward out of the door; then he turned and walked down the steps.

His footsteps grew quicker when he reached the ground. The morning air was invigorating, and his concerns over what Snow Deer might have on her mind disappeared in his excitement about preparing his land for planting.

Suddenly, all that he could think about was his garden, which plants would go where, and how many. He always looked forward to seeing that first tip of green breaking through the freshly tilled, black Illinois soil.

Then came the fun and pride of watching it grow!

When he reached the garden area, he stopped and placed his hands on his hips and gazed at length at it. His eyes gleamed as he imagined how it would look in mid-summer. This year it was good to know that he would be planting crops not only for himself but also for his wife.

Whenever the word "children" popped into his consciousness, he swept it aside, for he truly feared now that he and Snow Deer would never have children. If they had not made a child during those long winter days and nights that were filled sometimes with endless lovemaking, then he doubted they ever would.

He went to the barn and grabbed a hoe.

After going back to the garden, where the dirt was pitch black, as though it was mixed with oil, he began feverishly breaking the ground with the hoe for the plants.

"I had so longed to have a son join me in the garden in the future," he whispered to himself.

He shrugged, and his eyes filled with sadness. "Now I doubt that I shall ever have either a son or a daughter."

Chapter Twenty-Seven

Snow Deer stood for a moment, just looking around the house, wondering how she might renew her lodge since it was nothing like the one she had lived in, at her village. The Cheyenne women always renewed their lodges in the spring, placing new skins on them, so that they stood white and pure in the morning light.

They rid themselves of everything inside the lodge and replaced it with new beds, mats, and cooking utensils.

Everything was exchanged for new!

"This is no tepee and there are no skins to whiten," Snow Deer said thoughtfully. "So I must do what I can to purify my house in other ways."

She gazed at the furniture, piece by piece, then looked at the open door.

Yes, she thought to herself. She would remove all of the furniture. Then she and Charles could go to Vienna and replace it with new.

She would even have new cooking utensils.

She would make new curtains and rugs for their lodge!

Smiling, eager to please her husband, and wanting to have the house emptied and cleaned before he returned home for his dinner meal, Snow Deer began carrying furniture from the house and placing it on the front lawn.

She began with the living room. Struggling, moaning and groaning, she dragged the heavy upholstered chairs and divan outside.

The bedroom was the worst of all for her. She was unfamiliar with how a white man's bed was constructed, so she didn't know how to take it apart. And she had to disassemble it to get it through not only the bedroom door, but also the front door.

She had no trouble getting the soft feather mattress outside. She stretched it out across the kitchen chairs in the sun.

Then she returned to the bedroom and finally managed to tear down the bed into several pieces that were not too heavy for her to carry.

After even all of the pots, pans, and dishes were outside and the cabin lay completely empty, she stood just inside the door peering at it, and she smiled.

Then a thought came to her. It was time for her to prepare her husband's noon meal, and she had taken everything she needed to prepare it outside!

She rushed back outside and searched until she had found enough kitchenware to prepare the meal.

Breathless, her muscles aching from having carried so many heavy pieces of furniture outside, Snow Deer went to the kitchen and proceeded to make a pan of soup for her husband. She had

277

made bread only yesterday. She sliced it and laid it on a platter with several pieces of cheese.

And after the cabin was filled with the wonderful aroma of coffee and potato soup, Snow Deer stretched a tablecloth out across the bare floor and prepared a place for them to eat their dinner by the fireplace. Although it was spring, the air still held a chill in it.

She laid another log on the fire. She fanned the surrounding flames with the tail end of her apron until they began spreading along the fresh log.

She then turned with a gasp when Charles came into the cabin and shouted her name in a way she had never before heard it called.

"Snow Deer!" Charles cried, gazing around at the empty house. He stared in disbelief at the tablecloth on the floor. On it sat two steaming bowls of soup, coffee, and bread and cheese.

Snow Deer turned to him. Seeing his confused look of dismay, and having heard the anger in his voice, she just stood there, her hands clasped tightly behind her.

"Lord, Snow Deer, what on earth have you done?" Charles said, coming into the living room. He stood with his hands on his hips as he again looked slowly around him.

"I prepared dinner for you, Charles," Snow Deer said, now understanding that what she had done to renew their lodge had actually angered instead of pleased Charles.

She again tried to draw his attention away from what puzzled and angered him. "Come and sit with me, Charles," she murmured. "The soup will soon be cold."

"To hell with the soup," Charles said, going to her. He gripped her shoulders with his fingers. "Snow Deer, I have put up with so many things that you have done without saying anything, knowing that you always have a reason for doing them. But today?" He flung a hand away from her, gesturing toward the empty house. "What on earth could you say that could explain away what you have done here today?"

"Charles, do not be angry with Snow Deer," she said, her voice quaking with emotion. "I have done only what is natural for a Cheyenne woman in the spring."

"And what on earth could that be?" Charles said, dropping his other hand away from her. He turned and looked again slowly around the room. "All I can see here is an empty house." He turned to her again. "Why, Snow Deer? Why did you do this? What Cheyenne custom do you blame this on?"

"Blame?" Snow Deer said, eyes wide.

Tears streaming from her eyes, she turned and rushed from the house.

She didn't stop until Charles caught up to her and grabbed her by the arm. He swung her around and drew her quickly into his arms.

"I'm sorry," he said, his voice breaking. "I shouldn't have been so—so mean about this. I know you have a good explanation."

"You are quick to be angry with Snow Deer today," she said, sniffling as she looked slowly up at him. "That is not like you, Charles. Why do you get so angry today?"

"It was just a shock to see everything removed from the house," Charles said. He searched her face and eyes, seeing a deep hurt in her expression. "I said I was sorry, Snow Deer. Will you forgive me?"

"There is nothing to forgive," she said, wiping tears from her face with the back of a hand. "It is just another culture difference that you were faced with. I should have explained to you about it before I actually did it."

"Tell me now," Charles said, placing an arm around her waist and walking her back toward the house. He smiled down at her. "Better yet, tell me while we eat. Working in the fresh air sure can stir up a man's appetite."

He looked again at all the furniture scattered about the yard. He smiled down at Snow Deer. "I'm sure you've worked up quite an appetite yourself."

He chuckled. "Lord, Snow Deer, how on earth did you manage to get all of this out of the house?" he said. "Do you have muscles in places I don't know about?"

"Perhaps," she said, giggling. She was relieved to hear Charles joking again. It always hurt her to hurt him. His hurt was her hurt!

Hand in hand, they went back inside the cabin. They sat down on the floor and began eating. Between bites, Snow Deer tried to explain this newest custom to her husband.

"And so you have renewed our lodge," Charles said, laughing softly. He took a sip of his coffee, then set the cup back on the floor. "I'll bring everything back inside the cabin. I don't want you lifting another piece of furniture. That isn't something a woman should do."

"The true renewal is not completed," Snow Deer said. "Charles, it is a custom to replace old with *new*. We must go to Vienna and buy new furniture and kitchen utensils. Then I will truly feel as though my spring has been made right."

Charles paled. "Snow Deer, you surely aren't serious," he said. "I'm not about to replace everything. It's all relatively new, as it is."

"But Charles . . ." Snow Deer said, stopping when he placed a gentle hand on her mouth, silencing her words.

"Snow Deer, it's time for you to realize that you can't do everything you wish to do only because you feel it is right because you are Cheyenne," he said softly. "You have been so good at adapting to life here in the white community. Today it is no different."

Then he smiled as something came to him. "Darling Snow Deer, perhaps your custom today, your renewal, is not so different from the white women's customs of renewal," he suggested. "Each spring my mother cleans her house from top to bottom. She washes all of her curtains. She, in a sense, is renewing *her* lodge, but not in such an extreme way as you thought it should be done."

"I have no skins to whiten, yet I *can* clean the floors and windows," Snow Deer said, her eyes dancing. "Yes, I can see how that kind of renewal could satisfy me as much as the one I have always done in the spring in my village."

"But this time you won't be doing it alone," Charles said, laughing softly. "If you think I'm going to allow you to scrub the floors and clean the entirety of this house as if you were a mere maid, you are wrong. I'm going to help you."

"You are?" she said, disbelieving that a man would allow himself to do a woman's chores.

"Most certainly," he said, chuckling. "Let's finish eating our dinner, *then* renew our lodge."

Feeling better about things, Snow Deer went with him and sat back down before the fire. She ate some more cheese and bread as she watched him ladle himself some fresh, hot soup.

"If you help me in the house, why can I not help you in the garden?" she suddenly blurted out. "I

281

do love to work with the soil in the spring, so very much."

Charles saw that, in a sense, she was trying to introduce a compromise between them.

And suddenly it did not seem such a bad idea.

While she was with him, she would not be so liable to think up something else to do that he wouldn't understand.

"Sounds good to me," he said, laughing softly.

She smiled over the edge of her cup as she sipped her coffee.

Chapter Twenty-Eight

Several Weeks Later

Struggling at making pie dough, having already thrown away her first try, Snow Deer watched her newest attempt fall into small, lumpy pieces again as she lifted it from the bowl to the floured surface of the table.

Frustrated, she turned her back to the mess. She slowly wiped flour and lard from her hands onto her apron. "This is one thing I will never be able to learn for my husband," she whispered.

She turned and stared dispiritedly at the bowl full of the strawberries that she had discovered growing wild along the railroad tracks behind Charles's parents' house. She had found enough for a pie. She had grown so excited to think about using them in a pie for her husband.

Now she knew that her excitement had been premature. There was going to be no pie! Sighing, she reached for a plump strawberry and plopped it in her mouth.

Panic seized her when she heard the sound of a horse approaching. She turned and stared frantically down at the lumpy pie dough, then looked at the door.

Charles! she thought desperately. Her husband was returning from Vienna, where he had gone for garden supplies.

"I can't let him see such a mess as this."

Her face grew hot with a flush as she ran and got a coal bucket from beside the stove.

She took it to the table and started to scrape the dough into it, but stopped with a start when someone knocked on the door.

She knew that Charles wouldn't knock on the door before entering. That had to mean that someone else had arrived.

Thinking it might be Jacob, and not wanting him to see her futile attempt at making a pie any more than she wished for Charles to see it, her hands trembled when she again started to scrape the dough from the table into the bucket.

But the persistent knocking unnerved her too much to continue worrying about the dough.

Sighing heavily, she went to the door.

Before opening it, she gazed down at herself, at the flour smudges all over the apron, and at the sticky goo on her hands.

She knew that her face and hair would be in no better shape. Surely she had flour all over her. She could even feel some of the dough sticking to her chin.

She flicked the dough away from her chin with a finger, then slowly opened the door, hoping that if it were Jacob, he would not ask to come in. She hoped that he had only come to tell her something, perhaps that Patricia wished for her to have tea with her this afternoon. They had begun having tea together quite often, of late. She enjoyed this pastime, especially when Patricia made tiny, sweet little cakes with white icing.

When Snow Deer saw who *was* standing on her porch, decked out in new fringed buckskin clothes resplendent with many colorful beads in the design of forest flowers, she stiffened and took a shaky step backward.

"Rain Feather . . ." she gasped, paling.

"Snow Deer, it is good to see you," Rain Feather said, slowly looking her up and down. He raised an eyebrow at her appearance, for the flour all over her puzzled him.

"How did you find me?" Snow Deer said in a rush of words. "Why are you here?"

"When I arrived in Illinois, I asked around about a Cheyenne woman who was married to a white man," Rain Feather said. "I was directed here."

"But why would you go to the trouble of finding me?" Snow Deer said guardedly. "Why are you in Illinois?"

"I am in Illinois to have council with another band of Shawnee," Rain Feather said, again looking at her, and thinking she looked anything but Cheyenne with her white woman's attire and strange way of wearing her hair. "My friend Blue Thunder has a village close to a large cave in a rock not far from the town named after the cave—the town of Cave-In-Rock."

"I have heard of the cave," Snow Deer said, slowly relaxing her muscles when she felt that he was no threat to her. "I have heard of the town."

"I have wondered often how marriage to a white man treats you," Rain Feather said, the amused look in his eyes unnerving Snow Deer. "I see that it does not treat you well."

"What do you mean by that?" Snow Deer said, stiffening again.

One of her hands fluttered to her hair, moaning quietly when she realized that several locks had again fallen from the bun.

And she could feel pieces of dough stuck to her hair.

"So much about you is different," Rain Feather said, his eyes slowly lowering, stopping to gaze at her stomach. "But I do not see you large with child."

Infuriated by his boldness, by his nerve to even speak of such a thing to her, Snow Deer started to close the door in his face, but stopped, for she knew that Rain Feather had to have seen her parents before leaving for Illinois.

Strange as it seemed to Snow Deer, her father and Rain Feather had become fast friends.

Yet she felt that the friendship might be a forced one on her father's part, for Rain Feather had finally found a Cheyenne woman from her father's village who'd agreed to marry him. That had brought the tribes together. They now even shared the harvest and the hunt.

She knew all these things from Becky's letters.

"No, I am not yet with child," Snow Deer said, unconsciously sliding her hands across her stomach and resting them there.

"It is good that your mother is with child again," Rain Feather said. He smiled. "It gives this old man hope that he is not too old to fill his young wife's womb with his seed. Children are important to me now, although I understand that I do not have but perhaps ten winters left of life on this earth. I will leave an heir behind to follow in my footsteps—to be chief to my people."

Snow Deer scarcely heard any of what Rain Feather said after hearing that Becky was pregnant. She was stunned, not only because her stepmother was nearing her fortieth year of life and her father was much older but because Becky had not written anything about it in her letters.

In her latest letter, which had arrived a few short weeks ago, Becky had asked Snow Deer and Charles to come to Kentucky, if possible, on a certain date, but did not say why.

That date was now only a few days away.

Until now, Snow Deer had not thought much about going. She had even written back and told Becky that she doubted that she and Charles could come. Charles had looked forward to spring, to doing all those things he couldn't do through the winter months.

But now? Thinking Becky might have had an important motive for asking them to come home, Snow Deer began to wonder if they could make the trip.

But surely Becky wasn't pregnant. It was probably just a mean joke on Rain Feather's part!

"You are surely lying about mother's pregnancy in order to upset me, perhaps because you have never gotten over my rejecting your offer of marriage," Snow Deer blurted out. "You are still a fiendish man. How did father ever allow you to marry one of our beloved Cheyenne women?"

She started to slam the door closed, but what he said next caused her to pause and stare at him.

"Your father is proud of being able to boast of being a father again," Rain Feather said. "He misses you. *They* miss you. This is why they decided to bring another daughter into their lives."

He smiled. "Of course your father would not

mind if the child was a brave, for Whistling Elk is too preoccupied with family now to do much with his father," he said. "Whistling Elk lives away from the village with his white wife, on his wife's parents' horse farm."

Snow Deer let what he said about Whistling Elk slip past her, her thoughts still on Becky. "Then mother really is pregnant?" she said, watching Rain Feather's eyes to see if she could see betrayal in them.

"Yes," Rain Feather said. "My wife, Pretty Face, stays with her now instead of traveling with me to Illinois. She will assist when your mother has her child. She is the one who talked your mother into having another child. . . ."

Although Rain Feather continued to talk, Snow Deer no longer listened. This was all too much for her to comprehend, for her to accept. The fact that Becky had not confided in her caused Snow Deer's heart to ache with a sudden sadness. She had never before felt so left out of her parents' lives!

And . . . and her mother was having a child and Snow Deer could not get pregnant herself!

She thought back to the times Becky had talked to Snow Deer about not wanting any more children after Burning Snow's birth. Becky had told her that after seeing Burning Snow's affliction, she feared having more children.

Yet now she was pregnant!

Snow Deer was puzzled by everything, but most of all, that no one had told her this wonderful news, for she had always encouraged Becky to have more children. Children were the backbone of a marriage. Their laughter brought so much to a man and woman's life!

But worst of all, it hurt Snow Deer to the very core of her being to know that it was not *her* encouragement that had caused Becky to move past those barriers that had kept her from being pregnant again.

It had been someone else.

It had been Rain Feather's wife!

"Snow Deer? Rain Feather?"

Charles's voice broke through Snow Deer's deep thoughts. She looked suddenly past Rain Feather, discovering Charles there.

Snow Deer looked from Charles to Rain Feather, then burst out the door and ran to her husband.

Sobbing, she clung to him.

"Has this Indian threatened you?" Charles asked, his hand sliding beneath his coat, where his pistol rested in its holster at his right hip.

Hearing how guarded her husband's voice was, and seeing his hand sliding toward his pistol, Snow Deer leapt away from him. She reached a hand out and stopped him from grabbing his pistol. Out of the corner of her eye she saw Rain Feather grabbing quickly for his sheathed knife.

"No, it's nothing like that," she quickly cried. "I am upset over something other than Rain Feather's visit. He has come as a friend, Charles. Not as an enemy."

She could tell by how Rain Feather's eyes narrowed that he had no good feelings toward Charles. She knew by his attitude toward Charles that Rain Feather still cared for her, for jealously was sharp in his eyes.

"Rain Feather, what are you doing here?" Charles said, dropping his hand away from his pistol. "What have you said to upset my wife?"

"I did not come to upset Snow Deer," Rain Feather said, stepping down from the porch. "But now that I have, I apologize and will leave."

Snow Deer sidled closer to Charles as Rain Feather swung himself into his saddle. She knew that she was being impolite by allowing him to leave without first asking him to come inside her home for nourishment before he traveled again on his horse.

But she was in no mood for polite conversation. She felt a hollowness within her. She was hurt through and through over Becky's not having told her about being with child.

When Rain Feather's eyes locked with hers, Snow Deer still could not find it in her heart to ask him to stay.

For too long he had been her father's enemy.

For too long he had driven her mindless by pursuing her!

It had been too good to be rid of him. She could not turn about and cordially invite him into her home!

She did not even smile when he nodded toward her, then rode off, his shoulders slouched, his spine twisted in his old age.

"I can hardly believe that he was here," Charles said, staring at the Shawnee chief until he rode from sight. "I must say, I was concerned to see him standing at our door."

Snow Deer gazed up at Charles; then, unable to deny the need to cry torrents of tears, she yanked herself away from him and ran into their house.

Blinded by tears, she ran to her bedroom and threw herself on the bed.

Charles followed quickly after her and knelt on the bed beside her. He lifted her into his arms and held her, slowly rocking her until her tears waned into soft, whimpering sobs.

"He *did* cause you hurt," Charles said. He had never seen Snow Deer this distraught before.

"What did he say to cause this?"

"I feel so ashamed," Snow Deer said, turning her weeping eyes up at Charles. "I should be happy for my father and mother. Instead here I am, behaving like a spoiled child."

"I don't understand any of this," Charles said. He gently gripped her shoulders and held her away from him so that their eyes could meet. "Tell me. Tell me everything."

"Becky is with child," Snow Deer blurted out.

"Why, I would think that would make you smile instead of cry," Charles said, surprised. "Why *are* you crying, Snow Deer?"

"I am so happy for my parents that they, in their middle years, are having another child," Snow Deer murmured. "But ... but ... they never wrote and told me. I ... I had to hear it from the likes of Rain Feather, instead!"

"Oh, I think I see now," Charles said, drawing her into his arms again. "Yes, I see why you would be upset."

"There is more," Snow Deer said, a sob catching in her throat. "It was Rain Feather's wife who convinced Mother to become pregnant again, not *I*. I so often talked to Becky, telling her not to worry about having another child that might be disabled. And even so, did not she and father truly enjoy having Burning Snow as a daughter? We all saw her as a blessing!"

"And there is still more, isn't there?" Charles asked softly, slowly stroking her back.

"Yes, there is more," Snow Deer sobbed out. "I ... I ... have wanted so badly to be with child, and here I am, still childless, and my parents, at their age, are ..."

"Shh, say no more," Charles murmured. "In time, Snow Deer, we will have children. The good

Lord above, and your *Maheo*, will bless us with a child when the time is right for us. Until then, we must focus on our happiness, take a blessing from it, for never could I have loved anyone as much as I love you."

Snow Deer leaned away from him and placed her hands at his cheeks. "Husband, I want to go and visit my parents," she said, her voice quavering with emotion. "Your crops are planted. Can we take time now, before the harvest, to go to Kentucky? I must see for myself why I was not told of this pregnancy."

"If you go, your hurt will be revealed to them," Charles said softly.

"No, I will guard my feelings well enough," Snow Deer said, nodding. "And it is *shame* I am feeling now over being hurt instead of being happy for my parents. I will show them my happiness."

"Yes, I am sure you will," Charles said. Then his eyes filled with amusement as he raked them slowly over her. "Lord, wife, what a sight you are."

"Because of my flushed face from having cried?" she asked, placing her hands at her cheeks, feeling their heat.

"No, I don't think so," Charles said, plucking a piece of dried dough from her hair. "I think you got more dough in your hair than in a pie pan."

Snow Deer giggled.

"Oh, Charles, I hope you do not mind never having pie made from your Cheyenne wife's hands," she then said, sighing.

"And so you tried again today, did you?" he asked, taking her hand and helping her from the bed.

"Do not even go and look," Snow Deer said, her eyes twinkling into his. "I am afraid you would

292

laugh too much at my terrible creation."

He drew her into his embrace. "Never," he said huskily. His fingers went to her hair and pulled out the combs that held it in its bun. As the hair fell down over her shoulders, he wove his fingers through it.

"I would much rather have you than pie anytime," he whispered, kissing the curve of her neck, and then the hollow of her throat.

"Charles, I am so . . . so sticky," Snow Deer whispered as he rose from the bed, pulling her up to stand beside him. He untied her apron and tossed it aside. Then his fingers went to the buttons behind her dress and began loosening them, one by one.

"I shall lick it off you," Charles said, his eyes taking in her heaving breasts as he dropped the dress away from her.

"You are a wicked man," Snow Deer said, gurgling with pleasure when he licked his way from one breast to the other.

Her fingers trembled as she reached for his breeches and unfastened them at the front.

As they fell away from him and lay in a crumpled heap around his ankles she swept a hand around his manhood and began moving her fingers on him.

The sensual feelings rising within him as her fingers worked on him, Charles held his head back and groaned with pleasure.

But when he felt that he might be getting too close to that brink of ecstasy that he wished only to have while inside the warmth of her folds, he reached for her hand and took it away from his hardness.

He swept his arms beneath her and lifted her from the floor. He kissed her as he laid her on the bed, then spread his body above hers.

In one thrust he was inside her.

Her hips rose and met his rhythmic strokes.

Her hands twined through his hair and brought his mouth even harder against her lips.

Her breasts pulsed as his hands kneaded them.

She closed her eyes when his mouth went to her breasts, his tongue flicking the nipples, first one, and then the other, causing red hot embers of desire to burn inside her.

She felt the curl of heat growing in her lower body.

She locked her legs around Charles's waist, riding him, sinking more deeply into a chasm of hungry passion.

Charles felt the heat rising in his loins, his senses reeling in drunken pleasure. He kissed his way up the slender, curving length of her throat and kissed her lips again.

With a sob of pleasure, she clung to him and rocked with him.

He rained kisses on her lids and on her hair, then swept his hands down again and cupped her breasts. He stroked them. He gently rolled the nipples against the palms of his hands.

Then, his whole body one massive pulse of pleasure, he held her close and whispered into her ear. "Now," he said. "Darling, now."

He plunged more deeply and swiftly into her as moans surfaced from inside him. Their bodies quivered together, rocking back and forth, the ultimate release coming in waves through them until they were both engulfed in intense rushes of pleasure.

Afterward, as they lay together, snuggling, Snow Deer rose on one elbow and gazed down at Charles. "You never said whether or not we can leave soon for my home," she said, her voice drawn.

Charles placed a gentle hand on one of her breasts, cupping it. "We *are* home," he said thickly.

Snow Deer's eyes widened, and then she smiled. "I know," she murmured. "And never again shall I refer to home being anywhere but here. But, Charles, tell me—will you take me soon to see my family? It has been so long since I last saw them. Perhaps they think *I* do not care enough. Perhaps this is why Becky did not find it in her heart to confide in me about the child."

"They are wrong ever to doubt you over anything," Charles said, drawing her down against him. He ran his fingers across her back, stroking her soft flesh. "Yes, darling wife. I will take you to Kentucky."

He quickly thought of something—of someone. "But I must tell you that my decision to take you there is not altogether an unselfish one," he said. "I, too, have someone to see while there."

"Your Cousin Elissa?"

"Yes, Elissa."

Neither he nor his parents had heard from Elissa for some time now. He had to wonder if she was still alive, or if consumption had finally claimed her.

He closed his eyes, softly praying that she was still alive—had perhaps even fought the battle and won!

Anger swept through him at the thought of Gerald and his selfishness. But then his thoughts returned to those times when, as children, he and Elissa had found such joy in being alone together.

He thought past that, to the deeper feelings he'd had for his cousin. He *had* loved her, in ways that were forbidden.

He felt blessed that Snow Deer had come along to wipe such wrongful thoughts and desires from his heart and mind! Snow Deer was now all that he ever thought about. His love for her ran so deep, it sometimes frightened him.

If he should ever lose *her* . . . !

Chapter Twenty-Nine

"I'm so glad you don't mind stopping off first at Elissa's before going on to your village," Charles said, giving Snow Deer a quick glance.

They had been traveling for three days.

To ensure his wife's comfort on the journey to Kentucky, Charles had purchased a new buggy. The two-seated buggy, with its padded black leather seats as soft as air, rode like a breeze above its elliptical springs.

The ferry had, only a short while ago, carried them and their horse and buggy across the Ohio River.

"I understand why you are anxious to see your cousin," Snow Deer said, fidgeting with a bead on the front of her fringed buckskin dress. She was dressed for her people now, not for her white neighbors. "I know how much you have worried over her welfare. But your mother said that she finally heard from Elissa the other day and that she was much better. Perhaps she will be even *more* better now."

Although she listened to Charles's response, Snow Deer was preoccupied with thoughts of their last three days of travel. When she had taken her Indian dress from the chifforobe and laid it on the bed beside the other clothes she planned to wear on the journey to Kentucky, Charles had stared at it for a moment, then had smiled in understanding. He knew that she would only be comfortable arriving among her people dressed as they dressed. He understood that she was wary over how her people might feel if they saw her dressed as a white woman.

The past two nights, they had stayed at inns, and until last evening she had worn cotton travel suits, her hair in a tight bun beneath pretty hats. She had known that to wear Indian attire might have caused trouble with the innkeepers.

Yes, she was keenly aware of the prejudices of some people. Even while dressed as a white woman, she had gotten more than second glances from those who also took lodging at the inns. The color of her skin revealed her Indian identity.

Certainly, everyone who saw her and Charles together knew that he had chosen someone from another culture to be his wife. It hurt her deeply when she saw and heard the ridicule of those who were against white men marrying Indians.

She had learned to ignore those who shouted obscenities at her, to hold her chin high as she reached over and cautioned Charles not to retaliate against the bad-mouthed bigots.

"What are you thinking so seriously about?" Charles finally asked, after leaving her for a while in her silent thoughts. "Would you rather I didn't go to Elissa's first? Is that what's bothering you?

If you feel that strongly about wanting to go on to your village, I understand."

Having not realized just how deeply in thought she had been, Snow Deer looked quickly over at him. "I am sorry, husband," she murmured. "What did you say? I was thinking of other things."

Charles laughed softly. "As if I didn't know," he said. "Darling Snow Deer, what's on your mind? Would you rather I didn't go to Elissa's first? We can go there on our return trip to Illinois if that would make you more comfortable."

"I *am* anxious to see my family, and my people, but I can wait until you see Elissa first," she said. She frowned somewhat. "But Charles, I do not wish to spend the night. I will be so close to my family that I would find it hard to sleep."

"We won't spend the night," Charles said, snapping the reins to send the horse onward. "We'll stay long enough to have dinner, then go on to your village. Is that all right? That we stay at least long enough to eat with Elissa?"

"Yes, that is fine," Snow Deer said. She reached over and placed a hand on Charles's arm. "But do not despair too much if you find her not well enough to set a table for us and serve us food."

She swallowed hard. "Charles," she murmured, "I think you should prepare yourself to find Elissa in bed, unable to do much else but talk with us. Although she is somewhat better, I am aware of the disease called consumption. It kills slowly. I once had a relative who died of the disease."

"I know how slowly it kills," Charles said. He sighed heavily. "But if Elissa *is* well enough to visit us out of her sick bed, do not concern yourself about her having to set a table and cook food for

299

us. She has maids and cooks. They do everything for her."

"Maids?" Snow Deer said, her eyes widening. "Cooks? I do not know of those things. I can guess what a cook does. But what does a maid do?"

"Maids wait on white women and spoil them," Charles said. He smiled over at her. "Rich white women, that is."

"Your cousin is rich?" Snow Deer asked, watching as they rode beside tall sunflower plants, their faces lifted toward the sun, reminding her of the day they had buried her husband's uncle in a field of sunflowers.

"Very," Charles said, then frowned when once again he thought of Gerald and how his women friends surely also took a free hand with the money that Elissa, not Gerald, had worked so hard for.

Charles could not see how Elissa tolerated him. She had never acted as though she truly loved him, even when they were first married. It seemed as though she had married him for the sake of marrying alone.

He had often wondered if she married Gerald out of desperation over not being able to have the man she truly loved. Charles didn't know if she had loved him as much as he had loved her.

"Now it is *you* who are in deep thought," Snow Deer said, watching Charles's changing expression.

Charles looked back at her. He felt a flush rise from his neck to his cheeks. His thoughts had tarried on a part of his life that his wife knew nothing about—his feelings for Elissa.

"I'm sorry," he said softly. "I just can't seem to get Elissa off my mind. I am anxious to see her, yet wary of it. If she told my mother that she was better only to keep my family from worrying, and she is near death . . ."

"If she is, you must accept it," Snow Deer said, placing a gentle hand on his knee. She paused, her eyes searching his, then spoke again. "Charles, is there something more you wish to tell me? It seems you have secrets you have not spoken of to me . . . secrets about Elissa?"

"How did you know?" Charles blurted out, his fingers tightening on the reins.

"Darling husband, I love you so much and know you so well, I can see inside your heart," Snow Deer said softly. "I have seen it before when you have spoken of your cousin. There are feelings between you, are there not?"

Stunned to know that she had come to this conclusion only by watching his expressions and listening to how his voice changed when he spoke of Elissa, Charles stared at Snow Deer for a moment.

Then he looked away from her. "How do you feel about it now that you know?" he asked.

"How do I feel?" Snow Deer said, drawing Charles's eyes her way again. "Husband, I love you. You love me. All things in the past that we both left behind are left there. Although I know you still carry feelings from your past with you, I know they are not the same as they were before you met me, or you would not have taken me for your wife."

Charles was in awe of his wife and her ability to look into things with such depth and knowledge and come away from those thoughts knowing and feeling so much, with so much understanding.

"I did love her, yet it was forbidden," he told her. "We were cousins."

"As it is forbidden in the Cheyenne culture to

301

love cousins," Snow Deer said softly. "Did she know you loved her?"

"Yes," Charles said, sighing. "She could not help but know."

He looked quickly at her again. "When I met you, I knew the meaning of *true* love," he said thickly. "Yes, I loved my cousin, but it was more of an infatuation. When I first laid eyes on you, I knew that you were placed on this earth for me, to fill my heart with a blissful joy no other woman could ever give me. Snow Deer, my love for you is so intense that every time I look at you, my pulse races out of control. It is true love, Snow Deer."

"I have always known the depths of your feelings for me," Snow Deer said, scooting over to brush a kiss across his cheek. "I have never felt jealous over your cousin, nor will I over anyone else."

"Thank God I have that off my chest," Charles said. He laughed throatily. "I wish I had done it sooner." He reached a gentle hand to her cheek as she sat there, smiling up at him. "I should have known that you would understand."

A wide spread of land, where a beautiful white fence stretched out for miles, appeared around the bend of the road and drew their eyes from each other.

"Look at the beautiful horses," Snow Deer said. Her eyes widened as she gazed at the many sleek horses grazing on the knee-high Kentucky bluegrass inside the fence.

"Those belong to Elissa," Charles said with pride in his voice. "Many of those are racehorses. Others are there just for breeding."

"There are so many," Snow Deer said. "She is a very wealthy woman, for do not horses constitute wealth in the white world, as they do in the Cheyenne?"

"Yes, Elissa is quite wealthy now because of her horses," Charles said, nodding.

As they rode farther and saw the huge, pillared mansion in the distance, Snow Deer became silent as she stared at it.

"Snow Deer?" Charles said, reaching over to take her hand.

"I know that I am staring and that I am quiet," Snow Deer said, giving him a quick glance. "I have seen homes like this, but never did I know anyone who lived in one. How can anyone need something so big? Our home is more than adequate, Charles. Why would someone want more?"

"Some people want more things than others," Charles softly explained. "As for Elissa living in such a grand house—it was a dream of hers to have something this big. She just happened to find a way to live her dream."

Snow Deer gazed at the house again as Charles drove the horse and buggy down a white, graveled drive toward it. She noticed how Charles was suddenly quiet as he eagerly looked at the house.

No, she would not allow jealousy to enter her heart over his eagerness to see Elissa. She would keep telling herself that it was Elissa's health that caused his concern. Nothing more than that.

As they pulled up before the wide, pillared porch, a stable boy came running from one of the stables toward them. Snow Deer felt as though she was dwarfed beneath the shadows of the huge home. She swallowed hard, feeling worried. This was a different world, one where she was uncertain of the rules. She hoped she would be able to present herself in such a way that Charles would be proud of her.

"Sir, I shall see to your horse," the young stableboy said, taking the reins. "Are you staying the night?"

"No, just a few hours or so," Charles said. "I would appreciate your rubbing the horse down and giving it a bucket of oats before we head out again on our journey."

Charles noticed how the stableboy kept staring at Snow Deer and knew why. In this area, most Indians stayed near their villages, except when on a quest for food. He fought off the anger that the boy's impertinence aroused in him. It was something he was getting used to, but resented like hell!

Charles hurried from the buggy and helped Snow Deer to the ground. He placed a reassuring arm around her waist and walked with her up the long flight of stairs.

They stopped just as they reached the porch and the door swung open and Elissa was there, her cheeks pink with health, her body not wasted away from consumption as Charles had expected.

"Charles!" Elissa squealed as she went to him and flung herself into his arms. "Oh, Charles, it is so good to see you!"

Snow Deer clasped her hands together behind her and watched her husband hug the lovely woman with the strawberry-colored hair. No. She would *not* allow herself to feel jealous. She had heard the truth in her husband's words when he had explained how he felt about Elissa. She was confident that Charles's feelings were only affection.

And when Elissa stepped back from Charles, their hands still intertwined, Charles could not believe his eyes as he stared at her. "Elissa, you are no longer sick," he said. "Lord, Elissa, I . . . I thought you might be dying."

"I thought I was," Elissa said, laughing softly. "But Charles, I received word from a friend in Saint Louis about a doctor who knew ways of curing the sort of consumption that I was fighting. Charles, I went to him. I stayed in his hospital for a short while and took his special medicines. Charles, I *am* well."

"Thank God," Charles said, once again hugging her. "Thank God."

Elissa looked sideways and gazed at Snow Deer, then stepped away from Charles and turned to her. "You must be Snow Deer," she said, extending a long-fingered hand toward her. "Patricia has written me about you. I'm glad to finally meet you."

Snow Deer accepted the kind handshake. "It is good to finally meet you," she murmured. "Both Charles and Patricia have spoken to me of *you.*"

Elissa gave Charles a quick, questioning look, then smiled once again at Snow Deer. "Come inside," she said, whisking the thickly gathered skirt of her silk dress up as she moved toward the door. "We shall have a mint julep. I shall have Kathleen prepare a special dinner for us." She stopped and turned toward Charles. "You will stay the night, won't you?"

"No, not this time," Charles said, again sliding an arm around his wife's waist. "My wife is anxious to get to her village. I feel guilty for having detained her for so long—"

"But first you had to see your cousin?" Elissa said, interrupting him with her soft voice.

"Yes," Charles said, chuckling. "We had to see my cousin first."

As they entered the spacious foyer, Snow Deer gasped. She could see a long corridor stretching out before her, with doors leading into many rooms, and then her eyes found the huge, winding staircase at the far end of the corridor.

Elissa turned to her and silently studied her. Never had Elissa seen anyone as beautiful. And it was obvious that she was sweet. Sweetness was something that Charles had always said he wanted in a wife.

Elissa felt a twinge of jealousy as her eyes slowly went up and down Snow Deer, knowing that Charles's hands were familiar with every lovely curve.

Then she turned away, remembering with a pang of regret how she had felt for Charles when they were children. It had been a forbidden love. It had been hard to accept that they could never be lovers, or marry!

"I have someone I want you to meet," Elissa said, forcing such thoughts of Charles from her mind. She again whisked the hem of her dress off the floor and rushed into the parlor.

When Charles entered the parlor with Snow Deer, he found a tall, well-dressed man there, his blue eyes lighting up as Elissa walked toward him.

Charles stopped and stared as the man swept her into his arms and gave her a big bear hug.

Elissa then swung around, her eyes beaming, as she smiled at Charles. "Charles, this is Dr. Elmer O'Neal, the doctor who cured me of my consumption, the doctor who is now my *husband*," she said, slipping a hand into one of the doctor's. She laughed softly when she saw Charles's reaction, knowing that he was wondering what on earth had happened to Gerald!

"Charles, I sent Gerald packing not long after I saw you," Elissa said, sending a slow gaze up at her husband. "Once the divorce was final, I married Elmer. I've never been happier."

Charles's head was spinning with the suddenness of this news. "Gerald is gone?" he said. "You are married again?"

"Isn't it grand?" Elissa said, giggling. Then she frowned. "Of course I had to pay Gerald a hefty sum to get him totally out of my life. Although he practiced adultery, I could not prove it without hiring a detective. I wanted none of that scandal. So I gave Gerald a large sum of money in return for his promise never to darken my doorstep again. He took it."

"The bastard," Charles said, sighing heavily.

"Come and have a seat," Elmer said, gesturing with a hand toward the plushly cushioned chairs and divan that were arranged beside the long row of windows, where the sun was drenching the floor with its golden light.

"Thank you," Charles said, his hand at Snow Deer's elbow as he led her to the divan.

"I shall go and tell Kathleen to prepare us those mint juleps," Elissa said, leaving the room in a rush.

For a moment there was a strained silence in the parlor, but Snow Deer hardly noticed. Her eyes were absorbing everything around her, the way in which Elissa lived. The room was large and beautiful in its broad spaces and long lines and soft colors.

Long mirrors filled the room with reflected light. Plump divans, luxuriously fringed and mounded with pillows, and many other chintz-covered chairs were neatly organized around the room. Ornate shelves were filled with books richly bound in cloth and leather. All doors and windows were open, inviting bird song and flower scents to fill the room.

Charles broke the silence, bringing Snow Deer's eyes to him.

"Is Elissa as well as she pretends to be?" Charles asked guardedly. "I have not seen her this robust and happy for years."

"For now, yes, I believe she has improved enough to say that she has beaten the ugly claws of consumption," Elmer said. He reached for a pipe that he had earlier rested on an ashtray.

"Are you saying you aren't certain she is going to continue to be this well?" Charles asked, his heart thudding inside his chest. If the doctor knew that she might not have completely gotten over the consumption, surely this man had married her for all the wrong reasons!

"No one is ever certain," Elmer said, placing the pipe stem between his lips. He casually lit the pipe. He took a few puffs, then held the pipe between two fingers and gazed at Charles. "But I am as certain as anyone can be that I have brought Elissa out of this and that she won't suffer from it ever again."

Charles nervously drummed his fingers on his knee as he glared at the doctor.

"I sense there is something more than Elissa's health that might be bothering you," Elmer said, narrowing his eyes at Charles. "And I sense it might be that you are wondering what my intentions are toward your cousin. Sir, I did not marry her for her money, if that is what is bothering you. I am from one of the wealthiest families in Saint Louis."

Snow Deer glanced from Charles to Elmer, then back again to Charles, feeling the tension gathering in the air.

She saw again how important Elissa was to her husband.

Again she brushed her concern aside, for would not she be as protective of a cousin if she thought someone was taking advantage of her innocence?

She folded her hands on her lap and kept quiet, glad when she heard the doctor tell Charles that he had married Elissa because he loved her.

"I stood by and watched Gerald treat Elissa like trash," Charles said, his jaw tightening. "I didn't interfere, but damn it, I will never allow that to happen again to her."

"You can rest assured that I love Elissa," Elmer said, smiling at Kathleen as she carried a tray of mint juleps into the room. He looked past her, raising an eyebrow when he didn't see Elissa enter after her.

"Where is Elissa?" he asked, directing his question to Kathleen, a petite lady whose hair was just graying.

"She's gone to her room," Kathleen said, handing Snow Deer a glass of refreshment, and then Charles.

Elmer took his own glass from the tray.

"She told me to tell you that she would be right down," Kathleen said softly.

"I see," Elmer said, nodding.

Charles looked over his shoulder, out at the corridor, then sipped his drink while slipping a hand over to his wife and squeezing her hand reassuringly.

Elissa hurried to her bedroom and opened a dresser drawer. She slid an envelope from inside it and took it to the bed and sat down and opened it.

Her eyes poured over the various letters that her father had received from Charles's mother throughout the years. Elissa had only recently read the letters, which she had found among her father's things. While going through them, she had discovered that Charles was adopted.

She still could hardly believe it. The man she had loved with all her heart and soul had not truly been forbidden to her after all!

Tears filled her eyes, for it had been hard to pretend to love Elmer in front of Charles while knowing that she would never love anyone but Charles!

She had already been married to Elmer when she'd found the letters, and Charles was married to Snow Deer.

But Elissa had decided that whenever she saw Charles again, she would disclose the truth to him and hope that he would still have her. She would divorce Elmer in a minute to have Charles!

But now, after seeing Charles's devotion to Snow Deer, and seeing how sweet Snow Deer was, and how devoted she was to Charles, Elissa knew that she could not destroy their world by revealing truths that might also destroy Charles. If he knew that his whole life had been built on deceit, he might not be able to accept such lies.

"No, I can't tell him," Elissa said, tears streaming from her eyes. "It is just another secret I must keep from you, dear Charles. Oh, how long I have secretly cared for you!"

Not wanting to return downstairs with bloodshot eyes, Elissa willed her tears away.

Scarcely blinking, she began ripping the letters apart, wanting all written record of Charles's parentage to be kept from him.

She tore the last shred of evidence up, stuffed the pieces back inside the envelope, then stood over a waste basket and dropped the envelope into it.

After striking a match, she dropped it onto the envelope. She watched it burn, then turned, and with her chin lifted high, went back downstairs and acted as though nothing unusual had happened upstairs in the privacy of her room.

"And how do you like the mint juleps?" she asked, whisking her gathered skirt around as she sat down beside her husband on the divan.

Her eyes wavered for only a moment as she gazed at Charles. Then she plucked the tall-stemmed glass up from the tray and took an eager drink.

"I have learned to enjoy many new foods and drinks this year," Snow Deer said, setting the empty glass on the table. "But this is the most delicious drink of them all."

Elissa smiled over the top of her glass at Snow Deer, her heart aching almost as much as when she had been told that she was dying of consumption.

She gazed over at Charles.

Their eyes met and held for a moment, then a sob lodged in her throat when she saw him look quickly away.

For a moment she thought that she had seen something in his eyes that she could remember seeing when they were teenagers out horseback riding.

She had thought then that he might love her as she loved him, but neither had spoken of such a love to the other.

Their feelings would remain silent now as well.

Chapter Thirty

Their stay at Elissa's house had lasted longer than originally planned and it was almost dusk when Snow Deer saw the outskirts of her Cheyenne village a short distance away. Her heart began to beat like wild thunder inside her chest. She was happy being married to Charles, but a part of her would always long to still be a Cheyenne princess, living among her people.

She had learned what sacrifice was when she left her people. But she had accepted her new world with an exuberance that she knew pleased her husband.

As Charles led the horse and buggy closer to the village, Snow Deer anxiously strained her neck to see it better. From this vantage point, she could see that the communal evening fire had been kindled, for its smoke mingled with the swirling gray columns rising from the lodges.

She could see that from all quarters of the village women were hurrying down to the river, or coming from it, with their supplies of water for the night.

Horses were being brought from the pastures to the village for safekeeping in the long corral that spread out behind the lodges.

She could hear the Old Crier riding around the village, shouting out to the people the commands of the chief, and giving them notice of what was planned for tomorrow.

"It is so good to hear the Old Crier," Snow Deer said, smiling at Charles. "His voice is like no other's. As a child, I was awakened so often to his voice. He is elderly and can hardly mount a horse anymore, yet he does not give up his duties to his chief because of age."

"Your father seems to be the sort of man who radiates great kindness toward his people. I can understand why the Old Crier is still loyal to him," Charles said. "Although he did not show too much kindness toward me when he knew of my intentions toward you."

"His frown bespoke his fear of losing me," Snow Deer said, reaching over to take one of Charles's hands. "Losing me to the *white* world, Charles. But as you know, he has since accepted my choice of husband. He *is* kind toward you. You shall see it in how he greets your return as you bring his daughter back to him, if only for a short visit."

"I wonder if your mother has had her child yet?" Charles asked, his eyes narrowing when he saw how that question put a quick look of hurt in his wife's eyes.

"I'm sorry, Snow Deer, for reminding you of something that pains you," he said. "But you will soon learn why your mother chose not to tell you

313

about the pregnancy. She surely had a good reason not to."

"Becky has always been so caring toward me," Snow Deer said, sighing. "She and I were like true mother and daughter. I doubt, while I lived among my people, that she ever kept any secret from me."

She swallowed hard. "And now this." She slowly shook her head back and forth. "No, I can't understand why. And I must not show her that I am hurt by her silence."

She sighed. "Yet I do not hide my hurt all that easily."

"You will do just fine," Charles said. They were now so close to the village that he could see the diffused glow of the fires showing through the skins of the lodges.

Beyond the cone-shaped lodges, everything was quiet in the shadows of evening.

Then something broke through the silence.

Hearing the haunting sound of a flute being played from somewhere in the hidden shadows of dusk, Snow Deer looked quickly at Charles.

"We have new lovers in my village," she murmured. "Do you hear how the brave is playing his love flute up on some hillside? How softly and mournfully he plays? As the flute lifts its thin cry into the sky, rising and falling in the breeze, does it not sound like a sad-winged bird?"

"Well, I'm not sure that is how I would describe it, but yes, it is hauntingly lovely," Charles said, nodding. His eyes twinkled as he caught Snow Deer still looking at him. "What are you thinking, beautiful wife?"

"That perhaps you might want to make a flute and play it for me sometime," she confessed. "Although a lover plays his flute before the woman marries him, would not it be nice to pretend you are playing a flute to woo me into your bed?"

Charles didn't get the chance to answer her. Beneath the soft rays of the moon, he saw many warriors leaving on their mighty steeds from the village, the rifles clutched in their hands gleaming in the moonlight.

"They do not know it is friends approaching," Snow Deer said, watching the approach of the horsemen. "They do not know it is I, their princess, come home for a visit!"

"Lord, I didn't know they met intruders in the night with weapons," Charles said, drawing a tight rein.

"Perhaps my people have been troubled by those who wish evil on them," Snow Deer said, her pulse racing when she recognized who was leading the warriors toward them. Her father! Her beloved father!

Under Charles's loud protests, Snow Deer leapt from the buggy and ran toward the approaching horses. "Father!" she cried, waving her hands in the air. "It is I! It is Snow Deer!"

Her voice traveled to Blazing Eagle. His eyes widened and his heart skipped a happy beat when he recognized his daughter in her full Cheyenne attire, running toward him.

"It is my daughter!" he cried, sliding his rifle quickly into its gun boot. "It is Snow Deer! She has answered my wife's bidding! She has come home to us after all!"

He rode onward, then drew his horse to a halt when he came up beside Snow Deer. He leaned down and grabbed her up onto his lap and fiercely hugged her.

"Daughter," Blazing Eagle said, his voice breaking. "Snow Deer, it really is you."

"Father, there was no time to send word that I

was coming," she said, reveling in the feel of her father's muscled arms and the familiar scent of his skin as she placed her cheek against his thick neck. "Father, I have so missed you. I had to come."

They embraced for a while longer; then, when Charles rode up beside them, Snow Deer eased from her father's arms and smiled at her husband. "It is Father, Charles," she said, beaming. She swallowed back a lump of happiness.

Charles nodded, then extended a hand to Blazing Eagle. "It's good to see you again," he said, his voice drawn as Blazing Eagle's eyes narrowed into his.

Charles could still see some resentment in the depths of the Cheyenne's eyes and doubted that Blazing Eagle would ever totally accept him.

"You are a kind man to bring my daughter to her father for a visit," Blazing Eagle said, accepting the hand of friendship. He circled his fingers around Charles's. "Come. Many besides her father will be happy to see my daughter."

Charles nodded again and slid his hand away. Then he felt a sinking sensation as he watched Blazing Eagle wheel his horse around and ride away with Snow Deer still on his lap.

"Lord, I feel as though I've lost her again to her people," he whispered to himself.

He was determined not to allow that to happen. His jaw tight, he snapped his reins and followed the procession of Indians to the village.

Having drawn a tight rein in front of Blazing Eagle's large lodge, he watched for a while longer before leaving the buggy, as the people rushed from their tepees, shouting, some sobbing with relief at seeing Snow Deer, and many clinging to her.

He scarcely breathed when he saw Snow Deer's mother come slowly from her lodge. She was so swollen with child, she could barely walk.

Her hands on the small of her back, each step an effort, Becky stopped and waited for Snow Deer to break away from her people. She knew to expect quite a shock from her daughter when she saw her condition. She now felt guilty for not warning her first.

When Snow Deer saw Becky standing there, so swollen with child, so pale and drawn from the pregnancy, she paled herself, for she knew that her mother might be in danger from having a child at such a late age in life.

But quickly her resentment, her hurt, were gone, as though a wind had come along and swept them away.

She broke through the crowd and ran to Becky. She eased into her arms and hugged her. "Mother," she said, her voice breaking. "Oh, mother, are you all right? You . . . you are so pale. You look so tired!"

Becky was surprised that Snow Deer did not show more surprise at seeing her pregnant! It was as though she already knew. Perhaps *that* was the reason she had suddenly decided to return home just prior to Becky's time of giving birth! Becky was relieved that her daughter held no harsh feelings over not having been told about the child!

"I'm fine," Becky said, gently caressing Snow Deer's back through her buckskin dress. "And you?"

Snow Deer slipped from her mother's embrace. "Mother, this is no time for you to be concerned over *me*," she said. She took Becky by her elbow and slowly ushered her back inside the tepee. "I

317

want you to get off your feet. We can talk by your lodge fire."

Just before she stepped inside the lodge, Snow Deer looked over her shoulder at Charles, who was now standing beside his buggy, surrounded by her people who, with her father, were greeting him in the cordial fashion of the Cheyenne.

She exchanged a smile with her husband, then went inside with Becky.

"Please sit down, Mother," Snow Deer said, leading Becky to a backrest.

But Becky shook her head. Instead, she went to the back of the lodge.

Groaning, she sat down on a pallet of furs before a trunk.

"Snow Deer, come here for a moment," she said, slowly lifting the lid of the trunk. "I've something for you."

"What, Mother?" Snow Deer asked, settling down on her knees beside Becky. Her eyes widened when her mother lifted a beautiful necklace from inside the trunk.

"Snow Deer, your father gave me this necklace when we were first married," Becky said. She spread the necklace out between her fingers so that Snow Deer could see its lovely design. "It is called a squash blossom necklace. The necklace represents fertility. Whoever wears it will be blessed with many children."

"Yes, I remember you wearing it," Snow Deer said, taking it as Becky handed it to her. "I remember you telling me that this necklace has been handed down from generation to generation, the first-born daughter of the family always receiving it as hers."

"Yes, and so now it is yours," Becky said, placing a gentle hand on Snow Deer's cheek. "Wear it.

You will then have many children."

Snow Deer's eyes widened. "Truly?" she said. "You think I will become pregnant if I wear the necklace?"

"Yes. Let me slip it over your head now," Becky said. She leaned closer to Snow Deer and took the necklace. With tears in her eyes, she slowly slid it over her daughter's head.

Then she arranged each of the silver flowers, with their turquoise settings, so that they lay against her daughter's chest.

"But, mother, I do not understand why you think this necklace will bring many children into my life when . . . when until now, you had only one child," Snow Deer said guardedly.

"I purposely avoided wearing it again until recently," Becky said softly. "I have hungered for so long for a child, but as you know, I feared becoming pregnant again. Burning Snow has had much to face in life because of her affliction. I felt it unfair to cause another child such pain."

Becky swallowed hard and lowered her eyes. "I have been so wrong," she murmured. "Burning Snow has been nothing but a blessing."

Snow Deer scooted over and twined her arms around Becky's neck. She hugged her. "Mother, I am so happy for you, that you have chosen to have another child," she murmured.

Then she leaned away from her. "But you do look so worn out, so—so drained of energy," she said guardedly.

"Pregnancy does that to you whether you are young or middle-aged," Becky said, laughing throatily.

Then Becky turned somber. "Are you hurt, darling, over my keeping my pregnancy from you?" she asked, her voice wary.

Snow Deer's eyes widened, and then she lowered them. "At first, when Rain Feather told me, I . . . I was deeply hurt," she said, then stopped when she heard Becky's deep gasp.

"How did you hear this from Rain Feather?" Becky asked, paling. "When?"

"He came to Illinois to have council with another Shawnee chief," Snow Deer said. "He searched and found me. He came for a short visit, and while there, he told me of your pregnancy."

"Did he cause you any trouble . . . besides telling you, something that caused pain inside your heart?"

"No. He came and left as a friend."

"Thank goodness." Becky sighed and reached a gentle hand to Snow Deer's arm. "He is a friend of our people, yet I still can't trust him. He seems so sneaky—so untrustworthy." Her jaw tightened. "Like *this*. He had no right to interfere in private family business."

"Mother, you send frequent letters to Illinois— why did you not confide in me about your pregnancy?" Snow Deer blurted out, the hurt there again, gnawing at her insides.

"Darling Snow Deer," Becky said, taking both of Snow Deer's hands, gently holding them. "I knew of your struggle to have children. I just could not brag to you about my pregnancy, when . . . when I knew you were still barren. Tell me you understand."

"I knew there had to be such a reason as that," Snow Deer said, sighing heavily. "And, yes, now that I know, I do understand."

"I had hoped that by the time we saw each other again, you would have had a child and I could then show you mine without causing pain in your heart," Becky said softly. "I was going to mail the necklace to you soon, darling. I was going to urge you to wear it."

Snow Deer's fingers went to the necklace. She felt the turquoise stones in each of the silver blossoms. She looked anxiously at Becky. "Do you truly believe it will work?" she asked.

Becky stroked her large belly with both hands. "It worked twice for me. So shall it work for you, as many times as you wish," she said. "Wear it whenever you wish to have a child. Like magic, the seed seems to jump inside the womb and start growing."

"I want many children," Snow Deer said, beaming. "Charles will be a wonderful father."

"Oh, darling, my child has just begun its nightly kicking," Becky said, giggling. She reached for one of Snow Deer's hands. "Darling, feel it. Isn't it a miracle?"

Snow Deer splayed her fingers across Becky's stomach. When she felt the rolling movement against her palm, and then felt something like a kicking against it, she smiled widely. "Yes, it is a miracle," she murmured.

"Snow Deer!"

The sweet voice of Snow Deer's sister behind her caused Snow Deer to turn with a start. She jumped to her feet and ran to Burning Snow and caught her in her arms as Burning Snow leapt toward her.

"Sister, sister," Burning Snow cried. "Is it truly you?"

"Yes," Snow Deer said, laughing softly as the child clung to her. "It is I."

"I was playing at the far side of the village when the Old Crier came by on his horse announcing your arrival," Burning Snow said, her eyes filled with delight as she drew away from Snow Deer and smiled at her. "I could not believe my ears!"

"Your ears heard right," Snow Deer said, turning to Becky when she came and stood beside her.

"Did you see Mother?" Burning Snow said, giggling as she turned to Becky. "Her tummy is so heavy, she can hardly move."

"Yes, heavy with child," Snow Deer said softly. She placed a hand on her sister's shoulder. "How do you feel about the child? About soon being a sister again?"

"I think it is the most wonderful thing in the world," Burning Snow said, beaming.

Tears came to Becky's eyes as Snow Deer gazed at her and smiled.

Chapter Thirty-One

Charles awakened slowly.

His eyes widened when he suddenly remembered where he was. He looked overhead and saw the morning light pouring through the smoke hole at the top of the tepee.

He gazed at the fire pit. He was surprised to see a fire, which meant that someone had come into the lodge and started the morning fire while he and Snow Deer slept.

He looked slowly around him, recalling last evening. Charles and Snow Deer had been brought to a newly married couple's tepee for their night's lodging.

Snow Deer had explained to Charles that it was an old Cheyenne custom for visitors to occupy the lodge of some newly married couple who would then sleep elsewhere. She had told him that this was an honor not only to the owners of the lodge but also to the visitor.

After settling in on blankets beside the lodge fire, Snow Deer and Charles had talked almost the entire night, laughing and embracing.

But they had not made love, thinking it would not be appropriate in someone else's lodge, on someone else's blankets.

Charles leaned up on one elbow and gazed over at Snow Deer. His love for her made him feel warm and mellow inside.

And, ah, how he enjoyed seeing her sleeping. She was, indeed, a princess in her loveliness and sweetness as her thick lashes veiled her copper cheeks, her lips slightly parted.

"Do you know just how beautiful you are?" he whispered. He gently stroked one of her cheeks with a thumb. "Darling, darling . . ."

His gaze lowered and his fingers went to the lovely necklace that she had worn to bed. Beneath the soft light of the fire, the turquoise settings shone like the southern sun.

Snow Deer had told Charles that she would not remove it, not even while bathing, until she became pregnant.

"Believe in your dreams, my darling," he whispered. "I shall also, for you."

When she smiled in her sleep, as though she had heard what he said, he recalled the last evening and how at peace she seemed while sitting among her family, eagerly chatting and sharing with them her experiences in her new world.

He had so enjoyed seeing her this contentedly happy.

He was glad that he had brought her home to spend needed time with her family. He was afraid that her longing to be with them might have built up inside her into something savage, had he not brought her.

The sound of women singing wafted through the skins of the lodge, reminding Charles of what Snow Deer's mother had planned for early this morning, even before breakfast. Snow Deer's mother belonged to one of the most important Cheyenne women's associations, called the quilling society, or *Meenoistst* in the Cheyenne language.

The women who belonged to this society created ceremonial decorations by sewing quills on robes, lodge coverings, and other things made of the skins of animals.

Snow Deer had told Charles that the Cheyenne women considered this work of high importance, and when properly performed, it was quite as much respected as were bravery and success in war among the men.

"Husband?" Snow Deer said, drawing his eyes to her as she sat up beside him, pulling a warm blanket around her shoulders. "The singing awakened me. Did it also wake you?"

"No, I was awake before it began," Charles said. He sat up beside her and reached for her. She snuggled into his embrace.

"Wife, I have enjoyed watching you sleep," Charles said huskily.

"Charles, how could you enjoy seeing me look such a sight as this?" Snow Deer said, giggling. "My hair is tangled and my lips are dry." She ran her tongue around the inside of her mouth. "I feel as though I have eaten cotton in my sleep."

"You look beautiful no matter the hour of day or night," Charles said. He looked at the entrance flap as the songs continued from somewhere not far away.

"I can hear Mother's voice above the others," Snow Deer said, following his gaze.

"I'm glad that you no longer feel slighted over her not telling you about her pregnancy," he said.

"I feel ashamed for allowing myself to be jealous over her pregnancy," Snow Deer said, lowering her eyes. Her hands went to the necklace. "I was, you know. I was . . . jealous."

"I would say that is only natural, since you have been wanting to have a child for so long yourself," Charles said, brushing a soft kiss across her lips.

When the songs stopped, Snow Deer looked quickly up at Charles. "You had best get dressed," she murmured. "Mother will soon come for you."

"I'm somewhat uneasy over the coming ceremony," Charles said, rising. He went to his travel bag and took out a clean pair of denim breeches and a shirt. "But I am touched that she wants to do this for me."

Snow Deer rose and picked up a dress that her mother had brought to her the previous evening, as well as many others. They were the clothes that Snow Deer had left behind when she left to find Charles.

This particular dress had always been one of her favorites. White as snow, it was made of antelope skin. Her leggings were of deerskin, heavily beaded and nicely fringed. Her moccasins were of deerskin and worked with porcupine quills.

She had made all of these things herself, on the long, cold nights of winter before she even knew such a man as Charles existed.

"Are you certain you can't accompany me to the quilling lodge?" Charles asked, buttoning the last button on his shirt.

"The ceremony is solely for you," Snow Deer said, slipping the dress over her head. "Only mother and the women who belong to the quilling society will be there."

She went to Charles and twined her arms around his neck. "What my mother is doing is quite an honor for you," she murmured. "It proves her total acceptance of you. The robe she has sewn for you these past months, while too awkward in her pregnancy to do much else but sew, will be something you can cherish forever. When you wear it, you can think of mother *and* my people, and how much they have grown to love you."

"But how could they love me?" Charles said, arching an eyebrow. "They don't even truly know me."

"Through me they love you," Snow Deer said, her eyes filled with adoration as she gazed into his.

"Charles?" Becky said from outside the entrance flap. "Snow Deer? Are you and Charles awake? It is time for the ceremony."

"Yes, Mother, we are awake," Snow Deer answered back.

Charles's pulse began to race.

He swallowed hard.

"Snow Deer, surely your mother would understand if you went with me," he said hesitantly. "I . . . I . . ."

Snow Deer placed a finger to his lips, sealing his words behind them. "Darling husband, my place is not with you this morning," she said, interrupting him. "But I shall be waiting for you once the ceremony is over. I am eager to see the robe my mother made for you. I know it will be beautiful. Did you know that she has made thirty robes of quill since her marriage to Father?"

Charles's eyes widened. "She has honored that many people with a robe in a ceremony such as will be performed for me today?" he asked.

"No," Snow Deer said, laughing softly. "Most were made to prove she was worthy of being a member of the quilling society. I believe you are the first to be honored by her with the gift of a robe."

"Not even your father has one?" Charles asked.

"Father owns one, but you see, this one today is the first robe since she has been accepted into the society that she has made to give away as a gift. While making it, her thoughts were on you . . . only you."

"I do feel honored," Charles said, squaring his shoulders proudly.

"Then go with Mother and show your pride to her when she gives the robe to you," Snow Deer said.

She took him by an elbow and ushered him toward the entrance flap. Just before he stepped outside, she stopped him and stood on tiptoe to kiss him.

"I shall be in my parents' lodge waiting for you," she whispered.

He kissed her, gazed down at her for a moment longer, and then left the lodge.

Becky took his hand and walked slowly with him toward the quilling society lodge at the far side of the village, away from the others.

His heart pounding, unable to shake off his apprehensions, Charles gazed at the ceremonial lodge. This lodge was not made of buckskin like the other dwellings in the village. From the outside it appeared to be a cabin similar to the one in which Charles and Snow Deer made their residence.

Once inside, he saw the difference between this cabin and his. There were no boards for flooring. The ground was the floor. And there was only one large room.

Nervous about the ceremony as he had approached the cabin, he had not noticed the smoke hole in the roof, nor the smoke spiraling from it.

But now that he was inside, he saw a fire pit far back in the floor, where soft flames licked around several logs.

Sitting back from the fire, along the side of the room, were many Cheyenne women, their friendly eyes on him.

"Come with me," Becky whispered.

She led Charles past the women. "Turn to the right," she softly instructed. "Walk around the edge of the room, to the back of the cabin. You will see a robe spread out on the floor. Charles, that is the robe I made for you. You will sit down on it. I shall sit beside you on the floor."

When Charles reached the outstretched robe, he saw its loveliness and was touched to the very core of his being by the hours it must have taken Becky to make it for him. The robe was embellished with many porcupine quills, dyed various colors, all of which were bright and gay. He knew that each quill had been softened and colored by Becky, then sewn, one by one, onto the leather.

Becky was lost in memory, thinking back to the time when she had approached the quilling society, requesting instructions on how to become a part of it.

She had been taken to one of the elder quillers of the village, who belonged to the society. The old quiller had asked Becky if she was pledging herself to the ornamenting of robes and other objects for her people. Becky had said that she was.

After receiving a gift of a quilled backrest that Becky had made just for her, the old woman had asked her to stand beside her by the lodge fire.

The old quiller had then asked Becky to hold her hands out in front of her, palms up and edges together. The old woman bit off a piece of a certain root, chewed it fine, and spat it on Becky's hands. Becky was then instructed in ceremonial motions, passing her right hand over the outside of her right leg, from ankle to hip, her left hand over her right arm from wrist to shoulder, her left hand over her left leg, from ankle to hip, and her right hand over the left arm, from wrist to shoulder.

Then her hands had been placed on her head and passed backward from the forehead.

Becky had then been told that she would be expected to give a feast. She must choose which section of the society she wanted to ask to the feast—those who ornamented lodge linings, backrests, robes, sacks, or stars for lodges.

She chose to ask the women who quilled robes to her feast, for that was where her main interest lay.

After she had been instructed as to these things, she had asked the crier to go out and announce the feast.

"What do I do now?" Charles whispered, drawing Becky out of her reverie.

She saw that he had done as he was told. He was sitting in the middle of the robe.

She sat down beside him on the earthen floor. "Charles, draw the robe up over your shoulders," Becky murmured.

He nodded and did as he was told, made somewhat self-conscious by his audience of women as they stared at his each and every movement.

One of the women came to Becky with wooden tongs. She handed the tongs to Becky and returned to sit among the other women again.

Becky used the tongs to pluck a hot coal from the lodge fire. She placed it on the ground in front of Charles just inches from the edge of the robe.

Then she slid her hand inside her front dress pocket and pulled out a handful of sweet grass.

Charles watched as she sprinkled the sweet grass on the hot coals; the grass soon sent slow spirals of smoke upward as it began to catch fire.

"Charles, with your robe over your shoulders, now bend forward over the coal and sweet grass and let the smoke rise within the robe and cover your body," Becky said softly. "This is to give you a good heart—to make you feel happy. This good heart and happiness, too, is my gift to you."

Charles smiled at her, then did as he was told. The smoke smelled acidy-sweet as it bathed his face and rose up his nostrils.

"That is enough," Becky said, plucking the coal up again with the tongs and returning it to the fire.

Charles lowered his robe.

He scarcely breathed as he waited for the next part of the ceremony.

His eyes widened when Becky reached for his hand.

"You can leave now," she murmured. "The ceremony is completed. The robe is now yours. When you wear it, know that it was made for you out of love and deep gratitude for caring so deeply for my daughter."

Surprised by the simplicity of the ceremony, yet glad to know that it was over, Charles smiled at Becky. "Thank you," he said.

He clutched the robe around his shoulders as he rose from the floor and waited for her to walk with him to the door. When she instead sat down among the other women, her eyes smiling at him as she silently said a good-bye to him, he went out alone.

Charles felt lighthearted and happy as he stepped out into the sunshine. His steps were hurried as he went to Blazing Eagle's lodge.

Inside, he found Snow Deer sitting with her father and sister on mats spread out on the floor beside the lodge fire. Platters, piled high with food, sat before them on the floor. It was obvious that they were waiting for him before partaking of the morning meal.

When Snow Deer turned her head and saw him standing there, she leapt up and ran to him.

She stopped and clasped her hands before her as she gazed at the beautiful robe, then looked up at Charles.

No words were needed at this time to describe how he felt about his gift. Snow Deer saw it in her husband's eyes.

"You seem pleased enough," Blazing Eagle said, breaking the silence in the room. His gaze swept over the robe. In his mind's eye he recalled so many evenings when he had sat and watched his wife's hands busy at work placing the quills on the leather.

Yes, it was a labor of love.

And he was glad to see that it was accepted in the same manner.

"I will guard it with my life," Charles said, smiling as he again gazed down at the robe.

Snow Deer took his hand and led him over beside the fire. She yanked on his hand as she sat down, urging him to sit beside her.

Charles removed the robe, carefully folded it, and laid it on the floor behind him as he sat down.

"And so you have today seen the importance of Cheyenne ceremonies," Blazing Eagle said, handing Charles a wooden platter for his food. "I can see by your eyes that not only are you pleased with the robe, but also by the way in which it was given to you. That is good. It is important that you participate in the customs of your wife's people. As I hope to one day come to your lodge and witness your ways of doing things."

"It would greatly please me to have you as a guest," Charles said, watching as Snow Deer piled his platter high with meat and fruit. There were also boiled eggs, which he thought must be turtle's eggs, from their size.

"After my wife has her child, and the child and its mother are strong enough for travel, yes, we shall come to Illinois and have family council with you," Blazing Eagle said.

He lifted a piece of venison to his mouth, took a generous bite, and began to chew while watching Snow Deer cater to her husband dutifully as she poured him a cup of coffee and handed it to him.

Feeling Blazing Eagle's eyes on him, Charles looked quickly over at him. "I shall draw you a map so that you know how to reach Bloomfield after you cross the Ohio River," he said, nodding. "It isn't that hard to find."

Blazing Eagle nodded.

His gaze then went to Snow Deer. "And, daughter, I see you are wearing the necklace of your ancestors today," he said. He broke off a small piece of apple and slipped it between his lips.

"Yes, and I feel blessed to have it," Snow Deer said, reaching her hand up to it, touching the turquoise stones.

"You will have a daughter," Blazing Eagle said, his voice serious. "When she is older, you will give her the necklace with your blessing. You will explain its meaning to her, as your mother explained it to you. She will wear it as eagerly as you are wearing it."

"Yes, I shall have a daughter one day," Snow

Deer said, now confident that she *would* have children. She would have daughters *and* sons! "I shall gladly give her the necklace so that she will give me and Charles grandchildren."

"It would be good to have great-grandchildren," Blazing Eagle said, smiling.

Then his smile faded. "You said last evening that you must start your return journey to Illinois today," he said. "Daughter, I would like for you to stay just one more day. There is a surprise I wish to share with you on the morrow."

"Surprise?" Snow Deer said.

She saw a pleasant gleam in her father's eyes, knowing that whatever he was talking about would be something wonderful.

That was the way of her father!

"*Huh*, a surprise, but I will not speak further of it, or it will not be a surprise, will it?" he said, chuckling.

Charles sat silently by, watching. He enjoyed seeing the love between this father and daughter. There was such a devotion between them, he knew how hard it must be for them to be separated.

"Can I have a surprise also?" Burning Snow suddenly blurted out, having been silent until now as she had sat politely listening and eating.

"Yes, also you," Blazing Eagle said, reaching over to stroke his younger daughter's thick black hair. "Tomorrow will be a good day for all our family."

Chapter Thirty-Two

The next day, the whole day long, Snow Deer waited patiently to see what the surprise was that her father had told her about. When she questioned him just after the noon meal, he asked her to be patient. He told her that later, as the sun began to set in the sky, the surprise would be revealed to her.

She spent the day talking to old friends while Charles went horseback riding with her father.

Yet while visiting her friends, she became concerned about Becky. She had looked very drawn today. She walked much more slowly. She talked little. She spent more time in her bed than out of it.

When Snow Deer had shown concern for Becky, she had been told to go on and enjoy her last day with her friends. Visits were scarce now.

While sitting with her friends later in the afternoon beneath the shade of an old oak, Snow Deer began to notice a change in the village. The older women were scurrying about, laughing and chatting amongst themselves while piling huge logs in the center of the village for the usual evening communal fire. Yet this time it was much larger, the size of a fire made for a special celebration.

After the big fire was built, shooting its vivid red sparks into the heavens, and then dying down to searing hot coals, whole sides of meat were placed on iron racks over the fire.

Snow Deer watched as drums were set up several yards from the cooking fire, the children gathering around them, taking turns pounding on them with long sticks with knots of buckskin tied at one end.

Then Snow Deer saw Charles and her father return from their ride. Her breath caught in her throat when she saw that they weren't alone. She could hardly believe her eyes when she saw the arrival of many of her relatives and family friends whom she had not seen for years. It was apparent now that her father and husband had not gone riding for the sake of riding alone. They had apparently gone and met the ferry to greet everyone and guide them back to the village.

Her heart beat rapidly within her chest as she rose quickly to her feet and began running toward those who were arriving in their separate horse and buggies.

Her eyes darted from one to the other—to her Uncle Edward and his wife Marilyn, who had traveled from St. Louis.

To Judge Newman and his wife, Waterfall, who had arrived from Boston.

And to Fish Hawk, her father's best friend from childhood, and his wife, White Water, who had traveled from as far as Wyoming to be here on this special day of renewed acquaintances.

When she reached them, and they were out of their buggies, she did not know whom to greet first. She was happy to see them all.

One by one, she hugged them, then stepped back and stood beside Charles. Beaming, she smiled up at him as he slid his arm around her waist.

"Did Father introduce you to everyone?" she asked.

"Yes, as each got off the ferry," Charles said. He enjoyed being a part of this gathering, where family ties seemed so strong and sincere. It reminded him of his own family, though it was small compared to Snow Deer's.

Blazing Eagle went and helped Becky from her bed. With an arm supporting her around her waist, he led her out to greet everyone.

Hugs and tears of joy were shared, and through it all, Snow Deer was just beginning to wonder how all of this had come about—that everyone would arrive while she was there.

It could not be for her that they had arrived, for their journeys had taken too long for them to have received word from Becky that she was there for a short visit.

No, they had come for another reason.

And as they still hugged and clustered around Becky, it came to Snow Deer just why they *were* there. It was to see Blazing Eagle and Becky's child, for it was due any day now.

Snow Deer looked at Charles. "It touches my heart so to see everyone here for Becky," she said, sniffling as tears flowed from her eyes. She flicked the tears aside with a forefinger.

"Yes, I was told they had come to share the excitement of having a new baby in your family,"

Charles said. "They met at an inn just across the river in Illinois. They spent the night, then left for the ferry the next morning. The letter you received from Becky, in which she asked you to come to the village was meant for us to be here as the others arrived."

"I wish she had told us that," Snow Deer said softly.

"But aren't you feeling better about things now, Snow Deer?"

"Yes, I suppose," Snow Deer murmured. Then she smiled brightly up at Charles. "Yes, I *am*."

Charles's gaze shifted when the wonderful fragrance of the meat cooking over the hot coals wafted to his nose. He saw that the meat was almost cooked. Also he saw many of the women placing huge platters of assortments of other foods on blankets on the ground.

"This is to be a wonderful night for everyone," Snow Deer said, also watching things being readied for the feast.

She looked past that and saw several young men and women congregating in the shadows, all of whom were dressed in fancy dance attire.

She then looked at the drums. Those who were in charge of the drums no longer allowed the children to touch them. They were standing over them, beating out a steady, rhythmic song with their sticks. Several men with rattles stood beside them, also playing their music in time with the drumbeats.

As the sun went behind the distant hills, and darkness settled down over the village, the bright firelight shone through the yellow lodge skins. Sparks came from each smoke hole.

But everyone settled down around the outside fire.

Laughing and talking, they shared the feast and the music.

Afterward, weaving dancers circled about the fire, their feet thumping the ground in time with the drumming.

"It seems like such a time of magic," Snow Deer whispered to Charles. She looked from one relative to the other. "And, Charles, it seems as though *Maheo* led me here at this time for a purpose. To be reunited with loved ones."

Snow Deer became lost in thought and felt a little sad at the thought of Whistling Elk not being there with his wife and child. But he had good reason. She had been told that Whistling Elk's wife was having trouble with her second pregnancy. She was not allowed to travel. And feeling that she needed him there, Whistling Elk stayed with his wife instead of joining his friends and family at this special time in their lives.

Snow Deer was trying to understand, yet wished with all of her heart that her brother had thought more of their family than this. Surely his wife would have been all right for one evening without him.

Charles's attention had been diverted. He had seen how Becky occasionally winced and grew pale as she placed her hands on the large ball of her abdomen. He had seen how a woman's labor pains could come on quickly. One day, while attending Sunday services in the Baptist church, he had been distracted from the sermon as a very pregnant lady had begun to look uncomfortable in her pew. She had behaved the very same way Becky was behaving now.

"Charles, what is it?" Snow Deer whispered, noticing how his eyes were intently on something. She followed his gaze. She covered her mouth

with a hand and gasped softly when she saw
Becky grab at her stomach, then emit a soft cry of
pain.

Blazing Eagle looked quickly at his wife. "Is it
time?" he asked, seeing how she clutched at her
abdomen.

"The excitement has brought on the labor
pains," Becky said, smiling through her pain up at
her husband. "Husband, take me to our lodge."

As he helped her to her feet, she saw that the
women of the village had already seen that they
would soon be needed, especially Pretty Face, Becky's dear friend, who still stayed away from her
Shawnee husband's village to be with Becky.

Several women rushed to their lodges and
grabbed their water jugs and went to the river for
fresh water.

Others scurried ahead of Blazing Eagle and
Becky and prepared her bed with fresh white
cloths.

Snow Deer rushed to her feet and started to run
to her parents, but Charles grabbed her hand and
stopped her.

"I believe we'd best stay out of the way," he said.

Burning Snow ran to Snow Deer and grabbed
her by a hand. "Mother is going to have her baby?"
she asked, eyes wide as she peered up at Snow
Deer.

"Yes, soon," Snow Deer said, watching Becky
disappear inside her lodge.

"Can we help her?" Burning Snow asked, peering intensely at the lodge. Then she turned anxious eyes up at Snow Deer. "Can we, Snow Deer?
Can we help her?"

"No, this is not the time for you or I to be in our
parents' lodge," Snow Deer said. She bent down
to her knees and drew Burning Snow into her em-

brace. She hugged her. "Sweet sister, soon we both will be sisters again."

"Will the baby be a girl baby?" Burning Snow asked.

"Which would you prefer, a brother or sister?" Snow Deer asked, watching the lodge and the women scurrying to and from it.

She then watched her father as he came from the tepee to start pacing. She knew that it was the custom that a man could not be at his wife's bedside when the child was being born.

She watched as Charles went to him and stood with him, their heads close together as they talked.

She watched as her Uncle Edward, Judge Newman, and Fish Hawk clustered about them, entering the conversation.

Snow Deer rose to her full height again when Marilyn, Waterfall, and White Water came to her. They all hugged again, then sat down on blankets beside the fire, their eyes occasionally glancing at Becky's tepee as they talked about their lives and their happiness.

"Are you content to live away from your people, Snow Deer?" Waterfall asked softly.

"I am content anywhere as long as I am with Charles," Snow Deer said, then gazed at Waterfall. "And you? Do you enjoy living in the large city called Boston?"

"Its largeness is what I do not like," Waterfall said. "But I have such pride in my husband. I watch him perform his duties as judge and know I could never wish to be anywhere but with him."

"And you, White Water?" Snow Deer said, reaching a hand over to take one of White Water's. "Are you happy in Wyoming?"

White Water frowned. She lowered her eyes.

Then a look of utter despair came across her lovely face. "I do not like Wyoming," she said, her voice breaking. "Indians are not respected. Fish Hawk and I . . . we have come close to being slain many times by whites who do not want us to have land of our own." She swallowed hard. "I even fear that while we are gone, the whites will come and burn down our cabin."

"How horrible," Snow Deer gasped, paling. "Why do you stay?"

"Because that is now our home. We have labored hard to make it what we want it to be," White Water said, defiantly lifting her chin. "We shall never give up our home or land to whites."

"What if they *do* burn your cabin while you are gone?" Waterfall asked guardedly.

White Water's eyes leapt with an instant anger. "We shall then build again," she said. The catch in her voice revealed her true feelings, her true fears.

Snow Deer was saddened by White Water and Fish Hawk's plight, yet her thoughts were drawn away from her sadness when she heard the sound of a baby's cries filling the moonlit night.

"The child!" Snow Deer said, rushing to her feet. "Mother has given birth to her child!"

Burning Snow ran ahead of Snow Deer. She didn't stop before rushing into the lodge, her father just ahead of her. Snow Deer stayed outside beside Charles, waiting to be invited in, yet she could hardly bear the waiting.

"It is a boy!" she heard her father say, pride deep in his voice.

He came from the lodge carrying the small, naked baby. He held it up for everyone to see as they gathered in thick clusters about him.

"My *naha*,—my son!" Blazing Eagle cried. "My son Running Elk!"

Snow Deer eased up next to her father. "Oh, Father, let me see," she murmured, melting inside when he placed her brother into her waiting arms.

Unlike herself and Burning Snow, she saw that this child had light skin, yet his other features were Cheyenne. He had dark eyes, a dark shock of hair, high cheekbones, and a prominent nose!

"He's beautiful," Charles said, bending low to take a closer look. He touched the baby's face. "Lord, he's so soft."

"I can hardly wait to hold my own child," Snow Deer said, slowly rocking her brother back and forth in her arms. "Running Elk. I love the name."

As the members of her family pressed close, Snow Deer had no choice but to relinquish her brother to other arms.

She watched the child being fussed over, then turned to her father. "Can I go and see Mother now?" she asked softly.

"Yes, both you and Charles can go inside," Blazing Eagle said, placing a hand on each of their shoulders. "She should be ready for visitors now."

As Snow Deer and Charles entered the lodge, Pretty Face and the other women who had assisted in the birth brushed against them as they left, their hands filled with basins of water and blood-soaked cloths.

Snow Deer stopped and gazed at the bloody cloths. She paled. She could not help but worry about Becky having lost so much blood.

"Darling, that is ordinary when a child is born," Charles said, thinking she might be concerned over it.

An involuntary shiver went through Snow Deer. "I want a child, yet I fear losing blood while doing it," she murmured. "It is a frightening thought."

"Women give birth every day and lose blood and

live to tell about it," Charles said, reassuring her. He took her by the elbow and walked her out of the shadows, over to where Becky lay on blankets close beside the fire.

Becky's eyes were filled with a peaceful bliss as she gazed up at Charles and Snow Deer.

"Did you see and hold your brother?" Becky asked, reaching for one of Snow Deer's hands. She twined her fingers through hers.

"Yes, I saw and held him," Snow Deer said, glad to see Becky's cheeks filled with color, whereas earlier today she had been so pale. "He is adorable, Mother. So adorable."

"Do you like his name?" Becky asked, looking from Charles to Snow Deer.

"Yes, it's quite beautiful," Charles said, almost in unison with Snow Deer as she also answered.

"The perfect name for a young brave who will one day be a leader of his people," Becky said, sighing.

When Becky's eyes drifted closed, Snow Deer nodded at Charles. "We should go and let her rest," she whispered, but stopped and looked quickly up as her father brought the child back inside the lodge.

Becky opened her eyes and held her arms out for the child. "I think it's time I feed my son," she said softly, gently taking the child and placing him in the crook of her left arm.

A quick panic leapt into Charles's eyes. He looked over at Snow Deer. "We'd best leave and give your mother privacy to feed the baby," he said.

"No, stay," Becky said, already sliding a breast free from the blankets and offering the nipple to the child. "Watch the child feed. It is such a glorious thing to see."

Savage Longings

Charles had never seen a child feeding at his mother's breast before. He had thought he might be uncomfortable and embarrassed by the exposed breast.

But the child suckling the breast was a beautiful sight to see. He could not stop watching the tiny lips taking nourishment, or stop listening to the sweet sounds of contentment that it made.

Suddenly he knew for certain that he must have a child of his own! He slid a hand over to Snow Deer and held it as they exchanged knowing, wondering smiles.

She placed her other hand over her squash blossom necklace. "We will, Charles," she whispered. "I promise you not only one child, but many."

He drew her into his embrace.

Chapter Thirty-Three

Snow Deer had tossed and turned in her sleep throughout the entire night.

Even now, sitting before the morning fire in her parents' lodge, eating breakfast with all of her family, she could not shake her dispirited feelings. Although Charles had finally agreed to stay a few days longer so that she could be with her family, the time had passed quickly. Today they were leaving.

Everyone else had left early that morning, their duties calling them back to their homes.

It was hard for Snow Deer to accept that it might be months, perhaps years, before she would see some of them again, especially Fish Hawk and his sweet wife. Wyoming was a long way from Illinois. She knew that she and Charles would never venture that far from home to see them.

And knowing about Fish Hawk's problems with the white community in Wyoming, Snow Deer doubted that he would leave home again for such a long time.

And Judge Newman? Snow Deer already missed him. She loved him as though he were a brother. Judge Newman's duties kept him too busy to leave often. She knew that it would be a long time before she saw him and his wife again.

And Becky's brother Edward, and his wife, Marilyn. At least it wouldn't be as long between visits with them. Edward had promised to come from Saint Louis within the year to visit Snow Deer and Charles at their home in Illinois. She could hardly wait for that visit. Edward and Marilyn were so dear to her, a true aunt and uncle in all respects. And she was eager for them to see what kind of homemaker she was.

She looked down at her platter of food and cut away a bite of biscuits and gravy with her fork. She could feel Charles's eyes on her. She realized that he had been aware of her sadness upon their first arising that morning. And no matter how much he held her and comforted her, she could not get past the melancholy of her good-byes.

"The women of the village were good to bring in breakfast," Charles said, interrupting Snow Deer's thoughts.

"The women will keep me well fed while my wife is away from her cooking pots," Blazing Eagle said, looking proudly over at his wife where she lay at the far side of the lodge feeding their son. He returned her smile when she caught him looking at her.

"I want to learn to cook," Burning Snow said, rushing to her feet and going to kneel on the floor beside her mother's bed. "Will you teach me how to cook, Mother, when baby brother is not requiring your full attention?"

"You truly wish to learn?"

"Yes, oh, yes," Burning Snow said, clasping her hands together before her.

Becky reached a hand to Burning Snow's hair, weaving her fingers through it. She was surprised at the difference in Burning Snow's attitude of late. Always before, when Becky had tried to teach Burning Snow how to cook even the simplest of things, Burning Snow had paid attention for perhaps five minutes of the instruction, and then her mind had strayed, taking her from the lodge to play with children far younger than she.

Now . . . was there truly a change in her daughter?

As before, when Burning Snow gave signs of becoming self-reliant, Becky could not help hoping!

"Darling daughter, I will be in bed for only a few days and then I shall be everything to you again," Becky said, tears of happiness filling her eyes.

"I am so glad," Burning Snow said, leaning over to embrace Becky.

"Charles, are you certain you must leave today?" Blazing Eagle asked, giving his empty platter to an Indian maiden as she came and collected those that were ready to be taken to the river for washing.

"Yes, and I think we'd best leave now," Charles said, handing his own platter to the woman. "I'd like to get across the Ohio on the ferry and get my wife settled comfortably in an inn before it turns dark." He reached over and took one of Snow Deer's hands. "Are you ready to leave?"

She willed herself not to cry. She forced a smile. "Yes," she murmured. "I am ready."

Snow Deer went to her mother and knelt down on the floor beside Burning Snow. "Mother, I shall miss you so," she said, leaning down and hugging her.

Then she eased away from her and gazed at her baby brother as Becky slid his lips from her breast, covered her breast with a blanket, and held the child out for Snow Deer.

Snow Deer sat down on the edge of the bed and took Running Elk within her arms. Feeling so much love for her baby brother, she gazed down at him as she slowly rocked him back and forth.

"Look at how big his eyes are," Burning Snow said, gently touching her brother on the cheek. "See how he looks at you, big sister? He is memorizing you because you will soon be gone."

Hearing her sister use such a big word as memorize, Snow Deer had great hope that her sister was growing out of her affliction. During Snow Deer's visit, she had noticed increased alertness on her sister's part. Yes, she even began to believe that her sister might have a future of her own with some lucky man!

"Yes, our brother is memorizing me," Snow Deer said, taking her sister's hand and fondly squeezing it.

Charles knelt down and brushed a soft kiss across Becky's brow. "We really have to go now," he said, watching as Snow Deer placed the child back in Becky's arms.

"I shall write soon," Snow Deer said, rising to her feet.

She turned and embraced her father, lingering in his arms until she noticed Charles nervously shuffling his feet with impatience.

Then she embraced her sister once again.

Everyone but Becky went outside.

Snow Deer held back tears when she saw the horse and buggy there, readied for travel. The back of the buggy was filled with gifts from Blazing Eagle's people. They were in sacks ornamented with buckskin fringe and painted with various designs in bright colors.

Then Snow Deer saw something more that had not been there when she had entered her parents' lodge for the morning meal.

Snow Deer gaped openly at the horses that were tied at the back of the buggy. She recognized them. They were hers!

She looked quickly up at her father, a question in her eyes. She could feel Charles looking, also, at her father.

Smiling, Blazing Eagle placed a hand on each of their shoulders. He looked from Charles to Snow Deer. "Daughter, you recognize your horses, do you not?" he asked softly.

"Yes," she murmured. "They were gifts from you before I was married."

"When a father's daughter marries, the horses given to her by her father before the marriage are still hers, are they not?" Blazing Eagle asked softly.

"Yes, that is the way of the Cheyenne," Snow Deer said. She glanced at the six lovely horses. She had always found it hard to choose a favorite from among them. She loved each one dearly.

But when she had left home to go to Charles, everything she owned had been left behind. She had not thought to claim the horses as hers, feeling that in a sense they might be a gift to her father for his understanding of her decision to marry a white man.

"Then they are yours to take with you to Illinois," Blazing Eagle said, nodding. He smiled over at Charles. "Because the horses belong to your wife, they are now also yours."

"But Blazing Eagle . . ." Charles said, attempting to tell the Cheyenne chief that he did not need the horses, that the Cheyenne were in more need of them than he and Snow Deer.

But Snow Deer had sensed what he was about to say and gave his arm a gentle yank, making him stop speaking and look her way.

When he saw her soft stare, he cleared his throat, smiled, and reached a hand out to Blazing Eagle. "Thank you," he said. "Thank you for the horses."

Again many hugs were exchanged and final good-byes were said.

After Snow Deer and Charles were down the road quite a distance from the village, and riding along the Ohio River, Snow Deer turned to Charles. "Was it not a wonderful time with my people?" she asked, drawing Charles's eyes to her.

"Yes, it was something I will always remember," he said. "I myself hated to leave. I feel blessed to be a part of such a family. I'm so glad that I got to meet all of them. Everyone seems special in his own way."

"Yes, very special," Snow Deer said. She sighed. "And, Charles, I no longer feel sad about having left them. I am eager to return to our home. That is where I belong. That is where my heart lies."

Charles heaved a heavy sigh. "Am I glad to hear you say that!" he said. "For a while there I thought you might be regretting having married me."

"Never," Snow Deer said. She scooted over close to him and rested her head on his muscled arm. "Take me home, darling. Take me home."

Totally content, Charles clucked to the horses to speed them on their way.

The Ohio River was still at their right side. A pine forest was on their left, where sunlight scarcely penetrated the dark tangle of interwoven branches. It was a place where men seldom went, and where animals were safe. Bickering jays had kept up a loud accompaniment to their passage, but suddenly there was a strange, awkward silence.

Charles looked quickly toward the forest, having noticed the quick silence.

Then he heard the fluttering of wings and ducked with alarm when a huge flock of bluejays swept from the forest, squawking as they scattered in all directions over the river.

Snow Deer leaned away from Charles. She stiffened when she saw how Charles kept looking at the forest and how he snapped the reins, sending the horses into a faster pace along the narrow path beside the river.

"Charles, what's wrong?" Snow Deer asked, looking over her shoulder at the dust that was being whipped up from the horses' hooves.

"I feel as though something might be in the forest," Charles said. "As though someone was here watching us."

"But . . . who . . . ?" Snow Deer said, gasping and paling when she saw several Indians ride out of the dark shadows of the forest.

"Charles!" she cried, reaching behind her for the rifle. "We are being followed! I believe they are Shawnee warriors!"

"Lord," Charles said, giving a quick look over his shoulder. When he saw about twenty warriors galloping after them on horseback, he turned and stared at Snow Deer. She was turned around in her seat, her rifle aimed at the Shawnee.

"Don't fire unless you're certain they are going to shoot at us," Charles cried. "Snow Deer, be careful!"

As the warriors grew closer, and Snow Deer was able to see who was their leader, she slowly lowered her rifle. "Rain Feather?" she said, eyes widening.

She reached a hand to Charles and shook his arm. "Charles, it's Rain Feather," she cried.

Charles looked over at her and saw that she had lowered her rifle. "Snow Deer, just because you see that it is Rain Feather doesn't mean that we are no longer in trouble," he shouted. "Show them the rifle. Make them know that we will not be taken easily! Lord, Snow Deer, I'd stop and threaten him myself except I must keep as much space between us as possible!"

"Rain Feather came as a friend to our home," Snow Deer said, reluctantly raising the rifle again and taking aim. "His wife is Becky's very good friend. She helped Becky give birth to her child. I just cannot see Rain Feather causing me trouble now."

"We can't take chances," Charles said, his heart racing. He sighed with relief when he saw the ferry waiting on the Kentucky side a short distance away. He snapped the reins again, sending the horses into a frenzied gallop along the riverbank.

"They are gaining on us!" Snow Deer screamed. "Oh, Charles, I don't care if it *is* Rain Feather. I cannot help being afraid now!"

"Remember not to shoot unless you see they are going to shoot at us!" Charles said. "Do they have their weapons drawn yet?"

"No, I see no weapons," Snow Deer said as Rain Feather came within inches of the roped horses at the back of the wagon.

Rain Feather sank his heels into the flanks of his horse and rode at a harder gallop, then stared, eye to eye with Snow Deer, as he came alongside the wagon.

"Stop!" he cried, now looking over at Charles. "Why do you flee from a friend?"

"Friends do not pursue others as though they are enemies!" Snow Deer screamed back at him above the noise of the horses' thundering hooves. "You were hiding in the forest waiting for us. How could we see anyone who hides as a friend?"

"Yes, I was there waiting for you," Rain Feather shouted back. "When word came to me that you were heading out today, for your journey back to Illinois, I came to meet you along the river to warn you of outlaws who have escaped from a jail in Paducah. They are the danger. Not the Shawnee!"

Charles looked quickly over at Rain Feather, feeling foolish now for having allowed the elderly Indian to frighten him. And he did believe him. There was no reason why the Indian would lie. Charles knew that if Rain Feather had truly wanted to harm him and Snow Deer by an attack, he would not have waited until they came so close to the ferry.

He sighed and drew a tight rein. His horses came to a shuddering halt.

"Now what is this about outlaws?" he asked.

"You must be careful on your journey home," Rain Feather said tightly. "Would you like an escort?"

Snow Deer was astonished that the Shawnee chief would be so generous. And she felt ashamed for having allowed herself to become so frightened of him! It was certain now that he was a true friend.

"Are the outlaws that dangerous?" Charles asked.

"Most say they are," Rain Feather replied, resting his hand on his sheathed knife. "We will escort you across the river and beyond until you feel safe enough to go on alone."

"Why did Father not know about these outlaws?" Snow Deer said, still not completely free of suspicion.

"I only learned of them a short while ago," Rain Feather said. "Your father may not know about them yet."

The sound of other horses approaching at a fast clip a short distance away drew Snow Deer's attention from Rain Feather. She strained her neck as she looked past the many Shawnee warriors behind the buggy, smiling when she saw her father riding with many of his warriors toward her.

"Yes, Father has heard," she said, smiling at Charles. "He has also come to offer a safe escort."

When Rain Feather also saw Chief Blazing Eagle arriving, he gave Snow Deer a lingering look, then wheeled his horse around and rode off in the opposite direction from the approaching Cheyenne.

After Blazing Eagle stopped beside the buggy, he stared at the retreating warriors. "Was that Rain Feather?" he asked.

"Yes, that was Rain Feather," Snow deer said, still watching the Shawnee chief riding away from her.

"Was he causing you trouble?" Blazing Eagle asked, drawing Snow Deer's attention to him.

"Trouble?" she said, smiling. "No. Instead, Father, he proved today just how much a friend to us he truly is."

"How is that, daughter?" Blazing Eagle asked.

She explained.

"Still, daughter, never trust that Shawnee completely, no matter what he might say or do to try

355

to prove his friendship to you," Blazing Eagle then said. "I cannot myself trust him that easily."

"Father, sometimes one must forget bad feelings of the past," Snow Deer murmured. "I am forgetting my mistrust of Rain Feather. I hope that you will, also. You are not usually a man who holds grudges long against anyone."

"Hard times have taught me many things I was not burdened with in my past," Blazing Eagle said, then walked his horse around to the other side, closer to Charles. "I offer you escort. Do you wish it?"

"Do you think the outlaws are truly a threat?" Charles asked.

"Yes," Blazing Eagle said, nodding.

"Then, Blazing Eagle, I would appreciate having your company for as long as you feel it is necessary," he said. "I want to keep Snow Deer from all harm."

"You say the right things," Blazing Eagle said, smiling and clasping a hand of friendship on Charles's shoulder.

Snow Deer saw the bond growing stronger between her husband and father. And she could never feel any more safe than now, with her husband and father joining forces to protect her. She could not have asked for anything more wonderful than the sight of them together, smiling and forming a bond between them like that of father and son.

Chapter Thirty-Four

It was early evening. The sun had lowered in the sky and dusk was just falling across the land when Charles and Snow Deer arrived home from Kentucky. They put their horses in the corral, took their bags inside their home, and then held hands as they walked down the road toward Charles's parents' home.

"I've missed them," Charles said, realizing he had never been away from his parents for any length of time. "I'm eager to see them."

"I have missed them also," Snow Deer said. "They are not just my in-laws. They are my friends."

Her smiled faded. "At first, though," she murmured, "your father did cause me some moments of pain."

She smiled widely again. "But that quickly changed," she said, sighing. "And he has never made me feel an outsider to the family since."

"One thing does concern me," Charles said, looking over his shoulder in the direction of his garden. "The garden wasn't touched while I was gone. Although I told him it wasn't necessary, Father said that he was going to hoe the garden, at least between the rows of beans and peas."

He idly scratched his brow and gazed down at Snow Deer. "He did neither," he said softly.

"Perhaps he took your advice and saw that it could wait until you returned home," Snow Deer said. "He is so busy with his own garden and his post office duties."

"Yes, and his livestock," Charles said, nodding. "Mother isn't much help doing anything outside the house."

He chuckled. "Even the flower garden," he said. "One might think the woman of the house would tend the flowers. But not my mother. She hates to get dirt beneath her fingers. She says it might contaminate the food she prepares."

He smiled at the thought of soon enjoying her fried chicken and dumplings, and another apple pie. She had stored bushels of apples in the cellar. They would be eating them prepared in various ways for months to come.

"She is delicate, your mother," Snow Deer said, peering at the house as they came closer. She stared at it. It seemed eerily quiet. There was no lamplight in the windows, and smoke spiraled from only one chimney—from the fireplace in Charles's parents' bedroom.

"Charles, doesn't your parents' house look odd?" she asked, still studying the windows. "There is no light. And why isn't there smoke coming from your mother's cook stove? I would think she'd be in the kitchen cooking your father's evening meal."

Charles stopped suddenly, noticing the things that Snow Deer had pointed out. His mind began to spin with worry. He remembered his mother's recent illness, and the fact that his father had recently looked tired and worn out, whereas he was usually a vital, healthy man.

"I don't like the looks of things," he said, slipping his hand free of Snow Deer's. He began walking again in the direction of his parents' house, his pace quickening the closer he came.

When he reached the small path that led to the front door, he stopped almost in mid-step, gasped, and felt suddenly faint when he saw a black wreath hanging on the front door. A black wreath meant there had been a death in the family!

"No!" he cried, then broke into a run toward the house.

Snow Deer stared at him for a moment, then ran after him. "Charles!" she cried. "Wait for Snow Deer. Tell me what has alarmed you so much?"

Snow Deer's frightened voice caused Charles to stop.

He turned and waited for her.

When she caught up with him, he took her hand again and walked more slowly toward the house.

"Charles, tell me what is wrong," Snow Deer softly pleaded. "Your hand is trembling. There are tears in your eyes. Why would there be? What did you see that I have not seen?"

Trying to hold on to some semblance of sanity while still not knowing which of his parents had died, Charles swallowed hard, then stopped and gazed down at Snow Deer. "Snow Deer, the black wreath on the door is there for only one reason," he said, his voice drawn. He saw her look past him, to stare at the wreath.

Then she looked up at him again, her eyes wide.

"Snow Deer," he said. "The . . . the wreath is there to show that someone . . . has . . . died in the household."

His voice broke. He hung his head, then turned and stared at the house. "Lord, which one?" he said.

"We shall go and see," Snow Deer said, her voice filled with a sudden sadness. She tugged at Charles's hand. "Come, Charles. Let us go inside. Whoever is left behind, alone, needs you. Needs *us*."

Guilt flooded Charles as he walked slowly up the front steps. When his parents needed him the most, he had not been there!

But he could never cast blame on his wife for having taken him from his home to hers to be with her family.

Fate was to be blamed. Only fate.

He looked heavenward, wondering why God worked in such strange ways. Throughout his years of being a son he had hardly been beyond yelling distance of his parents, especially when he had gotten older and felt responsible for their well-being.

But still, he should not cast blame on anyone that this had happened. Not on the Lord. And not on his beautiful, sweet wife.

This was the way of life . . . the twists of fate.

His hands trembling, Charles turned the knob at the front door.

Inside, he heard the total silence, and when he was not greeted with the familiar wonderful scent of his mother cooking something in her beloved kitchen, he could only guess that it was she who had died.

Night was well upon the land now, leaving only darkness in the house as Charles held Snow Deer's hand while he made his way through the living room to the hall that led to his parents' bedroom.

When he got near the opened door, he could hear soft sobs.

He recognized them.

They were his mother's.

His heart seemed to stand still at the thought of having lost his father. A knot formed in his throat. He stopped and closed his eyes.

Gritting his teeth, he hung his head in his hands. In his mind's eye he saw the special moments he'd shared with his father.

And now he was gone!

Charles would never see his smile again. He would never hear his laughter. He would never feel his father's strong arms around him in one of his generous bear hugs.

He would never play softball with him again, as they had, so often, before Charles had married Snow Deer.

"Father," he gulped out. Tears rushed from his eyes. "Oh, Lord—Father!"

Snow Deer heard and felt Charles's despair as though it were her own, for his despair *was* hers. She felt all his emotions, as though she and her husband were one, with one heartbeat, one soul!

And when she heard him speak his father's name in such a tormented way, she realized that he had just surmised that his father had died, not his mother.

"Charles? Is that you?"

Hearing his mother's voice brought Charles's head up.

His heart skipped a beat, for in his mother's voice he heard such weakness . . . such sadness . . . such loneliness and despair!

"Go to her," Snow Deer said. She gave Charles a soft shove toward the bedroom door. "I shall come in a short while. I will give your mother time to talk to you."

Charles took her hand. "No," he said softly. "I can't do this without you. Snow Deer, please come with me. I . . . need . . . you."

Snow Deer nodded, swallowed hard, and then walked with him down the hallway and into his mother's room.

Her eyes filled with tears, Patricia was sitting on the edge of the bed, just now placing a match to the wick of a kerosene lamp. Soon lamplight flooded the room as she placed the lamp on a table beside her bed.

Charles could hardly believe his eyes when he saw his mother in the soft glow of the light. She looked as though she had lost a lot of weight. Her clothes hung loosely from her body. Her hair color had changed almost overnight to gray. Her eyes were swollen and red from crying. Her cheeks were sunken in.

"Son," Patricia said, pushing herself up from the bed. She held her arms out for Charles.

Charles rushed to her and drew her into his embrace. He could feel the bones of her body through her skin. He could feel her trembling with emotion and weakness.

He forced back his need to cry, for he now understood just how badly his mother needed him.

She needed him to be strong!

"Son, he's gone," she cried. "His heart took him from us! It happened so quickly! He was there with me one minute, laughing and joking beside the fire as we played checkers. Then . . . he . . . clutched at his chest and . . . *died.*"

Charles was so choked up he could not find the words he wished to say to his mother.

He closed his eyes and held her.

Snow Deer stood back and watched. Tears splashed from her eyes. She wanted to go to them and hug them both, but their joined sadness was at this moment separating her from them.

And she understood.

Seeing the neglect of the house, and feeling the damp and coldness as the hours of the night deepened into something that seemed dark and sinister, with death looming everywhere, Snow Deer saw that she could be useful while her husband and mother shared their sorrow.

Turning, she went from room to room lighting lamps, giving the house life again.

Then she began lighting fires in the fireplaces and heating stoves until the house was warm and comfortable again.

While in the kitchen, standing over the cooking stove and relishing its warmth, she looked slowly around her. Things were spotless, as though nothing had been cooked there for days. This had to mean that perhaps Patricia hadn't *eaten* for days.

"I will remedy that," she whispered to herself.

She took a bowl to the cellar, gathered several potatoes and onions in it, then grabbed a jar of canned green beans and went upstairs to the kitchen and soon had potatoes and onions frying together in lard on the stove. She emptied the green beans in a pot and heated them up.

Then she did the one thing that she hated most of all—she tightened her jaw and went outside and caught a chicken.

Still grimacing over having prepared the chicken for frying, she carried it inside and washed it, arranged it in a large frying pan. Soon the house was filled with the aroma of chicken.

Proud of her accomplishment, Snow Deer set

the table with three place settings. She placed a pot of coffee on the stove, then watched over the stove as the potatoes and chicken continued frying.

Charles led his mother to the living room. They sat down together on the divan before the fire in the fireplace. He held her hands as she told him more about the events since his father's passing.

"He died the very day I left?" Charles said, swallowing hard.

"Yes, and there was no way I could get in touch with you so that you could return for the funeral," Patricia said. She patted Charles's hand. "Son, never feel guilty for having not been here. You had no power over what happened, or when it would happen. The Lord chooses when someone's time on this earth is over."

"These past days have been so hard on you," Charles said, drawing her close and holding her. "How have you stood it alone?"

"As you see, I scarcely did survive," she murmured. "If not for the women of the church, I might have starved, for I've never once entered the kitchen since your father's death. Food was brought every day. I . . . ate what I could, but only to please those who had taken the time to prepare it for me."

The wonderful aroma of food cooking filled Charles with love for his wife. He knew it was she who was in the kitchen preparing the meal.

He recognized the smell of fried chicken and smiled at the thought of the ordeal Snow Deer must have gone through to kill and prepare the chicken. Although she was used to killing and skinning forest animals, the domesticated ones seemed to her to be different.

Yet it was obvious that tonight she was doing

everything she could to help. She had seen how frail Charles's mother had become these past days while mourning the loss of her beloved husband. She had seen the importance of preparing a meal for her. She had seen that this was at least one way that she could help during this time of sadness in the Cline family.

"Snow Deer is such a sweet person," Patricia said, leaning away from Charles. She wiped tears from her eyes. "She's in the kitchen preparing supper, Charles." She rose slowly from the divan. "I must go and help her."

Charles started to reach out for her to stop her, thinking that she wasn't strong enough to help in the kitchen, yet he had second thoughts about it. If she busied herself doing something, that might help her place her constant sorrow over her husband at least temporarily from her mind.

He rose from the divan and followed her into the kitchen. He stood back and looked at what Snow Deer had managed to do. Before his mother was able to offer a helping hand, Snow Deer already had the food in bowls on the table. Steam from coffee spiraled from the cups. And Snow Deer was standing beside the table, flour smudges on her face and buckskin dress, smiling.

"Husband, I believe I managed to fry delicious chicken tonight," Snow Deer said, pride in her eyes.

Patricia walked slowly around the table, looking at everything.

Then, smiling her approval, she went to Snow Deer and hugged her. "Thank you, dear," she murmured. "Thank you, thank you."

Snow Deer clung to her. "I am so sorry about Jacob," she whispered. "So very, very sorry."

"He is in a much better place now than you or

Cassie Edwards

I," Patricia murmured. "It is only now that I can say that and feel resigned about losing Jacob to God."

She swung away from Snow Deer and reached for Charles's hands. "Son, your father *is* in a better place," she murmured. "I shall be able to place it behind me now. It just took me some time to accept that God has called him home, for I still wanted to think his better home was with me."

Charles drew her into his embrace. He closed his eyes as he held her.

She clung for a moment longer, then turned from him and stared down at the food on the table. She smiled at Snow Deer. "I am hungry for the first time since I buried my Jacob," she said, sighing.

Charles pulled a chair from beneath the table and helped his mother into it.

Then he went to Snow Deer. His eyes gleamed as he reached a hand to her cheek; with his thumb, he smoothed flour from her smooth flesh. "You are an angel," he whispered, brushing a kiss across her lips.

They all ate until everything but the chicken bones was consumed.

Then they grew serious again when Patricia reached over and took one of Charles's hands. "Son, your father and I had a long talk a few weeks ago," she said, her voice breaking. "We agreed on something. It's something that you need to be told."

She lowered her eyes. "We had thought it best left unsaid," she murmured.

Then she looked quickly up at Charles again. "But we both decided that it would not be fair to you not to tell you," she said. "I see the need now, myself, especially after seeing how quickly your

366

father was taken from us. I might also be called away one day soon by the Lord, and before that happens, you need to know the truth."

"Truth?" Charles asked, raising an eyebrow. "What sort of truth?"

Patricia eased her hand from Charles's. She wiped her mouth on her white linen napkin, then rose slowly from the table.

"Come with me, Charles," she said, laying her napkin aside. She looked over at Snow Deer. "Dear, you, also. You need to be there for Charles when I tell him. . . ."

Charles's thoughts were spinning. He felt strangely afraid of what his mother had to say, for she was behaving as though telling him might change things between them! He couldn't think of anything that would cause a distance between himself and his mother.

After they were settled on the divan before the fire in the living room, Snow Deer at Patricia's left side, Charles on her right, they gazed down at a photo album as Patricia slowly turned the pages. She took her time pointing out one relative, and then another, as though she was deliberately postponing whatever she had to tell Charles.

When she turned to a page where the photographs were yellowed with age and scarcely discernible from having been taken before the art of photography was perfected, she handed the album over to Charles.

"Son, take a long, close look at your father's brother Franklin," Patricia said guardedly.

Snow Deer saw and felt that something painful was about to happen to her husband. She could feel it in the way his mother was gazing at him, in the way her voice was quavering. Knowing this, Snow Deer slowly slid an arm behind her husband, reassuring him that she supported him, always.

"I can't see Uncle Franklin very well," Charles said, holding the album closer to the light. He held the album one way and then another, finally getting the lamplight on the photographs so that he could make out the facial features of his uncle and aunt, both of whom had been murdered when Charles was just a baby. He had never known them. But from hearing them talked about, he knew them to be kind and gentle people.

When outlaws had entered their house and killed them, it was said that the whole community had been shocked by their deaths.

"Now can you see his face clearly?" Patricia asked, drawing his eyes quickly to her. She could tell that he was puzzled over her insistence that he see Franklin's facial features. Yet she waited for him to study the photograph again before telling him why.

Charles studied Franklin's face, his dark eyes and hair, his jaw structure, and his straight nose.

Also, there were his lips. They, and everything else, seemed so familiar, and not because Charles had looked at these photographs often before. He had only seen them one other time, and that was when he was a child. He recalled how quickly his mother had grabbed the album away from him then, scolding him for taking it from a drawer in her dresser, one that she had always forbidden him to open.

Charles's heart skipped a beat.

His eyes widened.

His pulse then began to race frantically when he realized why there was something familiar about the face of his Uncle Franklin.

It was as though he was looking at a photograph of himself!

"Mother, I never knew I looked so much like Uncle Franklin," he blurted out, giving his mother a quick, steady stare. "You never told me and—and I was never allowed to see the photographs until now. Why now, mother? Why is it so important that I see these photographs now?"

Patricia stared at Charles for a moment, as though mesmerized by his question; then she rose quickly to her feet and went and stood with her back to him as she stared down at the fire.

"Charles, Charles," she said, her voice breaking.

Charles looked over at Snow Deer and saw how wide her eyes were, and how quietly she sat listening and watching, as though she might understand more about what was happening here than he.

Then he shoved the album aside and went to his mother. Gently he placed his hands on her shoulders and turned her to face him. "Mother, tell me what's going on here," he said thickly. "Tell me now."

Patricia broke down. She reached a hand to Charles's cheek and ran her fingers slowly over his facial features. "Son, you look so much like your Uncle Franklin because . . . because *he* was your father, not Jacob," she choked out, wincing when she saw utter disbelief leap into her son's dark eyes.

Charles's heart thumped wildly inside his chest. "What did you say?" he said, taking a step away from her.

"When your mother and father died, Jacob and I took you in and raised you as our own," Patricia said, sobbing between words. "I knew then that I

Cassie Edwards

could never have children of our own. You became our child."

Snow Deer stood quietly listening and watching, stunned speechless by what was being revealed to her husband tonight. When Patricia said that she had never been able to have children, Snow Deer's hand slid up and she curled her fingers around her squash blossom necklace. She clung to it, careful not to say or do anything that might interfere in these awkward moments between a mother and son. Her time to console her husband would come later, and she knew that there would be much consoling to do. She could see that her husband was struck speechless by his mother's words.

"You aren't my mother?" Charles gulped out, his face pale. "Father wasn't my father?"

"The night your parents were murdered, we were keeping you overnight, for, darling, we loved you even then as though you were our very own," Patricia said softly. "Your mother and father knew that I could never have children. They . . . often shared you . . . with me and Jacob. After you were weaned from your mother's breast milk, Jacob and I *often* kept you overnight. Sometimes for weekends. You were with us for one of those weekends when the outlaws went into your parents' home and . . . and killed them, leaving leaving you . . . orphaned."

"You and father . . . adopted me?" Charles said, all of this whirling through his brain, causing him to be dizzy from the realization that everything he'd believed about his life was based on a lie.

In truth, his whole life had been a lie!

Yet, knowing this did not change anything, for this man and woman who had taken him in and raised him, filling his whole life with such love and caring, would always be his true mother and father!

Suddenly, he felt no resentment toward them for not having told him. He had been happy. He had been loved. He had been nurtured. He had been raised in the church, a Christian from the moment he realized who God was.

He could not look back and see even one time when he had not felt blessed by having such parents as Jacob and Patricia Cline.

"Mother," Charles said, tears rushing from his eyes as he reached for her and drew her into his arms. "Thank you for telling me. It is only fair that I know."

"Your father and I chose not to tell you at first, but it just seemed to eat away at us more and more," she said, choking on sobs as they kept rising into her throat. "We knew that we did not have long on this earth. If we didn't tell you now, you would never know, for I don't believe anyone, except family, even remembers those long years ago when we took you in as our son."

"Family?" Charles said, easing from her arms. "Do you mean to say that . . . that Elissa knows?"

"No, Elissa doesn't know," she said. She placed a gentle hand on his cheek and smoothed his tears away. "But her father knew. We wrote often and sometimes in those letters you were referred to as adopted. It was our secret, Hiram's and mine. I was so proud of you. I had to tell the truth to someone besides Jacob."

"Then Elissa never knew," Charles said, sighing, realizing that had she known, and had *he* known, things might have been different. There had never been any true blood ties between them. They could have married!

Snow Deer crept over and stepped between him

and Patricia. She took Charles's hands and gazed up at him. "Darling husband, are you all right?" she asked softly.

Just that quickly Elissa slid from Charles's thoughts, for looking down at his wife, and seeing her preciousness, he knew that he had never loved Elissa as much as he loved Snow Deer, nor could he have ever loved her as much, even if he had known the truth!

Snow Deer was his reason for having been put on this earth! He loved her with a special, enduring love which made what he had felt for Elissa child's play.

"I'm fine," Charles said, sighing heavily. Then he smiled and swept her to his side, holding his other arm out for his mother.

Patricia leaned into his embrace. She gazed into the flames of the fire. Suddenly she laughed softly. "If your father were here, he'd bring out the corn from last year's harvest and pop us a big bowl of popcorn," she murmured.

She looked up at Charles. "Remember those times, son, when we'd sit by the fire and eat popcorn while the wind whistled down the chimney and snow fell in solid white sheets from the heavens?" she murmured.

"Yes, and father would then tell me to get the checkers," Charles said, chuckling.

"You have the most pleasant of memories of your father, don't you, son?" Patricia asked, swallowing back another deep sob.

"The best," Charles said softly. "I loved him very much. My father outshone all other fathers. I remember sitting in church as Father served communion, thinking he was the best of all the deacons who served with him."

"I remember one time when you and I were sitting in a pew as your father stood at the front of the church. The preacher was saying a prayer just before Jacob was to help serve the communion," Patricia said, her eyes beaming as she gazed up at Charles. "Charles, you were two years old, and *so* feisty, I could hardly hold you back at times. Well, when you saw your father standing at the front of the church, holding the communion tray, his head bowed while the preacher said the prayer, you decided right there and then that you wanted to be with your father. Before I knew it, or could stop you, you wriggled off my lap and started running up the aisle toward your father, shouting his name and bringing the whole congregation's eyes open to stare at you. Your father could have been angry. Instead, he set his communion tray down, welcomed you in his arms, then picked that tray up again and carried you with him as he served the communion."

She laughed softly. "I was at first embarrassed by your antics," she said. "But then I became so proud, for the love between father and son that was shown to everyone that day seemed even more important than the sermon that the preacher preached. It was beautiful, Charles. So beautiful."

"I have many, many such special memories myself," Charles said. He looked over his shoulder at the window, and saw how dark it was. Then he looked at his mother. "I want to see the grave."

"Go, dear, but I don't believe I wish to go with you," Patricia said. "I find it hard to stand by the grave and know Jacob is lying there." She shuddered. "It's too soon. I shall, in time, visit the grave every day with flowers. But not now, son. Not now."

Charles turned to Snow Deer. "Will you go with me?" he asked softly.

"You know that you need not ask such a question," Snow Deer replied, taking his hand. "Come. We shall go." Then she arched an eyebrow. "But where is the grave?"

"We have a family plot in the cemetery behind the church," Charles said.

He then looked quickly over at his mother. Their eyes held steady when he recalled the many times he had visited his Uncle Franklin and Aunt Kathryn's graves with his mother and father. All along, he had been visiting his *true* parents' graves and had never known it.

"Yes, son, go and visit your true parents' graves, also," Patricia murmured. "They lie just beside Jacob."

Charles nodded. He gave his mother one last, lingering hug before leaving, then walked from the house with Snow Deer, into the white sheen of moonlight.

"You are truly all right?" Snow Deer asked, gazing up at Charles.

He looked down at her. "Yes," he said. "The truth is, Snow Deer, I shall always feel that the two wonderful people who took me in and raised me as their son are my parents. It will take me a while to think of Franklin and Kathryn in any way other than as my aunt and uncle. If I had known them, truly known them before they died, it might be different. In a way, it makes it easier for me because I have no memory of them."

They went to the cemetery. Charles felt at peace at his father's graveside.

When he gazed at Franklin's and Kathryn's graves, something fleetingly seemed to touch his cheek. He had felt it before while visiting the family cemetery plot with his mother. He had always felt as though someone else was there! He shivered to think that now he guessed what it had always been! His true mother's touch reaching down from the heavens!

He rose shakily to his feet and took a step backward.

"Charles?" Snow Deer said, seeing Charles's strange behavior.

He turned to her. He started to her tell her his feelings, but felt as though they were best left unsaid.

"Snow Deer, let's go back to Mother's house," he said, grabbing her hand and half dragging her through the small iron gate that led from the cemetery plot. "We've plans to make. Mother needs us, *both* of us. I want Mother to know that we will always be near, now and forever."

Snow Deer nodded, yet she knew that something had happened at the cemetery.

It seemed spiritual, and so she would never ask him about it. She knew about spiritual feelings. At particular times in her life she had experienced them herself. She had not known that white people could feel such things.

She smiled, thinking that her husband's spiritual world was not all that different from the Cheyenne's, after all! Little by little, their lives seemed to blend into something more wonderful than she could ever have hoped for!

Chapter Thirty-Five

Several Years Later

Tomorrow was Christmas. There was an air of magic hovering over the Cline household. A green-shaded lamp on a table beside a plush tufted armchair made tranquil circles of light in the gathering dusk. A cozy fire crackled and popped in the fireplace as the flames wrapped themselves around the huge logs on the grate.

The living room smelled of fresh cedar. Charles stood back and silently admired the Christmas tree as his wife placed the last gleaming ball on one of the thick branches.

"I think this is the most beautiful tree we've ever had," Charles said, folding his arms across his chest. "I think the children will get their eyes full when they wake up in the morning, don't you, Mame?"

Snow Deer turned beaming, happy eyes to her

husband. She now answered to the name Mame, because it was *her* choice to be called something that made life easier for her school-age children. The name Mame raised no eyebrows and stirred no questions that might be awkward for Charles and Snow Deer's children to answer. She was, for the most part, called Snow Deer while at home, although Charles slipped up from time to time.

"Yes, the tree is very pretty," Snow Deer said. "And I can hardly wait to wrap the gifts. We have so many this year, Charles. So many."

"With four children, yes, there are many gifts," Charles said, chuckling.

He gave his mother a gentle hug as she came into the room, her cheeks flushed pink from her long day of cooking.

As he leaned down and brushed a kiss across her cheek, he could smell various aromas on her, from the cooking.

The entire house was fragrant with spices. Charles's mother had made many kinds of pies, and she had only a short while ago slid a huge turkey in the oven so that it would cook slowly through the night.

Tomorrow she also planned to cook a rack of lamb with potatoes au gratin, accompanied by pots of horseradish cream and blackberry-mint sauce.

Charles could envision the turkey and lamb now as they would appear on the dining table tomorrow. Everything would be nestled among heaping displays of pumpkins and maple leaves and served with a tangy apple-and-grape stuffing, and mashed potatoes, which would be ladled with apple-wine gravy. There would be orange marmalade, glazed brussels sprouts, and a carrot custard laced with a hint of vanilla.

And best of all, Charles's mother was going to

make his favorite hot rolls. Although his waist would suffer—he had gained weight these past years—he could hardly wait to put huge dollops of freshly churned butter on the rolls so that it would melt on his tongue when he took slow, appreciative bites of the bread.

"I see you've got a good start on your evening's tasks," Patricia said, laughing softly as she looked around the room, and at the boxes that were strewn across the carpet. "I shall help you wrap the gifts."

"No, I don't think so," Charles said. He gently took his mother by an elbow and led her to a plushly cushioned chair before the fire. "You've been on your feet long enough, Mother. And I don't see you getting any relief until tomorrow is over. You know that you won't leave the kitchen the whole day through, not to mention your being up half the night basting the turkey with cider."

"I can baste the turkey, if you like," Snow Deer said, bending to her knees to open a box. "Mother, there is no need for you to spend so much time in the kitchen when I am here to help you." She sighed when she took a doll with real hair from the box. She looked up at Patricia. "The doll is beautiful. Our sweet daughter, Zelpha, will love it, Mother."

"It looks like her, don't you think?" Patricia said, easing down onto the chair, her hands at the small of her back. She tried not to groan, but the ache in her back was too gnawing not to.

"Yes, it does look like our sweet Zelpha," Snow Deer said.

Snow Deer then firmed her jaw stubbornly. "Mother, I insist that I help more in the kitchen," she said, putting the doll back inside the box. "It isn't as though I am here for a visit. Charles and I and the children live here with you."

"Yes, and such a joy you all are to me," Patricia said, smiling from Charles to Snow Deer. Then she lifted her chin stubbornly. "But as long as I have breath in these old lungs of mine, I wish to remain in control of my kitchen."

Snow Deer and Charles exchanged quick glances.

"I don't mean to hurt your feelings," Patricia said, settling back in the chair and heaving a deep sigh. "But I do love to cook. I love to feed you and the children. That way, I don't feel as though I am a helpless old fool whose age is catching up with her."

Charles went and knelt down before his mother. "Mother, don't talk like that," he said, his voice drawn. "Please don't refer to yourself as a fool— or as an old woman. Why, Mother, I'd wager to say you'll live to be a hundred."

"Heaven forbid," Patricia said, laughing throatily.

Then she grew solemn. "It's so sad about Elissa," she said, swallowing hard. "All along we thought she was going to be well, and then . . . and then she was dead."

Charles sat down on the divan opposite his mother's chair.

Snow Deer sat down beside him. She studied his expression, seeing a look that had become familiar since Elissa's death. There seemed to be a haunted sadness in the depths of his eyes, a despair that she could not reach with her words, or her embraces.

Still she would not allow herself to be jealous, especially not over a woman who was dead. But she knew that her husband had loved this woman, perhaps even more than he had ever realized.

"And it was good of her to will you the largest portion of her inheritance," Patricia said, gazing at Charles, then at Snow Deer.

Charles nodded. He clasped his hands on his knees. "Yes, that was quite a surprise, to say the least," he said.

He thought of something more that Elissa had sent his way, a true gift from her generous heart—a purebred Kentucky saddle mare, as black as coal!

Charles wasn't sure if Elissa had realized that by giving him that special gift, she had found a way to leave a part of her with him.

"Her husband got very little of the inheritance," Patricia said, looking away from Snow Deer, afraid that talking about Elissa might be causing her pain. Still, Elissa's recent death needed to be discussed, once and for all; then it would be forgotten.

"He is rich in his own right," Charles said tightly. "He returned to St. Louis, to resume his doctor's practice."

"I feel that Elissa left the money to you, Charles, because of the children," Patricia said, picking up an embroidered piece from a table and busying her fingers sewing. "Four children, Charles. And now, because of the inheritance, they will be able to attend college and make something grand of themselves."

"I wish they could have known her," Charles said, picking up a pipe and filling its bowl with tobacco. He gave Snow Deer a soft look as he lit his pipe. He took several deep puffs, then took it from his mouth and held it between two fingers.

"Snow Deer," he said, his eyes steady on hers. "Darling Snow Deer, you don't resent Elissa's money, do you? Or our talk of her? You know that the hurt I have is deep because I've lost someone dear and sweet to me, yet only because she was just that—someone dear and sweet to me. A *friend.*"

Snow Deer reached over and took his free hand in hers. "I understand your deep feelings for her," she said softly.

"Yes, we are blessed with such an understanding between us—such an adoring, loving relationship," Charles said thickly. He chuckled. "And your squash blossom necklace was very kind to us, wouldn't you say? We have four beautiful children."

"Yes, four children," Snow Deer said, sighing. In her mind's eye she saw her firstborn, whom they had named Hiram Franklin after Charles's beloved uncle and his birth father. Then there were Clyde, Fred, and their only daughter, Zelpha.

She looked slowly around her, at the grandness of this room, and thought of the grandness of those rooms beyond this one. Shortly after Charles's father died, his mother had asked Charles and Snow Deer to move into her house to keep her from being lonely.

And Charles had gladly followed in his father's footsteps. *He* was now postmaster.

He had sold his blacksmith shop and small cabin, yet had retained his land and had hired someone to farm it, to keep the plants thriving on not only his land, but now also his mother's.

The Cline family was now known to be one of the wealthiest families in the county, but they never flaunted their riches. They were still admired and liked by everyone. When there was any social function in the county, they were the first to receive invitations.

Snow Deer smiled as she thought of the many

balls attended by her and Charles. No one looked at her as different now. With her pretty clothes and fancy hairstyles, she blended in as though she were one of them.

"Snow Deer, do you want to help me put the train track together?" Charles asked, drawing her attention to him. She found him on the floor, the toy train paraphernalia scattered in front of him.

"Oh, yes," Snow Deer said, scrambling from the chair. Not caring how unladylike she looked as she sprawled her legs out on either side of her, her skirt hiked up past her knees, she laughed and chatted with Charles as, piece by piece, they got the train track, and then the cars, in place in a wide circle on the floor.

"Shh," Patricia said, rising slowly from the chair. "You two are making quite a racket with all of your giggling. You might wake the children."

"I don't think I'd even care if we did—would you, darling?" Charles asked, his eyes dancing. "I think it'd be fun to let the children see things before they are wrapped, instead of after, don't you?"

"Well, yes and no," Snow Deer said, cocking her head first one way, and then another, in thought. "I love seeing their eyes on Christmas morning as they open their presents. When I was a child, Becky introduced our family to Christmas. I loved the new custom of exchanging gifts. I love it even more now, since we have children to share the joy of gift-giving."

"Hiram Franklin will love the train," Charles said, placing the caboose on the shiny tracks. "He talks of nothing else but wanting to be a train engineer when he grows up. I enjoy watching him stand down by the tracks waiting for the trains to come by. He has them timed. He knows exactly when each one comes during the day."

"Trains are dangerous," Snow Deer said, growing solemn, this being one of the very few things that Charles and she disagreed about. She did not want to see her lovely child ride a tipsy-topsy train. There had been many train wrecks these past years since more tracks had been built in the vicinity.

"Snow Deer, if one wishes to, one could find danger in most anything spoken of today," Charles said, rising slowly to his feet. He watched his mother leave the room in her slow, shuffling gait. Then he reached a hand out for Snow Deer and helped her up from the floor.

"If Hiram Franklin becomes a train engineer, then that means he will not go to college," Snow Deer said, her eyes pleading with her husband. "Darling, I thought you saw the importance of our children attending college."

"I see importance in allowing our children to do what their hearts lead them to do," Charles said, framing his wife's face with his hands. "Don't you?"

"Well, yes. . . ."

Suddenly the room was filled with beautiful music, floating from the library which opened right off the living room.

"Mother is delighted with her early Christmas present from us," Charles said.

He took Snow Deer by the hand and walked with her to the open door of the library.

They stood together and watched Patricia playing the foot-pedal organ. She looked angelic as she played first one Christmas tune, and then another.

"Come with me," Charles said, tugging on Snow Deer's hand. "I can't wait until tomorrow to show you what I have for *you* for Christmas."

He chuckled as they walked down the hallway

toward their bedroom. "Anyhow, there would be no way to keep it from you," he said. "When we went to our room to go to bed tonight, you might want to know what that copper thing is standing in the small room off our bedroom which was, until today, a closet."

"Copper thing?" Snow Deer said. "And what do you mean about the closet?"

"You shall soon see," Charles said, whisking her into their bedroom.

Having been anxious the entire day to show her what had been installed while she was in Vienna doing some last-minute shopping with friends, he hurried her into what he now called their "bathroom."

"A copper tub!" Snow Deer squealed, rushing to it and staring at it. "A true, actual, real copper tub."

She fell to her knees and ran her hands around the inside of the tub, feeling the smooth, shiny copper.

"Do you like it?" Charles asked, moving to his knees beside her. "I saw you looking at this tub while we were in town shopping a few weeks ago. I later inquired about it, what steps must be made to install it."

He reached up and turned a knob, causing water to run freely from the faucet. "Running water," he declared, his eyes proud.

"My word!" Snow Deer gasped, then slowly eased her fingers beneath the water. She giggled as she withdrew them as quickly. "It is as cold as ice."

"Yes, but I'll find some way to remedy that, darling," Charles said. "Until I do, I shall be the one to carry buckets of warmed water to this tub for you."

"You don't have to do that," Snow Deer said, giggling.

"That is a part of the gift," he said. "It will be my pleasure."

She leaned into his embrace. "Under only one condition," she said in a purring, seductive fashion.

"That is?" he said huskily, glancing toward the door and seeing that they had left it open. He would also remedy that!

"That you take baths with me," Snow Deer whispered, slowly pulling his shirt from inside his breeches.

"That's a promise," Charles said huskily. He could hear his mother still playing the organ. He looked at the door again.

He whisked Snow Deer up into his arms and carried her to the bed.

Then he went to the door and closed and locked it.

"Why, Charles, whatever are you planning to do to your wife?" Snow Deer teased, already pulling small wooden combs from her hair. She tossed them on the floor until her hair was completely loose.

She gave one shake, sending it in luscious, long waves across her shoulders.

She stood up and slowly undressed.

Then, as Charles disrobed, she crossed her wrists over her heart.

He now knew this to be sign talk for love from his wife.

After Charles tossed his last boot aside and was entirely nude, they laughed and both leapt onto the bed.

Cradling Snow Deer close, Charles ran his

hands up and down her spine, his mouth eagerly on her lips, kissing her.

She sucked in a wild breath of rapture when his hands slid around and he cupped her breasts in their palms, the nipples throbbing against his warm flesh.

Charles felt the heaviness of her breasts. They had grown larger from having fed four children, giving him so much more to fondle and caress.

His hands swept down across her belly, where he felt some stretch marks, also from pregnancy, yet not making her any less desirable when he looked at her.

He ran his hands over her belly, smiling to himself when he felt its flatness, marveling at how that had stayed the same about her.

Then his fingers wove through the thick, black hair at the juncture of her thighs and found the soft wet pulse of her sex. He felt a warmth spreading through him to know that she was as alive there as before giving birth to the children—perhaps even more so.

She was a sensual person, always ready to join him in bed at the first indication that he wished to make love. She was an eager lover. She put her all into the lovemaking.

Having felt the familiar stab of excitement between her legs as her husband's fingers touched her there, caressing her in slow strokes, Snow Deer swept her legs around his waist and arched her back as he shoved his manhood inside her in one quick thrust.

Clinging to his neck, Snow Deer returned his kisses with passion.

She rode him in a frenzy of quick, jerking movements, her hips undulating wildly against his.

She heard Charles groan deeply in his throat.

Her hips rose higher, taking him in more deeply as she luxuriated in the sensations that were overwhelming her.

She drew him closer to her body, his thrusts almost driving her to the brink, into delirium.

Charles swept his hands down to her buttocks. He dug his fingers into her soft flesh and lifted her closer. He could hear her breath quicken, and he knew that she was enjoying the waves of pleasure as much as he.

He slid his mouth from her lips and rested it on the soft curve of her throat.

He cradled her closer as his movements within her became harder, feeling himself going into that final, irresistible rhythm that would take them together to that moment of utter enchantment.

"Darling . . ." Snow Deer whispered against his hair.

Her hands swept down his back, then up again, his muscles tight against her palms.

She could hear a throaty growl coming from between Charles's lips.

She could feel the perspiration on his brow.

"I need to kiss you," he whispered, his voice low, urgent, his pace inside her slowing as he looked down at her with utter adoration.

Slowly, meditatingly, he kissed her cheeks, one at a time.

He kissed her brow.

He kissed the tip of her nose.

He kissed each nipple.

He kissed her eyes shut.

And then their mouths met, trembling, their kisses more tender this time, more sweet, more lingering.

Their bodies grew still.

Their lips parted.

Their breathing slowed.

Then he shoved himself inside her again.

His final, deeper thrusts caused Snow Deer to arch and cry out against his lips as an explosion of pleasure washed them in bright, vivid waves of rapture.

For a long time afterward, Snow Deer lay next to Charles in sweet exhaustion, her head nestled against his chest.

They listened to the organ music as Patricia continued to play one song after another. They were no longer Christmas songs. They were a mixture of Tchaikovsky's melodious waltzes, played from sheet music that Charles had gotten free when he purchased the organ.

"Your mother is quite good," Snow Deer said, breaking the silence between them.

"As a child, she had piano lessons," Charles said softly. He chuckled. "After she met my father, it seemed music lessons came last on her list of priorities."

"It is grand that she has remembered the art of playing," Snow Deer said, snuggling closer. She closed her eyes and thought back to when she and Charles had first met. Ah, what savage longings had been awakened inside her! She had never thought that she would be able to put behind her the responsibilities of being a Cheyenne princess.

This thought made her think of her sister, Burning Snow. Her mind had so greatly improved that *she* had been given the title of princess!

Snow Deer felt a soft, lazy sensation of warmth to know that her sister was so happy. And there was even a young man waiting for her to be his wife.

"You are in deep thought and smiling," Charles said, leaning up on his elbow to gaze at his wife.

"Do you want to share your thoughts?"

Snow Deer's eyes opened. She reached a hand to her husband's face. "I was thinking of Burning Snow," she murmured. "Everything has turned out so well for her. Is not that grand, Charles? For so long I doubted she would have any kind of a future except as a beloved child in my father's tepee."

"Yes, I'm very happy for Burning Snow," Charles said, taking her hands, pulling her up before him. He lifted her so that she would be on his lap, her legs straddling him. "But I am also happy for *you*. I know how excited you must be about your family's arrival tomorrow."

"This will be the first time my father will receive a Christmas gift from beneath our tree," Snow Deer said, laughing softly. "I can hardly wait to hand it to him."

"The weather is the only reason their journey is possible this year," Charles said, looking toward the window. "Thus far, no snows this winter."

"I hope the snows do not come until my family has come and gone," Snow Deer said, giggling as she fell away from Charles, landing on her back in the soft feathers of the mattress.

She gave Charles a wicked, sly smile. "Charles," she whispered, beckoning to him with her hands. "My husband, come to me. Love me again?"

He snuggled down over her, his mouth gently covering her lips, her breasts pressing against his chest as he slipped his arms beneath her and lifted her closer.

Snow Deer slid her lips away from his. "I can hardly wait for you to open *your* gift tomorrow, Charles," she whispered.

"You aren't going to tell me what it is?" he asked, his eyes dancing as he gazed into hers. "I showed you yours tonight. I would sure like to see *mine.*"

She leaned up on one elbow. "You would?" she asked, her eyes innocently wide. She jumped from the bed and grabbed her dress. "Come on. I'll show you."

Charles began laughing. "No, no, Snow Deer," he said, reaching over and yanking her dress from her. "I was only jesting. All I want right this minute is *you.*"

He took her by the hand and pulled her back down on the bed beside him. "You are all I ever want, my beautiful Cheyenne princess," he whispered huskily. "Only you."

Desire curling inside Snow Deer, she twined her arms around his neck and brought his lips to hers.

No, she no longer suffered from savage longings.

Instead, she found life with Charles and their children nothing less than pure enchantment!

Dear Readers,

I hope you have enjoyed reading *Savage Longings*. My next book in the *Savage* Series that I am writing exclusively for Leisure Books is *Savage Tears*. *Savage Tears* is about the Dakota Indians, known to some as the Sioux. This book is filled with much emotion, romance, and adventure.

For those of you who are collecting my *Savage* Series and want to hear more about it, you can send for my newsletter at:

CASSIE EDWARDS
R#3 Box 60
Mattoon, IL 61938

Please send a stamped, self-addressed, legal-sized envelope for a reply.

THANKS FOR YOUR SUPPORT!

Always,
CASSIE EDWARDS

SAVAGE PASSIONS

CASSIE EDWARDS

**Winner Of The *Romantic Times*
Lifetime Achievement Award
For Best Indian Romance Series!**

Living among the virgin forests of frontier Michigan, Yvonne secretly admires the chieftain of a peaceful Ottawa tribe. A warrior with great mystical powers and many secrets, Silver Arrow tempts her with his hard body even as his dark, seductive eyes set her wary heart afire. But white men and Indians alike threaten to keep them forever apart. To fulfill the promise of their passion, Yvonne and Silver Arrow will need more than mere magic: They'll need the strength of a love both breathtaking and bold.

_3902-8 $5.99 US/$7.99 CAN

ᵀᴴᴱ SAVAGE
S E R I E S

SAVAGE PRIDE

CASSIE EDWARDS
Winner Of The *Romantic Times* Reviewers' Choice Award For Best Indian Series

She is a fiery hellcat who can shoot like a man, a ravishing temptress with the courage to search the wilderness for her missing brother. But Malvina is only a woman with a woman's needs and desires. And from the moment Red Wing sweeps her up on his charging stallion, she is torn between family duty and heavenly pleasure.

A mighty Choctaw warrior, Red Wing is tantalized by the blistering sensuality of the sultry, flame-haired vixen. But it will take more than his heated caresses to make Malvina his own. Only with a love as pure as her radiant beauty can he hope to claim her heart, to win her trust, to tame her savage pride.

_3732-7 $5.99 US/$6.99 CAN

SAVAGE EDEN
CASSIE EDWARDS

Bestselling Author Of *Savage Passions*

"This is a magnificent, sensitive romance...one of her best!"

—*Romantic Times*

Alone in the Kentucky wilderness, beautiful Pamela trembles under the gaze of the silent Miami warrior—and hungers for his touch. To Pamela, the virile chief Strong Bear is the ultimate temptation. Melting in his sensual embrace, she dares to surrender her innocence—body and soul.

Pamela and Strong Bear share a forbidden love forged in a breathless rapture of mounting ecstasy. The gleam of her lover's strong, bronzed arms, the touch of his lips, and the heat of his flesh kindle the flames of her deepest desires. And when a murderous tragedy strikes Pamela's family, leaving only Strong Bear to blame, her yearning will not die. For only their passion will conquer all injustice—and free their hostage hearts forever.

___52097-4 $5.50 US/$6.50 CAN

WHO WROTE THE BOOK OF LOVE?
ELEVEN OF THE TOP-SELLING
ROMANCE AUTHORS OF ALL TIME—
THAT'S WHO!

MADELINE BAKER, MARY BALOGH, ELAINE BARBIERI, LORI COPELAND, CASSIE EDWARDS, HEATHER GRAHAM, CATHERINE HART, VIRGINIA HENLEY, PENELOPE NERI, DIANA PALMER, JANELLE TAYLOR

From the Middle Ages to the present day, these stories follow the men and women whose lives are forever changed by a special book—a cherished volume that teaches the love of learning and the learning of love!

ALL PROFITS WILL BE DONATED TO THE LITERACY PARTNERSHIP!
JOIN US—
AND CELEBRATE THE LEARNING OF LOVE AND THE LOVE OF LEARNING!